W9-CDZ-235

CYCLING

Books by Greg Garrett

FREE BIRD

CYCLING

Published by Kensington Publishing Corporation

CYCLING

GREG GARRETT

KENSINGTON BOOKS
http://www.kensingtonbooks.com

KENSINGTON BOOKS are published by

Kensington Publishing Corp.
850 Third Avenue
New York, NY 10022

All Kensington titles, imprints and distributed lines are available at special quantity discounts for bulk purchases for sales promotion, premiums, fund-raising, educational or institutional use.

Special book excerpts or customized printings can also be created to fit specific needs. For details, write or phone the office of the Kensington Special Sales Manager: Kensington Publishing Corp., 850 Third Avenue, New York, NY 10022, Attn: Special Sales Department. Phone: 1-800-221-2647.

Kensington and the K logo Reg. U.S. Pat. & TM Off.

Library of Congress Card Catalogue Number: 2003101663
ISBN: 0-7582-0531-7

First Printing: September 2003
10 9 8 7 6 5 4 3 2 1

Printed in the United States of America

For my beloved sons,
Jacob and Chandler

There's a lost soul coming down the road
Somewhere between two worlds.

—Bruce Hornsby, "Lost Soul"

The mere realization of one's own unhappiness is not salvation: it may be the occasion of salvation, or it may be the door to a deeper pit in hell.

—Thomas Merton,
The Seven Storey Mountain

1

It is mid-August in Waco, Texas, the Year of our Lord 1993. The mercury stands at one hundred for weeks on end, the grass goes first brown and then gray, and the parched ground cracks open. In fact, my grandfather, Jackson Bradford Cannon, Jr., called last night from his monumental home over on Austin Avenue to gleefully report the momentary loss of my grandparents' idiotic tabbycat Buster, who blundered into a chasm in their gigantic but poorly watered backyard.

"Should have seen it, Jackson," he said. (Although most people call me "Brad," my grandfather insists on calling me by our common given name; I am, of course, twice distant, JBC the Fourth. Anyway, Buster is the much-maligned cat.) "One minute he was there, the next, whoop, he was gone. I almost bust a gut laughing. Evelyn made me go and pull him out. Too bad the cracks aren't any deeper."

They are deep enough for my liking, and they are everywhere. It has been weeks since we had rain, and even some of the roads have begun to crack, mostly at the shoulders where the dry ground shrinks away from the pavement, but sometimes out in the middle of the thruway. The cracks are generally only an inch or two wide at the most, nothing noticeable for motorists, but they are potentially lethal for a cyclist, which is what I am, now and forever, even in these scorching August afternoons.

What in God's name am I doing out here? Why am I puffing up this hill in 105-degree temperatures, rivers of sweat coursing down my face, a big truck whooshing past me just inches from my left elbow? I'm not certain that I can explain it. But you are right in thinking that it's an odd time to be outdoors, let alone out riding long distances on a bicycle. Everyone else in the state of Texas sits inside in air-conditioned comfort, waiting for fall with the anticipation a snowbound Michigander must feel for spring. This afternoon, putting in thirty miles on my Specialized mountain bike, I could almost be the only living creature on the planet. The dogs, who in more temperate seasons charge out from their porches to defend their territories, now loll, panting, in the shade; the floppy-hatted retirees who normally tend their lawns and flower beds with meticulous loving care have been forced by water rationing to sacrifice their verdant St. Augustine and Bermuda for the public weal; the farmers who are in between harvest and sowing wouldn't set foot on a tractor for love or money.

I don't blame them. I shouldn't be out on a bicycle; I'm supposed to be writing, finishing a book that I have not yet even begun. Let me explain: Five years ago a New York publisher released my history of the Confederate invasion of New Mexico during the early years of the War Between the States. I didn't make this up; I first read about it in Shelby Foote's *Civil War,* and after I managed to graduate from Baylor University, a venerable Baptist institution, I spent three years rooting through the university's excellent Texas Collection, through the like-named collection at Texas Tech in Lubbock, through the Confederate Research Center up the road at Hill College. In those days I was still young enough, Southern enough, to be fascinated by military action, no matter how futile or ill-conceived—in this case, five hundred Texans rode up the Rio Grande expecting to conquer a territory almost as large as the state they'd just left—and to my amazement I filled up notebook after notebook with what I discovered in the collections. The end result was a book that has sold copies by the wagon load in Texas, sold fairly well across the South, and is apparently even bought by the occasional Yankee Civil War buff.

Following that, my publisher encouraged me to get to work on one of the two projects that I have at various times claimed to be writing—a book on the Texas Brigade and their service under Albert Sidney Johnston at Shiloh, or on the diplomatic relationship between the Confederacy and Mexico, depending on my mood. The furthest I ever got was to read a few books other people had written and decide that nothing I had to say was interesting enough for me to add, so I did not and have not. Although I know I ought to be nervous about this being discovered, I am not for two reasons: First, the whirlwind of takeovers and buyouts in New York City publishing has meant that five different editors have assumed control over my project in the last five years, and until the most recent, Eddie Todd, not a one of them has been around long enough to do more than call, introduce himself, and ask how my work is coming; second, while it seems that I must once have cared enough about something to write a book, I have no plans to write another. I have no plans, period. Consequently, as long as my slender royalties, my grandparents, and my occasional columns on Texas greasy spoons and honkytonks for *Texas Monthly* continue to pay the bills, I am free to pretend to fill notebooks with my research, free to court in my noncommittal way the women in my life, free to pedal to my heart's content through this superheated August air.

I am reluctant to admit that there is any tense save the present, and I am not here to recount my sad stories, but since we are recalling *temps perdu* with this rolling account of my brief authorial career, I suppose that now is as good a time as any to unload the other sordid details. Everything will all come out at some point; it always does. So I guess, as Jackson might say, it's better to slap a mosquito with a bang than let her suck your blood in silence.

Here it is then, the unsavory and unalterable past: To begin with, I have been married twice and divorced twice in the past seven years. If any blame is to be attached to such a record of connubial failure, it must fall squarely on my head. I have a problem letting people get close to me. Although it's unfortunate, I can't seem to help myself; life seems easier if I just don't care too much.

Different people have attributed my fear of intimacy to different things. My first wife simply opined that I was a son of a bitch and left it at that; my second wife thought my distance was the result of my artistic temperament; if pressed, I like to say that it comes from being born and bred a male in the great state of Texas, since this seems to shut off debate at a surface level. My grandparents, however, alternatively suppose that my reluctance to connect has something to do with my past, and so it is the dark highlights of my history I must reluctantly recount for you—at least in brief—if you are to have any hope of understanding.

When I was twelve years old, my beloved mother, father, and kid brother got knocked off of Interstate 35 and into eternity by a gravel truck. While this in and of itself seems sufficient to me to justify some lamentation—I seem to recall that this kind of thing knocked Hamlet on his ass—I recognize that not everyone agrees: Fathers die, Hamlet, and mothers and brothers, too. And so they do, an ineluctable fact of life that perhaps should not—in and of itself—be paralyzing. I can say this: It is true that I loved my family dearly, that the mere thought of their fate now is like a crunching blow to the stomach. All the same, what happened to them seems like a long time ago, like another life, and not even my life, but the life of some character I read about once and then closed the book on.

This is not, unfortunately, true of everything in my past. There is something else that might account for the spare and shuttered life I lead, although many of my more recent acquaintances do not know of it except as lurid whispered gossip, the kind people in grocery stores cluck about and people in churches shake their heads over sadly.

There are gravel trucks, and then there are gravel trucks.

When I was seventeen years old, I took my girlfriend Susie Bramlett out on a Saturday night to see *Urban Cowboy* and then to the so-called Health Camp restaurant for good greasy burgers and butterscotch malts. Susie was a beautiful redheaded outdoorsy girl with a laugh as big and bright as the night sky, and she laughed at me all the time, which was one of the things that made me love her madly.

I made jokes about *Urban Cowboy* all evening, even after we had parked on a deserted country road south of town to make out. I was telling her how stupid I thought it was for even Debra Winger to ride a contraption like that mechanical bull, and Susie had thrown her head back and was laughing that laugh when a big black Lincoln or Caddy that had been creaking its way across the plank-and-trestle bridge behind us pulled up alongside and a dark-haired man with a big gap-toothed smile leaned out the passenger window and pointed a silver-plated revolver at us.

I should have done something. Should have. But I sat, stupid and stupefied, and the man behind the gun stepped from the car, ordered us to get out, and handcuffed me to the steering wheel. Then he held a knife to Susie's throat and did things I cannot recount, for your sake as much as my own. When he was finished and her body lay splayed in the creek below, he climbed back into that huge black car and drove off into the darkness, where he remains.

They never found him.

To this day I do not know why he killed Susie and let me live; he was not doing me any favor, believe me. When her body had fallen from the bridge into the creek bed with a crash that still wakes me sometimes gasping in the middle of the night, he turned to me and smiled his gap-toothed smile, and left me standing, as perhaps I have been, ever since.

There is only one more thing I have to say, the saddest thing, and then I'll depart this unhappiest of subjects. It is Susie's eyes that remain with me long after I have had to resort to looking at the one picture I hid away in a drawer to recall the shape of her nose, the tilt of her head. In the one moment when I could bear to meet her gaze, her eyes were bright with the tears she had shed and wide with the horror she felt, but there was something else in them that shredded my heart so that it has ever since been strictly ornamental: I will always believe that, even in the midst of her own terror, she also understood what it had done to me to have to watch.

Sometimes in the golden moment just before I wake, I am permitted a life with Susie Bramlett. In these dreams we are always holding hands and laughing, gazing into each other's eyes while children orbit us like playful moons. In these dreams I am a normal man who works and plays and mows his lawn and loves his family, and not a person who stood by watching paralyzed while hideous things were done to the person he loved most. I could happily dream those dreams forever and never again open my eyes to this waking world.

Anyway, there you have it: the whole sloppily-wrapped package that now puffs up another long hill and that answers to the name Brad Cannon. I will confess that I am an unholy mess; it doesn't take Dr. Joyce Brothers to see that. In fact, everyone around me seems to know how I could be improved, but isn't that always the way? I can spot cracks in the well-ordered facades of other people, although—unlike them—I hold myself back from offering advice. What would be the earthly good of it?

Anyway, my life is not completely out of control, not completely without shape or form. Once a semester I come back and speak to history classes at my alma mater about my tiny corner of the Civil War; once a year I do a book signing over at the Baylor Bookstore, usually for Homecoming Weekend; once every year or two I return to the building named after my grandfather to talk to beginning writers in the English Department about the craft I have mostly long since abandoned except for the occasional cranky letter to the editor composed late at night and the restaurant reviews I write when the mood strikes me and the magazine publishes when the mood strikes them.

These columns are as much a fluke as my ever having written a book; upon complaining about *Texas Monthly*'s sparse coverage of the vast expanse between Dallas/Fort Worth and Austin, the editor as much as invited me to do better if I thought I could. So I started writing about the restaurants I like—places frequented by truck drivers and farmers and janitors, barbecue places and family taco stands and meatloaf shacks on small-town main streets and soul food restaurants hidden away in back alleys. I have no assignments or deadlines, which is probably fortunate; I write when I feel like it, generally when I come home exhausted and happy from putting away a good meal at a place I hadn't known existed.

My stomach is growling now just thinking about it.

The rest of my life can be summed up thusly: I see my grandparents, a group of buddies with whom I eat lunch once or twice a week, and the women whose lives I seem to drift through, or perhaps, more properly, drift in and out of, like the tide. My grandfather, who recognizes that I am drifting even if he can't exactly put his finger on it, tells me, "Jackson, what you need is to find yourself a good woman," but I have already been married often enough to know that the problem is with me, not with them, and that while they can entertain me for a time they cannot change my life, make me happy, or give me purpose. That I will have to do myself, if it is to be done, which I doubt.

Still, living so obviously without a purpose beyond riding a bicycle makes most rational people twitch in my presence, so when the question of my shiftless life comes up, I have taken to explaining my compulsive cycling in this way: "A few years from now," I announce, "I would like to ride in the Tour de France." I do not deceive myself; I have no more interest in or talent for that level of competition than I have current plans for the year 2020. I am too old, and—even riding thirty miles or more a day—too out of shape for such a grueling event. Still, as ridiculous as it seems, the story satisfied the first people to whom I told it, and so I now employ it at every opportunity. It is nice to be able to explain at least something about the way I live.

"How wonderful, Brad," they often say to me, their faces lit with the mere possibility of it all. "Oh, I'm sure you'll do it."

Their faith in me is touching; borne aloft on their false visions of me, I almost imagine I *could* do it, that I would *like* to do it. Then I come to this moment at around the twenty-five-mile mark when my legs decide that even thirty miles may be too much. So I shift up into the highest gears to climb an inconsequential hill, my thighs burning as though someone has injected something thick and viscous into them, and I start to laugh hysterically.

At such times, I almost believe it would be easier to try to live a normal life. Surely I could have come up with a better cover story, one without this much hard work and hardship.

When I rose at ten o'clock this morning it was already startlingly hot outside, and now my T-shirt is soaked through with my sweat and hangs from me with sodden weight. Although my ride includes several roads that offer some shade, and one wonderful half-mile stretch overgrown with towering pecan and oak and cottonwood trees that form a cool dark tunnel—all behind me now, alas—the Texas sun is lethal, and without sunscreen I would burn horribly. As it is, I am as tan as a lifeguard, and my brown hair is bleached blond. My grandmother believes I am courting skin cancer, but I tell her something else will probably kill me long before that can happen.

She does not, somehow, seem reassured by these words.

Then there's the summer wind, constant and powerful and no more cooling than the air around a blast furnace. Today I headed south initially, as I usually do, and the first eight miles of my ride went straight into the wind. The road I followed across rolling farmlands was raised and completely exposed—no trees at all except in the bottomland and only the occasional woodframe farmhouse or barn, all far back from the road and thus of no practical use to me—and the wind whistled across the pastures and past the white-faced Herefords and tail-swishing Appaloosas, rustled through the dark green fields of corn and one field overgrown with the beautiful lavender blossoms of thistles, through the towering power lines and the barbed-wire fences on its way to try and knock me off of my spinning wheels.

Despite all this, if I miss a day on the road, I find an unnamable anxiety building within me. It's impossible for me to spend a day indoors and not end up pacing like a big cat in a cage; although I'm not home yet, I'm already feeling a sense of dread at arriving there. Unlike most everyone else I know, television has never calmed me, and music or books are only a stopgap measure. When I spend too much time indoors alone it seems to me that I become too full of myself, that memories come swarming around my head like hornets, and that only by getting out here, straining, sweating, courting catastrophe, can I let the excess self squeak out of me like air escaping a balloon.

"One of these days you'll get squashed by a truck out there," Becky Sue Bradenton—the youngest of the current women—has told me, "and I'll have to spend my days nursing you back to health." She may be right, although I am strangely detached from everything her statement implies. I don't much care if I'm hit by a truck; although I can almost hear the rumble of the vehicle looming behind me, can imagine the sudden sharp impact, can even see the spot in the ditch where I'd wind up—next to that discarded pouch of Red Man—I feel indifferent to any fate up to and including death. Likewise, while some men might love to be fussed over, I have had a caretaker wife already, and I know from experience that I react badly to constant faithfulness. While I know Becky Sue will fuss wonderfully for a husband one of these days, I'm not inclined to let her practice on me.

If I should ever get hit by a truck, I hope it kills me instantly, and that my granddad sues the miscreant gravel company and wins a huge settlement.

It beats a number of alternatives, some of which I have already had the misfortune to know personally.

2

I do not live in Waco proper. Neither did David Koresh, for that matter, but who would ever have read the headline "Tragedy in Elk"? Waco, is—for better or worse—the logical setting for some stories, and as I know better than most, you cannot escape it just by leaving it.

It is a city of contradictions: once known as "the Athens of Texas" because of its many institutions of higher learning, it has also been a place chock-full of prejudice, ignorance, and idiocy; the westernmost bastion of the cultured and literate society of Southern cotton planters, it became a lawless cattle town renowned far and wide as "Six-Gun Alley," and people to this very day and hour still get shot down in the streets; a city of churches, the "Jerusalem on the Brazos" (according to Southern Baptists, for whom Baylor University is a Mecca worthy of pilgrimage), Waco often—even now, in 1993—demonstrates neither love nor charity, the races and classes are largely segregated from each other, and the last public lynching of a black man in America took place downtown on the town square.

Is it so remarkable that I'm a touch addled when for all my thirty years I've been an inmate of this asylum?

In late August, about the time school starts up again, the annual ant migration begins. For a day or so, the shimmering hot air is thick with just-hatched ant queens, off to explore new worlds, settle new colonies, perpetuate the species. I ride alert for the glistening wings in the sun that are my only warning. On the day when they are thickest, I try to ride in the center of the road to maximize my reaction time, but still they manage to land on my shirt, in my hair, in my mouth. They stick to my skin, slick with sweat and sunblock. As quickly as I can without up-ending myself in a ditch, I flick them off with thumb and middle finger; Texas fire ants are not to be trifled with. Still others glance off my sunglasses with a plink, and pinwheel, stunned, to earth.

I know that most of these new colonizers will not survive; one of my love interests, biologist Sandra Fuentes, has told me that reproduction in prodigious numbers is Nature's way of trying to even the odds somewhat for a species. And yet, for this one day, it's almost impossible to believe that next spring the entire world will not be carpeted by the fine black dirt of anthills.

Just before I arrive back at my house, I pass the ramshackle farmhouse which is the home of my elderly neighbors the Fabers and their coven of cats, and ride beneath the low-hanging branches of an ancient pear tree next to the culvert. I slow down enough to reach up and snap off one of the dangling green-golden pears. When I bite into the sun-warmed fruit it is crunchy and the juice fills my mouth with a sweetness like the purest honey.

Although the fruit will not last long—perhaps into mid-September—it at least is something I can look forward to, and that is important. Except for my daily rides, my calendar for August and most of September is disturbingly empty. Toward the end of September, I will go into Dr. Robert Forest's Civil War class and give my short prepared speech on Sibley's Brigade and the invasion of New Mexico. October is already stacked high, though, a book signing at the campus bookstore for homecoming and a talk for creative writers in the English department.

Of course, it's entirely possible that the only reason people keep inviting me back to campus is that they want to talk about ways the Cannon family could help out the university financially, although I hope that's not true for both our sakes: nothing they say to me could possibly help them for a long time to come. Jackson holds the checkbook for the Cannon Foundation, and while he indulges Evelyn's philanthropic inclinations to make

Waco a better place to live for all its citizens, he gives to Baylor only when he feels guilty about something and wants to get right with God.

Twice a week I also have lunch at a local landmark, a roadhouse called George's, with the motley gang of men who seem to be my only friends, and as sparse a life as it is, I feel strangely content about it. Things seem to be going well, which is to say that they are going nowhere at all. I have written two pieces for *Texas Monthly*, one of which will run in the next issue, one three issues from now. And the three women are all back in town, which is worrisome, but with the advent of school, they soon will be involved with activities to take their minds off me, which is a comfort.

Whenever women have the liberty to concentrate on me they begin to notice things they can't abide. I tend to last longer with women who are preoccupied. In small doses, I can pass for exotic, even fascinating; too much exposure to me eventually reveals the truth, that I am essentially null and void, a lost cause, too big a challenge to take on. When women finally recognize this, they leave, disappointed in me for not being what they thought I was, disappointed in themselves for not being able to change me into what they wanted me to be.

I guess I fool a lot of people, although I've always been motivated by good intentions. I have no desire to hurt anyone, although I usually seem to do just that.

But enough of this junior Freud hoo-ha. What about important things, like the weather? There is little change there, either. Every year I forget that in Texas the coming of fall does not mean the coming of fall, and this year it seems particularly true. Although we have had one good rain recently, the land is still parched, the tap water has a strange, brackish taste, and I am into my third month without even touching the Hot knob on the faucets; the ground temperature is high enough to heat the water as it comes into the house.

Despite a run on bottled water at the H.E.B. grocery store where I shop, I've managed to buy enough to get by, and I'll drink distilled water if they buy out all the so-called spring water. Why people pay for something that normally falls free from the heavens I do not understand, but since I myself have joined the bottled-water-quaffing mob, perhaps I have no right to be cynical about them.

Nonetheless, I am cynical, about bottled water, about people who drink bottled water, and about lots of other things besides.

On August 30, as I am just about to leave for my grandparents' to have dinner, Elaine Rosenbaum calls from New York City. Elaine is my literary agent as well as my second ex-wife, and she still calls once or twice a month to check on me. She became my agent and later my wife because she thought I had a passion, a gift; she eventually became my second ex-wife because she realized that I did not intend to write anything else of substance, that I was not in fact the purposeful artist with whom she thought she fell in love.

"Are you writing anything?" Elaine asks, as she always does, in that broad and slightly nasal tone of hers. "Besides your food pieces, I mean." Although she has remarried, she still takes a personal and financial interest in my life, and for my part, I still like her very much, so I am never ashamed to tell the truth.

"Not a lick. Not a drip. Not a tittle. Not even a jot." I pick up my car keys from the hall table and jingle them just a little, trying out the sound as a distraction.

"I heard from Eddie Todd today." She pauses. Ideally, I'm supposed to express some sort of interest in my editor here—an actual writer would—but I don't bite and she has to noodge ahead. "He asks me, 'Honestly, Elaine, just between the two of us'—"

"So you're snitching on Eddie Todd. Betraying his confidence. Honestly, you are low-life scum, Elaine Littman Cannon Rosenbaum."

She ignores me and returns to her discourse. " 'Elaine, just between the two of us, is Brad really working?' So I tell him, 'Yes. In his own way.' You are still carrying those notebooks around, aren't you?"

"Wouldn't leave home without them." I jingle a little louder.

"I don't suppose there's a word in them."

"Empty as Ronald Reagan's head," I say.

She snickers a little before she catches herself. "You're bad."

"I know," I say. Jingling hasn't worked so I try the straightforward approach. "Listen, I was just on my way over to Jackson and Evelyn's for dinner. Want to come?"

"Give me a rain check," she says. "The tollway to Newark is so crowded this time of day. By the time I caught a flight, dinner would be over."

"I'll give them your regrets," I say.

"I've got a lot of them," she says.

"Uh-huh," I say. I begin to eye the door, as though I could escape what's coming.

"You know, Brad, you were a fine writer. A damn fine writer." Her voice quivers when she says this. Passion? Anger? Regret? Probably D: All of the above.

"Yes," I say solemnly. "I was." We speak as we would speak of someone tragically dead and gone, some promising stranger who was cut down in the prime of art and life.

Her sigh is audible all the way from New York. It always is. "Good-bye, Brad," she says. "Be careful on that bicycle. Look both directions at stop signs. "

"I will be careful," I say. "I'll talk to you soon."

I replace the phone gently on the cradle, lock up the house, and creep out to my little Austin-Healey 3000, parked beneath the gnarled branches of a century-old live oak. One of the Faber cats is sitting on the hood again, and although the paint is old and there's not much damage it can do, I help this one off into free flight with my open hand.

The Healey starts up on the second try—not bad for a thirty-year-old English sports car—and I back into the road. After five miles or so, I reach the Waco city limits. I drive past cemeteries and housing projects and under I-35, which runs from Mexico, on my left, to distant Minnesota, somewhere on my right. I continue down 17th Street past small frame houses with Hispanic families sitting on their porch steps and beautiful brown children playing in the spray of a sprinkler, and as I cross over the railroad tracks on the overpass, I spy Mrs. Baird's bakery beneath me and inhale the stomach-tightening scent of fresh bread.

After I cross the bridge I turn left onto Franklin, pull into the parking lot of Lolita's Tortilleria, and climb from the car, which

I leave running in the No Parking area. Inside, I pull half a dozen Coca-Colas in battered glass bottles from the glass-doored cooler and haul them up to the front counter where Hector Portillo stands smiling. He is a wide and somewhat doughy middle-aged man with a head like a jack-o'-lantern and a crooked smile to match.

" 'Ey, Brad," he says when he sees me, "*que pasa*," his smile threatening to circumnavigate his crew-cutted head, and he calls back through the window into the kitchen. "*Aqui*, Mama. Es Brad." Lolita waves, her hands white with tortilla flour, and smiles a gap-toothed smile before returning to her work. A few of the customers—mostly Hispanic, with a cowboy-hatted Anglo here and there—look up from their booths, but I know none of them, and I turn back to Hector.

I think of Hector Portillo as my friend. I have known him since I was a kid. Once a week or so, usually on my way to Jackson and Evelyn's, I stop in here to pick up some of these Cokes, which are imported from Mexico and thus are made with pure cane sugar instead of cheap corn syrup like almost all the other soft drinks in America. Whenever I come in, I ask Hector about his family and he inquires about mine, although I am forced to admit that neither one of us really knows the other at all. His life is edged with dark corners—Sunday mass, Cinco de Mayo, Tejano music—that I will never be able to penetrate.

So I suppose that while we bear each other genuine goodwill—if I miss a week, the next time I pop in he asks after me with what seems to be real concern—we are not actually friends, not in the classic sense of the word. While I could throw myself into Franklin Avenue to pull him from the path of an oncoming truck, I could not share any of my darkest thoughts or deepest feelings with him if my very life depended on it.

This is not his fault, although he is a typically macho specimen of the Hispanic male. It is mine, and I couldn't say even this to him for fear that it would change things between us.

And if there's one thing I cannot abide, it's change.

These thoughts sadden me for some reason, and after he has opened one of the Cokes for me—the bottle cap clatters onto the white-speckled formica counter, the red cursive *Coca-Cola* and the slogan *Refresco* facing up—and put the other bottles in a white paper bag, I nod and make my exit silently.

In the car I tilt back the cold green glass bottle and let the harsh sweet bubbling liquid course down my throat. This is what Coke is supposed to taste like, the way it used to taste before everything went to hell.

I wish life could taste like this.

In the Healey I jog west one block and leave behind the restaurants and used car dealerships of Franklin as I turn left onto Austin Avenue and then travel under spreading oaks past ever-larger houses to my grandparents' redbrick, white-columned Colonial. I pull up in the driveway and glance back behind the house at the garage apartment into which my grandparents continually invite me to move. No thanks. I vault from the car like Speed Racer and head for the front stairs.

Since I'm late and Jackson insists on eating punctually at six, they are already in the dining room when I arrive, so I buss my grandmother's cheek and sit down between them on one side of the table, shake out my napkin, and use it to swab my forehead, which is wet with sweat from my open-air drive.

"Bradford," my grandmother scolds, but she is too happy to see me to let social niceties interfere, so she goes back to her salad.

"What's for dinner?" I ask. "I'm starved." Billie brings in a platter of chicken-fried steak almost as if I had called her, and she sets it down in the middle of the table, waggles her finger at me a few times for being late, and makes her ponderous way back into the kitchen for more food. She is a large black woman in her sixties, as well as the repository of most of my warmest feelings about growing up in this house.

"You young people should learn to be punctual," Jackson says, offering a wobbly plate. I put a good-sized piece of steak on it and then one on mine. "Then you'd already be eating."

"Papa," Grandma says, but I can handle him.

"Elaine called. Sends her love." They both nod approvingly, as does Billie, who catches this news as she brings in mashed potatoes and cream gravy. Elaine has been their favorite wife to date, and they wouldn't mind hearing that Owen Rosenbaum had shuffled off this mortal coil and left Elaine to turn back to me for solace. If such a thing were to happen, I would do my best to comfort her, but my grandparents both think too highly of me; they don't recognize that Elaine and I split up for good reasons, most of them having to do with me.

That's what grandparents are for, though; they are the familial equivalent of dogs, never questioning, always faithful.

"Tell her hello," my grandmother says. "Has she sold any blockbusters lately?"

"We didn't talk long. I was on my way out the door."

"How did the writing go today?" my grandfather asks, and he fixes me with a steady appraising gaze.

"I got in a little after my ride," I tell him. "I'm in a difficult section on Johnston's battle plan. Very technical stuff." I seem to recall that they believe I'm working on the Shiloh book, and while I am reluctant to spin a tale for them, Jackson's growing skepticism must be answered head-on, so as I dish out potatoes I keep a surreptitious eye on him.

"You could get more done if you put in some concentrated work at the computer instead of riding all over the country," he says, but I think I've pushed the stone back over that grave for the time being.

"Writing is hard work," I tell him. "And writing history for people like you is the toughest of all. I have to use very small words."

He smiles; Jackson loves for me to give it back to him, and I oblige him whenever I have the spirit for it, which is not as often as he would like. "You must have had a good day."

"Just fine," I said. "The wind wasn't too bad, my legs held up pretty well, and I didn't get chased by any dogs. Pretty much the best you can expect out of life." And I smile and take a heaping bite of mashed potatoes to convince them that I am being playful, rather than stating my current philosophy of life. Buster the cat wanders through the dining room on the way from nowhere to nowhere, and he doesn't even acknowledge my presence, which is fine with me; I have inherited my grandfather's antipathy toward cats in general and Buster in particular.

After dessert, one of Billie's chocolate cakes with the creamy icing I used to lick out of her mixing bowl and off the spoon, Jackson releases a satisfied burp toward the ceiling, and he is again free to devote his full attention to me.

"Your grandmother thinks that your days could be better occupied if you had a few more responsibilities," he says, rubbing his stomach absently.

"Like what?" I ask. My voice sounds calm to me, although I feel my insides constrict at the word "responsibilities."

Evelyn leans forward. "We know you're not interested in taking over the construction business—"

"Have to sell it off to some damn Yankee, I suppose," Jackson mutters.

"Maybe you could do a little more work with the Cannon Foundation," Evelyn says. "We're not going to be around forever, you know. Papa is slowing down." She raises a finger to silence him when he opens his mouth to protest, turns to him. "It's true. You forget things. People take advantage of you."

"I don't forget things," he says, and crosses his arms like a willful two-year-old.

"Someone at the Community Band called up last week and said Papa had promised them ten thousand dollars for a new sound system. He couldn't remember what he had decided to do. If he'd decided to do anything."

I shake my head in exasperation. "Doesn't Carly write down on the grant applications whether they're approved for funding or not?" I think that is the name of the pale secretary in front of my grandfather's office; I have never seen her do anything, including make eye contact.

"Sure," Jackson says. "But this fellow said he and I had talked about it. So I gave him the money."

"Write things down," I say.

"That's fine," he says. "I forget to."

I roll my eyes, an action that does not go unobserved. My grandfather chuckles and pushes his chair back from the table. "What do you say, son? Do you want to help out an old man?"

"Responsibility" is still caroming around inside my cranium, and probably this is what causes me to shake my head. "This is not a good time," I say. "I need to leave things open for the writing."

He shrugs—he has expected as much (or as little)—and we adjourn to the den, where they sink into their matching leather recliners and Evelyn flicks on the television. A Chevy truck commercial booms out of the speakers, and I reach across for the remote and make to turn it down, but Jackson stops me.

"I need it loud," he says. "I've got my hearing aids turned up and I'm still deaf as a post. My God, what a life." He leans back and puts his feet up. "If I get much worse you have my permission to put me out of my misery."

As soon as Evelyn sighs he realizes what he's said, his eyebrows come together to crease his face with an expression of physical pain, and he seems to collapse inward upon himself. "Ah, Jackson," he says. "I'm so sorry, son. Damn it!"

The reason the "put me out of my misery" remark echoes in the room long after it's been uttered is that it was my grandfather who gave the permission to shut off the machines. For a moment I can again hear the harsh guttural breathing of the artificial respirator that kept my father alive for over a month in the Hillcrest Hospital ICU. My mother and brother died in the crash, but he was a strong man, and he clung to life long past the point I would have given up. I haven't set foot inside a hospital since, and that's just one of the many places irradiated by my past.

I know it must have been hard for my grandfather to sign those papers; I would never have had the strength to do it. All the same, then and for a long time after I hated Jackson for letting my father die. I know now that it was the best of the bad options available, but still, after almost fifteen years, it is a snag in our family's history so close to the surface that we can sometimes discern the ripples.

My grandfather closes his eyes and shakes his head, and when I see his lower lip tremble a little, I turn my head away and get to my feet. He is getting old after all; he never used to let his emotions show like this.

"It's all right, Jackson," I say. "Don't think a thing of it." I pat his shoulder, then lean over to kiss my grandmother goodbye.

"Thanks for dinner," I say. "I'll call you."

And before something else can emerge from the waters, I am gone.

The car won't start—just growls a little, like a domesticated tiger—so I let it roll backward into the street and pop the clutch when I hit the bottom of the driveway.

That works. I speed along under the cool of the tall trees on Austin Avenue toward downtown, trying to concentrate only on the pressure of my foot on the clutch, the rounded smoothness of the gearshift beneath my palm. It doesn't work; even the throaty roar from the muffler as I accelerate and the torrent of noise from the radio can't distract me. I still see my father on his back, so full of tubes he looked like a science project run amuck, still see my grandfather sinking in on himself like a Macy's Parade balloon leaking air, and I know that I can't go back to my dark and empty home where the memories ricochet around the rafters. Not yet.

I need to see one of the women, feel arms around me, know that—for a moment at least—I'm not alone. I check the possibilities. I haven't heard from Madelyn Clark since her husband Colby came back from his summer studying John Milton at Cambridge, and her silence suggests that he is enjoying his return too much to leave home yet, damn him. Infidelity seems too complicated a thing for me to manage when the husband is on this continent, and so I ruefully mark her off my mental list.

I drive by Becky Sue Bradenton's apartment on Bagby Avenue. Becky has called me twice this summer: I have taken her to a movie once and begged off a second time on account of my writing. I'm sure she has had plenty of fraternity boys anxious to fill her time, so I don't feel guilty about this at all. Becky Sue will always have a full dance card.

I slow down as I pass her parking lot, see that her blue Honda hatchback isn't in its usual spot, shrug, and continue down the street toward the Baylor campus. Sometimes Sandra Fuentes stays at school and works in her lab or her office, but when I stop to use the phone at 7-11 there's no answer at either number.

She picks up her home phone on the first ring.

"Sandra Fuentes," she says in a voice as starched and white as her lab coats.

"It's me," I say, holding the receiver closer to my ear as a Dr Pepper truck lumbers past. "Brad. Can I see you?"

I can imagine the expression on her face currently—blank—as she goes internal to ponder the options, examine contingencies, weigh pros and cons.

After what seems an unreasonable period of silence where I start to wonder if we've been cut off, she says, "I suppose that would be all right, for a little while. I have an eight o'clock class tomorrow."

I feel a smile twisting my lips upward ever so slightly. Although she is the least comforting of the women, her matter-of-factness, her straightforwardness, can be dry and refreshing, a martini with only the slightest hint of vermouth.

Sandra Fuentes lives just outside Robinson, a small town through which I occasionally ride. The citizens there have been voting down bond issues to repair the streets since Hector was a pup—and what does that mean, anyway? My whole life I don't know what that means—so even the main streets of the town are awkwardly patched or blatantly unpatched, a surface suited to my mountain bike, maybe, but not to my little Healey. I slow down to twenty and still hit the outside edge of a pothole that could swallow my little car whole, and when I reach the dirt road and get off the pavement, I breathe a paradoxical sigh of relief.

She lives in an all-American house that looks like Ward Cleaver's, as unlike the house she grew up in in El Paso as I can imagine; it's almost as though she has invoked the starched-white ghost of Hugh Beaumont to defend her from her memories of single-room shacks and wind whistling through cracks and Anglo kids who made fun of short squinting brainy Tex-Mex girls. Whatever works, I say. I respect people who can bury the past.

The porch light is on when I pull up out front despite the fact that the sun won't set for another hour or so; it is always on. I knock on the storm door and a heartbeat later the front door is pulled open and I am looking down on Dr. Sandra Fuentes, who is all of five-two. She's let her hair grow out while she was doing her fieldwork in Tanzania, and the tropical sun has bleached it several shades lighter. When she lets me come inside, she gives me a Mona Lisa smile and pushes a long strand of hair over her left ear.

Her home is cool and dark, a haven for cats, of which she has somewhere between five and fifteen, depending on the status of her various rescue missions. Books and papers cover practically every flat surface, including the dining table, the television, and the sofa, where she clears a spot for us by transferring debris to the floor.

"I'm afraid I don't have much to offer you," she said. "Milk or water?"

"Water would be nice," I say. "I'm still a little dehydrated."

"You look tanned. Very fit." She says this over her shoulder as she walks into the kitchen. I hear the clatter of ice cubes and the tap running, and then she returns with a tall glass that is beautiful beyond all utilitarianism, blue and seemingly hand-blown.

"New glasses?"

Her face closes down like a garage door descending. "I thought I deserved something nice. My family's taste ran to jelly glasses."

Yikes. I take a sip, swallow, and change the subject. "Did you learn lots in Africa?" It is an obvious diversion, but I am still anxious for the touch of her hand, of her flesh on mine, and the path to Sandra Fuentes' heart does not pass through summer evenings colored by strumming Latin guitars and *canciones de amor* but through steaming East African jungles and gleaming laboratories. The Mona Lisa smile broadens then, momentarily revealing tiny white even teeth, and her hazel eyes behind her scientist glasses actually sparkle.

"Oh, where should I start?" she says. "So many things happened. I live among them, you know. The chimpanzees. At first even the older ones didn't remember me, but I won back a few of my old friends, and they convinced others, and after a while they accepted me as if I'd never left. My two graduate students couldn't get close until just before we left. They had to stay away. They took pictures, video. But I was right there among them. I saw everything. Birth, death, and everything in between."

Her eyes are wide and almost gleaming; her leg against mine seems to be trembling a bit. "It sounds wonderful," I say. "I'm sure you're writing up your results now."

"Of course," she says, but then she smiles slightly to defuse the touch of petulance. Of course she is writing up her results now; she is a scientist. "Every year I am more and more surprised by how few differences there are between primates and us. Genetically, you know, chimps and humans have a ninety-five percent congruence."

I know. This is one of her favorite topics. Cats ruffle papers at our feet, my ice clinks a little as it settles in my glass, and I take her hand and put it to my lips.

"I've missed you," I say, and it's true; there is no one in my life quite like her. She accepts the pressure of my lips on her hand, even squeezes my hand in return, but when I lean over to try and kiss her, she gets up and walks into the kitchen. She does not recognize, apparently, that we have been involved in foreplay.

I follow her. Unlike the rest of the house, the kitchen cabinets are free of books, magazines, and papers; she apparently needs someplace clean to prepare the cats' meals. I know it's not to prepare her own, because I once—and only once—made the mistake of asking if she ever cooked Mexican food. Honest mistake, you would think. Besides, I love a good chicken tamale so much that my interest in her would have soared skyward if she'd admitted she'd been making them since birth, that nothing gave her more pleasure than whipping up a batch of chicken tamales for some lucky man.

She did not make such an admission.

"Do I look like some Mexican señora who spends her life bent over a stove?"

I backed away from that question like a man scrambling back from the crumbling edge of an arroyo.

"No," I said, shaking my head violently. "Not a bit."

"There's sandwich stuff in the fridge," she growled. "I don't cook. I'm a scientist."

"Okay," I said. "I'm sorry."

"I'm a scientist. A professional. Other people cook for me." She stopped glaring at me. "Do you want a sandwich?"

"I'll fix it myself," I said, and she nodded with approval. I did not ask her about tamales again.

Sandra is angry at the whole world—generally including me—because she has had to work twice as hard as an Anglo male to be taken seriously; she is a rotten housekeeper in a home lousy with cats; she would sacrifice my life to save a monkey's any day; I don't have the slightest idea what she looks like under her jeans and "I'm Primed for Primates" T-shirt. All the same, I want to make wild monkey love to her there on the cabinet, to pursue sexual pleasure like a good primate, and I tell her exactly that.

She doesn't slap me and her jaw doesn't drop; neither does she pull me close and run her tongue across my face. "You watch too much television," she says, and she hoists herself up to sit on the cabinet, placing herself roughly at eye level with me now. I'm pleased to see that she is not offended; she seems instead to regard me as a wonderful specimen.

"I don't watch *any* television," I complain, which is mostly true except for the occasional sporting event and late-night eye candy. "I'm just telling you the truth. I thought scientists were looking for the truth."

"We're looking for *a* truth," she says, and she involuntarily lets slip a yawn before she swallows it again. It is not encouraging. "Or truths, even."

"Well, couldn't this be a truth?"

"It could be," she admits. She turns that over in her mind for a moment, and then, as if she wants to test a hypothesis, she puts her hands in my hair, tugs me close, and kisses me, her tiny teeth clicking against mine. Her mouth tastes of coffee with cream and sugar, bitter but beautiful, something worth waking up to.

I moan a little from the sheer sensory pleasure of it, and she pulls her head back and a little to one side to observe me.

Then she pushes me away. "You're a very strange man," she says. "I haven't figured you out at all."

"I'm remarkably complex," I say. "Really a fit subject. You should observe me more closely."

"It would take too much time," she sighs, "and that's one thing I don't have enough of." She slides down off the cabinet, takes my hand, and leads me through the obstacle course. Going down the hall, I have a momentary thought that she will turn left and walk me back to her bedroom, but she continues straight and deposits me in the foyer.

"Go home," she says. "It was pleasant talking to you, and kissing you, for that matter, but there is no room for you in my life. None whatsoever."

"Kiss me again," I say.

"Once," she says, "and only once." She tilts her head up, I bend over, and our lips meet. She doesn't kiss like you would expect a scientist to kiss, although actually I do notice a bit of exploration there before she draws back.

"Now go home," she says.

"You've aroused the primate in me," I say, for she has.

"Not my problem," she says, ushering me out. "Take a cold shower. Drive around the block. Ride your bike."

Which, of course, is what I wind up doing the next day, after a sleepless night spent watching quasi-sports on ESPN. Thank God for cheerleading competitions and Australian-rules football, or my nights would be unbearable.

3

When it rains during the second week of September, three days of cloud-ripping lightning, booming thunder, and huge drops pounding onto the roof of my house, I accept it as a mixed blessing. I cannot ride in the rain, but the cold front that passes through seems to have taken some of the edge off of summer, and when I get back on the bike the morning after, there is a damp coolness to the air and some of the leaves are even drifting down from the trees.

After I leave my driveway, I negotiate three miles of twisting, turning country roads before passing the Robinson Municipal Park—ball diamonds, a swimming pool, and the cemetery. Then I pedal like a madman across I-77 to avoid being a fly on some semi's radiator, and continue five wind-whipped miles through farmland to the turnoff that puts me back in the Texas countryside for the rest of my ride, with all that entails, good and bad.

On the positive side, there's very little traffic, so my odds of being squashed flat or bumped into the culvert drop dramatically. On the bad side, there are bad dogs.

Evil dogs.

I am by nature a dog lover, yin to my cat hater's yang. I don't mind the noise and frantic rush of friendly dogs; what gets my legs pumping is the fangs bared, growling treatment. Some dogs come barking out to say "Howdy," some to say "Get the hell away from my house," and while I am, as I said, seemingly indifferent to dying, I am responsive to pain, and there are four of the potentially pain-producing strain of canines two miles past my turnoff into the country, at the bottom of a long gradual hill.

They generally hear me coming a quarter mile away and run barking into the street, and I begin to pedal harder for my getaway. I've tried everything to dissuade these dogs: I've sprayed them with water from my squirt bottle; I've pelted them with gravel; I've stopped to confront them; I've kicked them hard in their snapping, snarling muzzles. None of these things has curbed their appetite for me in the slightest, so now I get up a good head of steam, put my feet up on the crossbar, and let them nip at the whirling pedals. So long as none of them gets under a wheel, we're all happy: I get past them without losing a leg; they've driven me out of their territory.

It's win/win for everyone.

The rest of my ride is clear sailing, with no challenges beyond the normal hills, gravel, and exhaustion. The wind rises for a moment, and for a few miles, as I follow alongside a dry creek bed, I ride through a yellow flurry of falling cottonwood leaves; they litter the damp pavement like lethargic frogs. Some of them glance off me, cool and wet, a wonderful moment of contact, and then I leave the canopy of trees behind for open country.

My front tire starts to feel a little mushy as I stand up to muscle my way up a long hill, though, and when I get off to check it, I can hear the high-pitched whee of air escaping. If I turn back now, I may be able to get past the dogs before it goes completely flat, but if not I will be walking the bike past them, and what's left of me afterward will be pushing the bike the ten remaining miles home.

I consider other possibilities. I check my watch—2:20—and quickly assess the whereabouts of everyone in my life. Jackson is at the foundation, Evelyn volunteering at Caritas, the local food bank, Sandra is in class, ditto Madelyn, and only Becky could possibly be free to come after me, which is fortunate, since she is the person I would have called in any case.

I lay my bike down in the culvert and cross the front yard of a farmhouse where an elderly woman is almost finished mowing the yard on a riding mower. Although I have never spoken to her, we have seen each other often, her working in the yard or the garden, me puffing past her house on the long incline. I wave at her and she cuts the engine and drifts to a stop.

"Trouble?" she calls.

"Yes, ma'am," I say. "Flat tire. You suppose you could call somebody for me?"

"You come on in here," she says, turning off the mower and leaving a patch of tall grass for later. "I'll get you something to drink, and you can dial it yourself."

"Much obliged," I say, following. I seem to have fallen into this dialect instinctively, but it seems right and proper, where "Thank you very much" would seem exactly the opposite, stiff and mocking.

"How 'bout some lemonade? Ice tea?" I hear her pull a glass from the cabinet.

"Water's fine," I say, and I dial the number while she fills my glass clatteringly full of ice cubes and runs the tap.

"Here you go," she says, handing me the glass.

"Thanks. Hello? Becky? Brad."

I sip, and it tastes clean, cold, and fresh. Well water.

"Hey," Becky says, and she can't—or won't—hide the shiver of pleasure my call has given her. "What's up?"

"Do you suppose you could come after me? I blew out a tire."

"Sure I could," she says, as though she's surprised I would even have to ask. I sense that there are few limits on what Becky Sue Bradenton would do if I asked her.

"I'm not sure if I can give you good directions. Hold on." I turn to Mrs. Koufax—I know her name from the battered black mailbox—and ask, "Can you help this young lady track me down? She'll be coming from down around Baylor campus."

"Why sure," she says. I sip at my water while she gives clear, concise directions, and when she's done she hangs up.

"Sounds like you've got a good one there," Mrs. Koufax says. "She'll be along directly. She cook?"

"Yes, ma'am."

"Clean?"

I think of Becky's immaculate apartment, the matched Laura Ashley comforter and curtains, the sparkling bathtub and toilet.

"Yes, ma'am."

Mrs. Koufax tries to hide a grin and can't, and something I

might even call a twinkle comes into her eyes, deep-set amid her wrinkles. "Kiss?"

Boy, does she; Becky puts her unharnessed sexual energy into kissing. Last time I saw her, I went home with bruised lips. "Yes, ma'am."

"Well there you go," she says. "She's the one." She holds her hands out, palms up, problem solved.

If only it were that simple. "I'll wait outside," I tell her, handing her my glass. "Thanks for your help."

And though Mrs. Koufax tries to coax me to stay inside, tells me her husband will be in off the tractor any minute for a break and would love to visit, I go out to the road so I can flag Becky down, and Mrs. K. hops back on the mower, finishes that tiny spot in front, and hurtles around the house to get started on the back forty.

When I see the Honda, I step out into the road and give Becky a wave. She pulls over, pops the hatch, and gets out.

"I'm glad you called," she says, stepping up to me and throwing her arms around my neck. "I have had the worst day." She is wearing cut-offs and a scoop-necked silk tank top, and I am tall enough to see down to her navel without half trying.

"Thanks for coming," I say, and avert my gaze. I give her a peck and disentangle myself so I can stuff the bike in the back.

"I have spent the whole day with William Wordsworth," she says, opening the hatchback. Her hair, pulled back in a ponytail, cascades like a blond waterfall down her back.

"Just so you don't spend the night with him," I grunt, a feeble joke, but one she likes, and that brings her up close to me again.

"Now don't you worry about that," she says and winks, and I read her meaning loud and clear, and when she leans over again to slam the hatch shut I can see paradise fully formed and there for the taking.

"You are a lovely creature," I say, regretting it the moment it passes my lips. These days, I am not a passionate man; by nature, I am disinterested in most things and bored by the rest, but I am also, as Sandra Fuentes would tell you in some detail, a prisoner of biological imperatives. Although my mind has absolutely no interest in preserving the species, my body, often to my chagrin, apparently does, and it is only with some difficulty that I stop myself from asking Becky to pull over into a secluded driveway I pass daily where the car would be hidden completely by tall dense pampas grass and manage instead to call out clear directions to my house. This is a victory for the mind, a triumph for the forces of reason, but I do not trust myself to preserve the peace, and when she drops me off at the house, I tell her I have work to do and don't invite her in. The kiss she gives me from the seat of her car as I lean in at her window almost makes me reconsider; I turn quickly and make for the door, not watching her as she backs out to the road.

With my ride cut short, there's little to do during the afternoon, so when the mailman drives past, I go out to collect the mail immediately. It is a usual day's haul, about half a dozen catalogs, a few bills, and a cream-colored envelope that has a return address on the back flap that I recognize as quickly as the graceful handwriting that put it there, and another kiss, the last greedy, desperate kiss Madelyn Clark gave me before Colby came home from England presents itself in my memory: as I turned to leave her house, she called my name, stepped to me, took my face between her long graceful hands, kissed me as though her very life depended on it.

It is not like Madelyn to write, and for a moment I debate throwing the thing away unopened. If there's one thing I can't abide, it's surprises. Then I feel her hands framing my face; reason loses this battle. I run my index finger up under the flap and pull out an invitation, also on cream-colored paper, to—of all things—a party honoring Dr. Colby Clark on the publication of his book *God's Rebel: Miltonic Puritanism and the Commonwealth.* Before I can crumple the invitation, I see two lines penned at the bottom: *Please come. I miss you.*

Every instinct tells me to stay away: Colby and I do not like each other and have always treated each other with the exaggerated civility that masks such antipathy in polite company; Dr. Martin Fuller, the septuagenarian head of the Baylor English department will instantly go to work on me about the endowed chair that he hopes to leave as his legacy to the university; the rest of the invited guests will rightfully wonder why I'm there, and Madelyn and I have never talked about alibis, subterfuges, or explanations, since I don't think either of us has the energy or the deceit for them.

Still, instincts or not, on Saturday night I show up at the front door of the house in the faculty-fashionable suburb called Woodway, a bottle of what I think is good champagne—it was expensive—in hand as a house gift. I am decked out in a jacket and tie, a little moist under the arms, and not just because of the temperature. I have not seen Colby since I began sleeping with his wife, and I wonder if that will be printed across my face when he opens the door, if he will call me out, if there is some Yankee equivalent to pistols at dawn. I strive to make my expression as blank as the pages of one of my notebooks, inhale and exhale with complete consciousness of the act—the steadying influx of oxygen spreading through my chest, the calming sigh of carbon dioxide escaping—and then I press the doorbell.

I count five more such breathing cycles before the door opens and Dr. Colby Clark stands smiling gravely in front of me, a handsome dark-haired man in an elbow-patched tweed jacket and blue open-necked oxford shirt. "Hello, old man," he says, holding out his hand. He spouts such Anglicisms regardless of how recently he has sojourned in Britain, and I am accustomed to this affectation. I shift the bottle from right hand to left to briefly take his hand, slightly firm grip, one pump.

"It was good of you to come. Madelyn says she has got to know you better over the summer, so I told her to be sure and invite you." His gaze is steady but not intent, and his half smile does not seem to convey more than the usual irony at our meeting. I stop counting my breaths.

"Congratulations on the book," I say, and offer the bottle.

He chuckles. "It's not so much, really," he says. "The next one is coming out with Cambridge Press, of course, and that will be the important one. But it's nice to see one's work in print, as you know."

Before he can accept my token gift, we are overtaken by other party-goers, some of the religion faculty, if I remember correctly, probably some of Madelyn's professors in the Ph.D. program, and Colby turns to greet them.

"Run that back to the kitchen, will you, Brad? There's a good chap. Madelyn will be glad to know we have more bubbly." And while Colby accepts more congratulations, I go in search of Madelyn.

The living room and dining room are already filling with people, and as I prepare to enter the kitchen, a hesitant tap on my shoulder turns me around. It is Dr. Fuller, once my teacher, still chair of the English department, ultimate product of the repeal of mandatory retirement for university professors. "Good evening, Brad," he says, and I take his cold and quivering hand.

"Dr. Fuller," I say, nodding. Becky has Dr. Fuller this semester for Romanticism, and she reports that he has twice fallen asleep in the midst of his own lecture, a lecture probably delivered from the same yellowing index cards he read from when I sat his class, when my father took him.

"It's such a pleasure to see you," he says. "I hope we'll soon be attending a similar party for your new book. How's it progressing?"

"Slow but steady," I assure him, and excuse myself on account of the champagne. His deferential manner confirms that he'll be back later. "What a wonderful thing it would be to have an endowed chair in English," he will say, wistfully. "An ongoing memorial. Yes, that's what it would be, affecting the lives of students for generations. A fitting memorial."

I do not want to talk about memorials. Perhaps I can escape before he works up his courage, since I can't imagine staying long at this party.

Can't imagine it, that is, until I enter the kitchen and find Madelyn grunting with frustration at a champagne cork. She is wearing a black high-waisted dress with sleeves that come to about midforearm, a strange but nonetheless attractive look.

"I can help you with that," I say, and she almost drops the bottle she's holding.

"Don't do that," she says. "Sneak up on me like that, I

mean," but all the same she gives me a sad smile that does not quite reach those huge brown eyes. Then she trades me her bottle for mine, and once she is within arm's reach I am suddenly overcome by her scent, an unaccountably sweet smell like the cookie dough Billie used to let me eat by the spoonful, a smell of sugar and vanilla, and I recall that the last time she and I were together in this kitchen we were drinking Foster's lager from chilled glasses to cool off at four a.m., and remembering that, it is all I can do not to lean into her dark hair and breathe her in.

We are thinking along similar lines. Her eyes dart to the door—no one there—and then her index finger rises to pass lightly across my hand twisting the cork before dropping back to her side. "I was afraid you wouldn't come."

The cork comes off with a muffled pop, and I hand the bottle back to her. "There you go," I say, as I hear someone approaching from behind. "How's that?"

"Good show," Colby says from the doorway. "I am falling behind on my hostly duties, am I not? Thanks for standing in for me, old man."

"Any time," I say, and nodding to Madelyn, I leave mumbling something about mingling with the other celebrants, although to me there is only one person in the house worth seeing.

It is almost an hour before I have another opportunity to speak to her, and that is in the company of two of her religion profs as she refills champagne glasses. My time in between is spent filtering from group to group of English faculty who are busily invoking the shades of Milton scholars past and present to demonstrate that they recognize the importance of Colby's achievement, the stately critical procession he joins: C. S. Lewis, William Riley Parker, E.M.W. Tillyard, A.S.P. Woodhouse, James Holly Hanford, John M. Steadman, John T. Shawcross. These sonorous names sound vaguely familiar; I may have cited them when writing a paper for my Milton class ten years back, but it is the same sort of familiarity that I might have for the name of a kid who moved away in second grade, a recognition without any true remembrance.

After wading through three successive groups of such Miltonic conversation and falling splat into a deconstruction of the Pauline epistles, I seize the approaching Madelyn like an explorer sinking in quicksand.

"They say you're doing good work," I tell her, and so they did, earlier. She never seems happy about her doctoral studies, and admittedly, her interest in women and world religions is not particularly admired by the mostly-male faculty, but they do recognize her gloomy brilliance; despite this, she has the lowest self-esteem of any smart person I know. She also secretly worries that being the wife of a faculty star might somehow bring her special treatment from his colleagues at the university, a condition I have tried to tell her that I know from experience to be untrue.

"I failed three classes at Baylor," I told her late one night, holding up three fingers as though she could see them in the dark, "and my family owns the school. Is that the sort of special treatment you're thinking of? Give them a little credit. You're a brilliant woman."

But then—and now—she is hard to convince. "You're awfully nice to say so," she says, as she refills Dr. Warden's glass. "I'm just barely keeping my head above water."

"Nonsense," he says. Warden is a short, red-faced man with a tonsure of white hair. "You're one of the best students I've had in that Luke/Acts class in years."

She smiles, a skeptical pursing of the lips; she would like to believe it.

Colby, who has drifted close by, momentarily shoulders his tweedy way into our little circle. "Madelyn is quite snappy, with her women warriors and goddess talk, is she not? Always makes for an interesting diversion." He smiles at her and pats her shoulder, but this civility does not mitigate his words, and when he passes we are left in uncomfortable silence and I feel heat rising on the back of my neck. If I were Madelyn, I think I would accidentally spray bubbly down his trousers.

But I am not, and what Madelyn herself does is smile weakly, drop her eyes to the floor, and disappear. Warden, whom I know slightly from sharing the elevator in the Tidwell Bible Building, an architectural abortion that houses the history, religion, and philosophy departments, shakes his head. There is a pregnant pause, and he tries to take up our original, pre-Colby conversation. "Madelyn hardly ever talks in class, but what she does say is very insightful. I'd like to—"

It isn't working, and our downcast glances prove it. He breaks off to take a sip, shakes his head again—what we have just witnessed is beyond his powers to repair—and resumes his deconstructive treatise on the Letter to the Ephesians where he left off.

"Excuse me, gentlemen," I say, after only a minute or two of this. It's true that I'm not much interested in any discussion of the Apostle Paul, whom I have never liked—I prefer to take my coffee and my Christianity without dilution or addition—but mostly I've decided that if I can't see Madelyn alone for just a moment, pass something other than polite cocktail party conversation with her, then I want out of this place.

I follow Madelyn back into the kitchen, and find her leaning over the counter, head down. This time she does not seem surprised to see me. "You shouldn't be here," she says without looking up. "You don't belong in the same house with him, with these people."

"Tell me about it," I say. "I don't understand most of what I hear and I don't care about the little I can understand. Do you want me to leave?"

She raises her head, lifts her hair back out of her eyes, and improbably, shows her dimples in the first genuine smile she's displayed tonight. "No. I want them to leave. Am I awful?"

"Yes," I say. "Awfully beautiful." On the pretext of putting my glass next to the sink, I can brush against her, can breathe in that smell which is not perfume, she informs me, but surely has to be some edible soap or shampoo, since no human being can smell so wonderful.

"My God, I've missed you," she says, and she looks so desperately unhappy that I am about to kiss her when she suddenly whirls back to the sink.

"Not interrupting anything, I hope," Colby calls jovially as he enters with a tray full of empty dishes.

"I was just saying good night to the hostess," I say, nodding to Madelyn, who raises her head and nods back. "Congratulations again, Colby."

"Thanks so much, old man," he says. "Glad you could come and share in the celebration." His handshake is again perfunctory, and before I am completely into the dining room he is asking Madelyn if she can locate any more clean glasses.

Since there is no one else in this house I care to speak to, as the topography and population distribution allow I begin to push my way toward the front door. Dr. Fuller raises his hand at me from across the room, and while his wave means "Come back and talk," mine means "Hasta la vista, baby."

I walk out to the street and push the Healey away from the curb, jump in, build up a little speed going downhill, pop the clutch, and off I go into the darkness.

4

When I go out on the bike the next afternoon, warm with a powerful southeasterly wind, an alarming scent of death is in the air. I am not hypersensitive to smells—my consciousness of Madelyn's scent notwithstanding—but it seems that every few minutes, the overripe stench of rotting meat fills my nostrils and I have to gasp for air through my mouth.

I have known this smell from my youth; our German shepherd, Roxy, used to supplement her diet with roadkill until she herself got hit by a truck and completed the cycle. She was a loving dog, even when she had been out feasting on five-day-old armadillo. When we got home from school, she always came panting up to greet my younger brother Carter and me, and sometimes when we knelt to pet her the reek of death would hit each of us in the face and I could feel something sour rising in the back of my throat.

"Eugh," Carter always said, prune-faced. "You stink, Roxy."

And Roxy would wag her tail and pant happily, because she didn't know any better, thought we were complimenting her, recognized her name. Whatever.

That is the very smell that the wind whips up from the culverts, out from the ponds, across the fields. I know there must be a logical explanation: the weather change may have made animals more active, hunters and prowlers included; a few hundred thousand of the billions of crickets currently infesting Waco may have crawled into a communal grave. I just chalk it up as a statistical anomaly, part of my price of doing business. Things die, and unless you're in the city, where there is somebody to complain to and a sanitation worker to haul death away, it can lie under the sky for a while. If you can't stand the stench, get out of the country.

Still, it's unsettling—I have a flash of Susie Bramlett lying broken in the creek before I can stuff it back in its cage—and I feel something bitter rising at the back of my throat each time the wind shifts, something that bears only coincidental resemblance to the Wheat Chex and milk I eat each morning before I set out.

At the bottom of their hill, the dogs are waiting for me as if I am carrying the carrion smell with me, which perhaps I am. I let a Chevy Blazer precede me down the hill, hoping they will chase it instead of me, but it smells of oil and exhaust and I smell like meat, and guess which they prefer?

They pursue me with unusual vigor today, three on one side, the black mongrel on the other, so close to my whirling pedals that I could reach out with my foot and touch any of them, and they don't stop—past their house is a half mile of open country, flat blacktop but straight into the gale, and by the time they finally give up and trot happily back, I have moved past exhaustion and gotten my second wind.

I ride on through the shady grove, continue past the Koufax farm, past the Cottonwood Baptist Church, a Texas historical landmark like the Mooreville Methodist Church a few miles ahead, but a mile or so on, I am bucking the monstrous headwind again with the biggest hill on my route still to climb, and I decide to cheat: stop, squeeze a little water over my head, catch my breath.

Just up ahead is the Cottonwood Cemetery, a tiny graveyard that straddles the road. I have ridden by a hundred times and never given it much thought; there are, after all, several graveyards along my normal ride and others close by on alternate routes. Since I'm already stopped, I push my bike into the section of the graveyard on my right. Both sides are open to the road, no fences or gates, and I can see right away that the markers are very old, the German settlers who populated this area, mostly, born in the mid-nineteenth century and living until the 1940s or 1950s, some of them. As I continue to push my bike farther into the cemetery the markers grow more archaic, the names and dates and Bible verses engraved on them more difficult to make out. At the rear of the cemetery, overgrown by brambles and trees, it looks at first as though a solitary marker is all that holds off the forces of nature, but I look closer, and ten feet inside the dense undergrowth I see the tops of other gravestones that no one can even get to now; these people are doubly dead, in body and in memory, and unaccountably I shiver at the thought.

A truck passes on the road, and without really knowing why, I hide from it, keep a tree between the two of us as if I'm afraid to be caught here. It just seems like I must be doing something wrong, somehow, and it's not until he disappears down the road that I get back on my bike and set off to conquer the hill.

At lunch the next day I meet the guys down at George's. Wallace Dent and Richard Collins are already seated at our circular booth when I come in. Wallace is a history professor from Baylor. I took his Greek and Roman History, the facts of which he interpreted more coherently than his baseball lore. Last week, for example, he tried to make a case for the designated-hitter rule shortening careers in the American League, and as much as I abhor the D.H. and would use any ammunition to blow it out of the water, Wally's logic didn't hold up. Sometimes I think he argues out of sheer perversity; in any case, I hope his scholarly articles are better reasoned than his baseball arguments. He is short and stout, about five-five and one-eighty, and is all but bald save for a few tufts of hair sprouting from his forehead that put me in mind of Charlie Brown. Outdoors he wears a floppy fishing hat with colorful lures stuck in it, but now it rests on the ledge behind us, a potential hooked menace to anyone leaning back unawares.

Richard is a sportswriter for the *Tribune Herald,* the kind of guy who always seems to be on the fringes of the group, in but not of it, even when he's seated at the center of the table, surrounded by the other men. He is generally quiet except to be caustic, a man who dreams of a job with a big-market paper where he can cover the major leagues instead of high school sports. I would not call him handsome—for whatever my judgment is worth—but he has a melancholy presence that is noteworthy. He reminds me of his namesake in *Casablanca*, Bogart without the saving graces of Bergman: lonely, bitter, and a little too intelligent for his own good. Despite the protestations of the waitresses, his unruly salt-and-pepper hair hides beneath a black Colorado Rockies cap that he wouldn't doff for royalty.

I like Richard very much, although I do not think I know him at all. This is our unspoken rule here at George's: we are free to be comrades but not to be friends, and personal lives, outside the narrow bounds of strict reportage on women, kids, and bosses, are strictly off-limits.

Margaret and Dee, the two gum-snapping waitresses in our end of the building, wave as I slide in next to Richard, and Dee comes over.

"What can I get y'all?" she says, pulling her pad from her apron pocket.

"How's the barbecue plate?"

"Same as always," she says, already writing it down. "And iced tea." It is not a question, but I nod and hand her the menu.

Richard is winding down on the topic of the day, center fielders. "Devon White covers a lot of ground; so does Otis Nixon. Van Slyke still has the best arm. But for me it's a toss-up between Puckett and Griffey. They can both do it all, in the field and at the plate." He sits back, picks up a cracker, and uses it to scoop a recalcitrant piece of green salad onto his fork.

Hugh Kromer slides in on the other side of Wally wearing thick horn-rimmed glasses and the obligatory retiree brown coveralls. He's a sixtyish widower whose kids all live on the East Coast now except for a daughter my age who circulates in the stratosphere of Waco high society. "Not a one of 'em could hold a candle to the Mick," he says, launching into his Mantle-is-king argument before he even knows what the argument is about. Eating with these fellows gives me the greatest sense of security short of an encounter with God—you can pick up the conversation at any point and know you really haven't missed a thing.

Before Dee can bring my platter, our final member, tall and gangly Ronald Sloan, arrives. He is fresh from the courthouse, where he is writing a story on a local murder trial, and his knit tie is pulled loose and sleeves rolled up in classic reporter fashion on his amazingly long arms. Of all these guys, Ron is the only one I knew in distant history; we played football together in high school. Like me, he also remained here and attended Baylor while all our classmates escaped Waco, went off to Texas and Texas A&M and territories even farther afield.

My relationship with Ron is no deeper than with Wally or Richard, but it's different in that we know each other: he knows my family and my story. I know that he is also supposed to be working on a book, but that unlike me, he will finish it, will probably go on to bigger and better things like novelist Thomas Harris, who also used to cover the crime beat for the *Tribune*. It's just a matter of time. When David Koresh stood off the feds outside town, Ron's dispatches were picked up by the AP and sent worldwide, and to be honest, I don't know what's keeping him here.

"Am I too early for a Big O?" he asks Margaret, inquiring about the afternoon special, draft beer served in a glass roughly the size of a wheelbarrow.

"I'll get you one, hon," she says, patting his arm. His tankard and my barbecued brisket appear on the table simultaneously, and we toast each other, raised beer to raised fork.

"If it hadn't been for those knees," Hugh is saying to a not-unfriendly audience, "Mick, he would have broke every record in the books. Power from both sides, great speed."

"Ah, but he's no Mays," Ron Sloan sighs, setting down his Big O carefully on the now-crowded table and running his hands through his unkempt black hair. "Mays had more range, better speed, and hit a lot more home runs."

"660 to 536. Hell, Ernie Banks had 512," Wally murmurs. We nod in appreciation of his feat.

Hugh counters with leadership. Ron parries with the over-the-shoulder catch. It is a pleasant way to pass the day, and my lunch—not remarkably tasty, but remarkably cheap—is gone before either runs out of ideas, leaving the floor at last open for Wally, which is always an adventure.

"Oh, sure, Mays and Mantle," he says, looking around at us. "Obvious choices. But what about Cesar Cedeño?"

"Cesar Cedeño?" Hugh huffs. "Jesus Christ in a jumped-up sidecar."

"I think I need another Big O," Ron calls over to Dee. "Make that two."

"No," Wally says, hands raised. "Hear me out. Remember when he hit over four hundred in the Cardinals' stretch run in '85? He carried that team once they picked him up. And what did they do? How did they show their gratitude?"

"By releasing him," Richard says, without even a hint of a smile. "Guys, let me out, will you?"

While Wally continues spinning his tale in praise of mediocrity, here personified by one Cesar Cedeño, Richard gets some change from Margaret at the register and goes over to the pinball machines. George's has two, an Addams Family machine, good, with lots of gimmicks, and an ancient one that doesn't work well and nobody ever plays.

With Wally obviously vaulting off the deep end, though—I don't know if Cedeño ever played a game in center field—even a broken pinball machine starts to look pretty appealing, and I excuse myself to go and join Richard. I plug my quarter in, and at his first break in the action, he looks across at me. "That Wally, huh?"

I am trying to return a carom with the crippled right flipper, and the best I can manage is a feeble flap that barely keeps the ball in play. "I'm going to go back and advocate Jerome Walton," I say, and he chuckles approvingly.

"Rookie of the Year and thirty-game hitting streak," Richard recites as I try once again to get my flipper to work. These are details I don't remember, if indeed I ever knew them. My family attended major league games passionately in the Seventies, made pilgrimages to all the new state-of-the-art turf coliseums in Pittsburgh and Cincinnati and Philadelphia and St. Louis. All our family vacations revolved around baseball, which—next to his family—was my father's great passion. I knew how to read a box score before I knew how to read. Most of my knowledge of the sport dates back to that decade of Bench, Clemente, Stargell, Killebrew, Rose, Palmer. I can fake my way through baseball since then, and at least nod at football and basketball trivia, but honestly most of it is as unfamiliar—and unfulfilling—to me as World Cup soccer and world-class rodeo. All the joy is gone out of it.

I lose my last ball and lean over to watch Richard, who seems to be playing well, is flicking the ball at targets that light up and make important noises. "You know, Brad," Richard says, without taking his eyes off the game board in front of him, "I've always figured we had a lot in common. Far as I can tell, there's nothing important to you but your bike and your writing."

I grunt affirmatively; even if we spoke the whole truth here at lunch, I wouldn't want to distract him by a correction. Dee puffs past behind us with an order of chicken-fried steak and big sweating glasses of iced tea.

"And I don't have anything except Audrey and my writing," Richard goes on. Audrey is the only woman in Richard's life, excepting Dee and Margaret; she is a nine-year-old Golden Retriever he rescued from the pound six years ago. When the final ball at last slips between his flippers, he stands at the machine for a moment, then turns to me, and his gaze has a directness I have not seen there before.

"Come outside with me for a second," he says. "There's something I want to show you."

"You won a free game," I point out.

For a moment, he can't process what I have said. It's as if I have spoken to him in Chinese. At last he says, "Hugh can have it," and he leads me out to the parking lot where his beat-up yellow Firebird sits, and the south wind blows garbage up the street behind us, and he produces a large stiff manila envelope from the passenger seat and passes it across to me without a word.

I fight the wind to slide out a set of what looks like X rays, and when I hesitate, Richard says, "Go on. Hold one up and look at it."

It is a strangely intimate moment, looking at someone's insides. When I hold up the first sheet, both hands holding it tightly so it won't flap in the breeze, even I can see that something is wrong. On what I take to be the liver, I can see a huge opaque spot, almost perfectly black and round.

My mouth goes dry; I don't want to ask. When I look up, he nods.

"I just came from the doc. It's too late to operate, to do chemo. To do anything." He relates this information matter-of-factly, then looks away, clears his throat.

I don't want to know this; I don't know why he's telling me; I don't know what I'm supposed to do. I feel as though I am sinking into that dark hole, and it is only with an effort that I tear my eyes away from it and push the sheet back into the envelope.

"I'm sorry," I say, and I am, more than I can express. Although perhaps it would not be a great tragedy if it were to happen to me, I genuinely like Richard, and would not have this happen to him if I could somehow prevent it.

He shrugs. "It's not so bad. I'm not really in any pain yet." Then he smiles sadly. "Most of the things I wanted to do with my life I never would have accomplished anyway."

"That's not true," I tell him. He is no older than my dad was. Young, still.

He waves off my feeble attempt at comfort. "It doesn't matter. There's only one thing I still want to do, and maybe I still will. Hell, maybe the two of us can do it before I get too bad. I'd like to see the Rockies play at Mile High Stadium. Drive through the New Mexico desert, into the Sangre de Cristos, up into Colorado. That would be something, the trip and the game." Behind us a huge cardboard box—about the size of a refrigerator box, and so, I assume, empty—makes its clomping end-over-end way up the street toward wherever the wind is going.

"Have you told anybody else?" I ask, handing him the envelope and trying to get him thinking about something other than taking me off on some final Thelma and Louise baseball junket.

It does jar him out of his reverie. He snorts, in fact. "Who else would I tell?"

"But the guys—"

"I guess they'll know soon enough." He tosses the envelope back down onto the seat and lets a sigh escape him. "Soon enough." He slumps back against the car, and for a moment I get a preview of what is to come. He looks twice his age, defeated, skeletal.

"Come on back inside," I say. "Sit down for a minute. Argue with Hugh. You'll feel better."

He nods, pushes himself up off the car, straightens his cap. "You're probably right." We walk back inside and resume our seats, where I don't understand a single word spoken in the few short minutes before I can reasonably get up to leave. I make some sort of excuse—God knows I have no pressing business—wave to them all, nod at Richard, and head for the exit, my heart pounding.

I climb into the Healey, start it up, and almost back right into a huge black Suburban, which gives me a good long blat of its monstrous horn. I let the noise wash over me, let the truck disappear from my rearview, and then I back into the street, off on a drive.

I don't have a destination; I simply go all afternoon in the same fuzzy-headed stupor, drive like I had demons on my heels, crisscrossing an area that I discover—when I sit down later with a calm head and a road map—to be the size of a small state. I drive all that hot, blustery afternoon and into the night, past white frame churches and emu ranches, soul food restaurants and barbecue shacks and taquerias, pecan orchards and feedlots, deserted main streets and sagebrush plains, limestone bluffs and sluggish green rivers and high-tension lines strung from towers marching across the rolling countryside like Martian tripods come to destroy us utterly. Far off to the north and west, I see a line of gloomy thunderheads carrying their precious water away to Dallas or Shreveport. I rocket across bridges made of rusty iron and bridges of concrete, I crest hills where I can see for days and traverse impenetrable leafy green tunnels where trees overarch country lanes.

I stop for gas and a twenty-ounce Dr Pepper at a little mom-and-pop gas station outside Corsicana—Fruitcake Capital of the World—and make a similar pit stop some hours later in Dublin, home of the only Dr Peppers in America still made with cane sugar, although even this delicacy does not raise my spirits. I recall white dust boiling up behind me on a deserted gravel road and a dead white-tailed deer lying haggard and fly-buzzed in a culvert and turkey buzzards overhead circling, circling, and the velvet sunset painted orange and red and purple across the western sky and the high wispy cirrus clouds like something unutterably beautiful about to disappear forever into darkness.

Death is in the air.

I am somewhere near Robinson when I happen to look down

at my left hand, white-knuckled on the steering wheel, and at last become aware of the pain shooting from it up my arm. I make a left turn that suddenly seems familiar, and the next thing I know I am standing at Sandra Fuentes' perpetually-lit front door with bugs flitting around my head and I am knocking, knocking with that same insensate spasming hand, while over my head, the upper limbs of her pecan tree thrash about in the wind like a giant has taken it in his head to shake something—or somebody—out of it.

At length, the door opens, and she steps forward, a tiny presence blinking at me in the dim light.

"Brad?" she asks, although why she has to ask this I don't know, since she's standing right there in front of me, looking right at me, staring, actually. Her hazel eyes are bright and clinical behind her glasses and I am so close that I can see myself reflected in them, and in those eyes I can see that I am lost and alone and that the world behind me is a very dark place.

Her hand rises to my arm, but her eyes never leave mine. We stand there for how long I do not know, saying nothing, studying and being studied, silently comprehending loneliness and despair. At length her lips move slightly in what is not a smile but, rather, a signal of recognition, and she nods. "Come in," she says softly, with unexpected gentleness, "Come inside," and she takes my poor throbbing hand in her two small hands and pulls me gently through the door, pulls me from the wind-tossed darkness to safety.

"You don't have to be afraid here," Sandra says as she does this. "Everything's going to be all right." And she leads me down the hallway and back deep into the house to a place I have never seen, a quiet place without cats or papers or clutter. On the wall is a large terra-cotta crucifix, and beneath it is the oak headboard of her bed. She lays me down and holds me and speaks tenderly to me, and for a few moments, at least, she is right.

I am not afraid. And everything does seem to be all right.

5

It is becoming harder and harder to empty my mind during my rides, let alone during my long nights; since seeing Richard's insides, I can't seem to recover my equilibrium. I skip lunch at George's the following Tuesday because I don't think I can simply sit there and listen to Richard sardonically poke holes in somebody's eloquent argument for Pee Wee Reese's shortstop sainthood as though nothing has changed. I will scream, lose control; they will have to use nets to restrain me.

Richard is dying. Dying! He is being eaten alive by himself, by his own traitorous cells, multiplying and remultiplying every second of every minute of every one of his remaining days, and he wants me to pretend as though no such mutiny is taking place? Worse yet, he supposes I might like to drive him—a dying man, for Christ's sake—across the desert and through the mountains, to dance cheek-to-cheek with death one more time, and the truth is, a truly decent human being would do it.

I add five miles onto my afternoon trek, which diverts me at first. Whenever you assay new roads on a bicycle, opportunities for adventure are endless: new vistas, new surfaces, maybe a new bridge or two. Despite what happened to Susie Bramlett, I still have a soft spot for country bridges, plank or rusty iron truss structures with romantic views of slow-moving creeks and overhanging cottonwoods. It's also possible to get lost or pedal gamely for miles only to come smack up against a dead end. That's how I made my all-time record ride, fifty-five miles or so, not because I felt like a bicycle behemoth on that particular day but because I got lost and had to keep retracing my steps.

My five new miles turn out to have something even more interesting than any of the above. A mile and a half down the road, I see a sign—Bridge Out—and a smile breaks across my face for the first time in days. Sure enough, at the two-mile mark up ahead I discover a rickety old structure without side rails spanning—more or less—an overgrown ravine that may or may not hold water. The road's barricaded official end point under the low-hanging branches of pecan trees is littered with Miller Lite cans and Lone Star bottles, and here and there a used condom glitters colorfully in the sun. This is a happening place.

I dismount to lift my bike over the barrier placed across the road and push it through the chest-high weeds and gingerly onto the creaking planks of the bridge. Ahead I see a spot where they've given way completely, and yes, there is water down below. The bridge seems solid enough to hold the two hundred pounds or so that the bike and I represent, but the fact that I'm not completely sure of that makes my heart pound happily in my chest.

I feel—for the first time in a long time—completely alive as I step out alone onto the rickety planks, wheel my bike to the center, stand there with my eyes closed, my face raised. The sun is warm as it filters patchwork through the trees, a crisp clean scent rises from the water, and I am the only person alive to it.

The Out bridge becomes my favorite spot along my new route, and in the days that follow, I dally there, dangle my legs over the side, listen to the wind rustling through the leaves like the flipping pages of a hundred empty notebooks. I take out my water bottle and sip a little. Sometimes I can hear a distant truck rattling along State Highway 7, somewhere beyond the trees and the hills, but mostly I hear the wind, and the slight chuckle from the creek below, and the exhilarating creak of the bridge beneath me.

I am close to exhaustion now when I reach home in the evening, and for the first week or so, I actually sleep at night.

"I should have done this months ago," I tell Elaine, who calls while I am watching the Braves battle for the pennant. "So simple, really."

"What happens when you get used to thirty-five miles? Do you jump it to forty? Fifty? I worry about you."

"One day at a time, dear Elaine. Deal with the future if it comes."

"If? What happened to 'as'?" To be expected, I suppose. Elaine lives for the future. She gets paid when people finish books, when publishers release books; half her life is made up of anticipation.

"A guy I know—a friend, I guess you'd say—has cancer. It's going to kill him." I can say this to Elaine: she is fifteen hundred miles away, a disembodied voice on the telephone.

"I'm sorry," she says. It is all anyone can say, but from her it soothes. "Is it anyone I know?"

"Nope. I don't really know him that well myself. Now I guess I never will." I listen for a moment to the white noise on the line, a distant wail like the wind, before plunging forward. "Elaine, am I a bad person?"

There is a moment of hesitation now on her end as she tries to calculate how honest she can afford to be. "No, Brad," she says, and again comes that pause. "You're not bad. Not really. You're—rootless. Apathetic and morose. But not bad. Not in the sense of genuinely evil, I mean. Why do you ask?"

"He—this guy with cancer—asked me to do him a favor. A big favor. A dying-man's-last-request sort of favor. And I've avoided him. I don't want to do it. I can't." There; I have spoken it, and now it is true and tangible: I am not a decent human being.

"Oh, Brad. How awful. For both of you." We share a moment of silent commiseration. Then she returns to her usual crisply efficient self. "Well, you have to talk to him. Tell him that you don't think you can do it. If you hide out, it's not going to do either of you any good."

"Yes," I say. She is right, as she so often is. "I'll tell him." On my television, Brave third baseman Terry Pendleton snags a hot grounder, whirls acrobatically, and throws to second to start a double play, and the moment makes me feel so good that I tell Elaine so.

"Don't overexert yourself," she says, and then there is a buzz on my line—call waiting—and I excuse myself.

"Hi," Madelyn Clark says in her quiet voice. "How are you?"

"Okay, all things considered," I say. I turn off the TV sound with the remote control as the commercials come on. "How are you?"

"Oh, fine," she says. "Fine. Only I miss you something awful. Can I see you?"

"Where's Colby?" I ask. Surely he can't decamp for Cambridge again already; it's only a few weeks into the semester.

"Here," she says. "He's in his study, on the computer. He won't be out for hours."

"I don't like the odds," I say. "He'll come out, discover us, beat me to death with a riding crop or a bumbershoot or some such."

If I didn't know her better, I'd swear that the bubbling sound emerging from the phone is a giggle. "I didn't mean here, you idiot," she says. "Can I come by? I told him I had things to do. He grunted. It's all settled."

All settled, that is, except for the fact that I don't have people over to my house. That's why I didn't invite Becky Sue in when she rescued me and brought me home; I moved into this restored farmhouse when Elaine and I drifted apart, and it has been my Fortress of Solitude. I have a view out across a pasture that explodes with bluebonnets and Indian paintbrush in the spring, and in the winter I throw big cedar logs on the fire and sit all night watching the flames dance.

"I don't know," I say. It is the exact wrong thing to tell Madelyn Clark, only slightly less damaging than "Get lost." Although she doesn't hang up, it is as if the phone has gone dead. All of a sudden, there is no one on the other end.

At last she says, "I see," and her voice has the lifeless quality of a recording. "Well, I'm sorry to have bothered you." She is half a second away from replacing the receiver in the cradle, and I see her doing it, sliding her hand back from the telephone, sitting in silence as the afternoon shadows lengthen.

"Madelyn," I say, with unaccustomed force. "Wait!"

And although she says nothing, the receiver does not drone into my ear; she is still there.

"Pick up some Corona on your way," I say, and she says, "I'll be right over."

What in the name of all that is holy and inviolate has possessed me? A rendevous—here—with a married woman, no less? I've read those nineteenth-century novels. What's next for me? Scandal? Exclusion from high society? Throwing myself under the wheels of a train in adulterous despair?

Well, probably not. But I'm not pleased with this crack in the facade of my self-control. I do not want to need anything, to desire anything, to feel anything, and I'm starting to think that where Madelyn is concerned, maybe I do.

There is still time to get out, to make my escape. If the Healey will start, I could be halfway to somewhere else by the time she gets here.

And when she got here and I didn't answer, she'd be crushed.

So I sit right where I am, watching the baseball game, the sound still off, until she knocks tentatively at the door, as though she has read my mind, as though she really didn't expect me to be here after all, and I feel a dangerous feathery quivering in the vicinity of my heart and call, "Come in."

She pushes the door open, peers around the corner of it, her hair falling like a dark veil across her face. "I brought beer," she says, pushing it out of her eyes. "But they didn't have Corona." She carries her sack in and sets it on the table. "I can't stay long."

"I'm sorry to hear that," I say, without telling her—without really knowing myself—which of her statements I'm responding to.

She looks around approvingly. The house appears neat, as well it should; messes take too much energy. And this is my favorite room. One wall is a desk and bookshelves, one is mostly fireplace and mantel, one is mostly window. "This is a nice place."

"Thanks," I tell her. I shut off the TV and lead her back to my bedroom. Once we cross the threshold, she turns me toward her and kisses me, then she pushes me down onto the bed. After that, things get a little crazy. Clothes translate graceful arcs across the room: my sweats and T-shirt, her jeans, blouse, white bra and panties. These last come off quickly, and Madelyn tosses them toward the floor as if to disclaim them. Once, a long time ago, I teased her about her undergarments—all of them cream or white—and offered to buy her some naughty ones, red or purple, maybe, and she actually blushed. "Oh, I couldn't," she said, and quickly got my attention focused on other matters. I wasn't even speaking of getting her into any of those engineering marvels to be found in the Victoria's Secret catalogues, those male fantasies strapped onto women's bodies, but I didn't have liberty to explain, as I said, and the memory still seems to embarrass her.

It is already dark outside, and I make to turn on a light, but as always, she stops me. There are things she feels comfortable doing in the dark that she would never consider doing in the light. I think her underwear embarrassment is simply a manifestation of her inexplicable rejection of her body, maybe even of herself, but I did not carry a third major in psychology and even if I had, it wouldn't have prepared me to make such a judgment. No, it is just my conclusion based on the available evidence, although I don't happen to agree with it. I think she has an admirable body: small firm breasts, long slender waist, swelling hips, and I do my best to convince her of my admiration.

Later, we lie there in the dark, and unaccountably, her hand snakes across the short distance separating us and takes mine. "I'm glad to see you," she says.

"I'm glad to see you too," I say, although actually I can't see much of anything. A scuffling noise directly overhead startles Madelyn, and she jerks her hand away.

"It's one of those damn cats from next door," I tell her. "They get into the attic and chase mice."

"Oh," she says. "The Faber cats." I feel rather than see her roll over and check the clock. "I have to go." She throws her legs over the side of the bed, sits up straight. "I suppose I had better turn on the light."

"Unless you want to risk wearing some of my clothes home." I cover my eyes. "Okay."

The glare from the lamp is unpleasant, and we look away from each other as we both dress silently.

"I like your house," she repeats as we walk to the front door. In my literature classes, I learned that repetition typically indicates that a writer is trying to emphasize something, and so is Madelyn. What she is saying is, may I come back?

"It's very comfortable," I say. "For a bachelor, at least. I'm glad you like it."

What I am saying in return is less clear. I am balancing a tightrope between rejection and throwing the door perpetually open. I do not want the latter, and with her, it is always dangerous to even suggest the former, so before she can get away, I venture back out onto the wire. I pull her close, kiss her, and thank her for coming. "But we didn't get to have any of this beer," I say, looking over her shoulder into the kitchen.

"Well, maybe next time," she says, looking me straight in the eyes.

"Maybe so," I say, and I wave as she walks out onto the porch. Headlights flash by on the road as Madelyn Clark climbs into her car and goes home to her husband, and as she drives off I feel a sucking emptiness as if she's taken some of my internal organs with her. I go back into the den, turn the television up loud, and try to concentrate on the postgame show, but my mind is somewhere in the night on the road back to Waco.

It is another long night.

Naturally, the next morning early the phone rings, and with a groan, I lift it from the nightstand. It can only be one person.

"Where the hell have you been, son?" Jackson growls. I start to answer, but at my first syllable, he says, "Well, never mind that. Come for dinner tonight."

"Okay," I say. The alternative—a telephone argument with a half-deaf grandparent at six a.m.—would be potentially debilitating. I hang up and manage to go back to sleep for another few hours before another—or maybe the same one—of the Faber cats does a body slam on the ceiling just over my head. I get up, shower, shave, eat two bowls of cereal, and reread *The Green Hills of Africa* until lunchtime. It gives me visions of stalking the

Faber cats in khaki and a pith helmet. They are good visions. An elephant gun would leave nothing but a vague catlike smear behind.

I tell myself that I will only go to George's if I hit a convenient chapter break at noon, confident that the statistical chances of this happening are slim to none, but as I reach the last page of the wonderful chapter in which Hemingway shoots his first kudu, I hear the microwave's clock beep to mark the hour, and I am exiled by my promise. No matter what a louse you are in other places, with other people, when you go back on promises to yourself, you teeter on the edge of the abyss. There are few things I hold sacred, but this is one of them. If you can't trust yourself, who can you trust?

I sigh, set down the book, and go in to get my shoes and socks. Then I drive to George's, stand momentarily outside the door, take what is becoming, for me, a typical series of deep breaths, and pull the glass door open and walk in.

Richard is not sitting in our booth. In fact, although I am late and festivities should be in full swing, our group is skeletal today. Hugh is also missing, and Ron and Wally are somberly drinking, Big Os perched within the circle of their fingers. Although all of us are big fans of the Atlanta Braves, I cannot believe they are simply despondent over the Braves being beat by the Phillies for the National League championship, although it is true that the Phils are a graceless team of scraggly-bearded trailer-park trash.

I'm not upset about it either.

"Brad," they each say as I approach, and Wally scoots over a bit to make room for me in the corner booth, reaches behind me to scoot his fishing hat over.

Neither wants to meet my eye, but I wait expectantly, and after Margaret brings me a menu and a glass of water, Ron clears his throat and says, "Richard is in the hospital. It looks bad. Cancer. Hugh called, said he was going by. I thought we might go up later."

I am hit by simultaneous impulses that shake me like the Quake of '06: a cold hand seems to close around my heart at the same time as the realization that I am now off the hook shoots through some unfettered corner of my brain. The combination of the two is enough to make me dizzy and a little sick to my stomach.

I am not just a bad person; I am a bad person cursed with enough self-awareness to know it.

"Hey, easy, man," Wally says, and I feel his hand on my shoulder, steadying me, pushing me back against the seat. He and Ron both look at me with something like alarm on their faces; my own face tingles and must be bone white.

"I'm all right," I croak. "Just let me take a drink." I raise the glass of water, wet with condensation, to my lips, and my hand shakes only a little. I set it down and speak, although I do not look up. "When did it happen?"

"Last night," Wally says. He shudders a little himself, quickly raises his Big O to his lips, and drains it. It seems to make him feel better. "I just can't believe it. He knew. Why didn't he tell us?"

We sit for a moment, the jukebox playing the chorus of some old Tanya Tucker song—maybe "What's Your Mama's Name, Child?"—in the background.

"He told me," I say, and I sneak a glimpse up from the table. "Two weeks ago. Showed me his X rays. I don't know why."

They exchange glances. "Why didn't you tell us?" Ron asks.

The jukebox launches into "Delta Dawn." Somebody in here has a serious Tanya Tucker jones. But I remain silent. I have no answer for them. Maybe I should have told them; Richard did not forbid me. Maybe he even hoped I would help him break the news.

But I didn't. I couldn't. And I can see that I am not going to be able to eat lunch; at the moment, I feel even more queasy, and if experience serves, soon I will be hugging porcelain. This is what I get for sticking my neck even the tiniest bit outside my shell, for allowing myself to feel anything at all.

"I guess it must have gotten to be too much to carry around on his own," Ron says, finally.

"I guess so," Wally says.

They drink in silence for a few minutes. Margaret has reloaded for them and stands patiently to take my order. I shake my head at her.

"I gotta get out of here," I say. "I'm sorry."

"It's okay, Brad," Ron Sloan, hard-boiled crime-beat reporter says, and I believe him. "We'll give him your best." Both of them shake my hand somberly.

"You look like hell, hon," Margaret says as I rise. "You go on home and get some rest."

"Yeah," I say. "I'll do that."

And I flee. When I arrive home, I deny my roiling stomach and pull out my biking shorts and a T-shirt, and I am tying my shoes when the phone rings. In my present state of mind, I am surprised to find myself pleased that it is Becky on the other end. In fact, I am prepared to throw over my plans for the afternoon, although fortunately, it doesn't come to that.

"Do you want to go see the new zoo Sunday?" she asks. "I haven't been yet, and it's supposed to be great."

"Sure," I say. I like the Waco Zoo, and it doesn't hurt to have something to look forward to.

"I thought maybe we could go after I get out of church," she says. "Hey, do you want to go to church with me? We could go straight from there."

Subtle, but futile. Becky and my grandparents both attend worship services in the ornate hundred-year-old sanctuary downtown of Waco First Baptist, and even if I were inclined to go to church, which I am not, I have no interest in explaining to my grandparents why I'm suddenly in church, and sitting with a beautiful coed, no less.

"No thanks," I tell her. "I'll meet you at Monkey Island. Just inside. One o'clock?"

"Well, okay." Her voice registers a little disappointment, perhaps on several levels; not only am I not accompanying her to church, but this will be a meeting-each-other date instead of a going-together date, and we have had far more of the former, by my conscious plan. Becky Sue is gorgeous, pleasant, bright, but she likes me far more than I like her, and furthermore, she likes me for all the wrong reasons. She fell for me last year when I came and talked to her creative writing class, or, rather, she fell hard for an image of me, a case of imprinting gone awry like a baby duck following a human around, and nothing

I have done since can be admitted to her vision of me. My indolence and inconsideration simply slide off her oiled duck's back.

I have the responsibility of holding myself back, not letting her hurtle toward an Out Bridge just because she doesn't see it. Her affection for me is no more than a simple case of mistaken identity, and one of these days she'll realize her mistake; they always do. In the meantime, I must resist my biological urges and settle for small comforts.

Well. My behavior with Becky gives me some hope; maybe I'm not completely reprehensible after all.

I begin feeling even more like a human being during my ride, and when I get home, I shower again and dress for dinner. Billie fixes pork chops on Thursday nights, and I don't want to be late for pork chops.

I sprint up the front stairs and into the dining room of my grandparents, actually in time for a spinach salad with oil and vinegar dressing drizzled over sliced eggs and crumbled bacon.

"Well, well," Billie says. "The Prodigal returns."

"Lookin' good, Billie," I say, sitting down and shaking open my napkin. "How you been?"

"Go on with you," she says, although she is pleased to have me ask after her and her hand rises to my cheek and pats it. As always, she almost knocks me over. "These old folks here the ones you should be talking to."

"Ah, Billie," I say, "but they don't do the cooking." And she laughs and shuffles back into the kitchen while I rub my cheek.

Jackson waits until she disappears. "Where you been, son? What you been doing? You suddenly too busy to keep your dinner dates with your grandma and me?"

"I missed one time," I whine. I was supposed to come last Tuesday, but as I've noted, I fell down on a lot of my obligations on Tuesday. This would be the ideal time to tell them about Richard, to provide the extenuating circumstances, since this is one of the rare occasions that I actually have extenuating circumstances, but I hesitate. "Hospital" and "death" are loaded words in our family, like "abortion" or "child molesting" might be in someone else's. We do not introduce them lightly into conversation, certainly not for anything as frivolous as to excuse an absence at dinner.

"I'm sorry," I say. "I guess it slipped my mind."

Billie brings in the chops, the baked apples, the baked potatoes. Jackson tells a couple of jokes; Evelyn talks about her volunteer work; I sit silently and load up my baked potato with sour cream, butter, cheese, flood it with salt in hopes that I'll get hit by a massive coronary.

Everything seems so simple when I'm out on my bicycle; if only I could spend all my time out there.

If only.

6

After a couple of weeks of pleasant, almost fall-like weather, Indian summer has shot the temperature back up into the low nineties, and for my date with Becky at the Waco Zoo I pull on some khaki shorts and a polo shirt, hoping she will have sense enough to change out of her flowered Laura Ashley church dress before she comes.

As I pay my admission, it occurs to me that I am a cheapskate for having set up a meeting inside the zoo, but since I don't know if she's already here, it's probably best to stick to the plan, cheap as it may make me look. I walk inside, across the brick pavement, and down the wooden stairs to the wood platform that overlooks the pond and Monkey Island. At the far end of the platform, next to the ramp, a family is having a birthday party, and since the cake isn't being served yet, a dozen kids in conical paper hats run wildly, their small feet pattering across the planking.

I lean up against the railing and watch the antics of the tiny gray monkeys. Are these the gray monkeys of which Sandra speaks, the ones who can learn to swim? I resolve to ask her. Surely the zoo people would be up on monkey lore, would know which monkeys could escape their watery imprisonment and which couldn't. But to return to Monkey Island: these particular monkeys have a network of trees, climbing posts, and ropes upon which they can leap, brachiate, or simply sit, legs and arms dangling. The youngest one seems happiest on the ground running through the tall grass, his long arms flopping over his head or getting tangled beneath his feet so that he falls and rolls, gets up and sets out on his way again.

He isn't particularly light on his feet yet, although I suppose soon he will develop the skills his graceful elders possess, will make death-defying leaps look easy and natural.

Without warning, something or someone pinches me on the ass, and, if not for the railing, I would be in the brackish green water.

Becky Sue Bradenton giggles as she eases in behind me and throws her arms around my waist. "Did I surprise you? I saw you leaning over like that and I just couldn't resist. Am I bad?"

"Awful," I say. I pat her hands at my waist. "You'll make the FBI Ten Most Wanted, be on all the true crime shows."

She giggles again, her head turns, and her golden hair seems to fly in slow motion; Becky should definitely be selling something. I look down at her feet and see that she has on a pair of hikers and gray socks, scrunched down. Unless she has altered her fashion sense recently, she is appropriately dressed.

"Come around here and take a look at these guys," I say, and she pulls her arms out from around my waist and slides in next to me at the railing. She is wearing khaki shorts and a sorority T-shirt memorializing some party with a hoedown theme. She looks good. Maybe it's a simple matter, but her dressing down for the occasion gives me some new respect for her.

"How was church?" I ask.

"Fine," she says, and she doesn't volunteer anything else until she sees I am waiting for details. She never says much about church, although her parents are very religious, and I sense that she herself is, to a somewhat lesser extent. This is another thing I like about her. She is comfortable enough in her beliefs that she doesn't feel the need to preach to others. "The pastor talked a little about the Civil War today, if you can believe that. You might have found it interesting."

"I can believe it." The Civil War is complex, can be turned to lots of uses.

One of the older monkeys begins chasing the other from one end of the island to the other, and the chase is worthy of the finale of a Hollywood action film: narrow escapes, stunt leaps, dangling by fingertips. The tiny monkey on the ground watches with interest and then decides he wants to be a part of it, so he climbs laboriously up the nearest perch and swings onto a rope.

"You know," I tell her, "I admire your faithfulness. I'd like to feel strongly enough about something to do it religiously."

"Oh, but you do," she says. "There's your writing, and lots of other things, I'm sure."

"I'm religious about my cycling," I say in an attempt to be funny, and I suddenly realize that it's true. If asked to delineate my days, where I put my effort, my sweat, my occasional expenditures of capital, they all point in one direction. Where a man's treasure is, there his heart will be also.

"Are you religious about anything else?"

"Not a hell of a lot," I admit.

"When are you coming up to school?" she asks. She is wise enough to know when a subject needs to be changed.

"I'm giving The Lecture to Dr. Forest's Civil War class on Wednesday. That's probably it until next month."

"Do you want to have lunch Wednesday?"

"Dr. Forest always takes me to the faculty club. Payment, he calls it. Rain check?"

"Sure," she says. We stand for another few minutes watching, but the chase is over, and the three monkeys are now sitting comfortably and separately, letting out an occasional screech, grooming themselves like good primates. There is nothing more to observe here.

"Come on," she says, taking my hand. "Let's go see the elephants."

"Okay," I say. "I like elephants."

When I get home from the zoo some hours later, I can already feel sunburn tingling on my cheeks and forehead, and my stomach is in revolt from the hot sun, too many Dr Peppers, too much junk food, so I decide to grant myself a day off from riding. I take a long cool shower, sit down under the spray and let it pound on my head, and I feel a little better afterward. In fact, I stretch out on the couch and actually fall asleep for a while. The second game of the World Series is on when I wake up, and I watch the hideous Phillies whip up on the Blue Jays, then go to bed early, around eleven.

The next morning I sleep late, treat myself to a lavish breakfast of Wheat Chex and milk, and hit the road around noon to make up for my lazy Sunday. It is already hot, humidity in the high eighties, and the wind has picked up out of the south, so I start off directly into the teeth of it.

For some reason, the world is full of flying things: fluttering migratory Monarch butterflies and mated dragonflies zipping acrobatically across the roads; overhead, turkey buzzards soar, and I hear a sound like the creaking of a hundred rusty hinges, look up through the cottonwoods to the blue sky far beyond, and discover several squadrons of geese high above, circling in confusion. These last are worth watching, and I pull over to the side and crane my neck. The geese form up into wedges and start south, then double back on themselves, all cohesion lost. Maybe the heat has disoriented them; maybe the wind is causing them the same problems it causes me; maybe they have a faulty map, or some coup de flock is under way. At length, I lose interest in them, and when I emerge from my tunnel of trees a few miles ahead they have disappeared. On to Mexico? Stopped at some pond for refreshments? I can't tell, and in any case, they don't reappear for the rest of my ride.

It's just as well; I have little attention to spare. The steady wind calls forth all my strength and strategy. To present the smallest wind signature, I should stay seated and bent forward, but in that position I have almost no leverage, and as my thighs begin to burn, I have to stand on the pedals, use my arms and back to tug myself forward, although standing makes the wind resistance even more tangible and I slow nearly to a halt as it pushes against me.

As I pass the Cottonwood Baptist Church, the wind abates for a moment, giving me false hopes, because as I approach the big hill up to Mooreville the wind gusts back at least as strongly as before. Half a dozen turkey buzzards ride the thermals, circling almost directly overhead, but I am still moving; I don't think they are interested in me. I have an impulse to get off my bike, lie down on the road, and see how long it would be before they start to spiral down toward me—useful information I might need at some point in the future—but the truth is that cars and trucks also use this road, and it seems a lot more likely that one of them will come along before the buzzards take me seriously, so I turn my attention back to the hill.

It is as imposing as always. The road climbs several hundred feet in a quarter mile, and the last fifty yards seem to be almost straight-up vertical, although I recognize that this is a physical impossibility. In any case, the hill commands the valley, looms over it; any Civil War commander worth his salt would occupy this height as soon as he saw it. In fact, as I pump slowly up it, I always half expect to see cannon among the gravestones in the cemetery along the ridge to my left, a row of twenty-pounders set to enfilade an advancing line of troops.

The last yards almost do me in today; I shift up and up and up, begin to weave back and forth from one ditch to the other, and have slowed to the point that I am actually on the verge of climbing off and pushing. I am soaked when I reach the summit, and I sit panting in the shade of the huge oak tree next to the Methodist Church for a good twenty minutes before moving on. I have drained my water bottle only halfway through my trip, and so I make a rare stop at the little Mooreville service station, pour cold Dr Pepper into my bottle for consumption on the Out Bridge, and continue doggedly on my way. Fortunately the wind remains constant from the south, and it as much as pushes me the last few miles home.

I skip the Tuesday lunch at George's, although Ron calls me Monday night with news about Richard's condition, worse, and engross myself instead in Jane Goodall, read about Flo, Fifi, Flint, and her other chimpanzee friends. I hope to see Sandra Fuentes at school on Wednesday, and I want to bone up on her idol and mentor; I would like to be able to offer her something for a change.

Unfortunately, when I drop by her building Wednesday morning before I have to go over to Tidwell and divest myself of my lecture, she isn't in her office, and the Biology secretary tells me that she's speaking to an anthropology class in 212. I peer into a darkened classroom, lit only by the flash of projected slides, and hear a few snatches of recognizable Fuentes primate sexuality: "pinkening"; "presenting"; "mating." The class laughs at some witticism of hers, although all I hear is its conclusion: "Isn't that just like a man?"

It occurs to me then, as I loiter there in the hall of the life sciences building, that Sandra Fuentes' unhappy past and her present immersion in chimp life will almost certainly prove a potent bar to any human relationship. From what I'm hearing, female chimps don't seem to have a lot to look forward to in regard to romance: Chimpanzee males typically perform intercourse that lasts only ten to thirty seconds and often consummate the act of love while swilling down bananas.

I believe I could convince her that male chimpanzees are giving us, their kissing cousins, an unnecessarily bad rap, but while I'd like to wait for her so that I can uphold my species and my gender, I am expected over in the Tidwell Building.

Once there, since I get all the exercise any human really needs, I decide to take the elevator instead of walking the stairs. When the bell dings and the doors lumber open, inside is Madelyn Clark, her cold can of Diet Coke fresh from the machine in the basement.

"Morning," I say. Since people are passing by, that is about all I can safely offer.

She nods, recognizing this fact. "Hi."

I step inside, push THREE, and the doors slowly close. Someone comes running up at the last moment, but neither Madelyn nor I makes a move to press the button that will hold the door open. As the elevator begins loudly humming its way upward, I turn and consider Madelyn against the backdrop of the stained brown carpet, the dull finished metal surfaces; she is a wonderful surprise even in these surroundings. I whistle nonchalantly and tunelessly while she pushes her dark hair out of her eyes and a half smile curls her lips up slightly. My hand crosses the distance separating us and takes hers; I give it a quick squeeze as we jerk to a stop, feel the firm pressure of her squeeze in return, and then I step out into the third-floor hallway, where

Dr. Robert Forest waits patiently for me, and when I step out to meet him, the doors close between us again.

"Hello, Brad," Dr. Forest says, loudly, giving me a vigorous handshake and leading me down the hall to his seminar room. "Good to see you, son. How are things?"

Dr. Forest and his wife had a son who would be about my age; he died young, and I can't help but think that the two of them like to think of me as theirs. Several times a year they have me over for dinner, and although they are staunch Southern Baptists who approve of divorce roughly as much as they approve of Islamic fundamentalism, their affection for me has never wavered.

Nor has mine for them. Anne is a wonderful white-haired woman, generous and courtly, and Robert E. Lee Forest is as fine a specimen of the Southern aristocratic gentleman as remains. A graduate of the University of Mississippi, he often becomes a little melancholy in teaching this course—for as Shelby Foote has said, "Lost things are always prized very highly"—but Dr. Forest is nonetheless evenhanded in his approach. Although his preferred designation for the conflict is "The War for Southern Independence," in class he is more prone to use "War Between the States" or even "Civil War." And lest anyone misunderstand his nostalgia for the Antebellum South, he excoriates the Peculiar Institution of slavery and lauds Lincoln for the Emancipation Proclamation.

Unlike some unregenerate Southerners, you will never hear the words "Bluebellies" or "Damn Yankees" drop from his lips in referring to the foe; Dr. Forest honors the bravery of soldiers both North and South, for he recognizes that an epic battle requires a worthy opponent. For that reason, he is as likely to praise the bravery and ingenuity of Joshua Lawrence Chamberlain at Gettysburg as he is to honor the memory of his audacious distant ancestor Nathan Bedford Forest.

My talk, as always, goes well; Dr. Forest has built me up to legendary status, the sheer audacity of Sibley, Baylor, and their Texan soldiers commands attention far beyond my limited public speaking abilities, and the only question they ask that I can't answer has to do with what shape the battlefields are in today. I have to admit that I have never been to New Mexico, not even in the height of my enthusiasm—there were no major league baseball games there, after all—and that I wrote the book entirely from archival sources without walking the battlegrounds at Val Verde or Glorieta Pass myself. This doesn't seem to disqualify me in their eyes, and it probably shouldn't. It's still a good book.

But at lunch in the faculty club, Dr. Forest pumps me for information on the book I am not writing. Although he is intelligent enough to recognize that I should have finished it some time ago, his love for me makes him obtuse, and while I'm sure he has concluded that my comfortable life keeps me from working as hard as I ought, I don't suppose the awful truth of the matter has once crossed his mind. This is as it should be. Dr. and Mrs. Forest constitute one of the centers of my existence, one of the tent poles that keeps my gossamer-thin life poised above the ground, and if they ever lost faith in me—even though, admittedly, they have every reason for doing so—my world would be profoundly shaken.

"I think you need to come back and get the M.A.," Dr. Forest says after he has ordered—and paid for—both of our lunches. "With me to crack the whip, you could finish that book as a thesis. Don't you think it's time for you to change your work habits on this book?"

"Don't beat around the bush on this," I tell him. "Come out and tell me exactly what you think."

He clears his throat and drops his head slightly to hide the flush creeping across his face. I have discovered him being both ungracious and direct, and if I took the news to Anne Forest, his life would not be worth living for the next few weeks.

"Of course I don't mean that," he says, when he's recovered his composure, and I am pleased to see that he's smiling and that no harm was done on either side of the exchange. "It's just that," and he leans over closer to me as the waitress brings out glasses of iced tea and situates it on the table in front of us, "damn it, Brad, I want to see this book before I pass on to my heavenly reward."

"Now don't you worry about that," I tell him. "You've got a couple of good years left."

He squeezes lemon into his tea and follows it with several heaping spoonfuls of sugar; when he stirs his tea, his glass looks like a snow globe. "Maybe so, maybe so. But couldn't you see your way clear to letting me read a chapter or two? Surely my favorite student couldn't deny me that one pleasure."

Here it is again; he is pointing out the difference between my approach on the last book (the only book, actually) and on this nonexistent one: on the Sibley book, Dr. Forest read behind me every step of the way, helped with revisions chapter by chapter, suggested sources I had neglected, and I think his feelings are hurt by the fact that years have passed and he still hasn't seen word one.

I pat his hand reassuringly. I would not willingly bring him pain, and for a moment, I consider cooking up a chapter just to make the old gentleman happy. What then, though? Another? A third? I can see myself actually writing a book simply to soothe Dr. Forest, and that is an outcome to be avoided at all costs.

I divert the talk to other matters, Dr. Forest's impending retirement and his plans to tour battlefields during the spring and summer of every year. "Shall I send pictures from Val Verde?" he asks, and I nod, chuckle.

"People seem to want to know what the battlefield looks like these days," I say. "Pass the sugar, will you?" And the rest of our meal is pleasantly occupied.

Still the concept of change is echoing inside my head as I go out on the road later, and to prove that I am at least capable of it if I choose to be, when I reach the end of my driveway I turn right, toward town, instead of left, away from it. I traverse three pleasant miles of tree-lined blacktop, white-faced cattle grazing peacefully in pastures beyond the trees, before crossing State Highway 6 and following 16th Street into Waco past Rosemont Cemetery—this part of the world is lousy with graveyards—crunch and crackle my way for half a mile along the gravel road that 16th becomes just past the cemetery, turn left on Primrose, heading southwest, and then pedal frantically against a red light to beat a cattle truck across I-77 so that I can catch Old Robinson Road going south into the country.

Old Robinson is a pleasant residential street with big pecan trees and large lots, bigger the farther south I travel. I cross Highway 6 again and continue on my way past the acreages and ranches and horse farms, turn right on Gregory Lane, which looks promising, shaded and level, and reach for my water bottle. I've worked up a good sweat, and I can feel my T-shirt sticking to the back of my neck and between my shoulder blades.

Then I hear a yapping noise, in stereo, and a couple of tiny Chihuahua-looking dogs come pitter-pattering out of an open garage and into the road after me. I think to myself, You've got to be kidding, but they're surprisingly quick considering they have almost no legs at all, and since I've slowed to take a drink they're nipping at my ankles before I can get up a good head of steam.

"No!" I yell, which is the first line of defense against nipping dogs. "Go home." Well-mannered dogs usually stop in their tracks, look sheepish, and go home when I do this; I have a voice that is large out of all proportion to my size or importance on the planet. But these dogs don't lose a step, don't so much as hesitate in their absurd tiny-footed pursuit. When they keep yapping right alongside me, I go to Yellow Alert, which is a kick—no more than a gentle nudge, really, especially to these peanut dogs—to give myself enough room to really pedal without getting tangled up with one of them.

As my foot contacts the snapping squirrel muzzle of the one on the left, I hear a gruff male voice behind me yell, "Hey!" but I am too busy pedaling to look back, and with a few strong pulls I have left the dogs behind.

I am half a mile down the road and have all but forgotten about the dogs when I hear gravel spraying behind me and move over to the far right of the road to let a red Dodge truck pass.

It passes all right—chrome running boards, mud flaps, gun rack and lassoing rope in the back window—then sprawls to a diagonal halt like something out of the Starsky and Hutch shows of my boyhood. To keep from barreling headlong into the side I lay the bike on its side in the gravel while I bail out into the culvert.

Although I manage to land feet first, the judges would not hold up any tens, and I am—to say the least—intrigued to hear what this guy has to say when he climbs out of his truck.

What he says, this big bearded guy in his forties, muscle just going to flab, is, "Those were my wife's dogs."

He is standing across the truck box from me, and he looks at me with the same blank-faced stupefaction I must be reflecting at the moment, a display surely in stark contrast to the adrenaline squirting through my veins. He has on a greenish gray shirt with "Shep" written in red thread on his chest pocket and a gimme cap emblazoned with a rebel flag and the motto "We have just begun to fight."

"Don't you be mean to them dogs," he goes on, raising a finger as though he is giving me a public safety lecture.

"Listen, buddy," I say, with rigid control. "Once those dogs jump into the street they've left your territory behind. I've got every right to ride unchased on streets that my taxes help build and maintain."

His expression doesn't change; if anything, it becomes blanker. A constitutional law argument is going to be lost on this guy. "Okay," I say. "Listen closely, and I'll explain it in words of two syllables or less. If your dogs chase me, they could get under my pedals, under the wheels. I could get hurt. They could get hurt. And you may not care what happens to me, but I can see you'd care if one of them got hurt."

His expression says that if I didn't ride past his house the chance of their getting hurt chasing me would be reduced to nil. He follows it up by repeating, "Those were my wife's dogs," and then he starts rolling up his sleeves to reveal beefy tanned forearms.

"Hold it," I say, holding up both hands. "You going to fight me over this? Are you mental?" I step back from the truck box and raise myself to my full height.

Apparently he is. His sleeves all rolled up, he rotates his cap on his head and starts to walk purposefully around the truck. I stand ready for him, but I still can't help trying one last time to make him see the error of his ways. "Before you throw a punch at me, you better look at the facts, Bubba. I'm younger than you are, I've got a lot better stamina, and you may outweigh me some, but I run about one-eighty, and all of that is muscle. If you come around that truck, I'm gonna to do my best to make you regret it."

It's a good speech, and he stops for a second, looks me up and down, decides I'm telling the truth (I actually come in at around one-seventy, but this guy is no carnival weight guesser), and walks back toward the cab.

"Man, am I glad to see you come to your senses," I say, although why I feel led to say anything at all is beyond me; my grandmother has spent years pointing out that sometimes I don't know how to leave well enough alone. "I can handle rabid dogs, but I never thought a rabid owner would come after me." I lean over to pick up my bike, and that's why I don't see what he does next until I raise back up.

What he does when he opens the cab door is this: he reaches up to the gun rack in his window, pulls down his deer rifle, and points it right at me, so that when I raise up I'm looking directly into the dark aperture at the end of the barrel.

"You apologize," he says. "And say you ain't never gonna bother those dogs again."

It is only then that I realize my mistake, easy enough to do in Texas, westernmost bulwark of the Confederacy: I have been portraying the Imperious Confederate General Upbraiding Cornfed Subordinate, when the part I should have adopted was Hardened Gunfighter Staring Down Rival at High Noon. As I said, it's an easy mistake to make in Texas, where the two cultures mix uneasily and you never know whether a situation calls for Southern hospitality or Western hostility.

Up until this moment I have been ready for anything, for him to come around the back of the truck or for him to get in it and drive away, but suddenly, whether it's the influx of adrenaline or the strange gleam in his eye as he points the gun in my direction, I begin to feel a queasiness in the pit of my stomach. Is this what Sandra would call fight-or-flight biological imperative? Or could it be that, deep down, hidden in someplace that I haven't even seen before today, I really want to live?

We look at each other, neither one moving, and all I can hear is the wind whistling in the power lines and the pounding of my heart in my throat and the darkness at the end of the gun barrel seems to grow until it is big enough to fall into.

I have been here before.

I have almost decided that if he says it again I'll scream, but when he repeats, "Those were my wife's dogs," what I actually do is tell him, "Listen, I'm sorry. I didn't mean any harm." And at this, wonder of wonders, he nods solemnly, almost sadly, lowers his gun, puts it back in the rack, and gets back in his truck. I stand there and watch him turn the truck around, and when he is down the road, my legs suddenly give way beneath me and I sit down in the road with a start.

He might have shot me.

I don't know what is more disturbing: that I might have been killed by a grieving dog-loving Bubba, or that I care.

But this is neither the time nor the place to think about it. I clamber back to my feet, pick up my bike, and start riding away from the Chihuahua house with all deliberate speed. As I go, the migrating birds, which have been massed in the trees and along the power lines, scatter into squawking flight. I flush hundreds, maybe even thousands of them as I ride beneath them. It is a reaction out of all proportion to the threat I pose, but that seems to be my fate today. They swirl upward, then into the fields of corn like pepper from a giant shaker.

As soon as I can conveniently do it, I hang a left, pass through the patched streets of Robinson, and go home. It hasn't been a particularly successful experiment. Maybe there's something to be said for continuing to do the same thing, even if that thing is nothing.

7

October presents itself as my month to be in the public eye: In addition to the book signing and my short pep talk for young writers, the local public television station is reshowing Ken Burns' *Civil War* for their fund drive and they want me to come in and shoot some promos for it. I tell them I would prefer not to; I don't want to pose as some kind of expert on the Civil War—or anything else, for that matter—but I do have a certain local celebrity, like a guy who raises a giant watermelon or something.

"I can't do it," I tell my grandparents on the phone. "I'll have to get made up. I'll have to stand there and grin like a possum."

"Oh, get a hold of yourself," Evelyn growls. "It's the least you can do. This family has supported public television since you were a toddler."

"Never let it be said I didn't do the least I could do," I murmur.

"And going on TV might sell some books," says Jackson, ever mindful of the bottom line, who has commandeered the phone.

"Okay," I say, to them and to Kathy Spears, the station manager. I go in on a Tuesday morning, early for me, ten o'clock. They put some powder on my face, neck, and hands, clip a tiny microphone the size of a serrano pepper on my lapel, stand me up in front of a dark blue backdrop, and tell me to look into the camera and just be myself.

"Uh-huh. What exactly am I supposed to say?" I ask Kathy.

She brings her hands together with a slight clapping noise, and smiles. "We want you to tell them why the Civil War was so important. We want you to tell them why the film captures it so well. We want them to watch the series, love it, and send us money." Then she takes her hands apart, as if to say, it's that easy.

"Uh-huh." I lick my lips, struggle to keep my arms down at my sides, look into the dark lens of the camera. I do not expect to do well, and I don't remember much after "Hello. I'm Brad Cannon, and I'm here tonight to talk to you about two things: the most momentous event in American history and the most popular show in public television history. . . ."

When the red light on the camera goes off, Kathy breaks into applause; so does the cameraman; so does the audio tech.

"You were great," she says as she unclips my microphone and sets me free.

"Really?" I say. I am surprised; the possibility of greatness had never occurred to me. I blink a couple of times, as if to adjust my eyes to a new way of seeing.

"We ought to find something for you to do around here more often," Kathy says. "Maybe you could host a show on Texas history. What do you think?"

I think that all this is happening much too fast for my liking, and even though I am floating on their praise, we come back to the fundamental problem. For me to pose as a working historian—for me, in fact, to represent myself as anything except, maybe, a cyclist—is fraudulent. Duplicitous. I am a nothing, proud to be a nothing, and not about to lie to thousands of Central Texans about my ongoing nothingness.

"Not now," I tell her, shaking my head. "It's not a good time."

"Well, tell me when," she says. "You may think I'm not making a serious offer. But I am. You have a real ease in front of the camera."

"One promo does not a star make," I say, and she shakes my hand.

"Then come back some time and do another promo. We'll build up a body of evidence."

I am so pleasantly buoyed by the experience that I drive on to George's without a misgiving, although misgivings would normally be in character for me. We survivors at George's have been much more solemn since Richard was taken away from us, as though we are keeping a vigil outside his room.

But this is an infelicitous phrase. I have not actually been up to his room, although I hope to gather up the courage to do that soon.

I am the first to enter our booth. Shortly after I get seated, Hugh Kromer saunters in, unaccountably dressed in white shirt, gray slacks, and black polished penny loafers, and crosses the room.

"Geez, Hugh, what's the occasion?" I ask, as he slides into the booth. "You going to the prom?"

"Ah, nothing," he says, and he ducks his gray head for just a moment. If Hugh weren't sixty-plus years old, my diagnosis would be embarrassment, but surely he's outgrown that.

"You'd almost think Hugh was dressing up for somebody," a voice says, and we look up—way up—to find Ron Sloan.

Now red patches appear on Hugh's neck, and his blue eyes, huge behind his thick horn-rimmed glasses, look down at the table.

"I've missed something," I say as Ron takes a seat. "Why is Hugh dressing up for somebody? What somebody?"

"Doesn't a man have the right to dress any way he wants?" Hugh says with truculence, and then he signals Margaret for some water.

"Sure," Wally Dent says, as he plops heavily down on the other side of Hugh and places his prickly fishing hat somewhat more carefully on the shelf behind him. "As long as it meets community standards of decency. You'd think someone on the Phillies bench could tell John Kruk that he's got a hole in his pants you could drive a riding mower through."

"Hey," Ron says to me, as the table discussion shifts from Hugh's snazzy new look back again to the World Series. "Run outside with me for a second."

Even as the others are sliding out and getting to their feet so we can pass, I am wondering why. Then I remember the last time someone invited me to go out into George's parking lot, and I see again the looming black lump that is Richard's impending death.

And all of a sudden, I don't really want to get up from my seat; I feel a tingling shooting through my legs, and I don't think it's just static electricity from sliding across a vinyl booth.

All the same, I follow him out to his car, a huge vehicle from the days when Detroit made the largest cars on the planet. And there, in the backseat of the car, her paws up on the top of the half-opened window, is a golden retriever, about ten years old, to judge by the white on her muzzle, a lovely creature that can only be Richard's dog Audrey.

"I went by the kennel and got her this morning," Ron says, leaning over and smiling at her. "Richard told me that when he talked with you about—it—you said you'd take care of her. He asked me to bring her up today." He lowers his voice and steps back from the car, as if he doesn't want Audrey to hear. "You better get up to see him, man. He looks pretty bad. The docs say he's in and out."

So much for my feeling that I was off the hook. Sure, I could say, "He must have been out when he told you I'd take care of his dog," but is it really so much Richard is asking?

Audrey looks on, panting, as though she's waiting for me to make up my mind. At last I say, "Thanks for picking her up. Can I leave her here until time to leave?"

"Sure," Ron says. "I've got her leash and collar, and the kennel sent along some food. And Richard wanted his cap. It'd be great if you could take it up when you go."

"Great," I say. I haven't had a dog for twenty years, and Dad mostly took care of Roxy, even though Carter and I were supposed to, but how hard could it be? I remember pouring out a bowlful of Gravy Train, pouring on a cup of warm water, making sure Roxy had something in her water dish, bathing her every now and then. A dog is a dog.

"Oh, and I've got her medicine," Ron says. "She's got heartworm medicine, and sedatives for when it rains."

"Sedatives?" I fear a tone creeps into my voice. I've never heard of such nonsense, but I suppose if there is such a thing as pet therapists—and Elaine's little Shih Tzu sees one every week—could doggie tranquilizers be far behind?

"Rich said she tore up his apartment every time it rained. When a front's coming through, you've got to sedate her or she loses her shit."

"Uh-huh." I nod once or twice, take a deep breath, and let it out. Insane dogs on dope. Sure thing.

We go back indoors, and take a seat. "Brad's met Audrey," Ron announces, and the three of them take turns telling me what a good guy I am for taking her home with me.

"It's the least I can do," I tell them, and they smile, thinking something very different from what I mean.

Wally is telling a story about some poor sleep-deprived student in his class who happens to have dropped off with his head propped up on his hand. "I'd just said something about how the Spartans used to beat their slaves when his head slid off and hit the desk—crack!—and his legs flailed, he kicked the desk in front of him over, his arms flew up in the air, everybody in the class turned around to gawk at him. Complete silence, then everybody started laughing. He was red as a radish, so I felt a little sorry for him. 'Mr. Kent apparently has a strong humanitarian reaction to the thought of the Spartans beating their slaves.' I had his complete attention for the rest of the lecture."

The guys chuckle as they crunch on their iceberg lettuce.

"Thank God I never did that in your class," I say.

"That's because you just slept straight through," Ron says.

"Ouch," Hugh says, looking over to see how Wally will take this.

"Well, that would explain his final grade," Wally says.

"Ouch," I say, feeling like I've been hit by a richochet.

When I leave, Audrey is pleased to climb into my car, and as we drive out to the house, she hangs over the windowsill, her ears blowing back and tongue lolling. As we pull to a stop in the driveway, she spies one of the Faber cats on my front porch, produces a low noise, somewhere between growling and clearing her throat, and then clambers over the side and after the cat, who is so accustomed to a life of ease that at first he doesn't register Audrey as a threat. Certainly she is too old and slow to be a Class-A menace to cats, but she still has teeth, and when she bares them, the little calico scampers for his life in the direction of the fence.

Audrey is satisfied; she turns, beams in my direction, and sits down beside the porch steps to wait for me.

"Good girl," I say, and pat her head. If I'd known it was this easy to get rid of the Faber cats I would have hired an Audrey years ago.

She has been an indoor dog with Richard and the fences around my place are barbed wire with plenty of room to scoot under, so I have little choice but to show her inside. She sniffs her way around the living room, tail lifted high in interest, then surveys kitchen, bathroom, bedrooms, before coming back to the rug in front of the fireplace, circling twice, and collapsing into a heap on the floor. There is nothing subtle about Audrey when she lies down; it's slightly less graceful than a condemned highrise being dynamited.

"That's a good spot," I tell her. "It'll be nice this winter, when we make a fire."

I get down a couple of bowls for food and water, a temporary feeding arrangement, and go in to change for my ride. She follows me, wags her tail wildly when she sees me sit to put on different shoes.

"No," I tell her. "We're not going anywhere. Not now. I'll take you out later for a walk."

Uttering the word "walk" is a tactical error, for upon hearing it Audrey whines a little and places her head underneath my foot as I pull on the other shoe, nudges me. Then she steps back, looks up at me, pants, puts one paw on my knee.

"Not now," I tell her. I take a leak, closing the door so she won't follow me into the bathroom—some things do require privacy, after all—fill my water bottle, and walk to the front door, Audrey tailing me every step of the way. I have an irrational urge to tell her to stop following me, but it's not like she has anything else to do.

When I close the door between us, I hear her barking until I am out of the driveway, but as soon as I get out into the glorious fall day I forget about her and concentrate on the ride. The sun is warm, the wind is barely tangible, and I am comfortable wearing shorts and a T-shirt. These days will be rare, even with our mild winters, and I want to take full advantage, so I decide to add a little bit of distance, take in some new countryside.

When I get back home, I half expect Audrey to be waiting at the door to greet me in person; instead, what I find is her emissary, a small pool of odious yellow liquid on the wood floor just inside the door, a pool of liquid that I step in. My foot slides, and although I manage to catch my balance, my neck feels like I've been rear-ended.

"Audrey!" I yell, hopping to the kitchen sink on my clean foot, my head throbbing with pain. She is sitting in the corner, and she looks up at me reproachfully. This is new female behavior, and I am intrigued by it. Okay, she says, I'm not proud of myself, but it's really your fault. She's probably right. I should have let her go outside before I left; I just forgot to.

"Okay," I say, gently. Depending on whom I've talked to, people say dogs understand, variously, actual words or only tones, but in either case, I don't want her to misunderstand me: I'm not angry with her. "I can't leave you penned up all day long and not expect something like that to happen. Let me clean up this little puddle and we'll go outside, okay?"

She stands up and wags her tail a few times, tentatively.

"It's okay. Really. It was an accident."

I clean up the pungent mess, drop the towel in the washer, and take Audrey out the back door into the fields, where she trots about happily, tail raised, until she sniffs something intriguing and decides she would like to smell like it. Then she throws herself on the ground like a wrestler hurling an opponent to the mat, rolls with a strange swimming and undulating motion, paws now in the air, now thrashing in the grass, then positions her other ear over this secret scent and drops to anoint her other side.

She looks like she is having such a great time—and she looks so ridiculous doing it—that I can't help but laugh, and when she hears me laughing, her ears perk up, she leaps to her feet, and she trots over to have me scratch under her chin.

She is a good dog, pools of urine and psychopathic behavior

notwithstanding, and I can see how Richard grew to love her, Richard, who now lies dying, wrapped in the crisp white sheets of a hospital bed while I romp with his dog wrapped in the crisp fall twilight.

"I'm going up to see Richard tonight," I say, as much to myself as to the dog. This is good for two reasons: first, if Audrey does understand words, then I have made a commitment to her; second, and more important, even if she doesn't, I've made the same commitment to myself, and as I've said before, those are the only covenants I have ever managed to uphold.

That is what brings me back inside a hospital for the first time in almost twenty years. I walk across the posh lobby, Richard's cap clenched like a talisman, get aboard the elevator, which is slower, if possible, than the relic in Tidwell, and fidget my way up to the sixth floor.

I check at the nurses' station to ask if Richard is up for visitors. The nurse in charge is a tired-looking woman with a pen stuck over her ear and another one in her hand as she makes an entry on a clipboard.

"Last I heard," is her answer, without looking up at me.

"Thanks," I say, giving her my best smile, which she doesn't even look up to see. I don't know what makes me think I have to cheer up unhappy people who are supposed to be cordial to me as part of their jobs, yet I do it compulsively. The grouchy waitress, the crabby counterman at McDonald's, and my greatest challenge, the morose attendant at the Conoco on Highway 77—I am unfailingly cheerful to these people, even as they flounder in the slough of despair.

Shouldn't somebody be unfailingly cheerful to me, even if it's simply because I am passing over money?

The hospital smells exactly as I remembered it, ammonia and metal, and I could almost be a kid again, walking down this hall with Jackson and Evelyn to see if my dad is still alive.

I was thirteen years old. When I got up that morning, I had a family. My biggest concern was when my mom was going to let me buy the Led Zeppelin albums I wanted.

When Jackson and Evelyn had come to get me a few minutes

earlier, I was on the verge of having nothing. I didn't feel thirteen. I felt like I was six years old, like if my parents didn't take care of me, then what would happen to me?

I felt alone.

I almost reached up and took my grandparents' hands. But something stopped me, some pride or strength or sheer cussed perversity that said I was going to keep going no matter what, and I was going to do it by myself.

I wish I'd taken their hands. I wish I'd learned how to accept their help. Because that still small voice never told me how hard it was going to be to try to do it alone.

Jesus Christ in a jumped-up sidecar.

I stop in the middle of the hall, do my breathing exercises, shake off that memory. Things are the way they are, they can't be changed, and anyway, Richard's room is 610, two doors down, and the door is partially open.

I ease it open far enough to slip in, knowing what I will see, doing my best to control the desire to shudder.

Richard is lying propped up in bed, TV tuned to the Series, and he is watching it with what attention he can muster. When I come in, he smiles at me, and his right hand gropes for the remote, turns down the sound. Since that is the hand without IVs, I reach across his body to shake it, and he grips it with surprising strength and holds on longer than normal.

"How's Audrey?" he asks. He is pale and his face is drawn. He looks twenty years older.

"She's good. She's going to be just fine." He nods and lets go of my hand. I look up at the TV. I have been listening to the game in the car and I already know the score, but all the same I ask, "Who's winning?"

He shrugs, as though it's not important, or at the very least, is off the topic. "Thanks for taking care of her," he says. "You're a good friend."

"No I'm not," I say. "I let you down. I—"

He raises his hand and wearily waves away my objections. "Tell me about Audrey. Did you take her for a walk?"

"We went out and played in the field. And she chased a cat."

His eyes close now, but he smiles again. "Chased a cat," he murmurs. The faint smile stays on his face, but he's clearly gone under. I sit with him for some time, the faint noise from the television—crowd roar, the meaningless patter of the announcers, the elevated volume of the commercials—blending with the dull tones of chimes and pages and hushed voices from the hallway. Richard has lost a lot of weight in the short time since I've last seen him, and his face is etched with new lines.

I should have taken him on his road trip. What else do I have to do? And would it have been so bad? We could have pulled the top off the convertible, driven across the desert, through the mountains, bathed in the sunlight by day, chased the moon at night, breathed cool clear mountain air.

We should have done it. Soon he will be breathing pure oxygen.

Soon after that he won't be breathing anything at all.

I lean across, raise his head, pull the Rockies cap on over his matted salt-and-pepper locks, let my hand linger for a moment atop his head before I lean back.

A nurse, not the crabby one, gently taps my shoulder; without realizing it, I have fallen asleep, slumped over in the chair. "I'm sorry," she whispers. "Unless you're family, visiting hours are over."

I rub my eyes, look up at her—young, big blond Texas hair, freckles—and nod. "Thanks." I sigh. "I'll get going." Her eyes stray to the hat, and she gives me a sad smile that crinkles the corners of her eyes.

Next time we can talk; next time I will tell him how much I regret that we didn't go see the Rockies, that when he gets well enough we'll give it another shot. It will be a lie and both of us will know it, but still both of us will nod and agree that it will be wonderful, driving across the desert and through the mountains, that we'll go just as soon as he's well enough to leave.

I get to my feet. "I'll see you soon," I tell Richard, who gives no sign of having heard, and then I squeeze his emaciated shoulder, nudge the bill of his cap. "Good night," I say to the nurse, and she smiles again.

"Good night."

When I get home, I break the news to Audrey. "Get ready, old girl," I tell her. "He could go at any time."

Audrey hands me her paw, and I hold it, stroke it, and she smiles her doggish smile, as if to tell me that everything will be all right.

That night she dozes at my feet while I watch a movie on Cinemax about deadly clowns from outer space, a movie so god-awful terrible that it holds me transfixed with train-wreck fascination, and then she does her collapsing act next to the footboard when I finally decide to go to bed. She is asleep almost instantly, her regular but barely-audible snoring is so soothing I am wondering how I ever got to sleep without her, and before I know it, morning has come.

8

I do my annual book-signing the next afternoon at the Baylor Bookstore, and then I hightail it back to the house. Not only do I want to get in a fast furious ride before dark, but Baylor Homecoming has begun in earnest: twenty-five thousand alumni and their families have returned to Waco to pay tribute to their alma mater, to see old friends and professors, to walk the campus and point out sites that correspond to significant moments in their personal, spiritual, or sexual developments. I am always pleased to sell a few copies of my book—which is a good book, and was a true labor of love, and the yearly influx of alums allows me to do that—but otherwise I have little interest in homecoming. It's probably because, as I've said, for a weekend the equivalent of an additional small city crowds into our stores, restaurants, and public rest rooms, and I have more than enough people—and more than enough complications—in my life.

Evelyn should know this, and so she should also know better than to tell the former Cindy Metcalfe, my lovely but fickle first ex-wife, where I may be found during the weekend. All the same, there is a message on my phone Friday afternoon when I return home sweaty and sore from my ride that tells me exactly this. "I did let her know you were awfully busy," Evelyn says. "But she was only in town for the weekend, and she was just so anxious to hear how you were doing and she was so polite—well, I didn't know how not to tell her."

"Thanks heaps, Evelyn," I grumble. My own grandmother has sold me down the river. Audrey looks up with curiosity to see if I'm talking to her, but it's nothing she needs to worry about.

Rather, it's something I need to worry about. When the doorbell rings, I know without even looking outside who is going to be standing on my front porch.

"Come in, Cindy," I call. The door eases open slowly, and in she steps, pretty as a picture and twice as expensive.

"Well hello, Brad," she says, my name, as always, two sultry Southern syllables long, "I see you dressed up for me." I am wearing the pair of pull-string shorts and the T-shirt I biked seventeen miles in. I have not seen Cindy for four years—her last name is now neither Metcalfe nor Cannon but Wiesznewski, thanks to the huge Slavic Dallas Cowboy defensive end she married shortly after the demise of our storied marriage—but she looks the same, at least as she first walks in the door: big blond Texas hair sprayed high and wide, snub nose, high cheekbones, glossy lips. And she's still wearing the same musky perfume, the sensual scent of which—when we were dating, at least—was always in contrast to her actual inexperienced sexual self. Not all the expertly-applied makeup in the world, though, can hide the so-called laugh lines at the corners of her mouth, and when she offers her cheek for my peck, I see the beginnings of crows'-feet at each eye.

Perhaps it's to be expected; I have them too. But you know how it is: we fix people in our minds, and to us, they will always be a certain age. Cindy, for example, will always be the Homecoming Queen who insisted on saving herself until marriage.

In some cases, admittedly, this sort of photo-album mentality makes sense. My brother Carter will always be frozen at eleven, because that's the age he was when he died, and he'd only just developed the most annoying habit when he was ten. We shared a bathroom, and he had a habit of coming into the house at the last moment before he peed his pants and kicking the bathroom door if I was inside.

"Go downstairs," I would tell him.

"This is my bathroom too," he would say, and would kick the door again. If I didn't let him in, Mom would yell at me—Mom always took Carter's side—so whatever I was doing, I had to stop and let him pee.

I've never been able to get too comfortable in the bathroom; I still listen for that foot on the door, almost twenty years later.

It's a shitty thing to remember your brother mostly as an obnoxious little fire hydrant, because of course that's only a small part of the story. He loved me no matter how much I ignored him; he had this funny little thing where he'd read me bad jokes out of things he bought at school book fairs. And I'm sure he would have turned out all right, if he'd only had the chance to.

Dad and Mom will always be in their early thirties, the years when we traveled to baseball games, when we had such good times, when life didn't seem so complicated. My mom was a beautiful woman who didn't mind getting her hair mussed; my dad was athletic and handsome, more comfortable in a hard hat than a suit. One of my last memories of my dad is on a crunchy-leafed fall day, fading back into an imaginary pocket and preparing to throw me a wobbly spiral; I can see my mom chasing him, dressed in jeans and one of Dad's sweatshirts, giggling as she tries to tackle him, as he eludes her until the pass is in the air; can see them tumble then to the grass and roll, roll, roll, Roxy barking happily at them; can see the ball translate an arc through the blue heavens toward my outstretched hands as though something or someone had predestined it.

Dad was a lot like me, I now realize, quiet, funny, sad, charming. And Mom—well, I don't want to talk about my mom.

Perhaps I have fixed myself at a certain age as well, the age of that teenage boy who caught that pass and easily outran my brother to cross the plane of the goal line marked by the end of the house. Or perhaps instead it is that teenage boy a few years later kneeling handcuffed to his Camaro in the dark sultry Texas night.

Perhaps. But this is such a reasonable explanation for my behavior in recent years that I can scarcely credit it. If there is one thing I have learned about life, it's that the simple explanations rarely hold up. Look for complexity, look for difficulty, look for complications, and you will rarely go wrong.

Speaking of complications, Cindy—the Cindy Wiesznewski of the here and now, thirty years old and getting older by the minute—sits down next to me on the sofa, and I have no choice but to turn and look at her. She is taking in my new place, checking out the bookshelves, the computer, the notebooks. "You're still writing," she says, surprise and disappointment vying for supremacy in her tone.

"What did you think I'd be doing?" I ask. This way I can both avoid lying to her and hear an elaboration of her surprise. She's right to be surprised, of course, but I'd like to know why she thought she could be so sure.

"Oh," she says, and raises both her open hands, long red-polished nails facing me, "I'm sure I don't know. It's not as though I've spent much time considering it."

"Of course not," I say. Audrey gives the all-purpose deep-throated grunt I would like to introduce into the conversation at this point, and Cindy looks down at her with badly-concealed distaste.

"Since when do you have animals?" Cindy asks. During our short marriage, I once brought up the question of our getting a pet; I was given to understand that she had no intention of living in a barn.

"Audrey belongs to a friend of mine," I say. "I'm keeping her for him."

"For how long?"

It seems on the surface, at least, like an odd question, but it's one with an odd answer, so again, perhaps there is some kind of predestination at work.

"Forever. He has terminal cancer."

"Oh. I'm sorry." She purses her beautiful lips sympathetically for a moment before returning to the task at hand. "I don't suppose she could go outside."

"She's an indoor dog," I say. It is an impasse, although not an unpleasant one, since it seems like a win/win situation for me: Cindy will either get up and leave in a huff or she will accept the tangible furry presence of Audrey and stay on our terms, and I don't much care which she chooses.

"Do you suppose you could find another home for her? I mean, if you had a really good reason to?"

I don't ask what that reason could be; I am starting to have disturbing premonitions. Instead I simply say, "I made a promise to take care of her. I'm going to stick by it."

Cindy throws herself back on the couch with an audible huff of disgust. "You promised to take care of me, Brad, and look what happened. You disappeared into the library all day, the study all night. You can't blame me for leaving you." This should be a dead issue between us—as I said, we haven't even seen each other for four years—but all the same, she delivers this with surprising passion.

"I don't blame you for leaving me. You had every right to."

She looks across at me and bats those eyes. "And every right to come back?"

Okay, I'll admit it: despite those vague premonitions, it's a little much said out loud. When she sees my expression, she repeats it. "Do I have every right to come back? I know you're not married now, Brad, I know that Eleanor person—"

"Elaine. Elaine Rosenbaum."

"I know she left you. Your grandmother told me. She seemed a little—disappointed, if you want to know the truth." Her perfect lips twist sideways with something like disdain.

I feel a twinge of something unpleasant when I hear her say that Elaine left me. "It was mutual: Elaine hated Texas. I hated New York City." I leave out the matter of the writing, or lack of it, since I do not want Cindy to realize that this impediment to our own past happiness has been removed.

"Well, you're free, Brad, that's what matters." She leans closer, lays her long lovely fingers on my forearm, and when I look down at her hand to measure the distance to other parts of my anatomy, I can see her smile.

Still, I am not so completely a prisoner of my body's primate impulses that I can't interject, "But are you free? Last I heard, you were still married to three hundred pounds of steroid-soaked lineman." I have never met the man, but I have seen him devour opposing ballcarriers on television, and I have heard things about him.

Richard, in fact, one lunchtime filled me in on the important details concerning Cindy's current husband: Ed Wiesznewski, he said, could walk through my front door without bothering to open it; Ed Wiesznewski could pick up my car with me in it; Ed Wiesznewski could eat everything in my refrigerator and cupboard and still have room left for one of my legs. I do not understand exactly what Cindy has in mind here, but I do know that I do not want Ed Wiesznewski coming to the conclusion that I am trying to steal back our wife.

"That man is a big hulking slob, a p-i-g pig. That man's got no more refinement than I have measles. He hasn't said two words to me since training camp started. I think he's more interested in a good steak than he is in me. Can you imagine?" Her hand creeps across my arm, and to be honest, suddenly no, I can't imagine. I am starting to have difficulty framing my questions.

"Then why have you stayed with him?"

"Brad, honey, I'm here now. Doesn't a girl have the option of changing her mind when the circumstances dictate?"

Her roaming hand is activating—or reactivating—things over which I have no conscious control, not least among them my intense memories of this beautiful creature. I have thought about her often, and usually, I blush to recall, only in one context: I see her—us—in that room in the Windsor Court in New Orleans, the five-star hotel that was the only part of New Orleans we managed to explore on our honeymoon. In fact, we explored that room for the entire three days before we left on a cruise of the Caribbean, tried out the bed, the ample tub, the couch, the vanity, and other places it would embarrass me to mention.

"I want you to show me everything," she had breathed into my ear once the bellman closed the door behind him, "and I do mean everything." The first thing I showed her then she is just beginning to do with that encroaching hand in the here and now. She leans over and, slipping her other hand into my hair, pulls my face closer to her waiting lips. I can taste the salt—my sweat—on her tongue. Without even thinking, as though I have done it a hundred times before—which of course, I have, in another life—I slide my palm up across her flat belly and she arches her full breast into it.

I am simultaneously in two places, that ornate hotel room in New Orleans where we two young newlyweds discovered everything there was to learn about making each other feel good, and my not-nearly-so-ornate living room, where my first ex-wife, now married to a man almost exactly twice my size, is pushing me back horizontal on the couch and preparing to do another of the things she learned that weekend, one of my personal favorite things, in fact.

When the phone chooses this moment to ring, I cannot say I leap to answer it, but it does recall me strongly and solely to this one life I currently occupy, the life where Cindy and I have been divorced for seven years, and although she murmurs, "Let it ring, Brad," and is about to give me further encouragement to do just that, I sit up, push her hands away, and pick up the phone.

I can see that she is not pleased by this, which is as I remembered it; the former Cindy Metcalfe is used to getting her way in all things.

"Hello," I say, only slightly out of breath.

My rescuer is Becky Sue Bradenton, God bless her, who I haven't seen since our day at the zoo; she has been too busy working on a float for her sorority's entry in the homecoming parade. "I missed you at the bookstore today," she says. "How'd it go?"

"Sold about twenty books," I say. Cindy "humphs" at the word "books," shifts her weight away from me, and sourly contemplates the ceiling.

"Do you want to go to the parade tomorrow? Our float should look great."

"I'm sure it will." It always amazes me how people can invest hundreds of hours in building things out of tissue paper and two-by-fours that will be seen once and never used again. "I'm just not much for the homecoming parade. I haven't been for"—I look at Cindy, who refuses to acknowledge my existence—"about eight years. Too many people."

"Okay. I understand."

It's apparent from her tone that she doesn't, not really, but since she has unknowingly rescued me, I do feel that I owe her something. Besides, I am not insensible of the effect the conversation is having on Cindy.

"Why don't I take you out for dinner tomorrow night? Maybe we could run down to Austin. All the places here are going to be packed. We could take in some music on Sixth Street, maybe at Jazz—good bands and a decent crawfish etouffee."

"I'd like that."

"Call me when you get home from the game," I say. "I should be back from my ride by then."

When I hang up, Cindy has passed from examining the ceiling to studying the backs of her hands. They are nice hands, surprisingly strong and knowledgeable.

"So," she says, after the silence becomes so tangible you could walk on it. "I'm too late. There's someone else."

"I'm afraid there is," I say. "We're very serious." I put on a serious face.

"You didn't seem so serious about her before the phone rang," she purrs, and her hand slides unobtrusively back in my direction.

I stand up. "I was thinking about old times," I say. "But Cindy, that's all in the past. Go home."

She gets up too, faces me, and, strangely, smiles. "Well," she says, "that's someplace to start, the past. We've got a history." Then she walks to the door, knowing that I still can't help watching every movement. At the door she turns around, gives me her best pose, hands demurely behind her back, chest pointed skyward. "It was nice to see you, Brad. Maybe we can get together again sometime."

For someone who has spent the majority of her life as a virgin, Cindy squeezes more Mae West into that line than should be allowed. Still, I can appreciate the artistry, even if I don't want to buy the painting.

When I do nothing but raise a hand in farewell, she turns and pulls the door shut behind her. Not until I hear the car start up and back away do I sit back down again. I feel as though I have been in a collision, and touch myself to make sure I am all there.

"What was that?" I ask Audrey, who simply perks up her ears. She doesn't know. Some watchdog she is.

Except I don't know either. From now on, perhaps I would be wise to pay more attention to Elaine's telephoned admonition about being sure to look both ways. She is a wise woman, she knows me well, and unlike some ex-wives I could name, I think she has my best interests at heart.

I take Audrey out for a quick romp, and then I come in and get cleaned up. Although it's not my ideal Friday night date, I'm ready to go back to the hospital and see Richard. I never did finish telling him how sorry I was for the way I acted, or, rather, didn't act. Besides, the hospital is one place in Waco I can visit this weekend where I can be fairly sure I'll be safe from nostalgic alumni decked out in green and gold.

When I take that elevator up to Richard's floor and step out, though, I know immediately that something is wrong. I can feel it in the hollowness of my chest, the metallic odor in my nostrils that always means trouble.

When I find Ron in the hall outside the room talking to a young doctor, both their faces grim, I walk over to hear it for myself.

"You're also a friend of Mr. Collins?" The doctor extends a hand, and I shake it. Since I don't trust my voice, I simply nod and look down at his nameplate.

"It's just a matter of time now," Ron tells me and sighs, shakes his head. "You saw how he was slipping in and out? Well, he's out, maybe for good." He pulls his knit tie loose around his neck.

"Mr. Collins went into a coma sometime between five and six-thirty this evening," this Dr. Peterson explains. "I'm sorry to say the prognosis is not favorable."

Six-thirty; an hour ago. That's how much I missed him by, an hour. If I'd come here instead of going riding, if I'd come straight here instead of playing handsies with Cindy—

The doctor hasn't finished; there's more, and although he tries to put it as gently as he can, there is no sugarcoating this message. "Mr. Collins didn't indicate any next of kin on his admittance forms. If you're aware of any relatives who ought to be informed, I wish you'd let us know. I think we'll need to call them soon now."

"No relatives," Ron says, and he has to repeat the second word, which gets hung in his throat for a moment. "There's nobody."

"Just us," I say, and Ron and I look at each other, nod. We will have to do. Dr. Peterson nods in reply, tightens his lips into a dour farewell, and walks off.

We stand there for a time. A phone rings down at the nurses' station, and I hear a snatch of conversation, something about lunch breaks and a hair appointment. Finally I motion toward Richard's room with my head. "Can we see him?"

"They moved him," Ron says. "And you don't want to see him, man. He's on the machines."

"Oh," I say, and I stand there silently as a burly black orderly pushes a woman in a shower cap past. Ron is right: I never want to see another respirator, but I feel that I owe Richard something, something that I haven't in any way given him yet; maybe facing my memories and standing beside him in spite of them will help. I wish I'd done that with my dad.

Jackson didn't want to let me in to see my father after they'd put him on life support, but I think he would have changed his mind if I'd pushed a little. Still, I didn't push. That was the first appearance, I think, of the me I've turned into, the me who doesn't want to hurt so he opts for some distance.

My dad would have pushed, though. My dad wasn't afraid of anything—even getting hurt. I said some awful things to my parents the last year or two of my life. I told them I hated them, that I never wanted to see them again, that our family was fake, phony society retards just like Jackson and Evelyn.

And my dad was always the one who had to knock on my door and push it open gently after I'd slammed it, always the one who had to sit patiently on my bed looking down at my glowering self, waiting until at last I couldn't do anything else but look up at him.

"We love you," he would tell me when he saw me meet his

gaze. "Always have. Always will." I don't guess even he could bring himself to say "I"; still, given my family's vocabulary of caring it was pretty potent stuff.

"I'll be downstairs if you want to talk," he would say, and he'd squeeze my shoulder. He knew I didn't want to talk. I never wanted to talk. But maybe he also knew how much it meant that he would make the offer.

And that was the father I left lying by himself in a hospital room, lost, alone. Even being there to squeeze his shoulder might have meant something to him, wherever he might have been.

"There's nothing you can do," Ron says to me now, as though I've said all this out loud. "Don't tear yourself up."

I manage a grim smile. "Is it so obvious?"

"I know you, man." He rests a hand momentarily on my shoulder. "Don't tear yourself up."

I rub my eyes; I suddenly feel as though I've been awake for days, years, maybe. We're standing in the hall outside an empty hospital room and he's right, there is nothing I can do about that.

"All right," I say. "Thanks."

We turn for the elevator, wait patiently until it arrives, file inside. "I guess we ought to let the other guys know," Ron says as the doors close and we drop slowly down to the lobby.

"I'll call Wally," I say, and Ron gets partway into "And I'll get a hold of Hugh—" when he breaks off.

"They'll both be at that damn bonfire," he says. "And at the parade tomorrow. And at the game later."

"I can swing by Wally's house and leave a message for him. And maybe you can track Hugh down."

"Hugh and Caroline, you mean," Ron says, and despite the gravity of the moment, the density of the atmosphere, he cannot help smiling at my raised enquiring eyebrow. "Hugh's new sweetie."

"Hugh's new sweetie," I repeat as the doors open to the lobby, and then it hits me, and for a moment I just stand there, a goofy grin on my face. The doors close on us. Ron has to reach out to stab the Open Door button with a long finger and pull me bodily into the lobby. I am still shaking my head and smiling. Life does go on, I guess, even if I sometimes wonder how and why.

"Listen," Ron says, "Hugh has an answering machine. I'll bet Wally does. And anyway, that damn bonfire can't burn forever. How about you and I go have a few drinks in the meantime?"

"You're on," I say. We are neither of us big drinkers, and we have no regular haunts, so we settle on the bar in the Hilton, where we sit and have some beers and look out onto the Brazos River and the century-old bridge across it, once a toll bridge on the Chisholm Trail and the longest suspension span on the planet.

I have not eaten since breakfast, and quickly those few beers feel as though they've multiplied into half a hundred. "That's Waco in a nutshell," I tell Ron at one point, nodding out at the bridge, brightly lit over the dark river. "Used to be the longest suspension bridge in the world. The world, man. The Alico Building downtown used to be the tallest building west of the Mississippi. This is a place full of once-wases and might-have-beens and never-will-bes. A place where some guy with a souped-up black Camaro and a bunch of guns can claim to be Jesus and people are so bored or backward or stupid that they'll believe him. A place that's more fun to mispronounce than to say right."

"Here's to it," Ron says, and we raise our beers and toast the town of our birth and lifelong confinement.

I check my watch; the bonfire should be over, but I really have no desire to go looking for Wally; it has been a trying day, and I'd like to receive a little comfort, not pass out bad news.

"Excuse me for a second," I tell him. "Got to make a phone call."

I make two: I tell Wally's answering machine the bad news after the series of beeps; then I dial Sandra's number, knowing that she would no more go to a football pep rally than she would stir-fry one of her cats.

"Hello, sexy biologist lady," I say when she picks up. "Could you use a little company tonight?"

There is the momentary pause, the flicker of almost-audible

thought on her end of the phone. Then the readout: "I think you've had too much to drink, Brad. Why don't you call me back some other time, okay?" Her tone is not cruel, simply matter-of-fact.

"I'm not drunk, exactly," I tell her. "But a friend of mine is dying, and another friend is throwing alcohol on the homecoming bonfire of his sorrow, and I don't want to make him feel self-conscious by just standing by and cheering. But that phase of my life is over. Now I'd like to come over and talk to someone who doesn't shave her face. That's all."

"Listen," she says, and I stand a little straighter in an attempt to do that. "You can come by. After you sit for a while and freshen up. And here's how you'll know you're sober enough to drive over here: don't go out to your car until you completely lose the urge to call me 'biologist lady.' "

"You are a scholar and a gentleman," I say. "Thanks for being so understanding."

"Understanding doesn't enter the picture. I just want to observe you. Remember?"

The irritating thing about Sandra Fuentes is that I'm never really sure if she's telling the truth or playing along with me; the good thing about her is I don't think it really matters much, at least not as to how she treats me, which is, in either case, like an interesting specimen.

"Woman," Ron says—in reference to my extended absence—and I nod. "Sandra?"

"Only one home," I tell him.

"What a luxury," he says. "Man, I don't have such choices. I can go out with Val from Circulation, or I can sit home and watch ESPN."

"You ought to broaden your horizons. Circulation isn't the only game in town. Poke your head into Advertising sometime."

It's not funny, but we will laugh at anything just now, and he slaps his thigh, almost spills his drink, before getting hold of himself. "You know," he says, looking at me across the table with maudlin alcohol-amplified affection, "I used to hate your guts when we were kids. All the advantages. Sure, I felt a little sorry for you when your folks got killed. Hell, everybody did.

And—you know. Susie." He lowers his voice, almost whispers this, and I nod solemnly. "But you just went on like nothing had happened, like you didn't need for anybody to feel sorry for you, and I got back to hating you again. And then there was that day on the practice field. You remember it?"

"Oh yeah. I remember." It was a hot August morning, one of a series of two-a-day practices in the weeks just before school started. We had been doing what Coach Wheeler called tackling drills; they were hitting drills, really. Coach set up two tackling dummies to form an imaginary line of scrimmage, and then we gathered in two facing lines. The guy at the head of each line dropped into a three-point stance. Then when Coach blew his whistle, each guy tried to knock his counterpart into another time zone until Coach blew his whistle again.

Matchups were strictly luck of the draw; a quarterback could line up against a lineman, a freshman against a senior, and Coach could prolong the agony if he had some sort of obscure object lesson to transmit, either to participants or to observers. Each miniature contest came complete with shouted encouragement and admonition, and over it all, the booming baritone of Coach pronouncing judgment, a voice that could make you want to crawl into the cracked earth if you were its target. "I guess Roger would rather play with dollies than tough it out on the football field" was one of the more encouraging things I heard him say in this vein; other things he said were grounds for slitting your wrists, sticking your head in an oven, anything other than walking back past your peers to the end of the line, your face burning, your eyes fixed on the ground.

Oh yes, I remember. I push away my unfinished beer and order a cup of coffee.

"That was the year you tried out for flanker," Ron says. "And I was pissed off about how well you were doing."

"You were sure pissed off about something. Bad luck for me." I tear open a packet of sugar and empty it into the coffee, newly arrived in front of me. "Not only were you pissed off, but you outweighed me about thirty pounds in those days."

"Luck my ass," he says. "I counted how far back you were and switched places."

I raise my cup to him. I admire a man who knows what he wants and goes after it.

"Well, when Coach blew the whistle I tore into you, and I've got to give you credit. You didn't go down. I kept getting more and more pissed off, because Coach wouldn't blow the whistle. He just stood there making those snide comments of his, and you wouldn't go down. Remember?"

I can still feel the impact as we first hit, the clack of plastic shoulder pads against each other, can remember Ron trying to throw me to the ground like a wrestler, his strong hand wrapped in the slack of my practice jersey, through it all, our legs churning beneath us, trying to drive each of us ahead, over, through the other.

"When Coach blew the whistle and you were still on your feet, I just lost it. I shouldn't have done it, man. I'm sorry. You had every right to come after me."

"That was a hell of a long time ago, Ron." And it was; I don't even remember the last time I brought this to mind.

What happened after Coach blew the whistle, why this is something that two grown men might talk about in their cups years after the fact, is this: I turned around to trot back to the end of the line. Then I heard footfalls, turned half around, and Ron hit me square in the ribs and sent me tumbling groundward. I hit with a thud that almost knocked the breath out of me. I looked up at Coach, who was observing a distant cloud formation, and then at Ron, who clapped his hands together as though he were washing his hands of me, sniffed "Flanker," and turned his back.

That was a mistake; you should never blindside a guy carrying around a ton of repressed rage. Coach was still deciding if it was a duckie or a horsie he saw up there, and the same people who didn't warn me were also silent as I got to my feet and charged after Ron, although I'd guess they didn't warn me because I was an underclassman, and didn't warn him only because they couldn't believe anyone would do such a damnfool thing. Whatever, he didn't hear me coming, and I blindsided him good, hit him with what in a game would have been a blatant clip. When he hit the dirt and rolled onto his back, I climbed on top of his chest and started slamming his helmet against the ground. They pulled us apart before anything more than our pride had been damaged on both sides; it's hard to hurt a guy in full pads.

Ron is laughing about it now. "You had this crazy gleam in your eyes like you had lost your mind. I thought you were going to kill me."

I shake my head. "I lost something, all right."

He just laughs, although I do not join him; this teenage loss of control does not stand out as one of my finest moments. Such outbursts take too much energy; today I can scarcely believe I was capable of such a thing.

I check my watch when Ron finally stops chuckling. "I'm going to take off," I say, draining the last of my coffee. I do a mental check; Sandra is not "biologist lady." I am free to go.

"I think I'll sit a little longer," Ron says. "You go on."

We shake hands, solemn again, and I turn to go. At the door I stop to look back, and Ron is staring out into the night at the lighted Waco suspension bridge, at the pedestrians milling across it and along the Brazos River. He is looking into the night and for some reason he is shaking his head, and I feel an instant tenderness for him that could be the aftermath of too many Coronas or a growing feeling of attachment.

Because it is easier, I decide it is the former, raise a hand for a farewell he either does not see or does not acknowledge, and make my exit.

9

When Becky calls the next day after the Homecoming game—which Baylor loses to the TCU Horned Frogs, if you can believe that—it is probably unnecessary to remind her to wear a jacket. We both have been out in the forty-degree weather. I do though, because Becky has no wintertime experience with my car, and doesn't know that the Healey is inconsistently heated at best, or that a canvas top doesn't really serve as a good insulator.

"Okay," she says. "I've got an outfit I've been dying to wear."

"Good," I tell her. "Just so it's warm."

The weather has literally changed overnight: an arctic front pushed south into central Texas about the time I left the Hilton bar, prompting record low temperatures all across the northern half of the state, and the chilliness foreshadowed my reception at Sandra's, a scene I've gone over backwards and frontwards during my ride, a condensed version of my usual excursion that I endure wrapped in sweats and a windbreaker.

Things had begun well enough. She invited me in, cleared off a space for me on the sofa, shooed the cats out of our way, and invited me to tell her what was wrong.

I started off reminding her about my lunch group, told her about Richard's sickness and my conversation with Ron outside the hospital room. I left out some of the details—the X ray, the last request, the dog—because I always suppose that Sandra will appreciate a clinical, just-the-facts approach.

"Your friend Ron was right," she told me, hazel eyes blinking owlishly. "There's nothing you can do now. There's no reason to be so upset. There's not even anybody there now to appreciate the gesture."

"What do you mean?"

She turned to me, knees primly together, and spoke in the professorial tone she sometimes assumes, earnest with a mild trace of condescension. "Your friend is gone. All that's left is a collection of cells that bears a coincidental resemblance to him. Whatever you appreciated about him, whatever animated those cells, is gone for good. Vanished. Poof."

I got up from the couch, bit back my first response, something much more personal and condemnatory, and settled for sputtering, "That's a horrible thing to say."

She looked up at me with curiosity. "I didn't expect you to be so emotional about this, Brad," she said, and it is this more than anything else that set me off. I have been accused of many things in my life by many women, been labeled and maligned, and—often enough—been pegged right on the head.

But no one has ever accused me of being too emotional. I didn't like it, and so to prove her right, I stomped out to my car and drove home without another word, fuming all the way, muttering under my breath shameful epithets about her ethnicity and gender.

I was wrong to do this, even to think such things. I have been, as I said, turning our exchange over in my head, and perhaps my behavior was unfair. I was bringing—as they say these days—my issues into our exchange.

One of Jackson's sayings goes like this: *Don't go looking for jam in a jelly jar.* What does this mean? you ask. Well, Jackson usually says this after he has given some untrustworthy bastard one last chance to carry off a job successfully, to behave honorably, and he does neither. When he was younger, Jackson got mad, he got even. But as the years have rolled on, I think he has tried to take things in stride; perhaps this is a saying he invented to avoid ulcers or suffering a fatal cardiac arrest. In any case, it is a useful saying, and as he often is, Jackson is right. I went to Sandra expecting jam, knowing perfectly well, if I'd bothered to think about it, that she is not equipped to deliver it, that she is a jelly roll through and through.

After thinking in food metaphors all day, it's no wonder that I am ravenously hungry by the time I pick up Becky Sue Bradenton at her apartment, and not even the way she looks in her outfit—as good as promised, cream capri pants that show off her slender legs, ruffled blouse, purple blazer with her glistening hair falling across the shoulders, and a purple gaucho hat to top it off—not even this can fully distract me from my rumbling stomach.

During the hundred-mile drive to Austin, we have to almost shout over the throaty roar of my muffler and the whistling of the wind past my radio antenna, but we still manage to have a conversation. She remains upset about the football game, which seems to her almost to ruin the whole homecoming weekend. Not even the fact that their float—a takeoff on *Jurassic Park* called *Bearassic Park*, after the Baylor mascot—was named the parade's best can fully console her.

"You'll have to come see it tomorrow," she calls. "It'll be on display over in front of Tidwell."

"Maybe I will."

"Where are you taking me tonight?"

"Ah, wouldn't you like to know?" I give her my best Mad Scientist laugh.

"I hope there's lots of food," she says. "I haven't had anything since breakfast."

"Ditto," I say.

"You should take better care of yourself. You're supposed to be in training."

"Supposed to be." I ease off the accelerator a little—a Texas Highway Patrol car is tooling along a few cars ahead and has sadistically dropped his speed to fifty-five to see who has the nerve to pass him.

I do; the speed limit here is sixty-five, and once I sweep past him, the cars and trucks backed up behind him slowly begin to do the same.

Once in Austin, I find a parking place in the Seventh Street lot next to the old Driskill Hotel, a beautiful old Texas landmark that has hosted inauguration balls and political confabs, where Lyndon Johnson used to stay when he was in town. As we walk down Brazos Street across from it, we can see that some big do is going on up in the ballroom; black-tied gentlemen and women in evening dresses are smoking out on the terrace.

"Wedding," Becky says wistfully, and I trust her judgment on such matters.

We pass underneath the flags of the Mexican consulate and come to the corner of Sixth Street and Brazos, where we will be turning left, but before we can do that, a homeless drunk, his face a roadmap of broken capillaries, steps out of the shadows and toward Becky. He raises his hands toward her, speaks to her in a low, repetitive mumble, and I interpose myself, which is both gallant and unfortunate: His breath could dissolve most household plastics.

"Keep walking," I tell Becky over my shoulder. I hear her take a few steps and stop, but she is far enough away that only I hear what he's mumbling, eyes still fixed on her: "Can I have your hat, ma'am? I had a hat like that once, a beautiful black hat."

We have seen half a dozen homeless in the block and a half we've walked, carrying their belongings in duffel bags or trash bags, including an elderly gent who could be someone's grandfather leaning on his cane, a Hefty bag over the other shoulder. I have never been much for giving to individual homeless people; although I support my grandmother's organized work for food banks and shelters, I have never thought that one person could make much of a difference. But this—

This breaks my heart. I pull a couple of twenties from my jacket pocket and stuff it in his. "The lady's hat is purple," I tell him, holding him gently by the shoulders so he will look at me. "I don't think you'd want to wear it in the daylight. There's a hat store on Congress. Go get yourself a hat tomorrow, okay?"

His eyes do not quite focus on me—he still wants to look at that hat, and it does look lovely on Becky; if I weren't facing this way, I'd want to look at it too—but he murmurs, "Sure, okay," and then he drops his eyes to the pavement and walks up Brazos in the direction we have just come.

Becky takes my arm and leans close as we walk the half block to Jazz. "I saw what you did. You gave him some money, you old softy, you."

"He wanted your hat," I say, apologetically. "If he'd asked me for money for a cup of coffee I'd have kept walking."

I shrug and my voice trails off. I am ninety-five percent sure that tomorrow he will begin converting my charitable contribution to cheap booze. But that five percent—that seems to me a chance worth taking.

Jazz is pretty crowded, but they do have a table open against the wall that is halfway between the stage and the street, pretty much the best of both worlds. We take it.

They have a promo going for Bohemia, a good beer which, despite its name, is imported from Mexico. That makes it a momentary toss-up for me between that and a bottle of Dixie, a fizzling New Orleans beer I have grown to love in recent years. Becky, who has recently celebrated her twenty-first and thus become a legal drinker, asks for a Shiner Bock, a local brew that some people love and others think tastes like something you'd use to strip the lacquer off an old dresser. I flip a mental coin, balance the two-for-one Bohemia against the hundred miles I'll have to drive home, and settle for a single Dixie, at least to start with.

We order a half pound of boiled shrimp for an appetizer. When it comes, we settle into an easy rhythm—peel, peel, peel, talking all the while, take a bite of shrimp, nod with mouth full, take another bite, nod, begin again. It is this alternating pattern—we discover it works best to take turns talking and eating—which explains the following, a series of one-sided exchanges:

"We're having a formal the second week of November. It'll be at the Convention Center. I thought you might like to go with me. I'll make it worth your while." She smiles and pops a shrimp in her mouth.

"I'm sure you would. But I thought you were going to stop asking me to sorority functions. I'm an old man. You should be inviting some football hero or something."

She shrugs. "I forgot. And maybe I don't care for football heroes. Maybe I'm more the literary type."

"I've got a guy for you, then. Works for the Waco paper. Better writer than I'll ever be, and probably better-looking."

She takes a drink of her Shiner, messing up our rhythm; then she sets it down a little harder than she has to; gravity alone is usually sufficient for this sort of thing. "Are you ashamed to be seen with me, Brad, or am I ashamed to be seen with you? I can never recall which it's supposed to be."

"I think it's your week to be ashamed of me," I say, but levity doesn't work, and she doesn't pick up another shrimp, nor does she pick up the conversation, just crosses her arms and looks up toward the stage where the band is setting up, a beautiful pout spreading across her beautiful face.

I try another shrimp or two, but it's not nearly as much fun when it's just me. I push the plate away from me, agree with our gorgeously-ponytailed waitress that I need another Dixie, and then lean forward. It's a little late, but perhaps I can pull something back onto the playing field. "A guy would be an idiot to be ashamed of you. You're gorgeous, bright, funny—"

"You forgot sexy," she says. She doesn't look at me, but any response is a crack in the door, and I put my shoulder to it.

"And very sexy. Look around. All of these people are seeing us together tonight, although right now they're saying, 'Hey, that handsome couple is having a fight.' "

She turns back to me, and I can smell victory. "So how come you never take me anywhere in Waco?"

"Ah, but I do. In fact, my grandmother's spies saw us at the zoo. 'Who was the lovely girl you went to the zoo with?' she asked me the other night."

Our dinners are here, and I sense that all is right with the world. "Did she really say 'that lovely girl'?" Becky asks, but she is smiling as the waitress slides her half order of crawfish alfredeaux in front of her.

I am already a bite into my crawfish etoufee, but I can nod with the best of them, and I do.

"My parents keep telling me they'd like to come down in a few weeks. I'd really like for you to meet them." She looks up at me demurely, because she knows that I cannot refuse her twice in a row, that it would be a strategic error of the first magnitude. I wonder, in fact, if she didn't force a first refusal out of me to get to this point.

"Hmm. What have you told them about me?"

"I told them they should meet you because I'm pregnant and we're going to have to get married." It's all I can do to keep from spitting my food onto the table. Becky goes on to say, "What do you think I told them? I told them you were a writer, and then I told them how much I care about you." She says this last almost defiantly—there it is, I don't care what you do about it, but now you know.

"I'm not a writer," I mumble, picking at the weakest link of her discourse, but she steamrollers me.

"Of course you are. Don't be silly."

I am silly tonight; that's all there is to it. So I accept my role, eat some great food—including a piece of pecan-sweet potato pie for which I would ride twenty miles through a raging downpour—hear some pretty good jazz fusion from a band with a tremendous guitar player who picks like Al DiMeola, and drive back to Waco in a pleasantly-sated mood.

"Come in," she urges me, and after our conversation earlier in the evening, I don't see how I can avoid it, but I am a good boy: I keep my hands mostly to myself, and no clothes are shed by either party before I plead the lateness of the evening, a lame enough excuse but one that can occasionally be pushed through by sheer brazenness.

There is, of all things, a message from Sandra on my answering machine when I get in, an apology that she delivers as though she's choking on it: "Brad. Maybe I was insensitive. I hope we can talk again soon."

There are also messages from Jackson, commanding me to lunch the next day after church, from Elaine, and from Wallace Dent, leaving a message thanking me for leaving a message for him. I foresee a future of such communication. I will call him, thank him for thanking me; we may not actually speak in person again as long as we live.

I am obviously too tired to be thinking, and likely only to get myself in trouble. I climb into bed and am asleep immediately.

Sunday lunch at the Cannons is roast beef, carrots, onions, and potatoes, cooked together so that the juice of the meat soaks into all of it, and it is almost always great. Since Billie has the day off, this is one of the rare meals that Evelyn cooks, and like lots of other women across America, she sticks this combination into the oven before they leave for church, checks her watch nervously if the preacher preaches past his appointed time, and pulls it out as soon as they get home. God is generous, though, because I have never been for dinner in all these years when the roast has burned.

My summons for lunch, of course, is to fill in the grandparents on the recent details of my life, such as they are. I should tell them about Richard now, of course—these are my closest living relatives, after all—but "coma" is even more negatively charged in this house than "hospital," and perhaps I will be unable to tell them about Richard until after he dies, which could happen, apparently, at any time.

So I fill in details around the central story. "Well, I went out for a few drinks with Ron Sloan on Saturday"—and like the good Baptists they are, they both wrinkle their faces slightly at the word "drinks." They don't want to pronounce judgment but they likewise don't want me to think they approve of such decadence. "And I went out with a young lady last night. I took her to eat in Austin. We didn't dance, though."

Evelyn smiles wryly. "Well, thank goodness for that."

"I shot an eighty-six this week," Jackson says. He has recently returned to playing golf several times a week after laying off for some time after his heart attack, and further, he has pestered me to get back out there with him, as though I need more exercise.

"Come play with me on Tuesday," Jackson says. "We need another to make up a foursome."

"I'll come play with you in the morning, if you'll go riding with me in the afternoon." He doesn't take me up on this offer, so I follow it up by saying, "Tuesday is one of my lunch days. With the guys, you know."

"All right," Jackson says. "But you shouldn't let your skills atrophy like this. You used to be a great player." This is God's truth. I used to play with my dad every Saturday, and even as a youngster I used to outshoot him, even though he was a hell of an athlete. I could hit long drives off the tee that almost unerringly found the green, was a better-than-average putter, and sometimes I hit that zone that I recognized years later when I was writing well, that area where I was so into the moment that nothing but good things could happen.

I think it broke my dad's heart when I discovered teenage rebellion and stopped playing with him—I told him that golf was a game for snobs—although naturally he never said anything about it. My mom had the nagging gene, so a couple of times I heard how wrong it was of me to stop doing something both of us enjoyed so much. Then I learned to get up from the table when she came into the kitchen and head for my room.

My dad could have played professional baseball—he was drafted out of Baylor and everything—and I think he thought I could have gone on to play golf professionally. But he didn't nag. He didn't push. Maybe he just assumed that I would come back to it someday, that those mornings on the course with him weren't for nothing.

And maybe he was right. Maybe I would have come back, if they'd come back, which of course they didn't.

"Maybe I'll come out and play with you sometime," I tell Jackson, and then I throw out my barest conversational gambit. "Could I have another roll?"

"Who's this girl you've been seeing?" Evelyn asks as she sends the basket my way.

"I'm afraid you're not cleared for that kind of information," I say.

"Bradford—" my grandmother begins, but I am not about to divulge anything.

"I could tell you," I say, buttering my roll. "But then I'd have to kill you."

They know when to give up on this topic as well, and now is that time. "Maybe we'll meet her sometime," Jackson says, brandishing a roll at me. "Bring her for Thanksgiving."

"Bring her to the New Year's Eve ball," Evelyn says. This is her current project, a fund-raiser with monies to be distributed among her favorite local charities, and she has been after me for a month about coming, which I will probably agree to do just so she will leave me alone.

"Maybe," I growl. "Or maybe I'll just bring one of my ex-wives. Your directions were very good, Evelyn. Cindy found my house without any difficulty. And here all this time I thought Elaine was your favorite."

"Well Elaine didn't come looking for you, did she?" I can no more intimidate my grandmother than I could eat another bite of her wonderful roast beast, so dinner is suspended, we talk for a few minutes while we collectively clear off the table, and then I go home for a short nap.

It's hard to believe that now, in late October, it is already colder than it generally gets in November. I start a fire, pull my pillow off the bed, and settle down on the sofa with an afghan while Audrey dozes contentedly, sedated by her doggie downers, in front of the fireplace.

It is a nice way to spend a chilly, dreary afternoon, much better than bundling up against the wind and cold rain, and some part of me knows that, because I don't wake up until dark.

After Audrey and I go outside for a wobbly run and roll, I put another log on the crackling fire, put my feet up, and hold my book in one hand, rest the other on Audrey's side. It's too soon to tell, but I think I could learn to like this.

10

When Madelyn calls on the Friday afternoon of the second weekend in November, I have been luxuriating in the return of warm weather. After a week of miserable cold, the front pushed through and we have since been enjoying sunny days, highs in the seventies, cool nights in the fifties. It's the best of both worlds—shorts and T-shirt out on the bike during the day, a crackling fire at night.

"Hey," the voice of Madelyn says in my ear. "I'd like to make a date with you for next weekend."

"Hey," I say in return. "I hope this is Madelyn, because I haven't seen her for what seems like years."

"I know," she sighs. "Midterms and a lot of research. And I've been typing up the final draft of Colby's paper for the Milton Society meeting in Chicago."

"I don't suppose that meeting is next weekend, by any chance?"

"Yes indeed. How much of me would you like to see?"

I pause a beat to make the joke a little better; timing is everything, in comedy and in life. "All of you."

"You're on," she says. "Am I welcome at your place?"

"Sure," I say; I have reconciled myself to it, at least. Then I look across at Audrey and say, "I have a little surprise for you. I hope you'll like it." And I do hope so; since Audrey arrived, Cindy has regarded her with disdain, Sandra with disinterest, Elaine with disbelief, and only Becky with fastidious friendliness, a sort of "I'll pet you, but don't get any hair on me." In the short time she's been with me, though, Audrey has become an important part of my life, and I'd like for someone else to understand that.

"I like surprises," she says. She pauses. "As long as it's not new lingerie. You wouldn't do that, would you?"

"Not without your express consent." I check my calendar, which of course is as blank as one of my notebooks. "I'll look for you Friday night."

"Okay," she says. Now that it's been agreed on, she seems almost shy. "I'll look forward to it."

"I'll dream about it," I say, and I can hear the aural blush as she says, "Oh, stop it," and hangs up.

"We'll have company Friday," I tell Audrey, who has suddenly gotten to her feet and has started to pant and pace. "Try not to be jealous of her."

It's not jealousy; as I suspect, when I turn over to the Weather Channel I discover that our wonderful weather is going to take a turn for the worse, and that a cold front with possible thunderstorms is on its way.

"Okay, pooch," I say, and when I walk into the kitchen, as always, she follows. I take one of her pills, a small yellowish tablet called Acepromazine, wrap it in a slice of the processed American cheese product with which I am slowly poisoning myself, and let her gobble and swallow. I think I have caught it before she gets herself too worked up, which is good; if I don't, the pill doesn't kick in until she's worn herself out.

We have been lucky to date: only once have I failed to sedate her before a change in the weather, and on that day when it started raining while I was at lunch, I got home before she had time to do much more than destroy the rug in front of the fireplace. She is a lovely dog, and it's really a shame that she's so sensitive to storms. The medicine knocks her out for hours, sometimes all day, and afterward she still has traces of it in her system; it's sometimes three days later before she returns to being her usual genial self, and after being a prisoner of her own body for all that time she is usually wound up tight, bouncing off the walls.

"Shh," I tell her. "It's okay. We're just fine," and eventually I get her to sit at my feet. Then sometime later she plops onto the floor, her eyes begin to get red, and she is sedated into immobility. At such times, I would not want to trade places with her; for all my aimless motion, it beats being frozen in place.

The temperatures drop overnight into the low thirties, and they stay there through the next few days. When I go out on the bike, I layer: shorts and sweats, thermal socks, a T-shirt, a long-sleeved shirt, a sweatshirt, gloves. The wind howls out of the north in an unwanted preview of February, and I end up puffing the last few miles home with it searching out every gap in my clothes. My nose runs continuously, and I develop a new breathing pattern—in through my nose to momentarily suck back the snot on the verge of streaming forth, out through my mouth, a cloud of steam, to keep the mucus inside my head.

Once the front has arrived and her medicine has worn off, Audrey is playful. Dogs seem to like colder weather, to become much more active. In fact, dogs I have never seen before in months of riding run out to make my acquaintance, and I, for my part, try to become friends with them—I roll to a halt, speak gently to them, hold out my hand to be sniffed. I sometimes think I simply made a mistake with the dogs from hell; maybe if I'd struck up a conversation with them the first time they came after me—engaged them on topics of interest—our relationship would have taken a different path; maybe I would now look forward to that part of my ride instead of dreading it all the way into the pit of my stomach.

But those dogs have not chased me in some time, and the reason becomes obvious when I think to look for it: the barbed-wire fence around the property has been replaced by a chain-link fence, and although they still come barking wildly as I pass, they can't get out. They've dug here and there, and perhaps the fence won't hold them forever, but for the time being I can ride past and flaunt my freedom.

The new dog scents I bring home intrigue Audrey. She sniffs my hands, my legs, my socks, then does her best to mark me again as hers by licking.

"Stop it," I usually say, although I also usually let her get a few licks in before I pull my hand away. There is not enough affection in my life, and Audrey's is completely nonjudgmental, if sloppy. She doesn't care whether I'm a good guy or not, she doesn't care whether I write books or not; in fact, she doesn't seem to care about much of anything as long as her bowl has food in it and I give her a little attention every now and then.

She makes me want to believe in the existence of a loving God.

Other things militate against that, though; Richard lingers on in a coma. Ron checks on him several times a day, calls—when I don't see him—to update me. I don't know what to think. I can't say I want Richard to step off the planet for good and leave no forwarding address, but every time I think of him hooked up to that respirator I have to turn away and take up something else.

The group has continued to meet for lunch at George's, although on Thursday, Hugh clears his throat and makes a startling statement. "You know, this place just doesn't feel right without Richard. I think we should stop coming here." Behind his glasses, his eyes flit back and forth to gauge our response.

We have been sitting mostly in silence. Partly we are having trouble coming up with superficial sports talk: baseball is over, the Baylor Bears are having another lackluster football season, pro basketball has yet to begin and without new baseball player Michael Jordan will never be the same, and none of us has much to say on other topics. What is there to say? Our friend will soon be dead and none of us can do a thing but sit and wait for it.

Hugh's suggestion, coming after such a lull, is a conversational warhead exploding in our midst.

"What do you mean?" Wally says, at the same time as Ron says, "Stop coming here?"

I don't say anything, because I think I see what Hugh means; George's doesn't feel the same without Richard's silent ball-capped presence. I keep expecting to look up at him at that pinball machine where he used to religiously deposit quarters.

"Do you think we ought to stop meeting?" I ask.

"Hell no!" Hugh says, and then looks around to see who has heard him. "I'm just saying that maybe we should try meeting someplace else. Someplace where I don't feel like I'm looking for him and not finding him."

"Like where?" Wallace asks. He is a creature of habit, has

been eating here since before I had him as a professor, and the thought of going anywhere else has him visibly shaken. His floppy hat is in his hands and he twists it like a rosary. I worry that he'll hook himself beyond redemption.

"Well," Hugh says, doing the blushing thing again, "there's a little soul food place on Elm that I've been to a couple times lately. Martha's Place. Best smothered pork chops I've ever eaten."

The others receive this news in meditative silence; Elm Street is an almost exclusively black part of town, may be foreign territory to some, although I have been to Martha's many times, as well as its near neighbors, the dueling barbecue stands owned by feuding brothers.

"Who'd you go with, Hugh?" Ron asks. "It wouldn't be Caroline, now, would it?"

Hugh faces him squarely, although by the rapid blinking of his eyes you can see he'd much rather be ducking his head. "Do you fellows want to try it out or not?"

"Sure," I say, and the others nod.

"How about if I drive on Tuesday?" Ron says. "I've got the biggest car."

"That's true," says Wallace. "I've noticed aircraft trying to land on it." He is being hyperbolic, but only just; if any manufacturer ever made a larger car than Ron's Eldorado, I hope never to see it coming down the road toward me.

"Why don't we meet at my house?" Hugh's house is relatively central for all of us, and we make tentative plans to gather there around eleven-thirty on Tuesday. Then I announce my plans to leave, pleading work, and they trail me outside to make sure the Healey doesn't need a push to get started; it is notoriously slow to crank in cold weather.

"You doing anything tomorrow night?" Ron asks, as we file out. "I thought we might go grab a bite."

"Amazingly," I say, "I've got plans this weekend. How about if I catch you next week?"

He nods, flips me a thumbs-up.

"How's Audrey?" Wally asks, fishing lures jangling from his head. Wally, who owns three dogs himself, would probably have provided a better adoptive home, and he stands ever ready to offer advice or consolation.

"Fine," I say, as I get ready to climb in the car. "We got through that stretch of bad weather without her completely destroying the house, and now she's feeling better." The car starts right up—a cheer rises from my assembled friends, who turn and go back indoors—and off I drive.

When Madelyn knocks on the door Friday evening I have a good fire going, although that hasn't stopped me from tinkering with it. "Come in," I call, and Audrey gets up, yawns, stretches, and goes to investigate this intrusion.

They meet in the door to the living room, and it is Madelyn who lets out a surprised yelp. "You've got a dog!"

She comes into the room, hands me a six-pack of Corona, and drops to the floor where she can be at Audrey's level. "Hello, sweetheart," she says, and Audrey wags her tail so frantically that it almost lifts her off the ground.

"She's shedding," I warn, although I can see that it doesn't make any difference; she and Audrey are literally rolling on the floor together. Madelyn ends up on her back, with Audrey standing over her and holding out her right front paw to shake. "I had a dog once," Madelyn says, rising to an elbow. "Colby won't let me have a pet. His allergies." She reaches up and ruffles Audrey's coat with both hands. "I haven't seen the man so much as sneeze in ten years of marriage."

"So I guess you like her," I say when I can gain her attention for a moment.

"I love her! What's her name? Where did you get her? How long have you had her? Why didn't you tell me about this gorgeous puppy?" This last in puppy talk, high-pitched and cute.

Audrey's tail is still in frantic motion; I think she knows we're talking about her, and in any case, having another adoring person in the house is pretty exciting.

"This is Audrey. The rest is kind of a long story," I say.

"Oh," she says, dropping her head back to the floor and reaching up to scratch Audrey's tummy. "Audrey the mystery dog. Did you get her from a secret admirer?"

She is positively giddy, a word I would never have associated with Madelyn, whose state of most profound happiness some people have mistaken for clinical depression.

"Sure. I found her on the front step with a mysterious note. 'I LOVE YOU SO MUCH THAT I'M GIVING YOU MY DOG. Signed, Adoring You in Silence.' "

"She's a beautiful dog. Yes, you are, Audrey. A beautiful dog." And then, at long last, she gets to her feet. "And you're pretty spectacular too." She slides her arms around me and holds me tight. I hang onto her long past any welcome. "Are you happy to see me?"

Happier than I can properly express; happier, probably, than I should tell her. I let my fingers glide through her dark hair. "Very."

When we break, she goes to put the Corona in the refrigerator, "for later." Then she stretches out on the couch and pats the seat next to her, beckoning me to join her.

"I love the fire," she says. She and Colby do not have a fireplace in their house either; probably says he's allergic to smoke. She kisses me once, then whispers, "Why don't you put a big log on the fire? A really big one."

The fire looks like it's doing just fine, and from an inveterate fire-pesterer like me that admission means something. "Why?" I whisper back.

"Because it may be a while before you get a chance to put another one on," she says, and I rush to do her bidding.

It is a lovely evening, although I have to admit that it's strange to sleep with another person again. During the summer, I never stayed over at Madelyn's, but would depart after a decent interval. I thought that such a thing was probably best, both for secrecy and for sanity: making love certainly requires a certain degree of trust, but I think sleeping with another person requires even more. People should work up to it; only people who understand each other well should attempt it. It is an act of the greatest possible faith to fall asleep next to another human being.

So what does it mean that Madelyn and I awake together in my bed on Saturday morning? Well, I suppose it means that we have crossed some threshold, although what exactly that might be I do not know. Whatever it is, it's certainly pleasant. We both awaken slowly, gradually, and it is comforting to feel the warm reality of her body on a chilly morning. I slide my hand over her rounded flank, and she groans and rolls to face me, but Audrey has other plans entirely, and she comes to the side of the bed, tail thumping against the dresser, and emits the now-familiar whine that means she needs to go outside.

I pull on a pair of sweats and a T-shirt and pad to the kitchen door to let her out, then yawn my way back to the bedroom where Madelyn is sitting up in bed, blanket pulled around her shoulders like an Indian princess.

"What shall we do today?" I ask. "I am at your disposal. Not that I want to be disposed of."

"Don't you worry about that," she says. "You're much too precious to discard."

"Well," I say, feeling a flush come up my face. "What shall we do?"

"Well," she repeats, shrugging, causing the blanket to slide partly off her shoulders and me to slide back into bed next to her, "our options are kind of limited, aren't they? It's not like we can run into Waco, go shopping, have dinner."

"We could go out of town," I say, nuzzling that bare shoulder. "Someplace where nobody know us. Casablanca, maybe."

"Hmm," she says. "A road trip? It's tempting. But what would we do with Audrey?"

"She's okay by herself for the day. If we went away overnight I'd need to make arrangements, maybe leave her at a friend's."

"Let me think about it over breakfast," she says.

Ah, breakfast. I show her where the cereal is, let in Audrey, who is scratching at the back door, and restart the fire. Then we all sit crunching in the living room, Madelyn and I on our Chex, Audrey on the dry dog food.

At length I ask again. "What shall we do today? I should probably ride this afternoon since I didn't get out yesterday, but other than that, I'm open for suggestions."

"I have one," she calls, setting her bowl in the sink and coming back to sit down next to me. "I'd like to talk today. You said you had a story to tell me about Audrey. I think, for a change, I'd like to sit and talk."

"Talk, huh? What are you, some kind of pervert?"

"Come on," she says. "Wouldn't it be novel?"

"Okay," I say. "You start. What's been happening with you?" I know from hints she has dropped that she is still working on a prospectus for her dissertation on the Lilith figure in Judeo-Christian thought and doctrine, and that her failure to put her many thoughts into a concise and coherent framework is frustrating the hound out of her.

She makes a sour face. "I don't want to talk about that."

"Ah," I say. "Defeating the whole purpose, aren't we?"

"I don't want to talk about me. I want to hear about somebody I like whose life is going well."

"Don't you like Colby?" It strikes me that of the three of us, he comes closest to fitting those requirements.

"I especially don't want to talk about Colby," she says and rolls her eyes as if to say, Thanks for reminding me, he had almost slipped my mind.

"Are the religion faculty giving you a hard time on your prospectus?"

"I don't want to talk about it," she says, and immediately contradicts herself. "No, they're being awfully patient. It's my fault. Really. I can't seem to figure out how to get down what I want to say."

"I find that a little hard to believe," I say, and reach a finger across to sort of chuck her playfully under the chin, something I have seen other people do to each other and would like to add to my repertoire of intimate gestures. I'm hoping to lighten the tone a bit, but levity is not welcome here, at least not at this moment, at least not from me.

"Look at all this," she says, warming to her subject, indicating with her widespread hands my bookcases full of notebooks. "How do you do it? It must be wonderful to know what you want to say and just say it. What's your secret? What's *his* secret? I typed up his paper for Chicago, and it was brilliant. Bloody brilliant. How can it be that everybody around me is full of words and I can't seem to write a damned thing?"

She is close to tears, and for an instant I teeter on the dangerous brink of honesty, of telling her that it's certainly no easier for me than for her, of letting her know at least this portion of the truth. These empty notebooks she so casually indicates as proof of my superiority—given her crisis of belief, shouldn't she be told that they—that I—that neither of us is as we appear?

The look on her face at this moment is an expression of yearning, an expression of need. She wants answers, or my support, or something I am not giving her, and perhaps that itself is an answer of sorts.

Something I am not giving her.

I don't know what pulls me back from the abyss of intimacy, but something unquestionably does. One minute I am looking into those liquid brown eyes and the thing I want more than anything else is to ease her pain, no matter what it costs me, but that feeling is as slippery as soap, as ephemeral as a soap bubble, and the next thing I know, I am retreating to safety behind a sort of circular truism—almost a Jacksonism—I regularly spout for the writing classes: "You have to write to write."

"I know," she says. "I just can't seem to do it. I can't seem to do anything. I don't *want* to do anything." She gets up and starts pacing, which rouses Audrey, who has been dozing. "I mean what's the point?"

I can only look at her; I could expect to hear myself saying something like this, but it's novel to think that there may be other human beings asking the same questions. I begin to see an entirely new Madelyn. "The point?"

She whirls back to face me. "Let's say I get my degree someday. What do I do? I can't teach—he's got no reason to move, they love him, but I'll never get a job here—and I'll never get my own church because I'm a woman. Why in God's name should I get a Ph.D. in religion?"

Some thinly-buried part of me that is completely flip—or perhaps a deeply-buried part of me that is the exact opposite—wants to suggest that perhaps that last question is another that contains its own answer, but now is even less than before an occasion for levity, and when I have no more slogans, we both sink separately into morose states as sad as those microwave dinners for singles.

However, when Audrey stretches and comes wagging over to

us, Madelyn immediately brightens. After a few minutes of petting and ridiculous dog-talk—"Yes, you're a pretty dog, aren't you? Yes you are! Yes you are! A pretty pretty dog," and Audrey delighted to have someone else pay attention to her, wagging so hard her tail is thumping against the bookcases—Madelyn looks up at me with a new smile on her lips. "Let's go for a walk, Brad," she says, "and you can tell me all about this wonderful dog."

"I hope you're back in a really good mood," I mutter, but all the same, I go to get Audrey's leash; of all the various people close to me to whom I could tell this story, I sense that Madelyn is perhaps the only person who could—who would—understand it. "All right," I tell them both, "let's go," and I open the door.

11

The day when Richard Collins—or that collection of cells that superficially resembles him, if you believe Sandra Fuentes—finally dies does not seem to be a distinctive day in any symbolic way. It is the Tuesday of Thanksgiving week, which could be meaningful, perhaps, although I don't know how. Early in the day, we go as a group—Wally, Ron, Hugh, and I—by the hospital, and look in on Ron before going to lunch at Martha's—or rather, they check on him while I wait in the car—but he does not miraculously regain consciousness, recognize anyone, provide meaningful last words. No, he just lies there as he has for a month, inert as a turnip, and I don't need to be inside with them to imagine the rhythmic hum of the machines that are sustaining his vital functions, pumping blood through his veins, mechanically inflating his lungs with oxygen.

I know exactly what they sound like.

Thank God for lunch. I have the pork tips smothered in gravy, and four vegetables: pinto beans, spinach, glazed carrots, and yams. Everyone else takes the meat loaf as their main course. We talk mostly about our plans for the upcoming holiday. I'll be having dinner with Jackson and Evelyn, Hugh is celebrating with the adult children of his new lady friend, Ron will go over to his folks', and Wally and his family are flying back to Pennsylvania. It looks as though Richard—although this is not said by any of us—will be celebrating Thanksgiving in his usual fashion, alone. Maybe I am the only one to think about such things. I hope so.

All of this information about Thanksgiving is transmitted be-

tween bites. We sit at Formica tables, on mismatched chairs, but no one complains about the ambience. There is a momentary scuffle for the last piece of corn bread, but Wylie, a stoop-shouldered older gentleman who waits on us expertly, sees the impending conflict and brings us another plate.

Later that afternoon I'm a little lethargic—what I often feel after eating at Martha's is something akin to drunkenness, as though I should be sleeping off my lunch—but nothing of tremendous significance sets it off as somehow important either. The wind shifts around to the northeast as I ride, cooling things off in a hurry, and it occasionally gusts through the electric lines, making them whistle in addition to their usual cool-weather hum.

My old enemies, the fenced-in dogs, show some interest at my approach, but their every bid for escape has so far been thwarted; as I pass the angry canines I can see that although they've dug under the fence in spots, so far all the holes have been refilled. In any case, they're not going to redig them fast enough to catch me, and I'm afraid I'm not very gracious about letting them know it.

The message I've been expecting from Ron is on my machine when I arrive home. "He's gone, Brad," it says. "Funeral Friday. Can you be a pallbearer?"

Yes, I can, and I will. If I can't bear to haul him dying across a desert, I can at least haul him dead across a graveyard; the doctrine of the least I can do is still strong within me.

After I check my other messages, I don't know how long I stand unmoving in the hallway next to the machine, but it is apparently quite a while: Audrey gets tired of me ignoring her and begins licking my hand, and that moves me back to the present fast enough. "Come here," I say, walking into the living room and taking a seat on the fireplace. She looks up at me, trusting as an ingenue in a Forties melodrama. "Audrey," I say, stroking her head, "I've got to tell you something, and you're not going to like it."

She pants expectantly.

I suddenly feel thirteen kinds of ridiculous. "You're a dog," I say, more to myself than to her. This is not, of course, the horri-

ble information I told her I had to convey, but Richard is gone, and nothing I tell Audrey is going to communicate that.

Maybe that isn't the point. Maybe it doesn't matter if Audrey understands, can possibly understand. Maybe there are other reasons to say it.

"Richard is gone," I say, still petting her. "I know he loved you very much, because he talked about you all the time. When he asked me to take care of you, he was trusting me with the most important thing in his life. I guess that means something, doesn't it?"

Always eager to agree, she wags her tail happily. It breaks my heart.

That night, Richard's burial arrangements are broadcast on TV; one of the local funeral homes runs a nightly commercial of sorts, just before the ten o'clock local news, where they display the names and times of their upcoming services against the accompaniment of a chiming New Age melody. They apparently think it both helpful and tasteful. I have always thought it tacky and tasteless, and never more so than tonight, but I have to confess that it gets out the information, because no sooner does the last note chime than my phone rings.

"Hello," I say.

"That was your friend, wasn't it? The one who was in the hospital." It's Becky, and she's calling from someplace where there is loud country music in the background.

"Yes it was," I say, loud enough that I think she'll be able to hear me.

"I'm going to call my parents and tell them I can't come home for Thanksgiving. I'm going to stay here with you." She is a little maudlin and sounds as though she has had a few drinks, but the sentiment is a noble one, and I thank her for it.

"I wouldn't hear of it," I continue. "Go home to your folks. Have some turkey. I'll be all right."

"I won't go if you need me," she says. "I mean that."

"You go on," I tell her. "That would be too big a sacrifice. I wouldn't dream of it." The wonderful thing about courtesy is that by using it you can often get what you want regardless of what that is.

"Well," she says, wavering and then toppling, "all right. But I'll try and come back early. I know! Maybe my parents can come back this weekend. They're still asking about you."

This information clangs me upside the head with a cast-iron skillet. I have completely forgotten about meeting Becky's folks, mostly because she hasn't mentioned them since our night in Austin; I've assumed, incorrectly, that I was home free. "Maybe" is all I can think of to say back to her.

"I'll talk to them," she says, "and call you back. Are you sure you're up to it?"

I don't recall being asked in the first place, but it's a little late to split hairs. "I'll try to be."

There is a short pause, a line of Travis Tritt in the background, and then she says, all in one breath, "If you need me call me I love you 'bye." The tone in my ear after she hangs up is in the same key as the song. This is the sort of superfluous detail you notice when you don't care to think about anything else just yet.

Finally I hang up; try as I might, I can't get my memory to reconstruct the conversation any differently. Why did she have to say that word? She doesn't know me well enough to say it. If she did, she'd know better than to say it. "This is bad," I tell Audrey, who plops to the floor next to my feet. "This is very bad. She said the word. This is very bad."

I did not intend to lead Becky on, but apparently I have, and apparently it's time to make that clean break before I hurt her even worse. Maybe I should just start completely over, a clean slate, begin with an entirely new woman or women, give up on all three of these: let's face it, things haven't turned out the way I planned, and maybe I should just cut my losses, admit that life has gotten too complex again.

Except—

Except I like them, all of them.

Except they seem to like me, after their own fashions.

How did things get so complicated all of a sudden? I've done my best to avoid complication, to avoid even thinking about complication, and all the same I'm confronted by a set of difficulties that won't go away by ignoring them.

Becky is a problem I cannot solve at the moment, so after a late snack—cookies and milk, a dog biscuit for Audrey—I take some Henry James into the bedroom and read until I'm drowsy.

The next day I look forward to a good long mind-numbing ride, but when I go out to the garage my bike sits forlornly on two flat tires, a disaster of biblical proportions.

I have only one patch.

My alternatives are simple enough—go to the store and get more patch material or new tubes, take the bike to the shop to get both fixed, patch one and pump up the other and hope for the best—but all the same, simple decisions or no, I stand paralyzed into terrified immobility like a lifeguard suddenly confronted by a pool full of drowning swimmers.

Finally I patch the back tire and overinflate the front. Because of the end of Daylight Savings Time—a conspiracy against night people if there ever was one, giving the morning people an hour of daylight that we sleep through—I don't have enough time to run to the store and back, fix the tire, and still ride, and if I take the bike to the shop I won't get it back until at least Friday because of the Thanksgiving holiday. This way I've got a pretty good shot of getting in a short ride, at least, before the front tire goes flat, and then I can go get another patch or even another tube tonight or tomorrow at one of those grocery stores that stays open on Thanksgiving.

Since I have so little time to spare, I explore a new route that will take me about twelve miles in all, and I stop at the top of every other hill to press a thumb against the front tire.

I take a dirt road, packed and a little muddy because of recent drizzle, and the front tire throws up a fine thin stream of spattering mud that lightly coats the inside of my legs and occasionally gets flung against the underside of my chin. I taste grit mixed with sweat when I lick my lips. The culverts are full of leaves, mostly brown but some few colored brilliant yellow because of the brief freeze we had back in October.

I make a shifting mistake of some kind at the top of a hill and the chain slips. I have to stop and put it back on, and when I dismount to do that, I hear the barking. My first impulse is to get a running start and hop on the bike, coast down the hill to safety before I finish my repairs, but then I detect the frantic note of happiness in the barking, and sure enough, here comes a mother and her litter of pups, around a year old. She is jet-black, but her pups range from black to spotted, and a couple have brown patches. Sandra would have a genetic field day here.

They leap on top of each other to get a chance at my outstretched hand—it looks, with all the black puppies, like a cheerful bubbling cauldron of tar—and they yap happily around me when I turn back to stretch the chain into place.

"I've got to be going," I tell them. Although I would love to stay and play for a bit, my tire is already feeling a little mushy, and I can't afford the extra time.

The last mile or so, the front tire flattens visibly against the road, particularly when I lean over the handlebars on a hill, but I make it home safely and am feeling good about my decision. I have a lot of leftover energy, though, and so I take Audrey out for a long walk and end up half dragging her back to the house. She always starts off well: she'll run with me for a mile or so, but she overdoes it, uses up her reserves. I forget sometimes how old she is, because the puppy she hasn't been for eight years never seems far from the surface.

While we're walking slowly back home, Elaine calls to wish me a happy Thanksgiving, and when I hear her message, I call back to wish her the same. Thanksgiving was our favorite holiday, perhaps because it was one we could agree on celebrating without offending the religious right in either of our families.

"Hello," Owen Rosenbaum says, sourly. I have never met him, only spoken briefly with him on the phone, and he seems nice enough, if a little dour. Certainly he seems to be a sport about Elaine's continuing interest in my well-being.

"Good evening, Owen," I say, exaggerating the Texan a bit because he seems to like it. "This is Brad Cannon, calling from Texas to wish y'all a happy Thanksgiving."

"I'll get Elaine," he says, and the receiver clunks onto a hard surface.

"Hello, Brad," Elaine says, beaming through the phone. I never call, or hardly ever, and any interest in the world outside my house heartens her. "I hope you have a wonderful holiday."

"It's certainly going to be a memorable one," I tell her, in a tone that does not go unnoticed.

"What is it? What's wrong?"

"Too much to tell you over the phone. Let's synchronize our watches—I'll meet you in twenty minutes at the 42nd Street entrance to the Transit Authority."

"You wouldn't catch me dead there," she says. "Hustlers and pimps. How about the bar at the Carlyle?"

"Snooty and pretentious," I tell her. "How about that great Italian place off Third?"

"Kitchen fire," she sighed.

"I guess we'll have to forgo a face-to-face this time."

"It's nothing bad, I hope. Evelyn? Jackson?"

"They're fine," I say. "I'll tell you someday. Nothing I can't get through, I suppose."

"I've got to go," she says. "Owen is taking me out to dinner. Call later if you need to talk, okay?"

"Okay," I say. "You too."

She laughs. She has taciturn Owen wrapped around her finger, and her life finally seems to be going just as she would like. "All right. I'll keep that in mind."

I can't claim the same sort of contentment, and there's a lot of empty space left between hanging up the phone and showing up at my grandparents' for one of Billie's epic Thanksgiving meals. I sigh, stoke the fire, and settle into the chair with mail-order catalogs. For a few minutes, at least, I imagine that I'm living a different life, somewhere where the world is populated by smiling handsome people in the latest clothes whose houses are full of designer furniture. The death of a few trees is a very small price to pay for that kind of contentment.

Thanksgiving dinner is served promptly at one o'clock, or at least has been during each of my thirty years, and the menu has never once changed to accomodate frills, fads, or the latest health warnings. I can name every item in this dinner even as I am driving to the house to consume it: a huge turkey, a smoked ham, corn-bread stuffing, gravy with giblets, mashed potatoes, baked yams, cranberry sauce, broccoli and rice casserole, various salads—none of which I'll touch until I'm sure I've devoted as much space to the main course as I can manage—and those desserts on which Evelyn will collaborate, pumpkin, sweet potato, pecan pies, two or three different kinds of fudge, and a lemon pound cake so moist you can barely coax it off your fork.

It is also a special dinner because it is one of the three days—the others are Christmas Day and the anniversary of her entering service—when Billie joins us at the table. This is another tradition that stretches back into prehistory. After she eats with us, Evelyn helps her package up a pile of the leftovers for her family, and Billie leaves to celebrate again with them.

Since Billie is not serving, we fill our plates buffet style with those items that won't fit on the table proper, then sit for the prayer. As always, Jackson asks if I'd like to offer the blessing, and as always, I use courtesy to my advantage: "You're so much better at it," I say. "Go ahead."

"Bow your head," he commands. "Dear Heavenly Father, we thank you for this bounty, for the many blessings you've given us, for family and good friends."

"Amen," Billie says, getting warmed up.

"Thank you for our great nation and our great state."

"Thank you, Jesus."

"Be with our president and the congress. Give them wisdom."

"Wisdom, Lord."

"Bless this food to our body's use for thee, and forgive us our many transgressions."

"Lord, Lord."

"Protect us through the coming days, and help us to know your perfect will for our lives so that we may serve you better."

"Praise God. Thank you, Jesus."

"We ask all this in the name of him in whom we place our trust, your perfect son, Jesus Christ."

"Amen," we all say. We know Jackson's prayer by heart, but it is a good prayer, and as a deacon at First Baptist, he has rendered some version of it on more than one occasion, sans food references, of course.

"Praise the Lord and pass the potatoes," I say, which is another family tradition. It was more appropriate when I was eight or nine, but I have my part to play in the holiday drama, and I don't want to fall down on the job. I was the first small person to enter these adult tableaux in many years, so I had a monopoly on cute, at least until Carter got old enough to stumble around. Then I lost the best seat at the table at Thanksgiving—next to Billie—I lost the Santa hat—which goes to the person who hands out presents at Christmas—and I had to sit glumly waiting for Carter's short legs to carry my cool stuff across the room from the tree.

But I remember my parents smiling after Carter had turned a three-year-old's thanks—"God, I like turkey"—and climbed into Billie's ample lap—how he found room between her and the table, I will never know—and I even remember thinking to myself one Christmas that Carter made a good elf with that hat, even if it slid all the way over his eyes. Every package he dragged over to me was delivered with his complete unadulterated joy.

Damn, I had a nice family.

"There you go, Little Bit," Billie says, sending me this year's mashed potatoes, whipped with butter. "And I 'spose you'll be wanting some gravy with that." It is not a question, because the gravy is following just behind it.

This dinner is one of the great primate delights, and the fact that it's repeated annually actually gives me some hope. Set aside the past, if such a thing is possible; I can see how a future populated by Thanksgiving and Christmas dinners could be worth living for.

"Tell Jackson what's going on with your New Year's Eve dance," Bradford urges Evelyn, and Billie seconds him, "Yes'm, tell him."

"You'd best be lining up that pretty little girl of yours for New Year's," she says, "because I'm throwing a shindig to beat all shindigs, and everyone's going to be there."

"What little girl?" I ask, since it seems the surest way to distract her from her train of thought.

"Why, that little girl from the zoo," she says slyly. "I hear she was a gorgeous little thing."

"She is that," I admit. "But she's a little young for me, and too serious for my liking."

"Lord, who wouldn't want to snap you up?" Billie says.

"I could give you a list," I say. "But I'm afraid it would burn out my computer."

"Well, bring whoever you like," Jackson says. "But bring somebody. Your grandmother has been working her—well, she's been working hard to set things up—and you should be there to represent the foundation."

"Ah, Jackson." I sigh. I thought this had been shelved for the time being, and here it jumps up again. "I'm just a private citizen these days. I can't possibly two-step if I'm a representative of anything."

"You are a Cannon, sir," he says. "And that means you have civic responsibilities. Duties to the community you cannot ignore."

"I'll come to Evelyn's party," I say, motioning with my fork for emphasis, "but only as a private citizen. That's my final offer."

"And you'll bring someone," Evelyn reminds me, and I suddenly see that once again I have been out-negotiated. I have to learn to recognize that with me, people start from extreme positions and work me toward what they consider their reasonable demands.

"Okay." I sigh. "I'll find someone. I may have to hire someone off the streets."

"Merciful God," Billie says, even though she knows I'm joking. Maybe she's worried that God doesn't.

"How about eighteen holes tomorrow?" Jackson says, now that that's settled. "I've got a nine o'clock tee time."

"I've got plans," I say. "Maybe next time."

"Now what could be more important than spending some quality time with your granddad?" Jackson asks. It is not rhetorical.

"I have to go to a funeral," I say. A silence descends on the table like fast-dropping fog.

"I'm so sorry, dear," Evelyn says. "Who is it?"

"My friend Richard Collins," I tell her.

"The sportswriter?"

I nod. "Cancer. It was the best thing really. He was in a lot of pain toward the end."

I laugh then. "Did you know I'm keeping his dog now?"

"No kidding," Jackson says, and he laughs himself. The world is full of wondrous possibilities. "What kind of dog?"

"Golden Retriever. She's a gorgeous dog, Jackson. You'll have to come by and see her."

"I'd like that, son."

After dinner we adjourn to the den, and while Evelyn helps Billie carve the turkey and slice ham, I have Jackson to myself.

"You want to watch some football?" he asks. "Dallas is on today."

"Sure, in just a second. Can I say something first?"

He settles back in his recliner, and raises his hands, palms out, as if to say, fire away.

"You know, Jackson, Richard was on life support for weeks."

He immmediately drops his gaze to his slippers, so potent is the phrase "life support" within our family mythology.

"It was horrible," I say. "Horrible. Nobody should have to linger on like that."

He looks up at me, and I nod. "It's no way to live. It's not living at all, really. Just putting off the inevitable. I guess what I'm saying is that I think that you were right when you told them to turn it off. I think you did the right thing."

He raises his head and I can see his eyes glistening as he bites his lower lip. "Do you think so, son? Really?"

I nod. I am ready to bury this with my father, as I should have years ago. "Hell, it was the only decision you could make."

"Thank you, son," he says, and I can see that there is more he wants to say, but suddenly Evelyn appears from the kitchen, and he just smiles a regretful smile and asks, "Did you get everything packed up?"

"I had to help her carry things out to the car," Evelyn says. "I think they'll have a nice meal this evening."

"We were just getting ready to watch some football," I say, to help cover for Jackson. "And then maybe we can have some dessert at halftime."

"When do you have to leave?" she asks.

"I'm yours until four," I say. I picked up another inner tube and replaced the front tire this morning, and I'm going to have to start working off this incredible dinner. In the meantime, though, I intend to sit back in the comfortable silence of people who know each other well and don't feel that they have to fill each blank moment with conversation. Jackson turns on the TV with his remote, the Cowboys appear from blackness, and I settle comfortably back on the couch and rest a hand on my happy stomach.

12

The days between Richard's funeral and Evelyn's New Year's party constitute a bleary blur, a dreary dream full of half-glimpsed Christmas lights and shining solicitous faces peering down at me. It's not that I'm walking through life in my usual noncommittal stupor; this is an entirely new stupor, an actual stupor, and I am a victim of circumstances mostly beyond my control. Honestly.

Here's how it happens: after the funeral on Friday, after the Saturday dinner with Becky Sue Bradenton's parents, on Sunday I ride out into an overcast day that first begins to spit cold drizzle and then, when I'm around seventeen miles from home, erupts into a full-fledged great-grandmother of a late fall Texas thunderstorm, which at first only concerns me slightly because I remember I've left Audrey roaming free at home, and then concerns me more because my body temperature begins to drop toward absolute zero, and at last concerns me greatly because I get blown clean off my bike and make a bad landing on the flooded pavement before I finally reach home with what feels like my last dying gasp.

But I'm getting ahead of myself, and it's important that events follow in succession in narrative the way they do in life. First, of course, comes the funeral: Ron, Hugh, Wally, and I are pallbearers, and after the church service, we are enjoined to haul Richard's earthly remains and the huge metal coffin enclosing them to the gravesite. Hugh is sixty-seven years old and Wally has a bad back, which means Ron and I are left bearing the brunt of the weight, and my God, this coffin is heavy. From the hearse to the grave is maybe thirty feet, but every step of the way I fear the worst. The wind flaps the top of the funeral home tent, and an untenanted folding chair picked up by this wind whistling in from San Angelo or Amarillo lands three graves over. As we lurch through the sparse stand of mourners, the cords of my neck are standing out against the knot of my necktie, and both my biceps—I have both hands on the handle—begin to cramp with the strain. If it weren't such a solemn occasion, I sense that we would just drop this coffin where we are—ka-boom!—and collapse into hysterical laughter atop it. It seems like something Richard would approve.

When we finally flop the coffin onto the contraption that will lower it into the grave, I look down at my hands and see the huge painful red indentation in both of my palms, one last tangible reminder of Richard, although it will fade shortly and all will be as it was before. When we step back from the grave, I find myself standing next to Evelyn and Jackson, who have kindly agreed to come out to this funeral service for a man they never met.

"If he was important to you, Bradford," Evelyn told me while we watched football, "he's important to us."

"Any man who trusted you with his dog had to think a lot of you," Jackson said. "We'll come see him off." He has had to give up his golf game to do it, but this was probably a good decision in any case, since the wind would bring his tee shot right back in his face.

I expect and am prepared to see them; I do not expect Madelyn Clark to appear among the small group of people directly across the grave from me, but there she is, pale, dressed in a plain black dress, one hand holding her hem down against the lewd wind, and as beautiful as I have ever seen her.

I am going to have to rethink my stance on that stupid funeral home commercial; it is obviously hugely effective in getting the word out.

In my surprise at seeing Madelyn there, I'm afraid I don't pay as much attention to the service as I should. It's not that I don't try; I do at least hear the words of the homily, but they patter off me like rain off a tin roof, clatter away from me before I can seize them. I give up, stand instead looking toward the priest, a vantage point that lets me watch her every motion, lets me recognize that she is doing the same to me, lets me lose myself in those brown eyes.

At the conclusion of the ceremony, I thank Evelyn and Jackson, agree to come for dinner early in the next week, shake hands soberly with my friends, and drift slowly toward my car so that Madelyn can walk alongside me, almost close enough to touch.

"I hope you don't mind," she says, when we are a decent distance from the other mourners.

I turn to her. "Are you crazy? I'm glad you came. I just can't believe you did. Where's Colby?"

"Writing, of course. Somebody in the family has to."

We have reached her car, and to pause long beside it will mark my behavior as unusual. I hold out my hand, take hers, and simply say, "Thank you."

She smiles sadly and squeezes my hand in return before letting go. "Friends are important. We shouldn't forget them."

"Friends are important," I repeat. "I'll talk to you soon, okay?"

She nods, and a pause of tangible weight hangs between us; I can't speak for her, but I realize from the familiar fluttering in my rib cage that what I would most like to do at this moment is take her in my arms.

"I know," she says, and that sad smile is back for a moment. "But people would talk." She opens her door, gets inside, and waves with one finger before turning her attention to the road ahead and driving away.

I ride aimlessly that afternoon, pedal out past deserted farms and abandoned barns and fields lying fallow, strike out deep into the countryside trying to lose myself in new sensations, and I am partly successful; the sound of my tires humming on the pavement soothes me into a waking half sleep in which nothing exists but my body, an engine pumping, and the bike, a steel and rubber extension of myself, the two of us one, occupying the only real spot on the planet. I ride that day without fatigue, without soreness, without conscious thought: when I arrive at home as the sun is setting, in the chill of evening, I can't honestly recall all the places I've been.

I have been gone for four and a half hours, have probably covered fifty or sixty miles; on another day, I would be awfully impressed with myself. On this evening, though, I go in and let Audrey out—she's been worried about me, I can see, because she's not sure she wants to go outside, let me out of her sight—and fix myself a sandwich, which I chew and swallow mechanically, without noticing its taste or texture.

Becky calls at six to tell me she's back in town, and to ask if tomorrow night at seven would be all right to meet her parents. "I thought we could go to the Elite," she says. "That's an authentic Waco landmark, isn't it?"

"Elvis ate there," I say. "Sure. That'll make a better impression than the Branch Davidian Complex, wherever that is."

She snickers, about all that sally deserves. "I'll ride with my parents, so I can show them how to get there, make sure they don't kill themselves." This is not just idle talk; the Elite Café is located next to one of the few remaining traffic circles in Texas, and to say that neophytes have trouble negotiating it is like saying that Floridians may have difficulty driving in blizzards. "You can take me home after, if you'd like."

"Uhmm," I say, which sounds affirmative. For any other heterosexual male, it would be; I'm simply not that anxious to be alone with Becky Sue Bradenton; I know what people who are in love are supposed to do when they get off by themselves, and I'm not sure I ought to test my willpower so. I mean, really, I'm only human.

Again I wonder why Becky couldn't just find some good-looking premed student and fall in love with him. There must be plenty of guys who would do anything to get her attention. Ten years ago I would have done Tom Sawyer acrobatics for a girl like her.

"Dress up a little," she says. "I want them to be impressed by you. Wear your black and white houndstooth jacket. And those gray khakis. You look really nice in that."

"Okay."

Audrey barks once, briefly, at the back door, and I hang up the phone and go to let her in. She comes over to my chair, her tail tucked back between her legs, and I can tell that she senses a front moving in. I should hire her out to predict the weather; she's twice as accurate as any of those bozos on TV with all their Doppler radars and computer models of the jet stream. Audrey the Weatherdog. Big bucks, fame, handsome boy dogs, dog food commercials. It would be quite a life, for her, at least.

"Let's go in and take some medicine," I say brightly, as though I am communicating something of almost transcendent wonder, and she follows me eagerly into the kitchen. When I give her the pill wrapped in cheese, she accepts it as her due, not as anything suspicious on my part. "Good dog," I say, and I congratulate both of us on a job well done.

It doesn't take long, though, to see that those congratulations are premature, that I've given her the medicine too late for it to do any good. She's already gotten herself worked up, panting, trembling head to tail. It's horrible to watch, really. She shivers uncontrollably, and when I sit on the floor next to her, her awful fear-breath hot in my face, and throw my arms around her, she shakes me too, so powerful is her terror.

I sit up with her until she exhausts herself, sometime after four-thirty in the morning, and it's when she finally conks out and I wander in to lie down that I realize how exhausted I am too. We sleep, the both of us, until early the next afternoon, and for a moment I imagine that it's too late for me to ride, if I could move, which I cannot. My legs feel as if they're carved from wood. When I get up to walk into the bathroom, I catch my image in the mirror, and it would be frightening if it weren't so absurd: I look like one of those old Western stuntmen sashaying bowlegged away from a knock-down drag-out, a brouhaha.

"Great," I croak. "This should make a good impression." I take a long hot bath, soak until the sweat pours down my forehead, and when I get out, I can at least move without creaking. Then I shave, brush my teeth, floss, put on deodorant.

All this activity hasn't fazed Audrey, who lies unmoving at the foot of my bed, only her shallow breathing demonstrating that she's still among the living. When I fill her bowl with food and come back to check on her, she does raise her red and bleary eyes to mine, but otherwise she doesn't budge all afternoon.

"I've got to go out," I say later, after I get dressed. "Becky's parents. Try not to destroy the house while I'm gone." She raises her eyes again as if to say, *Don't worry.*

I dress, slap on a little of the Ralph Lauren cologne Becky got me for my birthday, and run my fingers through Audrey's fur before I leave. She sniffs idly at the new scent on her hair, then settles back on the floor. "I'll be back soon," I say. "Be good."

I have only a few miles to drive to reach the Elite. Becky and her parents are waiting inside, and after she introduces me, she tells me we'll have to wait a few minutes for a table to open up, never pleasant under the best of circumstances. But I have bought into this evening and all it entails, and I will endure.

Becky's father, Jim, is a doctor, brisk, trim, efficient in manner. He shakes hands with two firm pumps and a quick release and regards me with a sort of smug detachment. Suzanne is a Texas trophy wife, perfectly coiffed, her face stretched tight. At first, she does most of the talking.

"We've been so anxious to get together with y'all," she says when we're first introduced. "Our Becky has told us so much about you I feel like we know you already."

"It's a pleasure for me too," I say.

Jim sniffs audibly. I can't tell if he's calling my statement into question, as he properly could, or it is simply part of his overall persona.

The hostess calls our name, miraculously, and we follow her back to the table. Jim pairs off with me; we are, I presume, going to talk manly talk, while the womenfolk hang back a pace.

"So you're a writer," Jim says. "I didn't know such things existed."

I get a lot of this. Texas is not what you would call a literary culture, and writers are exotic creatures, like rodeo clowns. "I wrote one pretty good book," I say, and shrug. I'd like to stick to honesty as far as possible tonight, and this at least is true.

"Well," he says, "I'm a little apprehensive about that, about my little girl getting involved with someone who doesn't have a steady job. I understand you've got a little money coming in, but do you honestly think a writer can support a wife?"

I stop walking and just stare at him for a second; Suzanne actually bumps into me, then spouts apologies.

It's amazing how mad you can get in just the time it takes to walk to the back of a restaurant. Put aside the fact that it's a stupid question, and that I have no intention of marrying his daughter; what knots my stomach is the matter-of-fact arrogance of this son of a bitch, his automatic and completely unwarranted dismissal. He doesn't know me well enough yet to dismiss me.

My first impulse is to tell him, "Sure I can support a wife. I've supported two so far," but I sense that this would be a tactical error. And really, I don't want to cause trouble. I like this place, the food is good, and a man can stand anything for a few hours if he knows it's going to end at some point.

The hostess seats us at a table in the back room across from a large party with several small children. Suzanne beams indulgently at them; Jim scowls, rug-rats; Becky's so busy watching her father's reactions to me that she doesn't even notice them.

"So," Jim says, as soon as the waiter has taken our orders for iced teas around the table and two orders of the fried mozzarella sticks, "Becky says you're writing a book now. How long have you been working on it?" He's not going to let this rest even though I sense it's a bone he and she have already picked almost clean.

"Quite a while now," I say. "The first one took three years."

"It's still in print, too," Becky says. "I've got a copy of it back at the apartment I can bring to breakfast in the morning."

"How nice," Suzanne says. She's never met a real writer. Still hasn't, actually, but she doesn't need to know that. "Just think, Jim, Brad here has his book in bookstores all across the country."

Jim is not impressed. "Well," he says, squeezing a lemon into his tea, "it just seems like an awful strange way to go through life. What sort of—"

"He's a good writer, Daddy," Becky says, looking back and forth between us. "Not everybody has to make people well."

"What's your specialty, Jim?" I ask in a voice that is just barely polite enough.

"Internal medicine," he says.

"Uhmm," I say. I make a production out of stirring sugar into my tea, momentarily take a leave of absence from the conversation to see what will happen.

"Becky told us once how y'all met," Suzanne says, jumping in to restore order, "but I suppose it has slipped my mind, silly me."

"We met after a lecture I gave her creative writing class. She asked some good questions, and after, she wanted to talk about writing for a little longer, so we went across to the Union and had a Coke." I flick my eyes over to Becky and she catches my signal, tags me so I can leave the ring.

"He was so inspiring," Becky says. "I mean, I'm not a real writer, I could see that already, but he made me want to be one all over again. It took a while after talking to him for me to come down."

"Well I'm glad it wore off," Jim says, from behind his menu. "There's no point in chasing rainbows, Becky. Teaching is a fine solid occupation."

"I'll try the Cajun pasta," Suzanne tells our now-hovering waiter, swiftly, as if to obscure Jim's remarks.

I order the chicken-fried steak, which is awfully good here, and ask for all the fixings on my potato, and we settle back into the crosscurrents of conversation that dominate the rest of our evening together: Jim Bradenton's nobody's-good-enough-for-my-little-girl digs, Suzanne's skillful interventions to cover the tension in a veneer of civilized table talk, Becky's caught-in-a-revolving-door attempts to satisfy both the father she adores and the wretch she thinks she loves.

And that wretch? I sit back, enjoy a good meal which is made even better since I know Jim's pride will not permit him to let me pick up the check, speak when spoken to or when it's obvious I must, and suffer only from a low-grade resentment against this cocksure ass that mars my usual pleasant sense of uninvolved unfeeling.

After dessert—even though the massive chicken-fried steak, potato, salad, and rolls have filled me near to bursting, I have the chocolate pie, heated, with a scoop of ice cream, and coffee since

Jim is paying for it—we look around at each other, all of us recognizing that it has been a perfectly dreadful evening, and Suzanne smiles at Becky and me and concedes, "Well, I suppose we ought to let you two lovebirds have a little time to yourselves."

As soon as the words clear her lips, I look at Jim, smile meaningfully, and say, "Yes, ma'am, we'd like that very much."

I make a show of going for the check, insist once, as etiquette demands, and then thank Jim for treating us to such a wonderful dinner. "It must be wonderful to have a real job," I smile and say, which is a pretty good exit line, so I make it one.

Becky and I are silent for a time as we drive along the I-35 access road back toward her apartment.

"I'm sorry he didn't like you," she says, finally, as we turn down the street to her apartment. "He's never liked any of them, if that'll make you feel any better."

"That's okay," I tell her. "I shouldn't have let him get to me."

"You were just fine." She sighs, leaning over to plant a kiss on my jaw, just beneath my ear. "I'll bet he'll respect you for standing up to him."

I think it's unlikely that Jim Bradenton and I will ever meet again, which makes the question largely moot. In fact, if there were a graceful way to express these sentiments to Becky, to show her the mistake she has made, is making, I would do it. But the moment doesn't seem right, and it rapidly seems even less so. We pull into her parking lot, she whispers, "Come up. I've got a surprise for you," and then she winks, and whether I'm still thinking it would be nice to show Jim Bradenton a thing or two or my inner primate has seized the controls, I get out of the car and follow her inside.

"Have a seat," she calls, going on into the kitchen. I ease onto the sofa to the sound of clinking, and Becky brings in a bottle of red wine and two stemmed glasses.

"Is this okay? I've got coffee if you'd rather, but I thought you'd earned a drink. I know it's been a tough few days."

"It has," I say. I open the bottle for her and she pours, the liquid deep red and aromatic.

She hands me the glass, settles back at my side, takes a sip, then brings her lips close, chilled and fragrant and sweetened by the wine, and I can't help but taste them.

She sighs breathily with satisfaction, pulls away for a moment to take my glass and set both glasses down on the table, and then she returns.

I am apparently not the only one who feels tempted to show Jim Bradenton a thing or two, even in absentia. Her hands creep into my hair, which is long now, since I haven't been to the barber for a couple of months; she nuzzles me beneath my ear, and my hands rise to meet her, pull her body against mine. She complies; in fact, she contributes her own pressure, eases me horizontal back onto the couch, and once we're there, she takes my hand and raises it to the top buttons on her blouse.

"Go ahead," she says. "It's part of the surprise."

"What do I get if I do?" I'm trying to be cool and flip, but at the moment I am anything but, and she can tell.

"Everything," she says, and her lips return to my throat to encourage me further.

Well, I've always liked surprises. With awkward thumb and fingers, I undo a few buttons, sneak a peek past her busy blond head, and see black lace and the impressive underwired curve of her cleavage.

"Wow," I breathe. This is unworthy of me; she is a beautiful girl, and the packaging should always be subordinate to the gift, but still, despite myself, I am impressed.

"I've been on the pill for over a month," she says, striving for matter-of-factness, bringing her hand up to undo a few of my buttons. "I thought maybe we could go in there." Her head inclines toward the bedroom at the same time as her fingers open a path of bare skin toward my belt.

I can feel myself struggling to stay afloat, aloof. "Becky, darlin', are you sure that's what you want? I mean, you've got breakfast with your folks in the morning before church, your dad doesn't approve of me, we may be rushing things—"

"You're so sweet," she says, running her index finger across my lips to silence my objections. What a complete and unquenchable idiot I am: all these polite attempts to head her off can only seem to her like the solicitous questions of a truly wonderful man, someone who cares deeply about her and her feelings. And I do care, really I do, but I'm not nearly so nice as she gives me credit for; I'm just nice enough to get by in polite society, and so, I suspect, is just about everybody else if the truth were admitted.

"Becky," I object, but she is simultaneously kissing me and peeling my shirt back over my shoulders; as I realize that, I also recognize that I am doing precisely the same thing to her, and at the touch of skin to skin, her belly against mine, the soft lacy mounds of her breasts insistent against my chest, I am a goner.

Tomorrow I can call myself names and rail at myself for making it even harder to let her down easy, and one part of me, the small element of rational thought not yet submerged beneath primate sexuality, knows that I will do just that. That part also informs me that I've been played like a big trout by an expert fly fisherman, that the flimsy underthings and the wine and the birth control all amount to seduction aforethought. But she feels so good, and my life lately has been so trying, and I am so tired, so in need of something, someone, that I stop trying to be noble and rational and instead slide my hands down and over her flanks and pull her even tighter against me.

Later, much later, when we are underneath her Laura Ashley comforter snuggled against each other—her apartment is a little drafty and it is cold outside—she assures me that while I am not her first, there haven't been many before me. She tells me this, of course, to make sure I know that this is a significant occasion, but not an earth-shattering one, one that has to mean everything.

"If you had one wish," she asks me as we lie cuddled close for warmth, "anything in the world, what would it be?"

"That's a good question." It's so good, in fact, that I can't answer it. I am no good at pillow talk. I suspect that she would like me to tell her I wish we'd gotten together years ago, grown up in adjacent backyards in Tyler, Texas, maybe, but if I actually had a life-altering wish I'd want to employ it for something more significant than winning a girl I don't completely want. My first reaction is to wish that no one had ever come up with the idea of the gravel truck, but this is purely selfish; even if a gravel truck happens to bump a lovely family off the interstate and into a bridge abutment every now and then, I'm sure they have done our great nation some lasting good. Since the only other thing I might wish for is Susie Bramlett, alive and in my arms and this also would not suit Becky's notions of pillow talk, I simply say, "I don't know."

When she slides from beneath the covers for another bathroom break, I begin to dress quietly, pull on my shoes while I hear the water running, and when she comes back out, I come as close as I dare to telling her that what we have been doing is a mistake. Jackson would tell me—would tell me, that is, if we ever talked about such things—that what I'm doing is stupid; an apropos Jacksonism for this situation might be "Never get up from the table while they're still serving dinner."

I notice, by the way, that most of Jackson's sayings revolve around food; it's no wonder he had that last heart attack.

Anyway: "I've got to go," I say when she comes out. "I've got to get home to take care of Audrey, and you've got to get up early."

"I wish you would stay," she says, and she makes as if to unbutton my shirt again; this may be something that would work with men her own age, but I can truthfully say that for me, that train has already left the station, is in fact on down the tracks and completely out of sight, and in any case, I'm not going to stay here all night.

"Becky." I take a deep breath and begin the speech. "I'm just not sure about all this. It's not that it hasn't been wonderful. It has been. You have. But that's not the point. I really don't feel like I can manage a relationship right now. Not the kind you deserve. I have—I had—" I shake my head; I can't finish it. "I've had bad luck," I whisper; it is the best I can do.

She's dressed only in the comforter, which she has wrapped around herself, but she manages a surprising amount of dignity as she sits beside me on the bed and raises a hand to my face. "Oh, Brad," she says. "Don't you think I know all that?"

I blink, rapidly, several times, just about the only response I can muster.

"I'm not saying I can live with this forever," she says, scuttling back under the covers and drawing them close about her. "But I have my eyes open, and I know what I'm getting into."

"Do you?" I ask, as gently as I can manage.

"More than you might think," she says, and maybe she's right; there are depths to this girl, certainly more than I ever gave her credit for. I even consider saying this, but decide against it.

Too honest.

I settle instead for "You're a good girl," and she giggles and says, "Not tonight I wasn't." Then she leans forward and gives me a quick peck before dropping back and pulling the blanket tight around her again. "Now get out of here. I'd just as soon you and my dad didn't meet on the front steps."

"I think you're right," I say, and I get up to go. "Have fun at breakfast."

"It won't be so bad," she says. "I'll talk to you soon, okay?"

"Okay," I say as I lock the front door behind me. Then I drive blearily home, wake Audrey to give her another dose of medication to make her sleep, and I myself drowse fitfully until midmorning. I keep drifting in and out of sleep, turning things over in my mind, and, even with that parting conversation, feeling as though I am some kind of snake in the garden.

Before I leave on my bike I check the Weather Channel, which informs me that current conditions in central Texas are cloudy, temperature in the low fifties, wind light out of the south, precipitation in the area but not directly overhead. I have on gray sweatpants, a T-shirt, and a thick dark green hooded sweatshirt that I've had since I was a Baylor undergrad, and I am warm enough as I set off.

In the first miles of my ride, though, before I reach the Dog Turnoff, I have trouble getting settled, getting comfortable. Maybe it's just that I'm too tired, but the bike today feels alien, unfamiliar. I get off several times, once to adjust the seat up a tiny bit, once to fiddle with the rear wheel, which is a little out of true and rubs up against one of the brake shoes with every revolution, a sound a little like corduroyed thighs swishing together, light, rhythmic, and ultimately maddening.

At last, everything seems to be in order. For a second, as I turn left off the farm-to-market road, it almost looks as if the sun might peer out from behind the clouds.

It doesn't but I don't really notice, because at the house near the top of the hill I used to pedal down wildly, something more amazing than nuclear fusion draws my eye. A dog is on the roof of the house, barking at me. On the roof. Of a house. A big dog. I stop and marvel.

He is there on the tilted roof, walks a few steps down closer to me, barks some more. I take a drink from my water bottle, decide that there must be a pile of something in the backyard he can climb up on to reach the roof, and then I hear the answering barks.

They are coming from the dogs down the road, my dogs, the evil dogs that I now can see are slithering, one by one, from the fresh hole under the fence and into the road.

Now it all becomes clear: I've been suckered; the roof dog is a decoy for the leg-chewers down the road.

Well, turning around seems silly, so I choose my usual approach: get up a good head of steam, steer straight toward the barking mob to drive them off the road, and raise my feet up off the pedals.

They don't get out of the way. Whether it's excitement—they haven't been after me in a long time—or something more sinister—I have done a lot of trash-talking while they were safe behind bars—they don't give ground; they just sort of fall in alongside me, except for one who charges ahead of me, chasing me from in front, as it were, looking over his shoulder every second or two to make sure I'm still back there.

I can hear a man yelling from the porch "You dogs get back here, damn it!" but they don't. If anything, they surge closer, and it's a miracle, if you believe in such things, that I avoid hitting the front dog, who suddenly wheels, probably to hurl himself at my throat. I brake hard, cut the bike sharply to one side, grazing the dogs there, and then stand on the pedals, pumping like mad while they chase merrily after me. They're having a great time; not even a sudden spurt of cold drizzle can dampen their spirits.

I can't say the same for me. After the surprise of running from them and that near miss, my heart is pumping wildly, and I feel a little sick to my stomach. The mist continues as I ride on into the tree-lined lanes, where the leaves have fallen so thick since I last rode that in spots they completely cover the road, and I crackle across them for two miles before emerging.

The rain comes in force, all of a sudden, after I've passed the Koufax house and the Cottonwood Baptist Church and Cemetery, respectively; from the spotty drizzle it changes to a celestial overflow just as I begin my ascent of the enormous hill. The water comes pouring frothily down the road, an inch deep in places, carrying leaves and beer cans and empty packs of cigarettes.

Then a sudden gust of crosswind knocks me off balance and off the saddle, and I fall gracelessly to the blacktop, my back and shoulder hitting with a splash and a thud. You'd think the cold water surging down the hill would cushion the landing, but it doesn't. I get up slowly, roll my shoulder painfully a few times, pick up my bike, and push it the last hundred yards uphill, my shoes and socks filling with water. And it's now that I have turned for home that I discover that the wind has shifted around to the north and is growing in intensity, throwing sheets of rain directly into my face for the whole last twelve miles. The wind alone would be sufficient challenge. It's like being locked in that stupid tackling drill with Ron Sloan, only Coach never blows the whistle. And with the rain? My pants, my sweatshirt, everything I am wearing is soon soaked through.

As I ride, I remember that some fabrics are reputed to hold warmth well even when wet—the catalogs say so, at least—but this distinction is unimportant now. Whatever the truth about these mythical fabrics and their properties in some Platonic sense, here in the real world I am freezing my ass off. My nose is running freely, whenever I stop pedaling for an instant my legs begin to shiver so violently that my knees knock against the crossbar, and my neck and shoulder begin to stiffen noticeably, although this may be blamed on my fall, not on the weather.

But what are my choices? I ride doggedly for home, feeling as if I have been dipped in arctic waters, the cold seeping below my skin and deep into my very bones. When I finally arrive, I content myself with the discovery that Audrey hasn't eaten the upholstery and stagger toward the bathroom where I run a steaming bath and try to soak the shivers and the aches away.

It doesn't work; what's more, I've begun to cough. I'm full to the brim with phlegm. When I get out of the bath, I lurch into the kitchen, heat some soup, eat a little, take a handful of aspirin and cold medicine, make sure Audrey is still comatose, and go to bed.

I feel more than half dead, worse physically than I can remember ever feeling, but in a way, I suppose the day has been a success: I wanted to avoid conscious thought, and I've certainly succeeded at that. I haven't thought about Becky, I haven't thought about Richard, and I fall asleep so quickly I might as well have been chloroformed.

When I wake up Monday, I still feel rotten, am so stiff I can barely move my head and shoulders, feel like I'm running a temperature. I am moving like a man underwater. Audrey is only slowly coming out of her trance, but she may get hungry, so I set out some food for her, just in case. I don't much feel like eating anything, so I have a glass of orange juice and some more cold medicine and climb back into bed.

Some time later I am awakened by Jackson and Evelyn, who sound as though they're far away, or maybe they're underwater too.

"I told you there was something wrong," Evelyn says.

"Open the pod bay doors, Hal," I say without opening my eyes.

"I think he's got a fever." She touches my forehead, her hand cool and dry.

"What's going on?" I say, and I open my eyes and try to raise myself up with limited success, which is to say none at all. My grandparents loom over me like I'm seeing them through a fish-eye lens.

"You didn't come to dinner last night," Jackson says.

"I forgot," I say, and then I think about that. "What night? How long have I been asleep?"

"You need a doctor," Evelyn says. "Maybe we should take you to the emergency room."

"Uh-uh," I say. "No way. I'm not moving." That last, at least, is true.

"Papa, stay with him," Evelyn says. "I'll go out in the hall and make some calls."

Jackson sits on the edge of the bed. "You had us worried, son," he says. "We called last night when you didn't show up. We even called early this morning. Didn't you hear the phone?"

I try again to raise up without success. "What phone?" I can turn my head a little, can roll my shoulders a bit, but I can't seem to do much more without searing pain, and Jackson sees the expression on my face and stands up in a hurry.

"Evelyn," he calls, wobbling a bit as he turns sharply to call into the hallway. "Evelyn!"

"Coming," she says, and she appears in the doorway. "Frank Custer is coming by on his lunch hour." Frank Custer is a cardiothoracic surgeon at Hillcrest Baptist Hospital, and I venture to say that this is the first house call he has made in a long time. But Evelyn knows Frank's wife from church, and the rest is history. For all Jackson's wealth and supposed power, it is always Evelyn who gets things done.

"Look at this," Jackson says to her, pointing at the sweat that has broken out on my forehead from my slight exertions. His hand is shaking, and Evelyn takes it in hers to steady it.

"It's all right," she tells us both. "Frank will be here soon." She goes into the kitchen, makes some broth, and with Jackson's help, feeds me some of it. I can't really taste it—I don't know whether that is a good or bad sign—but I can at least feel the warmth as it goes down, and I like the feeling spreading through my chest.

That's one of the last things I know for certain for some time. Some of what follows I recall dimly; everything else is related to me after the fact.

When Dr. Custer arrives, he takes my temperature, which is actually just a little above normal—"Maybe a light case of the flu," he suggests—then decides from the limited range of movement of my neck and shoulders, and from my swollen trapezius and other multisyllabic muscles that I've endured some sort of localized trauma.

"Good call, Doc," I murmur.

After he's done all this, he shakes his head and asks me when I last had a decent night's sleep.

"What year is it?" I ask.

"He's delirious," Jackson mumbles.

That offends me. "Actually, I'm trying to be helpful."

"We ought to get him into the hospital, run some tests, let them make sure of the diagnosis," Dr. Custer tells them.

"No," I say, and the recurring suggestion of a hospital almost gives me enough strength to raise myself up. Almost; I make it up about three inches and then collapse with a groan. "I'm not going into the hospital. People die in hospitals." I look across at Jackson, and I must seem lucid enough to him at this moment. "Please. Tell him. I don't want to go to a hospital."

Jackson looks at Evelyn, who is probably all for calling an ambulance and having them hoist me from my bed this instant; this is what grandmothers are for. "The boy doesn't want to go," he says to her, and the silence hangs over the room as Dr. Custer waits for a decision.

At last she asks him, "Is there anything you can do for him here?"

"If this is spinal, it's serious," Custer says. "He needs care, not just medication."

"The boy doesn't want to go to the hospital," she says, and shrugs. These kids; what can you do with them? If I could move, I would kiss her.

"Evelyn—" Dr. Custer begins, but seeing her face, he realizes that the decision, at least for the present, will stand. "All right. Here's what I can do: I can prescribe a muscle relaxer, and a painkiller, in case he needs it." He turns momentarily to me. "And strict bed rest. But I'd feel better if—" He stops again. "If he doesn't improve, we'll really have no choice. But for now, I suppose this will be tolerable."

Well, that doesn't sound so bad, tolerable; actually, that describes my life under the best of conditions. And it's not as boring lying in bed as I fear: the medication makes bed rest not a choice but a necessity.

After they've fed me again and given me my first dose, the two of them lift me forward a bit to fluff my pillows.

"How do you feel?" Evelyn asks me as they lay me back down.

"I feel fine," I say. "Open the pod bay doors." And the effort of saying that is enough to send me under.

When I regain myself again, it is to discover that Evelyn and Jackson have hired a home-care nurse, one Nancy Fagen, an extremely large middle-aged woman—not fat, just large—with dry, competent hands and an utter and complete sense of loyalty. Although she and I have not even been formally introduced, I am her patient and what I ask for, I get.

"You had some visitors earlier," she tells me, after she first tells me who she is and what she's doing there. "But I ignored them."

"Why?" I croak.

"You told me not to let anybody in."

"When?"

"Yesterday." She lifts me forward, seemingly without effort, exchanges pillows behind me.

"What about my grandparents? Are you letting them in?"

"Well of course," she says. "They're paying me. But nobody else gets in unless you want them."

"Where's Audrey?"

She pulls the old pillowcase off the pillow in her hands, begins putting on a clean one. For a moment I think, irrelevantly, that these can't be my pillowcases, which they aren't, since I don't have any clean pillowcases. "If you mean the dog, your grandparents are taking care of her."

"Good." I mean to backtrack and ask Nancy about my visitors. Were they young, old, large men who might be defensive ends for the Dallas Cowboys, beautiful brown-eyed women? I can't seem to frame my questions, though, and the distance between her and me grows as though I'm sitting in a wheeled chair being propelled backward down a hall at a high rate of speed until I lose consciousness.

During the time I am on medication I spend most of my time sleeping, and I have dreams, vivid dreams with all the sensory images intact. It feels like I'm reliving my whole freaking life again.

Some of the dreams are only momentary and drawn from memory: a sniff of roast, Sunday dinner at Jackson and Evelyn's, the casual flip of my mother's bangs after she adjusted the rearview mirror, my dad singing Franki Valli's "Can't Take My Eyes Off of You"—badly—in the shower.

I get flashes of Christmas caroling up and down Austin Avenue with my parents and grandparents. The air is nippy, but my fingers are warm in my new mittens. Evelyn smells like roses when she holds me close to her heart. I put a tiny hand up to pat her reddened cheek.

I watch my mother teach Carter "Itsy Bitsy Spider." He can barely sit up, let alone climb up the waterspout. While he is making the rain wash the spider out, I pick up some of his less-gnawed animal crackers from the floor and quietly put them in my mouth, one after the other. The kid doesn't even have teeth. Animal crackers are wasted on him.

My dad has bought a new Doobie Brothers 8-track, "Toulouse Street," at the mall and puts it in the car stereo. We roll down all the windows as we drive home and sing "Rockin' Down the Highway." My mom tells me not to tell my grandmother that I know this song. When we pull up at the stoplight on Valley Mills and Franklin, people stare at us. My parents laugh and take each other's hands and we keep on singing, even Carter, who thinks the lyrics are "walking down a highway."

They aren't snobs at all, really. What kind of snobs listen to the Doobies on 8-track? I don't know why I ever said that to them. I want to tell them I'm sorry, I was just a shitty selfish teenager, but no sooner do I get my bearings in one scene than I'm gone.

Some of the dreams are full-blown. One recurring dream takes place while I'm out on my bike. It's a warm, sunny day, no appreciable wind, perfect for riding. But I have a growing sense of discomfort, as though something is wrong, even though I can't figure out exactly what it is.

Then it hits me: there's nothing out here. No birds; no cows; no squirrels rustling the grass beneath the trees. No sign of life. That's spooky.

And then I hear the noise. It's the sound of a vehicle coming, a big one. I can hear the engine race, the sound of tires squealing as it takes a turn a long way off but drawing closer, closer.

I don't know why, but I realize that this is the sound of somebody who is after me. I've seen something, or I know something, and although I don't know what that could possibly be, there's no question that somebody is coming.

As I top a hill near the Out Bridge, I look over my shoulder and see a big black car, a Lincoln or maybe a Caddy. It's been a long time, but I know this car, its glass tinted and chrome gleaming, its engine growling like a beast of prey. It is two hills back and gaining ground. I bend over the handlebars, begin to pump frantically, the sound of the air racing past my ears not loud enough to drown out the car's approach.

The barrier is three hundred yards away and the car is gaining; two hundred yards away and I can hear the hum of its tires on the pavement; one hundred yards, and I can almost feel the glare reflecting off the opaque windshield.

And then, just when I'm sure it's going to run me down, squash me flat as a cartoon character, the driver throws the car into a screeching skid to avoid hitting the barrier.

I'm not under any such restrictions. I slow down enough to step off the pedals and on top of the iron barrier; then I use the momentum of the bike to swing it up and over. I hop back atop the saddle like a rodeo trick rider, rattle swiftly across the bridge, and repeat the maneuver on the far side.

He can't follow me now. Nobody could. I relax, turn to taunt my pursuers on the far side of the rickety span, and discover that the gap-toothed man has jumped out of the car. The sun glints blinding off his revolver as he raises it to open fire. I am a mistake that must be corrected, erased, expunged.

I hear bullets whistling to either side of me, cutting the dirt directly in front of me, slapping into the trees to my left. My God, there are a lot of bullets in that thing.

I stand on the pedals as I race away, begin pumping, swerve the bike left and then right, raise and lower myself to present a more difficult target, and it seems to work. The bullets snap all around me, but soon I have passed a curve, the shooting fades behind me, and I can slow down and finish my ride.

I have escaped again.

Then, a few miles later, I feel the hackles rise on the back of my neck as though I'm being watched. I turn around. The car is back behind me. How he got there is a mystery. Either he slid behind me from some side road I haven't noticed, or he's been airlifted there by chopper; narrative logic is not this dream's strong suit, and in any case, it doesn't matter. He is there behind me, the chrome grille smiling, the dark expanse of windshield sparkling in the sun as the car pulls closer and closer and closer.

This is bullshit, one part of me protests. If I'm going to be imprisoned in my unconscious for a while, why not a harem of naked women, their lush bodies glistening with oil as they fan me with palm fronds and feed me grapes and pomegranates? Where are the ninth-inning World Series homers off Nolan Ryan, the crack of the bat and the roaring crowd and the ball climbing into the upper deck as though shot from a cannon? Why can't I win the Masters?

And where is my happy life with Susie Bramlett?

I wake again to cold night, to Jackson and Evelyn dressed in their robes and snoozing in their recliners, lugged to my house by God knows who.

"Hey," I murmur groggily. "Hey. Old folks."

Evelyn, who still has her hearing, wakes and brings herself to an upright position with a mechanical clunk. "Hello, Brad," she says, shaking Jackson awake with one hand. "How do you feel?"

Like I've been shat from the digestive system of a giant beast, I think, but for Evelyn, the correct answer is "Awful. How's Audrey?"

"A lot better than you are," she says.

"Wha's goin' on?" Jackson yawns as he also rejoins the living. One white skinny leg protrudes briefly from his pajama leg as he climbs out of the chair and pads across to the bed in his slippers. "How do you feel, son?"

"I just asked him, Papa," Evelyn says. "He says he feels awful."

"Your temperature's fine," Jackson says, checking me with one of those newfangled ear-canal thermometers.

"How long have I been out?" I think I've become one with the bed.

"A couple days," Evelyn says. "You've been babbling. We fed you. Once we helped you into the bathroom."

"What about the other times?"

"Nancy is very good with bedridden patients," Evelyn says primly.

"Am I getting better? I don't feel better." And that much is true: I'm still stiff, and there is still dull pain back between my shoulder blades.

"You're getting plenty of rest," Jackson says. "Dr. Custer says that's what you need for your back."

"Who are all those strange women on your answering machine?" Evelyn asks, switching conversational channels. "I recognized Elaine, and I think one of them was Cindy—she asked if you'd changed your mind yet or something like that—but the others are a complete mystery. One of them wanted you to do a promo, whatever that is. The others wanted you to do things I'm not sure I can repeat."

"Who said you could listen to my messages?"

"The incoming-message tape was full, son," Jackson says. "You think I want to listen to your women? I've got troubles enough with this one. We've gotta be able to leave messages for each other, or for Nancy. Anyway, I wrote everything down for you. Do you want me to read them to you?"

"Later," I say, yawning, improbable as that seems, feels. "Later." I smile at them, my seventy-something grandparents, watching over me from their recliners, and drift back to sleep.

13

I finally bid Nancy farewell the week before Christmas. It's not that I've needed her round the clock this whole time, but I have needed her a lot, she has successfully screened me from the world, and to be honest, I've gotten kind of attached to her. The progress of my pneumonia encourages that attachment: even after weeks of solid bed rest, I am still so weak I can't get around by myself, and then the fourth week I need her to help me get back into my old routines: cooking, feeding the dog, pretending to write.

Eddie Todd calls on December 17; he has heard from Elaine—who has heard from Evelyn—that I have been deathly ill, and if I know Elaine, she probably exaggerated even my difficulties. This means Eddie probably thinks I am resting in an urn on somebody's mantel.

"Thank God, thank God," he says when he hears my voice. "Elaine Rosenbaum told me that you were on death's doorstep."

"I didn't get all the way to death's doorstep," I say. "But I was probably in death's driveway."

"Thank God," he says again. "Elaine tells me that you were on the point of a breakthrough in the book when this happened. That it may set you back a spell."

Bless you, Elaine. "Right," I say, regret staining my voice. "A breakthrough. I had a flash of inspiration when I was riding home in the storm, and I hoped against hope that I had written it down, but I checked my notebooks when I was strong enough and there was nothing there."

"Are you sure? You've looked everywhere?"

"Everywhere," I say. "There's nothing. I'm positive."

There's a moment's silence, and I can almost see his lips scrunching. "Well, this is bad. My bosses, you've got to understand, Brad, they're businessmen. They're starting to say to me, maybe this guy isn't going to write this book. I tell them it'd be a damn shame if we didn't give you every chance to. Was I right to do that?"

I have never met Eddie Todd, and it is typical of writers whose initial editors move on that they are abandoned, become publishers' orphans in whose work no one has any investment. That's why I cannot imagine why Eddie would waste his time so championing me.

He is standing up on my behalf, and I am letting him down.

Well, I think, join the club; stand in line. I didn't ask you idiots to champion me. "I appreciate what you told them, Eddie," I say. "I hope to recapture that inspiration. But I can tell you that now is not the time."

"I can understand that," he says. "Take it easy, take it nice and slow. But remember, I can't hold these guys off forever. They're not book people. They don't care how good a writer you are. They just want numbers, and they'd just as soon sell shitty books as good ones, if you know what I mean."

I know what he means. "Thanks, Eddie," I say, and we hang up, me in Texas, Eddie in Manhattan.

Manhattan. It's strange to realize that there is a world going on outside my walls. I have hardly set foot outdoors in a month's time, have seen no human beings other than Nancy the Nurse, Jackson and Evelyn, and occasionally, my reluctant doctor. Audrey herself has only ventured out for nature's call; she senses that something has been wrong about me, and once I'm back among the walking and talking, she doesn't want to leave my side. When I eat breakfast, she plants herself at my feet, under the table; when I take a bath, she comes in and lies beside the tub.

But there is a world outside which has advanced inexorably toward holiday gift-giving as I lay oblivious to crowded malls and tacky Christmas lights.

I am a lucky man though, if for no other reason than that

Evelyn Cannon is my grandmother and personal shopper. "I didn't know if you'd be up and around in time," she tells me on the 18th, when she shows up at my place with a full shopping bag, "so I picked up something for everyone on your list. Even me. I didn't know any of the women on the answering machine, but I thought about the messages and I listened to their voices. I got Chanel for Becky. I got crystal for the mystery woman who didn't leave her name. She sounded sort of melancholy, and I thought maybe having something beautiful to look at would make her happier."

"It might," I say.

"And the last one, that Sandra woman, she was brisk and no-nonsense. Short messages. She's a busy woman. I got her a nice leather appointment book."

"Not bad," I tell her. "What did you get yourself from me?"

"Oh, I can't tell you," she says, hustling me out of my own bedroom so she can wrap presents. "I don't want to spoil the surprise."

She calls through the door. "So which of these women will I get to meet on New Year's Eve?"

"You know, Evelyn," I call back, "you may have noticed that I've been kind of busy being in a coma."

"You have to bring someone to my party."

"Jesus Christ in a jumped-up sidecar."

"What?" she calls.

"I'll work on it," I say.

"See that you do," she says. "I've already bought your tickets."

And of course, she has. I consider Evelyn a kind woman—which is why she did my Christmas shopping—but she is also hard as nails and has no intention of letting me weasel out of this commitment—which is why she did my Christmas shopping. I had planned on handling the challenge of Christmas the same way I normally handle problems, by ignoring them until they go away. Now, thanks to Evelyn, I have gifts to hand out—or at least, one gift, Becky's, since I don't imagine Colby will be too keen on Madelyn accepting an expensive gift from me, and Sandra and I have not spoken for what has stretched now into months.

It is that, strangely enough, which compels me ask Sandra to Evelyn's ball. A Christmas gift and a New Year's Eve date with Becky will transmit signals of the type directly antithetical to the ones I need to send her; while Madelyn may be at the party—everyone in Waco with even the slightest pretension toward a position in society above that of dogcatcher will be there—I think our arriving together could also send unfortunate signals. So it is Sandra Fuentes, Our Diminutive Lady of the Primates, on whom I call, Sandra whom I all but beg to accompany me to the gala to avert Evelyn's wrath.

Our telephone conversation does not begin promisingly. "Not much for answering our phone messages, are we?" she says once I've managed to get past the biology department's suspicious secretary.

"I have a note from my doctor," I say.

Chilly silence. I can almost hear her blinking behind her glasses.

"Honestly, Sandra. I've been really sick."

"And then your dog ate my number."

"No—" But I bite back my first response; it is so rare to have a valid excuse for something I have done—or more likely, didn't do—that I don't want to waste this one. "Really, Sandra. It's not that I didn't want to call. I've had pneumonia. I was bedridden, icy hand of death clutching at my heart, that kind of thing."

She makes some sort of skeptical *tsk* noise, and sits for a moment in reflection. I'm not totally suprised by this skepticism—when I stopped by Lolita's for some Mexican Cokes, Hector Portillo was huffy and hurt, was willing to believe my long absence was a personal insult, that I'd found a new and better Mexican Coke supplier, almost anything except the truth. At last she says, "Why would you make all this up?"

"Exactly," I say. "I would make up a better story. This time I'm just relating the unvarnished truth."

"I'm sorry you've been sick," she says. "I wish I'd known. Maybe I could have done something."

"Hold that mood of guilt and obligation," I say. "Go with me to a dance New Year's Eve."

"I don't dance," she says. "I'm not the least bit musical."

"My grandmother organized the charity ball this year. She'd like for me to go. I'd like to take you."

"I don't think so."

"Why not?" I ask, and my exasperation comes through, I think, because Sandra begins explaining to me in her unctuous professor voice: "Brad, I don't feel comfortable at social functions under the best of circumstances. How do you suppose it would make me feel to be the only brown person at a redneck social function?"

"They're not rednecks," I say. "Most of them aren't, anyway. And I'll bet you won't be the only person of color—"

"How enlightened of you," she murmurs dryly.

"It'll be fun," I say, although like her, I have my doubts. "Please."

"I'm sure I have nothing to wear—"

But I sense her weakness. "I'll help you pick out something," I say. "Come on. Be a sport. Think of the opportunity to observe man as a social animal."

"I don't like to think of man as a social animal. Really, Brad, I don't feel comfortable at these things."

"Me neither," I say. "I'll be right beside you, I promise. I'll take good care of you."

The Sandra silence, and it seems to last forever. Then she sighs and I know my grandmother will be placated. "All right. I'm not going because I want to. Just so you understand that. I'm going because you asked me to."

"Thanks," I say. My grandmother won't care why she's going, and right now I'm not sure that I do either. "Do you want to go shop for dresses?"

"I'll find something," she says dryly. "I'm not completely incompetent in social situations."

All of which is to explain how I end up going over to pick up Sandra at seven o'clock on New Year's Eve. We have agreed we will take her car, since she says she is unused to heels and doesn't want to climb out of a sports car. I pull up in front of the house, walk up beneath the perpetual porch light dressed in my tux, and ring the doorbell.

The door opens slowly, almost shyly, and then she stands before me, sans glasses and elegantly attired in an Empire-waisted yellow satin dress that seems to make her dark skin glow.

"Wow," I say, and nod admiringly, and I almost believe she blushes. "No glasses?"

"I got fitted for contacts," she says, stepping out and locking the door behind her. "It feels like someone wedged petri dishes under my eyelids." She wobbles uneasily on her heels. "Damn these shoes," she says, and takes my arm for support.

I shrug, look down at her feet, and intone: "Shoes, I damn thee." It earns me a wan smile as we set off for her vehicle, a huge green Ford Bronco. I can't see how this is going to be any easier to climb in and out of than the Healey, but I also see that this is not a time to bring up such matters. I boost her up on the passenger side, climb in, ease the seat way back, and turn the key.

The voice of some woman singing a Tejano ballad, sad and heartful, fills the cab, and Sandra quickly reaches over to the stereo, ejects the tape, and tosses it beneath her seat like something shameful.

"What's that?" I ask. It sounded like Selena, and I'd like to know why Sandra considers a Tejano singer a guilty pleasure.

"Nothing," she says, and fiddles with the radio until we are bringing in classic rock from Dallas, "Knights in White Satin." We listen to the Moody Blues in silence as I drive down I-35, take the University-Parks exit, drive along the Brazos River and past the Waco Suspension Bridge, and turn into the parking lot across the street from the Waco Convention Center.

I go around to help her out, and she stands for a moment looking at other cars arriving, at Waco society pouring forth to mingle. Her expression is pensive, her eyes look naked and defenseless without her glasses, and she sneaks her hand back onto my arm.

I pat it reassuringly. "It'll be fine," I say. "I bet you'll know some people here."

She totters across the street; I expect at every moment that she will topple from her heels and go facedown onto the pavement. "I doubt it. All the people I know are home tonight with kids or sitting in front of their computers." She looks wistful about this last.

We present our tickets at the door, drop our coats in the cloakroom, then push through the crowded lobby and on up the stairs to the ballroom. At one end of the room an orchestra is setting up, while at the other, a jazz trio—piano, string bass, drums—is already playing. A few intrepid souls are dancing—the rhythm section is strong and the beat is insistent, although every now and then they switch time signatures, which momentarily throws the dancers for a loop, and they glare up at the drummer as though he has had a seizure.

"How about a drink?" I ask, steering Sandra toward the bar.

"Club soda will be fine," she says. I get a glass of champagne for myself and we head off toward a table to talk of great apes while the cream of Waco society—Cotton Princesses and Symphony Belles and string-tied old gentlemen and the occasional hoop-skirted matron—sweeps past. I have been frantically cribbing Dian Fossey, and Sandra is more than willing to discuss her work, which she both admires as ground-breaking and deplores as being flawed by Fossey's emotional involvement with her subjects.

"She buried Digit when he was killed. And some of the other gorillas. Outside her hut, if you can believe that. Refers to them as 'friends.' "

I sip. A woman passes wearing a hat primarily composed of ostrich feathers. "People can get attached to animals."

"Oh, that's not the point." She waves off my observation as an irrelevancy. "I love animals, and I think my own subjects are remarkably intelligent. I prefer them to most people. But a researcher has to remain aloof, apart from the thing studied. The closer you get to it, the greater the chance that your observation will in some way shape the outcome."

"The Heisenberg uncertainty principle."

She raises her hand in shock—why are people surprised when I know things like this?—and topples her club soda. She looks frantically left and right, the crimson rising in her cheeks again, but we are not observed as we wipe it up. I have a perverse curiosity what you put on a club soda stain; maybe more club soda?

"I don't suppose it would hurt to have a little champagne,"

she calls after me as I depart for the bar, so I bring back two champagnes and we continue talking about gorillas as the music continues, as the crowds ebb and flow around us. Occasionally someone jostles up against the back of my chair, but mostly we are able to sit undisturbed.

Sandra is talking about how gorilla social structure differs from chimpanzees, but part of my mind—and apparently, part of my attention—is awake to the possibility that Madelyn might suddenly appear, and Sandra, ever observant, spots my lack of focus and stops in midsentence. “Who are you looking for?”

Sneak that I am, I’m ready with a lie. “My grandparents. They asked me to bring you by to say hello.”

“Oh please,” she says. “I don’t want to meet anyone.”

“They’re very nice. Harmless, really.”

“I’m sure they are,” she says. “All right. Get me another glass of champagne and I’ll think about it.”

So I do, and we talk while she drinks, and at last I haul her slowly across the crowded ballroom in search of Evelyn. The jazz trio is playing that Charlie Brown theme Schroeder always plays, “Linus and Lucy” I think it’s called, the one with the rolling left hand on the piano while the right chords the melody, and it makes me want to break into dance like Snoopy. I’m a good dancer, actually, but I see that Sandra demonstrates no such rhythmic impulses, so I restrain myself and try to walk slowly so as not to pull her off of her heels.

Too late I see Dr. Martin Fuller, venerable King of the English Department, quavering into my path, he and his considerably younger trophy wife waving at us like tourists arriving in port. “Hello, my boy,” he says, and reintroduces me to his wife, as he does every time we meet; we have been introduced somewhere between fifty and a hundred times, by my estimate, and she and I share the usual smile and nod before I introduce them both to Sandra.

He shakes her hand. “Fuentes,” he says. “Fuentes. Mexican name.”

“My parents were born in Mexico,” she says. “It’s an American name now.”

“Sandra teaches biology at Baylor,” I babble into the conversational pause, and I notice with some consternation that she immediately rises in their estimation when the Fullers discover she is a peer instead of my cleaning woman.

"You're in the biology department, then. How wonderful. I always loved biology, slugs and phytoplankton and such. Byron has a poem about—"

"Sandra does research on chimpanzees," I say. Phytoplankton?

"They are so adorable," Mrs. Fuller says.

"Yes," Sandra says, tight-lipped. "They are."

"We must be going," I tell them. "My grandparents are waiting."

"Ah," Dr. Fuller says. "Give them my best. Tell them we really must get together some time and talk about their past generosity—"

"Of course," I say, and we disengage ourselves from that conversation and hurry on our way.

"He's exactly what you led me to believe," Sandra remarks when we're out of earshot. "He must be three hundred years old."

"He's a semiliving legend," I agree.

My grandparents are seated at a table near the orchestra and have just bade good-bye to Marjorie Herring, wife to a third-generation doctor. She is wearing an evening dress about three sizes too small for her considerable bulk and looks like nothing so much as a sequined sausage; I bite my tongue hard as I accept her greeting to keep my expression serious.

"Hello, Brad," Evelyn calls, and we approach. I make the introductions, everyone shakes hands, my granddad informs Sandra that he passed through Panama during World War Two and saw his share of monkeys, and when they are involved in what looks like a conversation, I ask Evelyn if she'd like to dance.

"Charmed," she says. I have contrived ways to dance with her every year since Jackson had his heart attack. I think he's milked that little cardiac arrest for all it's worth—he never liked to dance in the first place—but it's also true that he has a lot of trouble with his joints these days, so maybe it's best if he assigns me this one family duty.

"Excuse me for a few minutes," I tell Sandra. "Tradition must be observed."

Her eyes widen, she looks as though she is about to say something, then she bites her lip, nods, and turns back to Jackson, who is going on about his war experiences.

The song is "What'll I Do?" a nice waltz, and I take Evelyn's hand and put my other hand on her waist. She seems lighter, frailer every year; if it's true that old folks lose calcium from their bones, perhaps this is an explanation, although perhaps it's that as we age, bits of ourselves evaporate away, escape us like mist rising off a pond.

"Your friend Hugh Kromer was asking after you earlier," Evelyn says as we enter the flow of dancers, about twenty couples, and I sweep her across the floor.

"Who's he with?"

She catches my smile and returns it. "Caroline Curry, the sly dog."

"How old is she? Hugh's not robbing the cradle, I hope."

"Oh, hardly. She was a freshman the year I graduated. Almost old enough to be your grandmother."

"Maybe I'll catch up to them later," I tell her, and that would be pleasant. None of the rest of my group are likely to be here, since Ron wouldn't be caught dead in formal wear even if he could afford it, and Wally has so many kids he has his own charity to collect.

"She's the appointment book," she says, and catching my blank expression, continues, "Sandra. She's the business-like one. From your answering machine."

"Oh, so you caught that. Yes, she's very matter-of-fact."

"She's attractive, in an odd sort of way."

"She looks good in that dress, although I think she's more comfortable in a lab coat."

"Who wouldn't be? These shoes are pinching my toes."

"It's nothing serious," I say, as the band strikes a coda just before finishing. She looks at me quizzically and I explain, "Between us. She's interesting, that's all. And very intelligent."

"Well," Evelyn says. "I don't want to pry." Which is her way of saying that she does, that she'd be pleased to hear any little piece of information I'd like to pass on to her, but that she just doesn't feel comfortable admitting it. We finish the song and I step back to give her a slight bow, which always makes her laugh with delight. As we walk back toward Jackson and Sandra, we are intercepted—blindsided, if you prefer—by Colby and Madelyn Clark, and surprisingly, it's Colby who steps forward and calls my name.

"Brad, old man," he says, and he gives me that handshake of his, slightly firm, two pumps, "I'd be indebted to you if you'd grant Madelyn a turn on the dance floor. She has been after me to dance all evening—which I can't do to save my soul, you know—and then when we recognized you out there, I knew you were my salvation."

Uh-huh. When he breaks for air I introduce them both to Evelyn, and then I turn to Madelyn.

"Would you do me the honor, Mrs. Clark?"

She nods solemnly.

"I'm going to visit the bar and the loo, not in that order," Colby says. "Have fun. Pleasure meeting you," he says to Evelyn, and then he turns and enters the throng.

I wave at Sandra and make a motion toward the dance floor. Her face is a mask, but Jackson still seems to be in mid-story, so I lead Madelyn out. The floor is more crowded now, and the song is "Night and Day."

Her hand on my shoulder seems uncommonly warm, unusually heavy; it seems determined to make its presence felt, although I know that Madelyn is doing nothing more than resting it there. This is the first time we've been in each other's arms in over a month, and both of us seem aware of the incongruity of coming together now in the midst of this crowd of people.

"How's Audrey?" Madelyn says, after a stretch.

"Doing very well," I say. "She'd love to see you, I'm sure."

"You're sure?"

"I am."

"And you're feeling better? I was awfully concerned about you."

"Be hard to feel any worse than I felt and still get up again," I say. "How'd you hear about it, anyway?"

"Oh, friend of a friend of a friend of Colby's. Everybody at Baylor hears everything about everybody. It's like any small community."

"I thought maybe Dr. Fuller had told an English faculty meeting to hit their knees and pray, because if I died, their chance for that endowed chair would be going to the grave."

"Nothing so dramatic," she says. She motions toward Sandra with the barest motion of her head. "I'm surprised. I expected someone a little more decorative."

"A blonde with killer curves and a Pepsodent smile, if they still make those."

"Right," she says. "I'm impressed. With you, that is, for avoiding the easy call. Good choice."

I hum along with the band for a bit, with the trumpet playing melody, then break softly, unconsciously into the words of "Night and Day."

"Do you now?"

"What?" Her question jars me; for a moment I have been caught up in the music, the two of us floating almost effortlessly to the beat.

"Think of me?"

"Sure," I admit. "Too often, probably."

"Brad?" she says into my shoulder.

"Uhm-hmm."

"What do you think will happen to us in the New Year?"

I shake my head. "I couldn't possibly say. I couldn't have predicted anything that happened to me this year."

"Do you ever—" She stops, reloads, looks up at me. "Do you ever wonder what it might be like—" She purses her lips; this is harder than she thought. "You know. If—"

I try to help her out. "If we had another life? Or if we were different people? Or if we had met ten years ago in a bus station somewhere?"

"I've never been in a bus station in my life." But her sad smile tells me I have hit the mark.

"Madelyn. Maddy. I can't see the point of thinking so hard about things that can't be changed. It's speculation. Maybe. Maybe not. Maybe we would have fallen in love. Maybe we would have walked right past each other. Maybe we met when we did because we needed to know each other now, not ten years ago or ten years from now."

The band finishes, but segues so smoothly into a new song that I think we can claim one more dance as a continuation of the first. Madelyn nods and smiles her assent, and Sandra at least seems to be hanging in there. Jackson is introducing her to some neighbors from across Austin Avenue, the blue-haired Reynolds. They own a string of dry cleaners and a bunch of small yapping dogs, and one of the few things I can imagine them having in common with Sandra is that they're all standing there excreting carbon dioxide.

"Maybe you're right," she says, after we adjust our tempo to the new piece, which begins to sound suspiciously like a big band arrangement of "Deacon Blues."

"Maybe I'm thinking too much about what-ifs."

"If you're thinking about me as part of your what-ifs," I tell her, "then I know you are. I know you're unhappy—and believe me, that's something I know a little about—but I'm no solution to that. I'm no better than Colby or any other man in this room, and for you to think of me—or me to think of you—as the cure-all for a rotten life, that's just not going to work."

"I know," she says, although she doesn't sound completely convinced.

It *is* "Deacon Blues," although we seem to be the only people young enough to recognize the melody the baritone sax is picking up. The orchestra is a pretty good group, mostly students and faculty from the Baylor School of Music, plus some pickups from the Waco Symphony, and they're having a good time with this.

I experiment with a twirl—"Hold on" is all I tell her before I do it—out and back.

"That was fun," she tells me. "Where'd you learn to dance, anyway? I thought real men hated to dance. Colby wouldn't dance if he were standing on red-hot coals."

"My grandmother had an old woman come out and instruct me in ballroom dancing prior to my first formal season."

"And you still remember it."

"I remember lots of things." But this song too is winding down and I'm surprisingly tired, and what's more, I have to turn her back over to the waiting Colby.

"I enjoyed it," I say. "Thanks."

"Thank you," she says. "I've danced. Now I can call it a successful evening." Colby leads her away, and I return to the table where Jackson and Sandra are still talking.

My grandfather turns to me as I approach; Sandra Fuentes, surprisingly, does not. "Jackson, Sandra here was telling me that Fuller cornered you on the way over. That formaldehyded old relic. I've put a roof over that man's head and he's still after me to pay the utilities."

"Well, something like that." I turn to Sandra and roll my eyes a little in Jackson's direction. "Sandra, would you like to dance?"

"No," she says.

"Can I get you something to drink?"

"I think I'm ready to call it a night," she says, and she checks her watch to punctuate it.

Jackson leaps in. "But it's only an hour until midnight. We'll have a big countdown, lots of lights—"

"Thanks, Mr. Cannon," she tells him, her curt tone counter to her pleasant words. "I've had enough socializing for one night."

My grandparents look at me; I shrug. "I'll see you tomorrow," I tell them. "We're still on for the bowl games, right?"

"Right," Jackson says, and Evelyn chimes in, "You come on over whenever you're ready."

Sandra and I make our arduous way toward the exit of the ballroom—now that it's approaching twelve o'clock the crowd is beginning to build—and down the stairs. Nowhere in our progress from table to stairs to cloakroom to parking lot does a word pass between us. I look quizzically at her a few times, as if to invite comment, but she doesn't respond, and her expression is as inscrutable as usual.

We have been driving for a good ten minutes before she turns to me. "I didn't realize it was customary to park your date with your doddering relatives."

"I didn't think you'd mind for a few minutes."

"It was more than a few minutes."

I miss the rush of air in my convertible, the roar of my exhaust. Silence in the Bronco is filled by no such diversions; it floats between us, dark and tangible.

I look across at her, arms folded, legs primly and firmly together at the knees. "I'm sorry. I thought you and Jackson were having a conversation."

"*He* was having a conversation. Brad, I didn't put on this getup to listen to your grandfather try to remember his war experiences."

I can feel my lips go tightly into a straight line, the semblance of a smile before I growl, and rein myself back, try once more. "I thought he might have something interesting to tell you."

We are entering Sandra's driveway now, and I'm glad to be here because it means an end to the evening. I'm not sure exactly what I've done wrong, but Sandra has a firm grasp on it. Before I can even think about going around to open her door, she is out and wobbling toward the house, and that's what finally sets me off. This hasn't been such a walk in the park for me either; why does she get to have the tantrum?

She reaches the front door, fumbles in her purse, and of course doesn't have the keys; I do. I walk up, proffer them, and she snatches them out of my hand.

"You knew how I felt about going tonight," she says without looking up at me, working the key frantically in the lock. "How could you leave me there—to dance with that woman? How could you make me an even bigger laughingstock?"

A vacuum forms in my chest, sucking all my air into it, and robbing me of the chance to respond nonchalantly "What woman?" before it's too late.

"I knew it," she says when I don't answer, don't spout disavowals. She throws open her door and it bangs against the inner wall. Then she kicks off her shoes one at a time, and they soar, shiny yellow projectiles, into the hallway.

"What are you talking about?" I finally manage. It is too little, too late.

She whirls, and in the poor lighting there seems to be a glint in her eyes; in another person I would suspect tears, but surely that's a misreading.

Surely.

"Everyone in town knows," she says, looking at me like the pathetic creature I am. "Everybody's heard about it except the husband, who must be an idiot. An idiot like me. I didn't want to believe it. But I watched you together. Watched you dance. Then I knew."

I long to launch denials, but I find that I cannot; Sandra is a scientist, she's accustomed to weighing data, making judgments, pursuing truth. She knows when she finds it. "How I feel about her has nothing to do with how I feel about you."

The tears in her eyes now are large and luminous. "I thought we shared something, Brad. I thought we could help each other."

I shake my head and feel myself visibly sag, as though some vital life force has seeped from my body.

"Do you think you're the only person who's ever suffered? Who's ever had to deal with a terrible past?" As she becomes more angry, her words become more sibilant, more Spanish. A Sandra I have never known is taking shape in front of me, but I remain silent, head down, gazing at her tiny stockinged feet on the concrete.

She raises my head, none too gently, by putting her finger under my chin. I am forced to look into her eyes, and I do not like what I see reflected there.

"I can't help you or anybody," I say when I can stand it no longer, and I drop my face, turn my head. "I don't have anything to give. I'm sorry."

"Sorry," she says, and she spits it out as though she can scarcely bear to have the word in her mouth. "You're a coward, Brad."

"I'm sorry," I say again, but she has raised her hand in dismissal before I even finish.

"A coward," she repeats, and she turns and walks quickly, shoulders slumping, head down, into the house. The door closes firmly between us and every lock locks. I can hear her sobbing, hear her slump to the floor, and although I know she can't hear me, I speak.

"I know," I tell the door. The wind has picked up and I can hear it in the tops of the trees. She's right. I am a coward.

I get out of there, head for home with the throaty roar of my exhaust and a thousand demons pursuing me, and I ring in the New Year reclined ragdoll on my couch, in the presence of Audrey, Dave Letterman, and a growing flotsam of empty Corona bottles.

"To auld acquaintance," I mutter when California hits midnight, and I offer the West Coast a first toast for their brand-new 1994. "Should it ever be forgotten, let's hope it never comes to mind."

And I raise another bottle to that sentiment, feel the cold yellow liquid course down my throat and filter up into my brain, even though I know better than most that forgetfulness is a complete and utter impossibility.

14

As the new year rises from the ashes of the disastrous old, I have discovered a gaping chasm in my path, a virtual Grand Canyon stretching to the horizon of my worldview: I've always believed that whatever else went wrong in this world, whoever else betrayed me, however consistently I might betray myself, one thing I could depend on was my body, lean and muscular and self-sufficient, and now that belief has been proven as unreliable as everything else I thought I knew. It's not that my body has never disappointed me before—it sweats more than I'd like and doesn't hold alcohol well at all. It's not that I'm one of those people who claims never to have been sick a day in his life—I've had all the standard childhood diseases, plus a broken leg and cracked ribs—but I've always relied on my body, trusted it to handle any challenge I encountered without complaint or assistance. The exposure of the illusion of my physical invulnerability as just that, an illusion, has had a profound effect on me. I find that now I'm approaching life with a degree of hesitancy and trepidation that seems excessive even for me.

I begin cycling again only in stages, with very short rides, careful not to overdo it, and even then I am amazed by how my strength and endurance have fled. I depart on the first warm day in January intending to do ten miles and manage only two, and the last of that, dismounted, pushing, puffing back into my driveway; I spend the week that follows huddled near the fire as cold rain patters against the window, as Audrey snoozes in narcotic slumber. In earlier days I might have put on a poncho and ventured out into the wet, but now I sit motionless, remembering the awful cold of that last rain, feeling it start at my feet and seep up my legs like poison creeping through the veins toward the heart.

Thus the second part of my New Year's crisis, the far wall, if you will, of my Great Rift: I have built myself an identity, such as it is, with which I cannot now identify.

If I am not a cyclist, what am I?

The answers to that question—particularly given New Year's Eve—do not seem promising and so I try to avoid asking myself again. I spend the January days drowsing on the couch in front of the fire, nights drinking beer in front of the television, and although I rarely manage to get out on the bike—rarely manage to move from the sofa, in fact—I still feel so tired each morning that all I want to do is roll over and go back to sleep.

Which I often do, if not always. The scattered elements of my schedule, the occasional dinners with Jackson and Evelyn, the Tuesday/Thursday lunches with my gang, assume a new importance in my new life. I seize upon them as a man sinking in quicksand—even if the sensation of sinking is not altogether unpleasant—might occasionally seize upon a tree limb or root to prolong his descent.

When I visit, my grandparents don't seem to notice anything different about me, which makes me think I must have been worse off than I'd imagined; I've abandoned all pretense that I'm writing, cycling, or, for that matter, living, and they don't say a word. I don't have the energy left to lie, and if anybody asked, I would tell them the truth, the whole truth, nothing but.

But nobody asks. Evelyn says, "You're looking so much better," Billie tries to fatten me up—I've lost a good twenty pounds—and Jackson begins to pester me again about playing golf with him.

"I don't feel up to it," I tell him, and that is God's truth. I don't feel up to anything.

Which may be why my lunch meetings begin to loom so large in my life: I don't have to do anything. I can simply sit back, nod, listen, chew my food, and know that my friends will understand if I don't have anything to say.

They have all gotten past the difficult part—acknowledging

that something pretty bad took place in my life—although not without some grunts and stammering on their part, and it is Ron who has the most difficulty.

"I thought it was happening again," he tells me privately one day before the others arrive. "Like Richard all over again. I thought maybe I was a jinx or something."

I shake my head. "Don't attach so much importance to yourself," I tell him. "While I was lying there trying to kick the bucket you never once crossed my mind."

That seems to makes him feel better. Now the four of us can sit at Martha's, leaning against the wobbly table, and I can pick at my meat loaf while they talk about whatever they like.

At one of our meetings early in the month, they—we, I suppose—make a decision of some import, even if at first it seems mostly symbolic. Ron proposes, after our lunch orders have been taken, that we consider expanding our roster, calling up a new player.

"I sort of mentioned you guys to Terry Stephens," he says, and I nod briefly. Terry is a sportscaster on local news, used to be an All-American safety at Baylor. I met him once, briefly, some years back when they were trying him out on the early morning news and I went on to plug the book. He was intelligent, asked good questions, and did his best to put me at ease, which I rarely am early in the morning. We could do a lot worse.

"He's that black fella on the news," Hugh says, stroking his chin, and for a second we all hold our breath. Hugh comes from a generation—Jackson's generation—when good Southern men could casually and without conscious thought be bigots of the worst kind. But what he follows this with is "He's damn good on football. What does he know about baseball?"

"He wants to learn," Ron says, and we look at each other and nod in agreement. So let it be written; so let it be done.

We are not trying to replace Richard, and that's not really Ron's motive in proposing Terry. It's just that we seem oddly incomplete, a pie with a piece missing, and although I feel some anxiety about auditioning a new member, I also recognize our need.

My need.

There is an empty space that needs to be filled.

For the time being, though, I am prevented from all my usual methods of filling—or ignoring—that space. I'm afraid to venture out into bad weather on my bike, and only slowly build up to any sort of distance on the days I can go out.

And although I see Madelyn and Becky early in the new year—Sandra won't return my calls, although I continue to have hope—for now, the biological imperative, that drive to procreate, whatever it was that formerly allowed my body freedom to override my brain, seems to have disappeared, which complicates both relationships more than I would have thought.

"We've got to be more careful," I tell Madelyn when she first shows up at my place after my illness, as if that is some sort of explanation for why I won't get naked. "People are talking about us."

"I don't care," she says, and she kisses me ardently. Madelyn is the only person I know who can match me desperation for desperation; sometimes I don't know whether to applaud her or be scared out of my wits. "Do you?"

Well, no, I don't, but at the moment I don't care in a different way than she doesn't care, and things as a result are not so great between us. As I feared, she naturally takes my lack of interest in sleeping with her to mean there is something wrong with her, and she retreats into herself, or more properly, back to her house, from which she doesn't emerge for the rest of the month, at least so far as I am concerned.

Becky doesn't go quite that far—I'm not sure how much of herself there is to retreat into yet—but she too is mystified. Our first time out since my illness, a Wednesday night after she gets out of church, she takes me to Buzzard Billy's, a Cajun restaurant in an old warehouse near the river, and forces me to eat crawfish. Around us, college students are tossing back Miller Lite and Shiner Bock and some frat boys over in the corner with a table full of empty pitchers are letting loose the occasional Rebel yell and laughing so hard at something that they can't seem to get their collective breath.

Becky's manner with me is easy, affectionate, and very possessive: when she laughs, she reaches across the table to place her hand lightly on top of mine. I look down at it. Our hands sit on top of an old Paul Dean baseball card; the tabletops all have such cards lying underneath a clear layer of shellac or laminate.

I move my hand off Daffy Dean, out from under Becky's hand. "It's sacriligious to cover him up like that," I say.

"Oh. Was he famous?"

"Not as famous as his brother. But he did all right for himself."

"So have you," she says, and there is her hand again.

Becky seems anxious to take things up right where we left off, to resume the relationship we seemed about to begin before I got sick, while I have stepped back several paces from that, from everything, and I'm sure it must seem to her almost as if we're getting to know each other all over again.

"I told my dad he was a quack," she says as I dive into the crawfish alfredeaux. The sauce is creamy with a hint of Cajun heat, and the crawfish is sweet and almost melts between my teeth.

I raise an inquiring eyebrow and speak when my mouth is free. "Why is your dad a quack?"

"Well, just a couple of days after he saw you, you were bedridden with pneumonia. How could he have sat right next to you at dinner and not seen you were an invalid about to happen? Some doctor," she huffs.

"How could he have foreseen the abuse his little girl was going to put me through later that night?" I say, just to see her blush; it is a handsome one.

"Now you stop it," she says. "Why if I even thought for a second that I was partly responsible for what happened to you—"

"Partly? You almost killed me, woman. I've given up sex for a safer sport. Cliff diving." This is good for her ego, so I let her go on thinking it; maybe I could try something similar with Madelyn.

"I wish I'd gotten the chance to take care of you while you were flat on your back. That would have been fun."

"For whom?"

"For both of us, maybe," she says, and then she dives into her food as if to shut herself up. We eat mostly in silence, a few remarks here and there on the other patrons or on our waiter, Frank, whose short dark hair stands straight up on his head. The frat boys in the corner have become morose as they continue to drain their beers sullenly, their silence now as startling as their earlier whooping. If we stay much longer I look for one or more of them to step over to our table and try to give me, the nearest male of the species, an ass-whupping.

"Do you want to come over?" she asks without looking up from her plate when we're working on dessert, a shared piece of sweet potato pie. "I'm wearing some more of those little things you like." And it's only here that she looks up, and faces me unblinking, and I can see, not only into those eyes, but all the way inside her.

What I see almost puts me on the floor: this girl loves me. She honestly does. I have seen that look in women before, open and trusting and devoted, have even observed it in pictures of myself that Cindy took during our honeymoon.

This gorgeous creature loves me.

Well, here is the acid test. A living man—that is to say, one with his wits and senses in the here and now—would find it impossible to resist such an offer from such a girl.

But me—I don't feel even the slightest nudge in that direction. What I feel mostly, is a sudden roiling in my stomach, which could be too much of the rich food, or could be deep-seated sadness over opportunities lost, over a gentle heart I will eventually have to break if I can just manage the cruelty that will be required.

"I've got to get home," I tell her, an expression that I hope is regret on my face. "This time you might finish me off."

She gives me another satisfying blush, and, outside, a kiss that in earlier days would have curled my toes before driving off with a wave.

Fortunately for the continuity of the species, my unwillingness to commit myself to another human being is not shared by everyone, and I receive a graphic reminder the following day at lunch, our last meal before Terry joins us. Hugh comes in twenty minutes late with a satisfied look on his bespectacled face, and it's really only a matter of who can get it out first.

"What is it, Hugh?" Wally asks, moving his hat so Hugh can seat himself.

"Gentlemen," he says, when he has given Wylie his order—beef tips with noodles, carrots, and turnip greens, "I have an announcement." He looks momentarily at me and smiles, as if it is a secret he and I share. I smile back; although I have no idea what he's about to say, his enthusiasm is infectious.

"Caroline and I are getting married in April. You're all invited. And a huge reception. Dancing. Food. Champagne. You'll have to bring your best girls." A wild round of congratulations, hand-shaking, and back-slapping breaks out that grows to encompass Wylie, the other patrons, and, eventually, Martha herself. The elderly black woman who does all this wonderful cooking shuffles out from behind her counter to throw her arms around Hugh and call him "darlin'."

"Best girl? My only girl," Ron observes sourly as the pandemonium dies down. "Brad is the only one who has the luxury of a decision, unless Wally is holding out on us."

"I won't dignify that with a response," Wally says. "Except to thank you for even momentarily considering the possibility."

"Did you hear from Evelyn and Jackson?" Hugh asks me. "I think Caroline let it slip to some of the folks at First Baptist."

"I saw the grandfolks Sunday for dinner," I say. "But they didn't mention it. I'm not sure they remember we know each other when they're not around."

Hugh looks surprised, maybe even a little disappointed. He likes to think that Jackson is one of the things that we share, since the two of them have known each other since college and he claims to have known me since I was in the cradle.

"Hey, don't feel bad," I tell him. "It doesn't mean you're not worth gossiping about. It's just that Jackson and I don't really talk about that kind of thing. Never have, really."

"I got the impression that you two were close."

"Well, we've been through a lot, and I guess we'd do anything for each other. But now that I think about it, I can't really say that I know him at all. And he probably doesn't know me any better." Actually, I know the latter to be true, but it's a strange realization to come to, all of a sudden, that you can know somebody your whole life and still not really know him, and a strange thing to suddenly share with these guys, although admittedly our conversations have begun to turn more toward the revelatory since Richard left us.

"Maybe nobody ever really knows anybody," Wally says; this may be the influence of the Greek philosophers he's getting ready to spring on Baylor sophomores. "I think Clara and I are close, but there are parts of her I'll never know, and probably couldn't understand if I got there."

"Well, it's too bad about you and Jackson," Hugh says, nodding his thanks at Wylie as his food arrives. "I'd say you're both missing out on a lot. Your granddad's quite a guy. Always has been.

"You know," he says, "we were freshmen together at Baylor in '46. He was a combat vet just back from the Pacific and I was a seventeen-year-old freshman. Lots of the other returned G.I.s talked big, tried to let people know how tough they'd been, impress the girls and such." Hugh leans forward to make his point. "But your granddad never said a word. Teachers would ask him in class, he'd say he'd served on Guadalcanal and the Philippines, and he wouldn't say anything else. That's how I knew that he'd really seen things."

There is silence at this, and we sit for a moment imagining what it might be like.

"I always thought your granddad was sunk deep in himself," Hugh says, and you can see by his face that he's drifted back decades. Behind those horn-rimmed glasses his eyes have gone opaque to the present. "Of course he was lots older than the rest of the freshmen, so he didn't go in for bonfires or chants. He'd go to the football games, but he'd sit off by himself if we let him. I think when he met your grandmother, it made all the difference. I think Evelyn saved him. I don't know from what, but I've always had the sense that she filled a hole in him, somehow. Saved him from himself, maybe."

More silence. Ron scuffs his big feet, and the next table over we can overhear two women talking about one of their sons who won't obey his teachers and is in danger of getting kicked out of school.

"What is all this talk?" Wally says with bluff heartiness, and maybe we need it; we have become a morose group all of a sudden. "Tell us more about the wedding. Or do you want to save it until Terry gets here?"

"I'll tell it as many times as I get to," Hugh says, his smile so big it threatens to divide his head, and we return to cheerfulness for the rest of our time together.

As well we should. We can see through the window that it's a beautiful sunny day outside, and when I'm ready to leave I actually take the top down on the Healey for the first time in months and hurry home to get on my bicycle.

I've worked up to only ten miles in my infrequent rides this month, riding when the weather has allowed, and it hasn't brought me much relief. Even on the rare days when the sun has been shining brilliantly—if low on the horizon—the landscape remains brown, or gray, the grass dead, the trees bare and dormant except for the live oaks. On my ride now I pass stands of dry pampas grass, twice as tall as I am, or more, and the rustling in the undergrowth as I pass is less and less frequent. But today is a day the likes of which I may not see again for months, so I resolve to get out and do my full thirty miles if I can possibly manage it.

When I reach the gravel road which is overhung by trees, normally one of the highlights of my ride, several truckloads of dirt and rock have been dumped at a bend that Bullhide Creek has been washing out, and the rocks—some the size of a canned ham—are impossible to avoid. For a good eighth of a mile I am vibrating across them, jostled up and down, my head bouncing uncontrollably like one of those figurines with the head on a spring, shaking like a maraca.

My head starts to hurt and will not stop, a pounding in the back of my head where the skull and spine meet, accompanied by a familiar pain that shoots through the back of my head whenever I turn my head to left or right. I deviate from my route to the I-35 access road, where I stop at a convenience store for aspirin and a Dr Pepper to wash it down with.

As I push open the door to the clanging of a cowbell, Tejano music is playing over the store speakers, and I find the culprit behind the counter, a Chicano girl who has black-painted fingernails and is wearing a Selena T-shirt.

I ask, "Is this Selena we're listening to?" and her weary face suddenly lights up like the Vegas Strip.

"Oh, do you like her?" she asks as she begins ringing me up. "I think she's wonderful."

"I knew someone who did." It is bracing to speak of Sandra in the past tense; I knew there was a good reason I avoided using it.

"I'm sorry," she says, seeing my reaction. I hand over the emergency twenty I carry in my shoe for such times.

"She's not dead," I say. I look closer at this girl's name badge as she's getting my change and see that her name is Maria Elena Fuentes. She is about twenty, a little on the chunky side and made up garishly for my tastes, but she has a hundred-watt smile that makes me think I wouldn't mind getting to know her better, and I do seem to have a slot open now. "Her name was Fuentes too," I say. "Isn't that weird?"

She snaps her gum and shakes her head. "There must be a hundred in the Waco phone book." She counts the change into my hand.

She's right. There's no connection between us, however I might reach for it. In fact, as much as I hate to say it, there's a gulf between us that small talk will never bridge. That I don't get Selena is just the tip of the iceberg.

A big old cowboy in a sweat-stained white Stetson throws open the door with a clang and calls out in a hearty voice, "Have y'all got any of them good beef fajitas left?" He says "Fajitas" with the emphasis on the first syllable. As he stomps across to the deli counter I take a handful of aspirin, wash it down with a long swig of Dr Pepper, and nod a good-bye to Maria Elena Fuentes.

It's still warm enough to take Audrey out for a long walk when I reach home, but each time my foot hits the ground, a pain shoots up through my spine and into my head, and I have to call an early halt, much to her chagrin. She pulls at the leash the whole way home, and once we get there she whimpers and tries to interpose her head to be petted until I yell at her—which makes my head hurt even more and probably serves me right—

and she goes to plop down in her spot in front of the fireplace with a deep-throated growl of complaint, less threat than a heartfelt expression of disgust.

My head doesn't hurt quite as much when I wake up the next day. Lying in bed seems to make things better, so I keep doing it, and keep doing it, getting up now and then to let the dog out or to take more aspirin, or occasionally to nibble on something.

I don't know how long I would have stayed in bed this time—as it is, I'm there for several days—but early one morning there's suddenly a thud above my head, which I recognize as one of those damned Faber cats in the attic again—followed by another thud, and another, as if several of them are up there giving a feline judo demonstration, and I realize that I've kept Audrey cooped up for so long that her deterrent value has completely disappeared.

"Well, we'll see about this," I say to Audrey, dutifully curled on the rug at the foot of my bed, and I roll out of bed, and back into life, such as it is.

I let her out to bark and chase and generally make her presence felt. Audrey scares off the cats, and the house again belongs to us. Eventually, after a period of some days, the pain in my head and the stiffness in my neck go away, so I figure I am cured, at least for the time being. In the end, of course, none of us is cured. Life is terminal.

Which makes me think I've been spending too much time around Wally; his stoic gloom is rubbing off on me.

And perhaps I would have gotten out of bed regardless of whether the cat—or cats—had taken over my attic. I don't want to miss Terry's first day with us, so I shower, shave, dress for lunch, and put the top back up on my Healey, since the day is sunny but brisk.

They are already there when I arrive, so I catch only the tail end of the introductions before being launched into them myself.

"I'm retired from Central National Bank," Hugh is explaining to Terry, with characteristic modesty; Hugh is the majority owner of CNB, although he makes it sound as though maybe he spent his career as a loan officer.

"And this must be Brad," Terry says in his deep hearty broadcaster's voice, turning to me and extending a large hand. As I remember, his handshake could crack walnuts, but I don't sense any malice behind it, just incredible vitality. "I thought I remembered you from a few years back." Terry has a thick neck, a sparkling smile, and he wears a tan sports coat and a Looney Tunes tie featuring Sylvester and Tweetie.

"You've got a great memory," I tell him, as I shove Ron over to make some room for myself at the table. "It's been five years or more since I was on with you to talk about my book."

"No," he says, shaking his head and smiling. "It can't be. It doesn't seem like I've even been on television for five years. What have you been doing with yourself in the meantime?"

I smile. "Not a hell of a lot."

We order. Wally has the temerity to advise Terry on his choices for the day, like he didn't grow up here in East Waco, never had good, solid, high-fat, cholesterol-filled home cooking.

"You know, from listening to the others talk," Terry says to me after his order is taken, "I sort of took you for the hub of the group."

My expression is intended to be polite with a hint of disbelief, a slightly raised right eyebrow. "That would probably be an overstatement." I am perhaps a locus of discontent, but other than that I could not claim to be the hub of anything.

"Okay," Terry says. "You and Ron knew each other in high school."

"True," Ron says. Martha and Wylie bring out our food as Terry continues.

"Hugh here has known your family for forty years."

"Forty-eight in August," Hugh says, counting on his fingers.

"And Wally says he had you in class as an undergrad."

"That's true," Wally says. "Undistinguished, but nonetheless, enrolled."

"Thanks loads," I tell Wally, but my mind is working double time. I had never stopped to think about this, but the implications are startling. Our group formed spontaneously over a stretch of months, as people eating by themselves or in small groups at George's found some common ground, began to drift together and adhere. But although none of them had known each other before, they all, strangely enough, knew me at least a little.

"And you and I met, briefly, a few years back," Terry says, holding up his hands, palms up, as if to say, *See what I mean?*

"That is strange," Ron says. "And pretty sharp of you to notice, man."

"Hey," he says. "I am a professional journalist."

"I'm not the hub," I say, finally, when it's apparent that I'm expected to say something. "If anything, I'm out on the rim somewhere." But the thought of all of us coming together blindly, yet with this most tenuous of connections—me—leaves me smiling at the wonder of it all. Perhaps there is order in all the seeming chaos of our lives if we can only puzzle it out. Sandra would say so, I know; her whole life is predicated on discovering that order. She certainly discovered what makes me tick.

"Gentlemen," Wally says, raising his iced tea. "And Brad. A toast. To completing the wheel."

"Hear, hear," we say. We bring our plastic iced tea glasses together with a clatter, and drink to the smiling newcomer in our midst, a gentle bear of a man, Terry Stephens.

"And to a long and happy association," he toasts in return, and we drink again, the tea for just a moment tasting like divine elixir, cold and sweet.

15

As February turns into March I am recovering, physically at least. The weather begins to improve along the inexorable march toward spring, and I am again riding daily, or near daily, although I spend the occasional gray afternoon dozing in front of the fireplace. I also still get occasional muscular stiffness or a headache pounding low at the base of my skull, mostly late in the evening after a stressful day, but I generally feel better the next morning after I've had some sleep. Since I've got my physical self back to some semblance of its previous condition, when I venture out for a lengthy ride on a warm day in March, I no longer have to concentrate on keeping my legs moving, and suddenly it is as if my eyes and ears are opened to a world I hadn't known—or had forgotten—was there.

Part of my new awareness comes from the fact that I really am seeing many things for the first time. Since most of the vegetable kingdom has been dead or dormant for months—the only green to be seen comes from brambles, briars, and hanging mistletoe—and the grasses, bushes, and trees lining the roads have had time to shrink back or blow away, it's now possible to see the detritus cast out over the past year. Just in the section of my ride from the dogs to Mrs. Koufax's house, off the tree-lined road I spy with my little eye the following: fast food packaging from Taco Loco, Taco Cabana, Taco Bueno, Taco Bell (why anyone in Texas would want to eat any of this faux Mexican food I do not know); plastic antifreeze and milk jugs; Styrofoam cups; a sofa, foam spilling from the weather-beaten brown cushions; beer and soda bottles and cans; tires, especially in the creek bed, which is cluttered with car, truck, and even tractor tires; something large and dead, judging from the stench as I pass over a culvert; a car battery; most of a car's windshield; a metal bed frame; a broken cassette cartridge, the glimmering brown tape draped across a tree; a dozen Folger's coffee cans of various sizes, green and red; a TV aerial, flung across a gulley like a flimsy jungle gym; a hot water heater, still glossy white; a faded green '69 Malibu.

Kinda makes you proud to be an American, the wonderful things we throw away.

Other things appear through the skeletal branches, the withered vegetation. Through the now-golden pampas grass on the north, the old abandoned house that I have known, instinctively, has been hiding all spring and summer behind its green shield, finally reappears, its two attic windows eyes, its porch mouth full of white pillar teeth.

While I am paying attention to the house, which is admittedly a spooky thing and probably better off overgrown and out of sight, a red '71 Ford pickup truck hurtles around the bend behind me, makes a last-second adjustment in steering to keep from knocking me into the creek, and bounces past, a musical clinking coming from the bed as bottle meets bottle. The three kids inside don't know or care that they've scared the wits out of me, appearing so suddenly like that, and my heart is pounding as I follow, at a considerably slower pace, in their wake.

With that mild upset out of the way—it is not, after all, a big black car—I continue to absorb the world as I ride onward, cross over from McClennan into Falls County just outside Cottonwood, pedal past the few houses and the old German Baptist church, puff up what I now think of as Commander's Hill. I stop and sit for a rest at the wooden bridge at the bottom of the hill, sheltered from the slight northern breeze, smack in the sun's warming rays, and I dangle my legs over the side, take a drink from my water bottle, feel it ooze cool down my dry throat.

With my preternatural awareness, I begin to sort out sounds from the seeming silence: the humming of trucks passing on State Highway 7, some miles distant; the lowing of the white-faced cattle behind me; the carbonated burble of the creek below; the far-off whine of an airplane, which almost blends into the whine of the gnats buzzing past my ears. I feel good, at peace, totally without conscious thought, and it is with real regret that I get back up to resume my ride.

As I coast downhill toward the Out Bridge I finally see the plane I heard earlier, and the suspicion that has been growing as I detect the faint bitter chemical smell is confirmed when I spot it. It's a crop duster, dropping low and out of sight over the fields, pulling up at the far end and wheeling back around like a turkey buzzard and dropping again to deliver his load.

Well, I'm willing to make my sacrifices for American agriculture; what's a few carcinogens between friends? I watch as the biplane swoops and soars, a creature from another age miraculously alive and aloft in ours, and again I let myself get so involved in one feature of the landscape that I neglect others of real personal importance.

Coming up the hill toward me from the Out Bridge is a pickup truck, a red '71 Ford, in fact, and by the time I'm aware of it, I can only observe that the three boys—I continue to think of them as such, even though as I pass I can see that they're in their late teens or early twenties—are sitting in positions of exaggerated nonchalance, guilty positions I know from my youth, beer bottles cupped out of sight in their dangling hands.

Well, I'm not here to make value judgments. Let them live their own lives, make their own mistakes. "How's it going?" I call, by way of greeting as we pass; then I ride down the hill, slow, stop, and get off to lift my bike over the barrier.

As I step out onto the bridge I see something glistening below, see that the bottom of the creek beneath my beautiful private bridge is now home to dozens of beer bottles, the sort of bottles that might, say, make a musical clinking when piled high in the back of someone's truck.

"Sons of bitches," I say, turning to trace the truck's progress up the hill. "Sons of bitches."

The first good rain will pick these up and float them off, which will restore this scene to its former beauty, but only at the cost of littering somebody else's view. My eyes burn, but whether it's from sorrow or anger I can't tell. My first impulse is to get back on my bike and charge after them, and I like to think that if they were skinheads vandalizing a synagogue, say, I would be on them in a flash. But there's no higher cause to be served here, just my own sense of outrage and a crazy biological insistence that pulses through my veins, telling me that these kids should be permanently expunged from the gene pool, that at the very least I should put the fear of God into them.

But there are three of them and one of me, they have vanished over the crest of the hill, and anyway, kids these days shoot people instead of just beating the shit out of them, their right to bear semi-automatic weapons apparently guaranteed by the Constitution.

It's not worth it.

The crop duster rises above the line of trees, wheels, and comes back around again, and I sigh and sit and watch.

Fortunately, other things in my life are more pleasant. As we draw closer to Hugh's wedding, the guys and I have decided—over his delighted objections—to throw a bachelor party for him, and all of us, Terry included, have gathered in secret—once at my house, in fact—to toss ideas around. Terry has taken to Hugh like to none of the rest of us, partly because Hugh has the largest store of baseball lore to dispense, and Terry really does want to learn the game.

"I saw Josh Gibson play once here with a barnstorming team," Hugh recalls in mid-March as I'm enjoying my smothered pork chops at Martha's. ("That's right," seconds Martha from the kitchen. "That was a fine man.") "Barnstormers used to come through here all the time, you know, black and white both. Babe Ruth played in Waco once, although of course that was before my time."

"If only marginally," Wally says through a mouthful of corn bread, which cracks Terry up. He's still getting used to the way we relate.

"Wisdom and experience, sonny-boy," Hugh says. "Read 'em and weep."

I drop into my straight-man role; since I can't practice it with

Sandra, I need to work it in somewhere. "Was Josh Gibson as good as they say?"

"I saw him hit one so far I lost sight of it. Really. Clean out of sight. In 1934 he hit the only home run ever hit out of Yankee Stadium. Man hit over eight hundred home runs, for crying out loud, four-time Negro League batting champ, and he was only thirty-four when he passed."

"Man, when you think what he could have done if he'd gotten to play in the majors," Terry says, and his voice trails off.

"Criminal," Ron says.

"A real shame," Wally says. We sit in uncomfortable guilty white liberal silence for a moment.

"He would have booted Babe Ruth's fat white ass out of Cooperstown," Terry says, and I sputter and almost choke on my food.

He's one of us now all right, for better or worse.

After Hugh pleads a tuxedo fitting and deserts us, we linger to finalize our plans. The wedding is in two weeks, the first Saturday in April, and we've set aside the Friday night before as our bachelor blowout.

"Now, we don't want to kill the guy before his wedding," Wally cautions. Since Hugh is a deacon in the First Baptist Church of Waco, we've ruled out strip bars and whorehouses. Wally has petitioned for a night of fishing on Lake Waco, cold beers in hand, dressed for comfort in fishing hats and sandals, wetting our lines for bass and catfish, and I admit that there is much to recommend this, maybe preceded by a big dinner at La Cabaña, my favorite Mexican restaurant. But at last, on Ron's recommendation, we decide to have the party at my place, grill some cow, lay in a stock of this new beer from Austin called Celis, wheat beer with just a hint of orange peel in it, which sounds as though it should make you projectile vomit but is actually amazingly good. Terry has promised a videotape of a 1969 game between the Cubs and the Phillies played at Wrigley Field—"Don't ask me how I got this," he says—and has also borrowed the tapes from this past year's Series from the station.

"That'd be nice," Ron tells him with a sad smile. "We weren't exactly able to give it our full attention when it was on."

"Then you'll enjoy it this time. I could watch that Joe Carter home-run over and over."

"Hey, who're you bringing to the wedding?" Ron suddenly asks me, as though it has just occurred to him, and everybody turns to hear my answer.

I blink and play dumb. "Who says I'm bringing anybody?"

"I've already asked Val," Ron says, as though that settles the question.

"From Circulation," Hugh says, as if I need reminding.

"Why do I have to bring somebody? Why can't I just come alone? Aren't I good enough?"

"No," they say in unison.

"Well," Wally says, "I can't come alone, which means that if you come alone, you'll be out in the cold. I can't desert Judy. You need to bring women so they can all get together and talk womanly wedding-talk while we talk manly wedding-talk."

"I'm in between women at the moment," I tell them.

"Oh, bullshit," Ron says. "Call Sandra."

"We don't seem to be speaking," I say, because this is the truth. "She won't call me back. When I went up to see her at school she literally locked herself into her office, leaving me to stand outside in the hallway making plaintive noises. Ten minutes later, members of Baylor's police force arrived to help me locate an exit. I do not take these as positive signs." They sigh. "I guess I could ask Becky."

"Do it," Terry says. "She sounds gorgeous."

"She is," Wally mutters; Wally has had her in class, remarked on her beauty and wit, and purses his lip in disgust at the unfairness of a universe that permits me to go out with such a creature.

Since the community would probably give us worse than Wally's disgusted lip if I were to take Madelyn—and since her husband probably already has dibs on her for such a soiree—I suppose that Becky is my port of last resort, but just thinking about the contrasts between the two gives me an unaccountable sense of urgency. I recently had a strangely significant dream, Madelyn and me in bed underneath a down comforter in some mountain cabin while Becky tapped frantically on the frosty windowpane.

I have to see Madelyn. Soon.

I remember hearing her say earlier in the year that Colby would be going to New Orleans in late March for the regional Christianity and Literature conference, so that afternoon I call the English department from a pay phone on Clay Street and tell the secretary I'm an old friend from Tulane and want to know just when Colby will be rolling into town. I have a momentary fear that she'll transfer me to his office and I'll have to hang up on him, but I also know this is a reasonably good gamble, since Madelyn tells me Colby rarely keeps office hours and prefers instead to spend his time in his research carrel at the library where he can't be disturbed by students.

There is a momentary shuffling of papers as the secretary clears a space on her desk big enough for the departmental calendar. On the sidewalk across the street from me, an old Hispanic man pushes a dark-haired baby in a stroller. He takes a last swig from his Coors Lite tallboy, crumples it in his fist, and tosses the can into a hedge without breaking stride. I would love to follow him, find out—in Paul Harvey's words—the rest of the story, but the secretary comes back on and the old man and his diminutive charge escape me.

"He'll be there Thursday afternoon," she informs me, and I thank her sweetly for being the bearer of such good news.

Then I go to the florist's and order a dozen roses to be delivered to the Clark household on Thursday afternoon. I write a short message that says, "I'll be home tomorrow. Please come see me," and seal the envelope.

When the knock falls lightly on my door Friday evening, I am there before the echo dies to open it, gather Madelyn inside, kiss her. She drops her bag to the tiles, puts both hands to my face, and returns my kiss with equal urgency.

It has been a long time. So long, in fact, that my body manifests signs of interest in human females in general and Madelyn in particular, interest in the possibility of continuing the species.

It has been a very long time.

Just as it is some time, in fact, before we even leave the foyer.

The kiss turns to something else, to clothes dropping to the cold tile floor, and we end up using the table that holds my answering machine in ways I'm sure its makers never intended. Elaine, her timing always impeccable, calls and leaves a message on the machine while we're flailing away right next to it, and Madelyn arches an eyebrow at me as beautifully as she arches herself toward me, as if to say, Aren't you going to answer that?

"Not on your life," I pant, and we go frantically on about our business.

Only then do we enter the house proper, buttoning and refastening, to where Audrey has been waiting patiently, and Madelyn drops to the floor and hugs her with an equal—if slightly different—intensity. "Hey, Audrey! I'm so glad to see you! Have you missed me?"

Audrey wags frantically in answer, for both of us. No one else will get down on her level, and I've been horribly inattentive in recent months.

"Want to go for a walk?" Madelyn asks, and Audrey recognizes the word, perks up her ears, and then, panting, goes off in search of her leash.

"Come with us?"

"I think I'll watch and admire," I say, as Audrey returns, dragging her leash; I knew that old dogs/new tricks thing was ridiculous if you wanted something badly enough.

"What made you send for me?" she asks, pausing a moment before she hooks the leash on Audrey's collar and the two of them become a blur toward the back door.

"Is that what I did?"

"I think so. I wouldn't have come if you hadn't."

"I missed your body," I say, and Audrey whines, ready to go.

"Come on," she says, and she makes as if to whip me with the leash.

"Okay," I admit. "I missed *you*. All of you. Your laugh, your mind, your sardonic wit, and the gorgeous fine-tuned body they all drive around in."

"Come with us," she says, smiling now, and clips on the leash, and Audrey gives a mighty tug, and I follow them—my two favorite girls—outside, to frolic in the pasture among the new-blooming wildflowers.

"Storms are coming," I explain later that night, when Audrey whimpers up beside the bed. Madelyn reaches over, finds Audrey shivering, and coos to her.

"It's okay, puppy," she says. "Everything's okay. We're right here. Brad and Madelyn won't let anything happen to you."

"It's no good," I tell her, and I roll groggily out of bed and pad into the kitchen, Audrey following. "She won't sleep now," I call. "She can't. I'll have to stay up with her for a while."

"Call me if you need a breather," she says. I imagine her rolling over, her perfectly rounded white shoulder sticking up out of the blanket, and I almost abandon Audrey to face her fears alone.

But I am made of sterner stuff, and furthermore, I know I have Madelyn to myself all weekend. I flip on ESPN 2, and together, Audrey and I sit, her shivering, me yawning, until at last she begins to imitate me.

"Why don't you lie down and go to sleep?" I suggest, and, wonder of wonders, she does.

And so do I. When I flip back the covers, Madelyn turns over, shifts her weight back over toward me without really waking up, as though it is the most natural thing on earth to welcome me back to bed, and I snuggle against her curved warmth. We sleep like that, in immediate contact, my back to her front, her arm pulled over my hips, and we awake hungry for each other, as though we have been pursuing each other in dreams.

After a hearty breakfast of cold cereal and a quick dog check—Audrey is still comatose—we return to bed, where we stay much of the morning and on into the afternoon. The metaphors stumble over each other in their eagerness to emerge—it is a marathon, a smorgasbord, a decathlon of love—but the language doesn't capture it at all, the experience of being so close to someone else, of being a part of someone else, of filling and fulfilling, of giving of myself and receiving from her.

Since words fail me, I can only draw on past experience, on comparisons, and announce that this day is the most passionate and fulfilling of my life, better than my adventurous first honeymoon, better than my tepid sex with Elaine, better than a night with Becky Sue Bradenton. Madelyn destroys me and then she rebuilds me, brick by brick, stone by stone. She uses her mouth, her hands, her whole body, and she demands that I be as attentive and as loving with her. When she is temporarily through with me, after finishing a back rub that turns into things far more intimate, I lie on my back, my arm around her, her head on my chest, her leg thrown across me, and for the moment, I haven't the strength to pick up my head, to move a muscle. And anyway, why would I want to?

I am off somewhere far away, drifting in a warm ocean, when I feel the wetness on my chest, feel Madelyn shudder in my arms. "What's wrong?" I ask.

"Why can't it always be like this?" she sobs. "Why can't we be this alive all the time?"

"Hey," I say, and I pull her close. "Hey." I understand completely: it would be wonderful if every day we could make love in such harmony, with such passion.

And, at the same time, it wouldn't. If we could always do this, wouldn't we get used to it, eventually? If all our days were equally beautiful, wouldn't they also be equally ugly? If the Texas wildflowers bloomed year-round, would we even notice them?

"Death is the mother of beauty," I murmur, so softly that perhaps Madelyn can't hear it, even though we are at this moment as close as two members of the species can ever be.

"Death is the mother of beauty," she repeats softly, and she stops crying, settling instead for a couple of deep sighs, which seem to have a steadying effect on her. The phrase is part of our shared heritage; like me, Madelyn was once an English major reading Wallace Stevens.

"Anyway, that was wonderful." She sighs, her final sigh, and she raises herself on an elbow to look at me, and, incidentally, brings her right breast, cinnamon-tipped, directly into my line of sight. "Can we try again later?"

It will have to be later; even this incredible view is not enough. "Let me call for my stunt double," I say, although I will do my best when the opportunity arises again since our time together is so precious. "Let's grab something to eat. I'm starving."

"I can see why," she says. "I'm a little hungry myself."

We dress, go into the kitchen, fix a late lunch/early supper of Jarlsberg Swiss, wheat crackers, sliced apples, and eat sitting on the stones in front of the fire.

"How's your prospectus coming?" I ask, and I know immediately it is the wrong question to ask. Instantly she is transformed: her smile disappears, her shoulders slump, her head tilts forward, her gaze shifts away.

"Not well," she says. "They turned it down."

"Turned it down," I repeat.

"They said it wasn't focused enough. That I was covering too many religions and periods."

"But doesn't the Lilith figure do just that?" As Madelyn has explained it to me, Lilith or her precursors are prominent in all sorts of beliefs over a span of thousands of years.

"Yes," she says, "and I thought I was writing the prospectus in such a way that it was obvious, but I guess I failed to demonstrate that adequately."

"Maybe they're just not progressive enough to understand it," I say.

"Or maybe I'm not intelligent enough to write it," she counters.

I know better than this; Madelyn has a B.A. from Sarah Lawrence and an M.Div. from Yale Divinity School. She's one of the brightest women I know, and this from a man who is inexorably, inevitably drawn to women brighter than himself. "I don't believe that for a second," I tell her. "If they'd give you half a chance—"

"It's not working," she says, and she sets down her plate and gets up to pace the room. "I can't pretend that it is. Maybe I'm not cut out for this kind of life. Maybe I was just meant to be an adoring helpmeet, looking on from the wings."

"I don't believe that either," I say, "and neither should you." I put down my plate and stand up so I can meet her on her level, talk to her the way she apparently needs to be talked to.

"Don't shout at me," she says.

"I'm not shouting. I'm just trying to get you to listen to me."

"You aren't listening to me. And why should you? You're a real writer. Both of you, both of the men in my life, doesn't it just figure?" She starts to laugh.

"Stop it," I say. Her laughter continues to rise. She's scaring Audrey; she's scaring me.

"What does it matter to you? After I leave you'll go back to work. 'Poor Madelyn,' you'll say. 'It's too bad about her. What shall I write next?' "

"Stop it," I say, and I raise a finger of warning. My head is pounding, and Audrey, her eyes bleary, totters to her feet and patters out of the room at her best possible speed.

"I'm probably good for your ego, aren't I? A smart woman you can look down on, can—"

"You're wrong," I say, angrily, through clenched teeth.

She turns to confront me. "Oh really? About what?"

"About me, for one thing. I'm not writing."

"Oh, not at this moment. Maybe not even this week. But you will, which is more than I can say for myself."

"No, I won't. Damn it, I'm not writing. Not now. Not seriously. I am not a writer."

She looks away from me and takes a deep breath; it's as though she can't bear to see me try to pass off such utter nonsense as truth. She's smart enough to know better, that look tells me, even if she isn't smart enough to write a satisfactory dissertation prospectus.

She doesn't believe me.

More to the point, she won't believe me. Not on this. My deception has been too successful, and now I stand on the verge of a decision: maintain it or destroy it.

The ultimate result of either choice is uncertain to me, but I can certainly see what my illusion of writerly success is doing to Madelyn in the here and now.

We stand in silence then, the only sounds the crackling of the fire and Audrey in the hallway settling into a heap with a groan. Madelyn stands leaning against my bookcase, looking out the window into the pasture, into the night. I look down into the fireplace, almost lose myself for a moment in the leaping flames, and when I break the silence, it is in a low voice; I find that I can barely speak.

"Take a notebook off the shelf next to your elbow," I say, without looking away from the fire.

"Why?" Her voice is tinged with suspicion, and, worse, with defeat. It is this last that tells me I am making the right choice, hard as it may be.

"Take a notebook off the shelf."

"Which one?"

"Any of them. Doesn't matter. Open it and tell me what you see."

From the corner of my eye, I can see Madelyn shrug, then slide one out, can hear the rasp of cover against cover.

"What does it say on the front?"

"March 1990."

"Open it."

I hear the rustling of paper as she opens it to the first page.

"What do you see?"

"Nothing," she says. "It's blank."

She pages through the book, slowly, at first, then more swiftly, flipping front to back, and when she's done, I feel rather than see her eyes on me.

"Pick out another one. Any one."

She does. July 1992. She looks in it. Nothing. And another. February 1993. Empty. I can't bear to look at her as she does this, as she flicks faster through the pages, and for a moment I imagine myself lost in the flames, flickering oranges and reds and blues all around me, a beautiful destruction, a lovely way to go. For aesthetic reasons alone it would beat a gravel truck any day of the week .

"They're empty," she says, wonder in her voice, and she sits down heavily on the couch. "Empty."

I lift my head, an action that takes every ounce of strength I possess, and meet her gaze. "All of them," I say. "Every last one." And I keep my eyes up, open, let her read in them what she will.

I want her to know, for once, the absolute truth.

The problem with this is what I can simultaneously read in her eyes and her furrowed brow: questions, doubt, and more than a little concern. She is wondering what kind of person would perpetuate such a ridiculous fraud, wondering if I'm totally and completely off my nut.

Maybe so; it seemed so simple at first. I started out with the idea that it was better to perpetuate a few little untruths than to hurt anybody, and then one day I looked up and saw that my whole life had become a lie.

But now, at least, the truth is out. Madelyn knows. Madelyn sees the real me.

And Madelyn is royally pissed off. "What kind of game are you playing?" she asks, and she rises from the couch. "Who are you? I thought I knew you, I thought we shared something special together, I thought—"

I feel a world-spinning sense of deja vu and open my mouth to protest, but she breaks off in midsentence and storms out of the room.

This is not the way I imagined this scene developing. I can hear her in the other room throwing her things in her bag. At last she stands in the doorway and takes a last look at me.

She shakes her head. "I can't believe you," she says—and I think she'd like to say much more—but she turns on her heel and walks out of my house.

So much for the truth.

I think I feel a relapse coming on.

16

I return to my riding in earnest—you might even say with a vengeance—and I begin to draw certain conclusions as I ride daily, past the fields turning green with corn and wheat, the budding trees, the sprouting bluebonnets and Indian paintbrush. These conclusions are limited, and maybe they don't have much relevance for anyone besides me, but they at least are conclusions that I feel I can stand on, can take rock-solid into my hands, can use in some way to ground my existence.

To wit: the best surface for bike riding is packed dirt, maybe with a little gravel or river rock, but not much. Dirt seems to give a little beneath the tires, and while I suppose it's prone to washouts and to washboarding, most of the time dirt roads remain smoother than either the concrete surfaces—which have seams and are rare on my ride in any case—and asphalt roads, most of which are no more than gravel poured on tar and start to deteriorate shortly after the road crews disappear. Both of these also absorb heat in the summer, and being roasted from the ground is simply a redundant indignity come August.

The worst riding surfaces are sand and gravel. Gravel can be downright dangerous, in fact, especially if you get up a little speed and then hit a loose patch. It's easy to lose control of your bike, to watch helplessly as you turn your front wheel frantically in the other direction and still slide off the road.

The best month for riding is October. Summer and winter are unpleasant for obvious if contrary reasons, and although the spring months are as mild as October, not only do they bring a rash of thunderstorms that can come up out of nowhere, the verdant explosion of spring sets off my allergies. Central Texas is reputed to be the allergy capital of the world, and I regularly return from spring rides through the country with my nose running and my eyes watering. Already, in April, I am going through three boxes of little green antihistamines a week, and some nights I can't breathe through my nose at all, just lie on my back snorting and snuffling until even ever-faithful Audrey gets fed up and deserts me for the living room.

Audrey is the sweetest dog I know. The meanest dogs I know are the ones currently penned up, down the street from the Amazing Roof Dog; the most pleasant are the puppies on the Out Bridge road who sometimes come swarming out to play. The best-looking female on my route is the little high school girl named Elizabeth something who lives in the house just south of the Koufaxes on Farm Road 2640. She drives a red Mustang and washes it in the summer months in the front yard dressed in cutoffs and a bikini top. I am apparently not alone in thinking she's quite a catch; a quarter mile from the house in each direction some beau has painted on the blacktop, in red spray paint, "Brad loves Elizabeth 4-Ever," and the writing is situated so that Elizabeth can read it no matter which way she turns from her driveway.

The nicest house I pass is the old tin-roofed farmhouse on the hill just outside Cottonwood with the porch on three sides and the great view. The most beautiful car I see is the old green MGB someone in Mooreville owns and occasionally puts up for sale.

The most repugnant excuse for a human being I can think of is myself.

It's nice to have articles of faith, no matter how small, to cling to. They are a comfort when the rest of the world seems arbitrary, mysterious, or downright cruel.

There are other small comforts: Audrey for dog-love; my grandparents for good food and mostly nonjudgmental acceptance; my circle of friends for a multifaceted view of what life might actually be like; Becky Sue Bradenton for her pleasant company and her great good looks, and the added fact that she is apparently the only woman in the world willing to talk to me.

But mostly, I feel as though it's back to me and my bike, and I behave accordingly.

This, as I said, does not mean that I don't have time for friends. I have nothing but time, really, so when Wallace Dent calls, panic-stricken, the Thursday morning before Hugh's bachelor party, I suppress my natural waking urge to yank the telephone out of the wall and listen.

"You've got to help me," Wally repeats. "I promised Eric a basketball goal for his birthday, opened the box this morning, took a look at the instruction sheets. It would take someone with a degree in engineering to put this thing together."

Eric is Wally's eight-year-old; it's his birthday. So I sit up, wipe the sleep from my eyes, and think out loud. "Jackson knows how to build things," I say. "I'll bring him over and we'll get this thing put up."

"But there's more, Brad. It says I need nine hundred pounds of concrete. Nine hundred pounds! Dry, no less! What am I going to do? Where am I going to get nine hundred pounds of concrete?"

I try to imagine what nine hundred pounds of concrete in eighty-pound sacks would look like. The mind rebels. "Maybe it's a misprint. Or something. We'll figure it out." I am not crazy about my chances with a complicated assembly, but I do at least feel competent—more competent, certainly, than Wally—to mix concrete.

Jackson always enjoys feeling needed—and enjoys taunting me about my lack of competence in the manly art of building things—so he is happy enough to accompany me to Wally's house. He insists on driving his old work truck, in fact, since he says we may need one, and it turns out that he's right. When we arrive, Wally is out front in his driveway with a huge, now-empty, cardboard box, a jumble of metal parts, and a complicated instruction sheet that he hands to me in wordless panic. While Jackson examines the parts, I read from the first page: "Concrete Required: Approximately 900 lb. (dry weight) equal to 7.1 cu. ft. of concrete."

"Surely that's a mistake," I say, and now I try to visualize

seven cubic feet of concrete. "Although they do say 'approximately.' I mean, we're not building a storm shelter here. They gave you the wrong set of plans."

"Keep reading," Wally says, the lures on his hat jumping up and down as he nods.

Sure enough, the manual writers are used to that reaction, because the instructions continue, emphatically, "Yes, 900 lb. (dry weight) is required to balance high forces encountered during normal play."

"What high forces?" I ask. "Whose normal play? Shaquille O'Neal's?"

"That's just a crock," Jackson says. He has looked over the backboard, the sections of pole, and the mounting equipment, and come to his conclusions. "They want you to sink the pole in a huge hole, then fill the pole, all ten feet of it, to the brim with concrete. It's worst-case ass-covering—pardon my French. See the fine print?"

The fine print informs us that if we fail to use the nine hundred pounds of concrete exactly as called for here, all warranties, written or implied, will be null and void.

"So their pole breaks and drops the backboard on my kids, crushing them, they're not at fault if we haven't sunk it in bedrock. I get it." Wally is pleased for a moment, the pure intellectual pleasure of sudden comprehension, but then he moans again, "Where are we going to get nine hundred pounds of concrete?"

Jackson takes a good look, and I see the old construction foreman in him that comes out now only on odd occasions. "Two-foot hole. About two feet in diameter. Brad, take the truck, go to Payless and get five or six bags of concrete. We probably won't need all that." He tosses me the keys, then turns to Wally. "You got a trowel?"

"No sir." I'm not sure Wally owns a hammer. It's probably safer, in fact, if he doesn't.

"Okay. And a trowel." He looks in Wally's garage. "And a wheelbarrow."

"You sure you don't want me to stay and start putting all that stuff together?"

Jackson tries to suppress a chortle and fails miserably. "Son, you'd be as useless here as a three-legged hound dog."

Which is true. I'd much rather drive than puzzle over diagrams and schematics, even though the cab of Jackson's old Dodge is drafty and the AM radio is even more static-ridden than the one in my Healey. On the way to the lumberyard, my best bet is a Tejano station and I'm determined to listen, to find the beauty in the chunk-chunk rhythm, the lickety-split accordian, the voices singing something about a dancing woman, which is as far as my Spanish will take me. Really, it isn't bad. But I have to be honest—it doesn't move me.

With the slender help of a skinny guy named Brett who works on the loading dock, I pick up six eighty-pound bags of concrete and dump them in the back of the truck, along with a wheelbarrow to mix in, and arrive back at Wally's as they are finishing up the backboard assembly.

"I thought you might have the hole dug by now," I say with bluff heartiness, but this is wishful thinking. Each of us has a role here, and my role—packhorse—is painfully obvious. Jackson has already appropriated handyman, and Wally is now his faithful assistant. So I unload the concrete and lug it to the driveway, next to the spot where Wally would like his hole dug. By the time I'm finished unloading it all, my lower back is killing me, but I'm not finished.

I get a shovel from the truck and start digging. First I cut through the sod—Wally has good dense Bermuda, just beginning to turn green and thicken out again—then through the topsoil and into the thick, claylike black soil that will make up most of my digging. It takes me a good half hour to get a decent hole. I sink my blade with enthusiasm, jump on it to sink it even deeper, but the dirt is so thick that it has to be carved out a little at a time, and the final few inches take forever; a posthole digger would be more appropriate, as I take no little pleasure in informing Jackson.

But at last my sore hands, sore back, and sore insteps have created a thing of beauty, a hole two feet deep and around two feet in diameter, and my task of mixing concrete can begin.

"How's it coming?" Wally asks. He and Jackson are working

on something called a "ratchet elevator system," which will allow someone more mechanically apt than Wallace Dent to raise and lower the backboard at will.

"Swimmingly," I grunt. I have added water to the dry mix, and am trying to stir it. It is certainly more resistant than any cookie dough or cake batter I ever helped Billie mix, and I'm already pretty sure I won't want to lick the shovel when I'm done, so the whole operation is without charm or cheer.

My granddad calls over after it's mixed, "Jackson, you need that first section of pole yet?"

They are finished putting together the backboard, and I have apparently been holding up our orderly progress. "Hole's almost full," I tell them, shoveling frantically. "Then I guess we can put the pole in."

Jackson walks to his truck and returns with a level about the time I am scraping the last few shovelfuls of this batch of concrete out of the wheelbarrow. "Save that," Jackson says. "We'll want to put a little inside the pole."

"But not nine feet worth," Wally says, hopefully.

"No. Just enough to stabilize it."

Jackson sinks the pole section down into the concrete, checks to make sure it's level and plumb, whatever that means, nudges it slightly left and right, back and forth, then stands back to approve of the work. "Looks good," he says, finally.

"Okay," I say. "Let's put the backboard on and finish up."

Jackson looks at me again and can't help laughing; it's heartwarming to be such a source of amusement to your closest living relative. "Son," he explains slowly, as if to an infant or an idiot, "the concrete has to cure. At least twenty-four hours. Maybe more. We'll have to wait on the rest of it."

"Judy and I can put it up tomorrow when she gets home from work," Wally says. "It's just putting these last bolts on, right?"

"Right," Jackson says, slapping him on the back. An unlikelier bonding I have never seen, but there it is. "Jackson, you want to drop me back at the house before y'all go out to eat?"

"Sure," I say. Wally piles into the cab with us, and then the two of us take my car to Martha's where we arrive early to make the final plans for Hugh's party.

The bachelor party is set to begin at seven, and so the next day I do my ride early in the afternoon, shower, clean up a tiny bit, and check the Weather Channel to make sure Audrey and I are prepared for any possibilities.

Ron is the first to arrive, and he comes in bearing an ice chest full of Celis beer and the hamburger buns I forgot I needed. I am mincing onions to mix with the hamburger meat.

"Hey," he says. He sets his load on the floor next to the refrigerator, and Audrey sniffs at it, then noses his pants leg. "Hey Audrey," he says, and scratches her head in a way that guarantees a wagging tail.

"Hey," I say. "Thanks for bringing the buns. I'd shake hands, but—"

"No sweat," he says. "Did you call the hookers?"

"Sure," I say, mincing furiously. "They should be here any minute."

He leans up against the counter next to me. "So what's up with you?"

I look over at him. "What's up? Nothing's up. Same old same old." I scrape the minced onion over onto the ground beef and begin mixing it in, the cool red meat squishing between my fingers.

"I didn't hear you say ten words at lunch yesterday. I mean, I'm used to you being quiet, but come on. You let Wally get away with that Mattingly argument. Since when does Mr. Speed agree with anyone about putting lard-butt Don Mattingly on an all-time best list?"

"Well, he wouldn't have been my choice," I say. "But surely he's stolen a base or two in his day."

"Two in his best year," Ron says, before he realizes how craftily I've shifted the subject. "We're worried about you. Is it the wedding?"

I suddenly see how my friends might naturally assume that anyone who's been married and divorced twice might be a little antsy in general about the institition of marriage, or perhaps might believe that Hugh's happy occasion is bringing back hurtful memories. Neither of these is true, I think. I have no deep feelings against marriage, and might conceivably marry again under the right circumstances; at the same time, I have enough current unpleasantness in my life—two women who run at the very sight of me, for starters—that I don't really need to go fishing for more.

"I'm okay," I say. "Really. Had a good ride today. And the wildflowers are gorgeous."

The door opens, closes, and Terry comes in laden down with videotapes. "I'll have a beer now," he says. "My God, what a day."

"Ice chest," Ron says unnecessarily, since Terry has made for it as unerringly as he used to make for an airborne football.

"Wally's picking up Hugh," Terry announces. "They should be along shortly."

I take the meat out through the back door and flop it onto the grill. The coals are white and hot, and the burgers send up a sizzle and a wisp of smoke as they land. It's going to be a good night. A couple of different kinds of chips are out in bowls, the beer is on ice, and there are bakery brownies from the HEB store with thick chocolate icing for dessert or midnight munching.

The doorbell rings again, and Terry goes to bring in Wally and our honoree.

"Hail, hail," Ron says.

"We who are about to die salute you," Wally—ever the Roman historian—returns. He then gives me a thumbs-up sign to answer my inquisitive eyebrow-raised look; he and Judy successfully negotiated the final stage of the backboard raising.

"What's cooking?" Hugh asks, and he comes over to where I am working, looks over my shoulder through the sink window.

"Get away from me before I smack you with my spatula," I say. "And somebody open a beer for me, huh?"

They settle in around the kitchen table, chairs scraping, sighs of relief to be off their feet.

"So how does it feel?" Terry asks Hugh.

"How does what feel?" Ron counters suggestively, and Hugh blushes deep crimson.

"I'm a little nervous," he admits. "I think we both are, a little. A lot of people are going to be there."

I take a sip of my beer. It tastes good and I take another sip before saying, "What could possibly go wrong? The worst that could happen is you make a complete ass of yourself in front of everyone you know."

"Now I feel a real sense of peace," Hugh says. "Thanks so much."

Audrey is wandering around demanding to be petted and generally getting underfoot, so as much as it pains me—and her—to do so, I put her in my room, out of the way, and go out back to turn the burgers.

"Hey Brad," Terry calls from the living room as I open the back door, "how do you like this computer?"

Ron is an IBM man from way back and probably views the computer on my desk, an old Macintosh LC II, as a relic from an alien civilization. I use it mostly to play games and write my food columns and the occasional letter to Elaine, although naturally it makes up a large part of the cover story into which I have sunk myself neck-deep. "It's a good computer," I say. "But I'm thinking about getting a new one soon." And I am, a bigger, faster one with more memory and a CD-ROM drive; there's actually a catalog on the desk with a model circled. I can call in my order and they promise to have the computer on my doorstep the next day.

I do love catalogs.

When the burgers have sizzled nicely, I take the first batch in and get everybody started. Me, I'm content enough drinking good beer and flipping burgers, so I stand amid the smoke and cook up all the patties before fixing my own and we all adjourn to the living room. There Terry, as is his right as successful hunter/gatherer, cues up our video trip back to Wrigley Field circa 1969 when I was six years old and my dad used to tell me about yesterday's games over breakfast as he read through the box scores.

We watch the ball game mostly in reverential silence. Ernie Banks hits one out onto Waveland Avenue, Ron Santo strokes two doubles, and Ferguson Jenkins throws a complete game. The Cubs beat the Phillies 4-2.

It is beautiful.

I'm on my fifth Celis as the game ends and feeling pleasantly fuzzy, and we lounge for a moment, satiated.

"How about some poker?" Hugh then asks. "Everybody got some change?"

"You're a wild man, Hugh Kromer," Ron says from somewhere to my left, although penny-ante poker may in fact be living on the edge for a deacon from Waco First Baptist. So we indulge him. He is the honoree, and besides, cardplaying is one of the manly arts. It's part of our genetic heritage, as impossible to disavow as testosterone, and further, is a Texas artifact like six-guns and longhorns, although we ultimately look less like off-color desperados in a border cantina than off-duty doctors in an episode of M*A*S*H.

"Okay," Wally says, some time later when it is again his deal, picking up the cards and shuffling awkwardly, as is his wont. "I've got another game for you."

"We're not playing Indian Poker again," Terry tells Wally, kindly but firmly.

"Okay," Wally says. "How about a game of Dr Pepper?"

We shrug and assent; Waco is the birthplace of Dr Pepper, and although this is another of Wally's silly games—in this one the tens, twos, and fours are wild, like the old Dr Pepper slogan that invited you to Pepper Up at ten, two, and four—and ridiculous poker hands are common, five of a kind and such, I am able to pick up my cards and remember that we are here to celebrate with a good man his forthcoming happiness and besides, I've got nothing better to do.

"I propose a toast," Wally says, much later, after I have lost almost all my small stake of pennies, nickels, and the occasional quarter. He too is getting pleasantly misty, and it's possible that Hugh will end up driving him home instead of vice versa. "To Richard, wherever he is." He looks up and his hat threatens to fall off his head. "Richard, if you can hear us, we miss you. You should be here."

"To Richard," Ron says, a maudlin shine in his eyes.

"To Richard," Hugh affirms.

We raise our mugs to Richard, and suddenly our future becomes clear to me. I see us, all of us as old as Hugh is now, sitting around a table drinking to absent friends, a roll call of the dead that will eventually tax our recalls to the breaking point. Each of us now seated here will follow Richard, some sooner than later.

"To Hugh and Caroline," I propose instead, raising my brown bottle. "May they have long years and great happiness."

"I'm on that," Terry seconds, and we drink.

Long years and great happiness. Well, hell, why not?

Surely somebody deserves it.

17

It would be nice to say that the wedding itself is anticlimactic, that Caroline and Hugh disappear into the sunset without any traumatic events to mar the proceedings.

It would be nice to say this, but, unfortunately, it would also be untrue.

It's not that anything goes horribly wrong, at least not for Hugh or Caroline, who are the people who really matter. The ceremony is held in the First Baptist Church sanctuary, of course, a beautiful domed space, perfectly suited for such a formal wedding. Hugh looks handsome, very dignified and hardly the worse for wear although we did keep him out until dawn. And Caroline looks lovely in the same wedding dress she wore when she married her first husband. Although some people might consider this either morbid or at least a curious lapse of taste, what Hugh has told us earlier is simply this: "She says her first marriage went wonderfully. Why mess with success?" And I can't argue with that. Ballplayers wear the same uniform during a winning streak. Why not a lucky wedding dress?

I wake up on Saturday afternoon about two. I have time to get in a ride before I start getting ready to pick up Becky, who expects me at six-thirty.

When I let Audrey out the back door for her pee and playtime I can see that it's a gorgeous sunny day, about seventy-five degrees, strong wind from the south, which is where the wind will come from for the next six months. When I get out on the bike I can also see that the sky is deep blue, not a cloud anywhere in sight. These all seem like good omens to me as I'm puffing through the first miles into the wind.

Nothing else on my ride indicates that anything is amiss. The dogs are penned up in their fence, I make it up the huge hill to Mooreville with energy to spare, and I almost coast home with the touch of wind like a gentle hand between my shoulder blades.

Audrey admittedly seems a little antsy when I return, and she follows me around the house whining and nudging me with her cold nose, but the Weather Channel says there is no inclement weather coming and no front nearby, so I tell her to just cool it, which she finally does by the time I leave.

I wear a dark wool-blend suit—it's hardly ever cold enough here to justify an all-wool suit—with a floral sort of tie, and I think I look pretty good. Since I so rarely make an appearance at my grandparents' church, I owe it to them to at least make a good impression on their peers, who hear—and probably believe—the worst of me.

The First Baptist Church of Waco has flitted in and out of this narrative, and although I have never had need to talk about it at length before, it is important at this point to establish a few facts. This evening—Hugh's wedding—will be one of the first times I have been inside the church in over fifteen years; although my parents and I were once members in good standing, I have attended only a few times since my family's funerals were held there. It's not the fault of the church, or the pastor—it's God's fault, if any fault is to be assigned. It's just that I couldn't help but remember the coffins—shiny metal on gleaming metal carts, the large ones for my parents at their ceremonies a month apart, and Carter's child-sized one, just about the right size for me—couldn't help but see them at the front of the church like a solar afterimage.

From that time on, First Baptist Church was haunted for me, and I wanted nothing to do with it.

I am not anxious to return.

Still, nothing good will come of putting it off. I knock on Becky's door promptly at six-thirty, and she opens it immediately. She is wearing a form-fitting navy dress belted at the waist and cut to about mid-thigh plus a single strand of pearls, carries a Dooney and Burke clutch purse, and looks absolutely tremendous.

"Ma'am," I say, offering her my arm, and she takes it. It is all I can do not to stare as we walk out to the car, and once we're safely ensconced inside, I break down and tell her.

"Da-amn," I say. "If you'll pardon my saying so."

"I'll pardon it as often as you want to say it," she says, and she puts her forefinger to my mouth in a loving way. "And you look very handsome. I bet we'll be the best-looking couple there." She is only half joking, and, I expect, only half wrong. We do look good together.

"I've missed you," she is saying, "but I have been awfully busy since I last saw you. Two papers, an exam, and a bibliography for Dr. Clark."

"Uhm," I say. I do not trust myself to say anything following that name, and I notice that she doesn't look back over at me until the conversation takes a different tack.

"They're going to have an orchestra tonight," I say. "Dancing. Drinking. Merriment."

"Not at the church," she says. This is not a question; all three of those things are stricken from the list of possible activities for serious Southern Baptists.

"At the convention center," I say. "The Brazos Room. It should be nice. It looks out onto the river. The bridge will be all lit up." And I just manage to stop myself before saying something about the New Year's Eve party to which I didn't invite Becky.

Perhaps she remembers all by herself. "You didn't say anything about going to the reception," she says airily. "Maybe I have plans for after the wedding."

"Oh, really?" She has plans for later about like Richard Nixon has plans for the election of '04, about like Pickett had plans for his charge beyond "Charge!"

"But I guess since you've asked so nicely and all." She gives me her best grin as I pass under the I-35 overpass and turn onto Fourth Street. "Did you say dancing?"

"I may have mentioned something about it."

"I love to dance," she says. "Are you a good dancer?"

"Tolerable."

We park in the lot to the north of the church, just across Fifth Street, and it takes a minute to find a space. A lot of people are already here. Hugh and Caroline are popular themselves, and between them they have a lot of kids who have a lot of friends. We pause for a moment to let cars pass, then cross Fifth and enter the church through the northwest portico.

"Where do you usually sit?" I ask Becky.

She points toward a section, but we are met by the ushers then, and I have to give her up to one of them, Hugh's nephew Ken, if I remember rightly, and follow her down to a pew near the front on the groom's side.

"I've never been this close to the pulpit in my life," I grumble, and a middle-aged guy in the pew in front of me turns around to smile his agreement.

"Well," Becky says, looking on the bright side, as she does so well, "we have a good view."

And indeed we do, for what there is to see. The ceremony is of the standard variety: love, honor, and obey, the kind where we are asked if anyone knows any reason why the couple may not be joined in holy matrimony. Since my only possible rejoinder is that marriage may be a bad idea in and of itself—at least it has so far proven to be so in my experience—I let it slide.

After Hugh has kissed the bride and the couple has been presented to us, we push toward the exit. I spy Ron up ahead, looking marvelously uncomfortable in a suit and tie, which I suspect is a clip-on, and also get a flash of Terry and his date, who are conspicuously brown among this white throng.

"There's Dr. Fuller," Becky nudges, and I look ahead toward the door, where he and Colby Clark are in deep conversation.

"Whoa up there," I say, stepping into a pew and pulling her along with me. "Let them clear out."

"Why? What's wrong?"

"Just trust me."

"Oh," she says, "okay," and we wait a moment, let another group jostle ahead of us. I don't see Madelyn nearby, but I can't imagine that Colby would come to such an occasion without her. Perhaps they won't go to the reception, but even as I think this, I realize that Colby will not miss the chance to schmooze with powerful people in more casual surroundings. The dean of the college will be there, the president of the university will be there: ergo, Colby will be there too.

"Come on," I say once Dr. Fuller has been joined by his wife and tottered down the steps. We go out to the car, then drive the five blocks to the Convention Center—in the year 1994, one does not walk any appreciable distance in downtown Waco, which at night bears a strong resemblance to Atlanta after Sherman burned it—and park across from it on the west.

"An evening of splendor awaits," I say as I open Becky's door and take her hand to help pull her out; the Healey must be pretty low-slung for someone wearing a tight dress, although it makes for a spectacular view for me.

"Thank you, Jeeves," she says in a similarly cheesy voice, and then takes my arm as we file in; it is reminiscent of Sandra Fuentes a few months earlier, but without the desperate grip.

Still, I recognize the similarity and although I am secure in the knowledge that this evening cannot possibly end as badly as that one did, Audrey's mood of doom before I left makes me suddenly and unaccountably nervous and my stomach tightens as we ascend the stairs to the ballroom.

The setup in the Brazos Room is so similar to Evelyn's dance that for a moment I have to look down, find Becky, and make certain I haven't somehow slipped sideways in time: circular tables, two stages, strategically-placed bars, and clumped groups of party-goers.

"Oh, this looks wonderful," Becky breathes, taking it all in. I tend to forget that although Becky Bradenton has lived a privileged life, it has also been a sheltered one. If Waco is some distance from the bright center of the universe, Tyler must be even farther into the benighted regions.

"Can I get you a drink? Wine, champagne, whiskey and water?"

"Oh, some champagne," she says. "When can we dance?"

"When somebody starts playing music," I say, she punches

me in the arm, and I get up to retrieve two glasses of champagne. A country band is tuning up on one stage, which means, I guess, that they'll be playing first. It's too bad. While I'm a pretty good swing dancer, most of the people here will wind up two-stepping or clogging up the floor with line dances.

Or maybe they won't. Most of these folks, after all, are Baptists, and most of the rest of them are still relatively sober. Maybe we'll have the dance floor to ourselves.

Or maybe we won't. As we're finishing our champagne, the band opens up with "Achey Breaky Heart," and suddenly it's a colony of lemmings speeding for the sea.

"I can dance to this," Becky says and looks up at me with puppy-dog eyes.

"Jesus," I say. "Okay. Come on." We shoulder our way past all the people doing the Achey Breaky and find a place on the far side where there's enough room to spin. Becky is a pretty good dancer. She's got a fine sense of rhythm, and she knows how to follow a man's lead, both of which are useful traits on the dance floor, and some—not me, necessarily—might argue, elsewhere in life. She can't, admittedly, twirl very well in that dress, but she sure looks good trying.

"Randy Travis," Becky informs me when the next song starts up, and after that, there's a slow one, and Becky slips into my arms and even though I'm trying to keep a discreet distance between us, there's unquestionably a body under that navy dress with which I can't help making stirring contact.

"You're a wonderful dancer," she sighs, her head on my shoulder.

"Thanks," I say, rolling my eyes. Idiot. I have been trying so hard not to impress her, but this one just sneaks up on me. The results are disastrous. Now I can see I might as well have plunged heroically into a burning orphanage, saved the spotted owl.

"I'm thirsty," I say when the dance is over, and we get more champagne and have a seat for a second. "I'm going to have to find my grandma in a second," I tell her, although I don't say that I'm going to take her out for a dance once I do; that would sound entirely too noble. I resolve to be a churl, an absolute unregenerate asshole for the rest of the evening; at the same time, I know I'm not going to have the willpower to carry out my resolution.

"Well I'm going to go powder my nose," she says. "How about if I meet you back here in just a second?"

So as she saunters off in one direction, I streak off in the other to find Evelyn. At last I spy my grandmother in deep conversation with a group of blue-haired society women from her church. I beg their indulgence, and drag her out on the dance floor.

"She's lovely," Evelyn says to me as I two-step her backward to some Bob Wills. "How old is she?"

"Not old enough," I say.

"Still," she says. "Where has she gotten off to? Have you lost another one already?"

"No such luck," I say. "She adores me."

"Uhm." No sympathy.

"No, Evelyn. Seriously. This girl would put my picture up in her bedroom like Donnie Osmond or something and talk to it every night before she goes to bed."

"How terrible for you," she says.

I spin her as an act of revenge and then steady her again. She is laughing.

"Well, if this one's too young, why don't you just find somebody closer to your age?"

"Not now, Evelyn," I say, and I threaten another spin. I think but do not say that I have found another one, only she's already spoken for, even if she was speaking to me.

"Your young lady is coming back," Evelyn warns as we file off the floor. "Would you like to introduce us?"

"I will," I say. Becky comes up expectantly, and I say, "Evelyn Cannon, Becky Sue Bradenton. Becky, this is—"

"Your grandmother," Becky says. "Sure, I can see the resemblance. How are you, Mrs. Cannon? Brad says such wonderful things about you."

Evelyn of course cannot truthfully declare the same, but all the same, she says, "And you're as lovely as he told us, my dear."

I am not the only one who recognizes the practical social value of a white lie.

"Bring her over to meet your grandfather," Evelyn commands, and points in the direction of Dr. Fuller, who has cornered Jackson next to one of the bars.

"Later," I say. The music starts up again, and Becky pulls me back out to dance.

"That's who I thought she was," Becky says when my ear is momentarily close to her face. "I've seen her at church and thought about going over and introducing myself, but I didn't want to presume."

"Of course not," I say.

"I mean, I figured you'd introduce me to them when you were ready to."

"Of course," I say.

After three more dances, we are again ready for a drink, and in any case, the country band is taking a break. We head toward the nearest bar as the dance band strikes up "Three Little Words," and I am concentrating on working our way through the crowd—a broad-shouldered and corpulent man in front of us wearing black cowboy boots and a gray suit seems to have taken it as his personal calling from God to stop traffic—which is the only excuse I can give for the way Colby and Madelyn manage to sneak up behind us without my seeing them, Colby in the lead and almost dragging Madelyn in his wake.

"Hello, old man," he says to me, strains for Becky's name, and settles for nodding his recognition. "Do grant Madelyn a dance so I can take her away satiated."

I look at Madelyn, who is hard-pressed to meet my gaze. "Would you like to dance, Madelyn, or is Colby forcing you to dance against your will?"

She looks at me then, at Colby, and nods curtly. "Please," she adds, not even looking me in the face.

"Will you permit Brad a short turn on the dance floor with my wife?" Colby asks Becky, a dazzling smile on his face. He can be a charming rogue when he puts his mind to it.

"Sure, Dr. Clark," Becky says, although she doesn't respond

to the smile, and her response is merely cordial. She looks at me to gauge my reaction.

"I'll be right back," I tell her. "Then we'll have that champagne."

"Okay," she says, her voice and her face neutral, and she takes a step backward. I take Madelyn's hand, which seems cold as a February morning, and we walk silently out to the mostly-deserted dance floor. The song has changed, or, more accurately, the orchestra has segued into another tune, something Gershwin-y that I'm sorry to say I don't recognize—maybe "Embraceable You."

Madelyn steps forward and I put a hand on her waist, take her hand in my other. She is stiff as cedar, and instead of our former grace together, dancing with her is now like wrestling sheetrock into place.

"How's Audrey?" she asks, at last, when the silence has become intolerable.

"She's fine," I say. "A little nervous, with the storms." I can't think of anything else to say, so naturally I babble on. "She's started shedding. Hair. Lots of hair. Everywhere. In the carpet, on the blinds, I found some in my cereal this morning."

"Good for her," Madelyn says, and there is silence for a few more moments, before she says, "You couldn't wait another week or two out of grief, I see. Jesus, you're all alike."

"What are you talking about?"

"Your little blonde welcome mat. Well, she's probably more your type anyway." I can see that again, without meaning to or planning to, in some unaccountable way I have hurt her deeply.

"I never said that," I say. "And I wouldn't. You're my type. You have been all along."

"Oh, save it, Brad," she says. "I wouldn't believe anything I heard coming from your lips."

I bite back my first bitter response, take a deep breath, look around. "Colby is watching us," I finally say, because I suddenly realize that he is and has been, intently.

"Colby's an idiot," she says, and she spits it out as venom. "He wants to catch us in flagrante. He always has been six

months behind when it came to what was happening in my life. I guess this is just another example."

"What the hell does that mean?"

Before she can answer—if she was planning to—the song ends, and she's out of my arms like I was runny-sored with leprosy. I pull back her hand and give her an exaggerated bow; I am not above cruel and obvious irony, even if only she will recognize it.

"It was a pleasure," I say as I rise and look her in the eyes, and she pulls her hand from my grasp.

"I wish I could say the same," she says, but she can't maintain her cool. "Jesus, I didn't realize you were such a bastard," she says, and she clamps her lips together for a moment to keep me from seeing them tremble. "I was wrong about you all along. I thought you were someone with his head on straight, someone who had goals—"

"You thought I was a Colby who would be nice to you."

I don't even see her hand before the palm contacts my jaw, but it's a good ringing slap, the kind almost guaranteed to rise above the low crowd murmur and draw all eyes to you. I don't know what is worse, the sting of my red cheek or the knowledge that we have become the entertainment in the brief lull before the band strikes up—and the bandleader's choice here is inspired, I have to admit—"You Took Advantage of Me."

Madelyn walks slowly and with complete dignity to Colby's side, where she takes his arm and the two of them disappear into the open-mouthed crowd.

I do not have the luxury of disappearing, although Becky comes forward and takes my hand and leads me to our table, and I am reminded again how for another man she could be the perfect woman, beautiful, smart, and loyal to a fault.

She hands me a glass of champagne—she has managed for herself—and draws up her chair close to mine and takes my hand, and I find myself telling her everything, absolutely everything, from the beginning.

"I'm sorry," I say, finally. "It's over now." And although no such words have been spoken between Madelyn and me, I know that these words are true, and that knowledge is as sobering as black coffee drunk in a cold shower. I say it again, as if to fully apprehend its significance: "It's over."

"I know," she says, and then she takes a deep breath, turns my face to hers, and says, "and I knew."

"You knew," I say. That slap must have jarred my brain; this I cannot yet grasp, and probably even repetition will not help, so I sit, blank-faced, and wait for her explanation.

"I've known for months. I saw her car parked in front of your house. Overnight." She can't quite say this and maintain her straight-on gaze. In fact, she turns away, hides her face, her shoulders shake, and she surreptitiously wipes away her tears before turning back around.

"I'm sorry," I tell her, and I am, again, as usual. "Come on. Let me take you home."

"We don't have to go," she says, and she raises her chin bravely, and I can see that if I ask her to, she will stick this out, will look everyone we meet for the rest of the evening square in the eye, will claim me without reservation or hesitation.

"Becky, you deserve better than that," I say, and I squeeze her hand. "You deserve better than me."

"I think that's for me to decide, isn't it?" she says. I don't know what they put in her drink the first time we met, but it should be patented and marketed worldwide. The planet would be a markedly better place to live.

"Listen," I say. "It's okay. Let's go. I'll make it up to you somehow. I'll think of something."

"I've got some ideas already," she says. I can see the gleam in her eye and I know that I'm going to have to get those ideas out of her head right away.

"Not tonight," I say, after we complete the gantlet and start down the stairs. "I don't think I'd be much good to you or anyone else tonight."

"Okay," she says. "But soon. Remember, you owe me, and I'm not going to let you wiggle out of your obligations. Even though I like the way you wiggle."

"I pay my debts," I say, and I will. Who knows? Without Madelyn in the background, maybe I'll even enjoy it. Maybe

Becky and I will live happily ever after. Maybe we were meant for each other.

Maybe, as Charlie Brown used to say, I will flap my arms and fly to the moon.

After I drop her off and kiss her good night, I drive straight home, even though I know I won't sleep. What's worse, there's nothing on either ESPN or ESPN 2, no worthwhile trash sports, nothing on any of the other channels that doesn't have some disturbingly personal relation to love, lost love, or simple primate lust.

It is yet another of the longest nights of my life—I begin to wonder if somehow I've been mystically allotted extra darkness hours—and I am profoundly grateful when the orange starts to spread across the eastern horizon. As soon as it is light enough, I go out to my bike and set off. At the turn where I should head toward my dogs I keep going straight on Farm Road 3148, down a long hill to the I-35 overpass, and then I cross over to the west access road and continue pedaling south. This access road goes, with an occasional break that can be negotiated, at least as far south as Temple, thirty miles farther on, and I-35 goes as far south, of course, as Old Mexico. Theoretically I could ride south until I either collapse bodily or wind up in another country, and I have half a mind to do one or the other. Maybe both.

At the top of a hill a few miles farther on, I reach a field radiant with wildflowers in the early morning light, Indian paintbrush and bluebonnets. The breeze carries a scent like a beautiful woman; my allergies kick into overdrive.

So I ride south sniffling, tears running down my face as though I've suffered the greatest loss of my life.

Maybe I have.

18

April goes; May comes; Audrey sheds; my grandfather pesters me to play golf; Becky and I become lovers again.

I relate all this simply to prove that I am capable of telling a straightforward story, of getting to the point, of eschewing—as they say—superfluous verbiage. But you know, somehow none of these blank-faced facts looks the least bit interesting without the details, without the embellishments, without a few sensory impressions here and there. So let's admit it: this is an experiment that fails, not one where the reagents blow up in your face, simply one where they lie there in the beaker and do nothing at all.

My way may be slower and it snakes its tortuous, sinuous way through the mountain passes, but the journey itself should be important, should it not? If I have learned nothing else from a life in which each day I spend hours traveling in a thirty-mile circle, I have learned this.

If not for the wildflowers, which are omnipresent, and have expanded from the well known—the black-eyed Susan and Texas thistle and goldenrod and various daisies—to varieties that I have to look up, Indian blanket and Mexican hat, lemonmint and basketflower, spiderwort and chocolate flower (a task for which I could certainly use the help of someone versed in the sciences, I might add, if such a person were still known to me) and the blustery breezes, and the spring showers—this is a lot of qualifiers, I realize, and the thrust of the sentence may have disappeared long ago—if not for all of these things, I would be perfectly happy as I pedal gamely around my circuit. The weather is warm, and thoughts of my winter illness are far away; it almost seems like something I dreamed, something someone told me about, certainly not something that ever happened to me.

Audrey, of course, doesn't take well to the spring thunderstorms, and I have to make two emergency trips to the vet just to lay in a sufficient stock of her doggie tranquilizers. The first time they don't believe me—or just don't listen to me—when I ask for as many pills as they can give me, because when I get home and open the envelope, only ten of them plink out onto the counter, and at her most paranoid, Audrey can go through these in a couple of days, like me with my tiny green antihistamines.

"Listen," I tell the pleasant little man behind the counter when I go back, "I need a lot of Acepromazine. A lot. Not a little. A lot." And I brandish a visual aid, a swatch of carpet Audrey has shredded in the grip of storm-fear. "This is what she will do to my whole house if it storms and I don't have enough medicine for her."

The envelope I carry home this time is bulging, although what both Audrey and I would certainly prefer is clear skies and no rain through August. Damn the farmers; my canine has a monkey on her back.

That, and she has become a serious source of fiber. She begins shedding in earnest in April when it first hits eighty, and she goes on from there exponentially. I get on my hands and knees in my bedroom and rake together softball-sized handfuls of her auburn hair from the carpet with my fingers, and there's more there that I'm not getting, lots more.

In fact, she keeps shedding, day and night, outdoors and in. It is a miracle on the order of the Galilean loaves and fishes; the mass of the hair she has shed eventually exceeds her total mass, and there is no sign of slowing. You would expect her to be Chihuahua-bald, but I can't even tell a difference.

Between her storm paranoia and her fallen follicles, Audrey drops off my list of favored creatures in April and May.

I'm not sure, to be totally honest, who would be up there. I myself am not the easiest person to get along with, and everyone notices it. My buddies think that including me in their banter, maybe ribbing me about cradle-robbing, will snap me out of it; Becky thinks that fulfilling what she imagines to be every one of my sexual fantasies will bring me back; Evelyn thinks I should get more involved with those less fortunate than myself, although at the moment I'm not inclined to admit that there are any such people; Dr. Forest keeps after me about coming back to school and finishing my book; Jackson wants me to go out on the links with him some morning and thwack a three wood off the tee, view the graceful parabola of white onto the distant green; me, I don't know what to think. Perhaps one of them—or all of them—is right.

So since I don't know what to think, I do what I know best. I eat, occasionally. I sleep, fitfully. I ride, faithfully.

None of these things, however, gives me sufficient comfort, however, and it is all I can do to keep Elaine Rosenbaum from hopping the next flight to DFW when she first hears my voice.

"What in God's name is wrong with you?" she asks, all adenoids and distress. "I thought I had heard disaster and distress in your voice before, but you have achieved new levels of audible grief."

"Nothing has happened," I tell her. "I'm riding my bike. I'm cleaning up after my dog. I'm having sex with a twenty-one-year-old English major."

"Back up," she says. "I think I was with you up to that last sentence. You're sleeping with a coed?"

"Not sleeping. Having sex."

"Well. Thank God for that." The distinction is lost on her. "Listen, Brad. I don't suppose you've considered writing your way out of this depression?"

"Sure I've considered it," I say, and I clam up. I just want to see how long she'll lean forward in anticipation before biting. I must be feeling at least a little better; my sense of timing is returning.

She bites. "And?"

"I rejected the idea completely. I did get a new computer, though. It has all the audiovisual stuff. Multimedia. They have great games for it. Lots of explosions and stuff."

"I'm sure," she says dryly. "You know, Brad, you're a very difficult person to feel sorry for. I was trying desperately to, and now I'd just like to strangle you."

"I know," I tell her. "It's not your fault. I've always turned away from sympathy. It's an unattractive character flaw, but there it is."

I can hear a rustle of papers, and her business voice comes on the line, the voice she always uses when she wants to draw the line between herself as my ex-wife and herself as my literary agent. "Well, you'll call me if you change your mind about that?"

"Absolutely," I say, and surely I would. "Hey, let's meet at the Met and take in the new wing. Some good art would cheer me up, don't you think?"

"Seen it. How about that little Mexican place we used to go to over by your grandparents' house? The one we used to walk to, down past the car dealerships and across the railroad tracks. Remember, we used to get those take-out chicken tamales?"

"Saltillo's?" I can't believe she remembers this place; when we went there, all I ever heard issuing from Elaine's lips were worries about exotic Mexican parasites.

"That's it," she says excitedly. "That's the place. I can taste those tamales. Is it still open?"

"It is. See you there in twenty minutes?"

"Synchronize watches," she says. She didn't escape our marriage scot-free, I can see; her old loving voice is back as she bids me good-bye. "Take care of yourself, Brad."

"I'll do my best," I tell her, although I know that this will be small comfort; she has seen my best. "So long, kid. See you on the road."

On the road is where I am every day now, rain or shine. It's good for me, really, or so I tell myself, to put myself through this misery. It beats other misery I could be putting myself through.

There are other kinds still out there, as I discover.

The first week of May, a slightly-overcast day which is supposed to be my window between two days of hard rain, I make my first leg without difficulty. The wind is, unaccountably, light and out of the west, which means it will be of little moment to me, since almost no part of my ride is directly into or away from it.

But the dogs are out. They are covered with mud as they emerge howling from the culvert into the road; digging their way under the obstacles their owner has left them is tunneling worthy of a World War Two prison camp escape, and I could admire such resourcefulness and determination were I not suddenly busy being the object of it.

It is immediately reminiscent of the last time they escaped, the infamous Lookout Dog on the Roof episode: they swarm me, the black mongrel charges out in front of me, and that's the last thing I can remember clearly.

I can piece together what must have happened next, of course; the possibilities are strictly limited. I am speeding down the hill, the dogs all around me, when suddenly the black dog turns, too close for me to avoid, let alone brake, and I hit him.

I hear him yelp, cut the wheel hard to the right to try and keep from running completely over him, feel the bump that tells me I have been only partly successful, and then my front wheel is somehow perpendicular to the frame, the handlebars wrenched from my hands, and I am skidding—it could be wet blacktop or gravel or the simple will of God, all of which are equally mysterious to me—and then the front tire finds traction again, bites hard, and the bike comes to a brisk halt. My body, however, keeps going, over the handlebars, and translates a less-than-graceful somersault into the culvert. I land flat on my back with an impact that for a moment recalls Ron Sloan, and I instantly regress fifteen years. Just after I hit, I remember thinking that I'm going to get up and kick his ass, coach or no coach.

But I don't do that. I don't do anything. I don't know anything.

And I don't know how long it is until I do know something, but it can't be too long, because I can still hear the dogs yelping, all of them—the one I ran over and the others keening in sympathy—and I suppose it will be only a moment before they stream over the lip of the ditch and down upon me to tear my throat out. I'm lucky they haven't done it already. That is a galvanizing thought, and my immediate impulse is to get to my feet, to at least go out swinging, to take a couple of them with me. Furthermore, I now recognize the strange sensation I've been feeling as wetness, realize that I'm lying ear deep in stagnant water, and thoughts of typhoid and water moccasins are close to the surface of what currently passes for my consciousness.

But I can't move. I'd like to; I will myself to. But the pain I've felt before in this vein, bad as it was, just doesn't compare. When I try to raise my head, there is an excruciating searing agony at the base of my neck, crystal knives shattering in my spine, and it's as though my skull weighs tons; I can't sit up. I can't even lift my head out of the water.

Neither can I roll over and slowly push myself to my feet. Lying at the bottom of the culvert, I am effectively wedged in between the sides; to roll over, I will have to risk my face sinking beneath the brackish water, and of all the horrible ways I can think of to exit the planet, this one would be way up there.

So I lie in the ditch and listen to the dogs scream and consider joining them. The water is chilly, I am in the worst pain I have ever known, and my immediate prospects for relief are not promising.

I've always been curious how I would react to extreme physical torment, the agony of a gunshot wound, say, or a car wreck, and I have the presence of mind to be somewhat pleased with myself. Unlike my canine tormentors, I don't whine. I take it like a man, whatever that means nowadays. I breathe shallowly, because to breathe deeply hurts more, for some reason; my breath whistles between my teeth, and the muscles of my stomach contract over and over as I try to double over with pain, and of course can't, since I can't sit up.

I have heard that angels sometimes appear to men and women in such dire moments; at this point I would be willing to settle for the extraterrestrials I read about in the headlines of supermarket tabloids, even if they kidnap me and do anal probes.

Then I hear a voice, and I concentrate: angel or alien?

"Are you all right?" It is the farmer who owns these dogs, and remembering the irate Texan who not so long ago wanted to rub me out for aggravating his pets, I am momentarily unsure if he is asking me or the dogs.

"My God, you should be more careful."

Definitely the dogs.

Except he is perched above me at the top of the culvert, miles away, it seems, although it can't be more than two or three feet, plus his not-considerable height. I observe that he is sixtyish, with a kindly face and wisps of gray hair escaping from beneath his feed cap. Dekalb, it looks like, is the brand name above the brim, an ear of corn with wings emerging from it their logo.

"I seem to be stuck," I tell him.

"Stuck in the mud?" He considers my position and the depth of the water, and while he seems willing to give me the benefit of the doubt, you can see he has his reservations about that as a theory.

"No," I grunt. "Stuck here. I can't move."

"All right," he says, and he shouts back to the house, "Call an ambulance, Doreen."

"Much obliged," I say, slipping into the proper dialect. "I don't guess I should move." I say this with genuine regret.

"Probably not," he agrees. "Where you hurt?"

"Neck," I say. "Maybe other places." I can't rightly say at the moment; that pain is so intense it obliterates any possible competition from weaker sources.

"I'm awful sorry," he says. "Those dogs are terrors. We do our best to keep 'em in the yard, but—"

"Yeah," I agree. "I know."

"Can I get you anything? Do anything for you while we're waitin'? Call anybody?" He's being awfully solicitous, and is probably a genuinely nice human being. Of course, it's also true that we live in the most litigious society on earth as well as the one with the highest per capita of lawyers, and I'm lying in the ditch across from his house with a pretty good claim to negligence, pain, and suffering.

"I guess you could call somebody," I say, but who? If I call the grandfolks, they'll start to get the idea that I'm a permanent invalid or a walking magnet for disaster, and they will nag me accordingly for the rest of my life, or theirs, whichever is longer. If I call Becky, she will nurse me, as she once promised to, probably to madness. I give Hugh's number; he's retired, he should be home, and sure enough, he is. By the time the ambulance arrives, he is there to gather up my bike and follow me to the emergency room.

I have a slipped vertebra in my neck, just at the base of my skull, and the emergency room doc hands me over to a specialist, some neuro-mensch who prescribes pain pills and a lot of bed rest. "If it doesn't heal up," he tells me happily, without looking up from my charts, "we can always go in."

"Great," I say. Even with the pain pills kicking in, I am lucid enough not to applaud the notion of anyone monkeying around with my spinal cord.

"I've got to call Jackson," Hugh says, when they turn me loose and he is driving me home.

"Negative," I say. "I'll tell him, in my own good time."

"Brad, I can't leave you alone," Hugh says. "You can't even get out of bed on your own."

"We'll call Becky," I say. If you're forced to have a nurse you should at least pick a beautiful one, and she should have some time on her hands now since she is finishing up her finals.

"Okay," he says. We arrive at the house and he helps me get out of the car—it takes a long time, since I can't seem to turn my neck. I have to turn my whole body instead, slowly, and slide out an inch at a time. It hurts. The so-called painkillers, I am discovering, are, at best, only kidnappers; they take the pain far enough away that I can't see it, but I can still talk to it by telephone.

"I'm going to get you some water and put your medication next to the bed," Hugh says. "Can you dial?"

"Push the buttons," I correct him, dreamily.

"Right," he says. "Here. Tell me the number."

I tell him the number, and then I seem to float off someplace. When I wake up, Becky is perched at my side, her hand feeling my forehead for fever—I don't have any—and I smile up at her.

"Thanks for coming," I tell her. "How're finals?"

"All done," she says, and waves her hand dismissingly as though to say it is the last thing on her mind. "Didn't I tell you? Didn't I always tell you this would happen out there? Well, here I am."

"Silver lining," I grunt. The pain is coming back, and when I try to turn my head a fraction to look at her my stomach knots up again. "Anyway, you said something would run over me. It was—other way around."

"Does it hurt?" she asks, her face furrowed with concern, her hand still on my forehead.

"Does childbirth?"

She gives me another pill and a glass of water, assures me as I drop off that she is taking good care of Audrey, and maybe she is. "Check the weather," I remind her, and then the next thing I know it is the next morning and the phone is ringing and Becky is answering it in her electric blue silk pj's, button-up top and pant bottoms, an outfit cut like men's pajamas although Julia Roberts would look at home in it.

"It's your grandfather," she says. "Can you talk to him?"

"I better," I say. I try to sit up, but there's no change in that part of my condition and it's all I can do not to gasp from the pain. "You'd better hand it here."

"I was going to ask you to play golf," Jackson says when I answer, "but now I've got other fish to fry. Who's that? What's she doing there? Is it the married woman who slapped you or the coed who adores you?"

"Adores," I grimace.

"And what does she mean 'Can you talk to him?' "

"I had a little accident on my bike," I say. "I'm pretty stiff. Becky came over to look after me."

"Stiff where?" he asks. "Wait. Don't answer that."

"Neck," I say, disregarding him.

"You been to the docs?"

"Yeah. Painkillers and bed rest, they say."

"Well I'll tell you what, son," he says, "this time if it's not better in a few days, I'm dragging you over to my chiropractor." Jackson has recently been visiting a bone-popper to relieve the back pain he gets on the golf course, and he swears by it.

"Maybe," I say, meaning "No way in hell," but three days later, when I still can't turn my head and there are no signs that I am getting better and several that I'm getting worse—I feel dull pain that keeps me awake even with the drugs—I let him take me to his chiropractor, Dr. Bennett.

At the intake, I fill out a form that has a diagram of the human body—"Mark the locations of your pain," and I do so—and a straight line continuum that runs from "No Pain" on the far left to "The Most Pain I Have Ever Experienced." I place a large "X" way down at the far right of the line.

I don't meet Dr. Bennett for half an hour. First a gloomy female technician takes X rays and develops them while I sit in a waiting room with a large horizontal padded table, leaning my head back against the wall, a position that seems to be the least uncomfortable I can find. At last, Dr. Bennett enters. He is a large, bearlike man in his robust fifties, surprisingly handsome and very well dressed. He has on a crisp white oxford button-down, a silk Repp tie, navy slacks, and Cole Haan loafers, and there is a slightly tangible scent of musky aftershave in his wake.

After he shakes my hand, firm grip but not a vigorous shake since he doesn't want to jostle me, he puts my X rays up on an illuminated board. "Here," he says, pointing to a disk in the forward view that even I can recognize is way out of whack. "Your C-7—that's the number-seven cervical disk—has slipped back and to the left. The pressure on your nerves is causing the pain, although the stiffness is probably muscular. Your muscles don't like it when your bones are misaligned. Were you in a car wreck?"

"Something like that," I say.

"Headaches? Any numbness of the arms, tingling?"

I nod before realizing what a mistake that is, and he writes down "brachial ridiculitis" and "peristesia," words I foggily resolve to look up some day and never do.

Then he explains what he will be doing to me, and I take in as much as I can through the fuzzing haze of the pain: he will not be popping things back into place like I've always heard; instead he'll be freeing them from the unnatural alignments they currently occupy, and with some exercise and toning, we'll hope that the body will be able to keep them in more natural positions.

"I'll want to see you every day at first," he says after he's positioned me facedown on the table and his big dry hands—unlike the rest of him, they smell of clean fresh disinfectant soap—have descended on either side of my spine. He pushes down with tremendous force, his fingers precisely placed, and I hear my spine crack, a sound audible in my ears and through my bones, and I curse Jackson for bringing me here. Before, I was only in excruciating pain; now I'm both in agony and permanently paralyzed below the neck.

"Relax," he tells me. "This will hurt at first, and there will be some residual muscular soreness. I'll prescribe some physical therapy that should help loosen up your neck muscles—they're frozen solid right now—some heat therapy and ultrasound, and some electrostimulation. Then I'll send you an ice pack to put on it at home."

He moves down my spine, from my shoulders all the way to my lumbar, popping along the way, each time compressing me against the table like you would knead dough against a countertop. Then he works on my shoulders themselves, around the shoulder blades, and he pushes with such vigor and the pain is so great and the noise is so much like a string of firecrackers going off inside my body that I grunt and drool onto the headrest. Then he turns me over on my back, takes my head in his hands, and in two swift and devastating movements, pops my neck, first left and back, then right and back.

"You've got very little range of movement there," he tells me, or I think he tells me. I am trying very hard not to occupy my body, which hurts so much at the moment that I would gladly donate it to medical science. "It's going to take a while to get it back to normal."

"You mean we're going to have to do that again?"

"Now, it wasn't all that bad, was it?" He helps me up—he has to—and rubs my shoulders briskly like a coach sending me out into the big game. "I'll see you again tomorrow. You can make an appointment with the receptionist. Here's the address of the physical therapist. Have your granddad drive you over there now, if he will."

"He'll have to," I say.

In marked contrast to the session at the chiropractor, which seems like pure Spanish Inquisition—just short of stretching on the rack and boiling in oil—the physical therapy is pure indulgence. After the therapist reviews Dr. Bennett's recommendations and assigns me some light neck and shoulder stretches to loosen up, one of his assistants, Holly, a petite woman who seems to be in her twenties but goes on to talk about her teenage kids, gives me a long massage while I lie on my stomach, turning me to liquid beneath her surprisingly strong fingers as she works on my sore neck and moves down my back. Then she does ultrasound—which feels mostly like almost uncomfortable warmth after the initial shock of the cold metal head—and the only thing I don't like—which is attach electrodes to my neck and shoulder muscles and stimulate them with low-voltage electricity; I feel like some kind of galvanic experiment, a twitching frog, my neck muscles spasming out of control. After I've endured that, though, she flips me over, wraps me in hot packs, and leaves me staring at the ceiling—white, textured, one vent blowing cold air—and listening to the greatest hits from the Seventies, Eighties, and Nineties, a tiny timer clicking away on my chest to announce to the world when I am done.

This is the routine I assume for several weeks: manipulation and bone-popping in the morning, followed by an hour of physical therapy, followed by alternating periods of applying the ice pack to my neck, followed by a long nap on my new orthopedic pillow after lunch. Although Becky goes back to her apartment after I am somewhat mobile, she is still around a lot, and so she tells her parents she will be enrolling in summer school instead of joining them at the cabin they've rented on the Blackfoot River in Montana.

"Brad needs me," I overhear her telling her father, who is certainly arguing against the idea, against lots of ideas: her staying here, first, then her taking care of me, and maybe most importantly, my reliance on a chiropractor, for God's sake, instead of an M.D., someone who has actually studied medicine.

"Give him my best," I call to her. He has suggested that I come up with Becky as soon as I'm feeling better and the two of us will go fly-fishing on the Blackfoot. He is convinced that you can take the measure of a man—determine his actual worth and truest self—by fishing a river with him. Although I would love to be standing in a frigid mountain stream casting for trout—it has begun to heat up here in Texas, and it will continue getting hotter for several months until either October comes or the entire state bursts into flames—I am reluctant to go because I think this idea of his is right on target, and while I'm not really concerned about him discerning the true me—frankly, I think he's got me pegged pretty well—I think I can say the same about him. I don't want to know the good doctor any better than I already do.

Wonder of wonders, I get better. I would not at first have believed it, but I begin to anticipate Dr. Bennett's big hands in the same way I look forward to Holly's tiny ones. When I lie there trustingly on the table and smell Dr. Bennett's hands, feel them take my head gently but firmly, for some reason, I think of my father. Maybe I am undergoing what psychiatrists, teachers, and health professionals call "transference," the movement of positive feelings related to a positive experience to the person who most directly seems to be the agent of that experience, but the facts are simple and incontrovertible, no matter what the AMA says, no matter what Wally says, no matter whether Blue Cross will pay for this or not: I was in terrible pain and now I am not; I could not move my head a fraction of an inch and now I can peer back over my shoulder; I was suffering, and now I am well, or almost well.

After three weeks of daily treatment, Dr. Bennett gives me the okay to ride my bike, drops my bone-cracking to twice weekly, and ends the physical therapy, to my regret. I have grown fond of Holly, would gladly hit on her, despite her kids, her husband, and her indifference to me as anything other than a patient. It's hard to believe that we could share something seemingly so intimate and actually be so distant, that her fingers on my flesh could mean so much to me and absolutely nothing to her, but that is the state of things, which is too bad.

I would like to meet another woman, and Holly and I have shared a lot of words, have talked of many things in the hours I have spent motionless and in her care. This is always the hardest part anyway, and it is the part I told Evelyn that I didn't have the energy for anymore. I am with Becky now. We are a couple in word as well as deed, purely by default.

De fault of whom? Who can say. Perhaps it's simply meant to be, one of those things that happens and for which no blame may be assigned. It certainly seems natural enough. In late May, without my really inviting her to, she ends up staying at my place all night, and before I know what is happening, she has established a beachhead, part of a drawer, and room in the closet, and space for her makeup on the bathroom counter. She is cooking breakfast for me before she goes off to class, we are going out to dinner at La Cabaña and Lolita's and the Elite Cafe, to the movies, country-western dancing at Melody Ranch; she buys me a bike helmet and makes me promise to wear it whenever I ride; she and I take Audrey out for long walks in the warm evenings, and then when we come back, she wants to make love every night without fail.

The guys are apoplectic with jealousy, except possibly Hugh, who is still honeymooning himself. "What a life," Ron says, shaking his head and wishing it were his own.

I wish it were his too. I should be happy. I know that. I understand why everyone says so. Sometimes I even seem to be on the verge of feeling that way myself.

I will agree, then, with everything and everyone: I should be happy.

I should be.

I certainly should be.

19

It is the nature of human beings to miss that which is gone, just as it is the nature of life to make sure that things rarely stay the same. For all my bluff "Death is the mother of beauty" nonsense to Madelyn—ah, Madelyn!—I long for solidity, sturdiness, steadiness, simple monotony, and my life in recent years has been a motionless quest for those qualities. Perhaps my whole life has been, with the exception of my brief period of artistic madness; how else explain that I have lived thirty years in the town of my birth and have not traveled more than a few hundred miles beyond its bounds since the death of my family, that once a week I still buy Cokes from a Mexican restaurant I discovered as a teenager, that I still eat Sunday dinner with my grandparents, that I am living with a woman who is sitting the very same college courses I took ten years past?

I can recognize this, can see it as ultimately destructive of soul and spirit, can even be afflicted by a sort of low-grade nausea in reaction, and all the same, I can say to myself that the life I am living now is better than taking a chance on some radical change.

The past nine months have been physically trying—and mentally, and perhaps spiritually, if one considers such things—but as I reenter August, I feel like I am finally back in fighting trim. I can climb the Mooreville hill without shifting into my highest gears or weaving drunkenly from side to side.

At home, Becky has taken over an entire closet in the guest bedroom and half of my bureau drawers. She's rearranged the contents of my kitchen cabinets so that they are more accessible, and has cooked for me almost every night in the two weeks before she goes up to spend a few weeks with her parents in Montana, fajitas and enchiladas and even—on one tremendous gustatory occasion—chicken tamales.

Her parents, incidentally, are of two minds—since they are two people—about Becky's news that we are living in sin. Her mother is trying to take a modern and completely non–Southern Baptist attitude toward it all—"Well, if you kids are in love and just can't wait"—while her father has rescinded his fishing offer and I'm sure has privately promised to pistol-whip me within an inch of my life. I'm a little surprised after all that to find Becky wanting to go see them. I can't imagine that the issue will never once come up, but her family is a huge part of her life and has a tremendous hold on her. What they think matters to her, and when they're not around she misses them terribly. On our shared dresser she has crowded side-by-side individual pictures of each parent, a picture of the two of them together, a picture of Becky between them, and a picture of those three on the slip-covered couch with their loathsome cat Sunshine. I don't have that many pictures of my family in the whole house.

I half expect—and more than half hope—that Becky won't return from the mountains, that her parents will convince her of the tremendous mistake she is making in throwing herself away on me, but Becky confronts that possibility as she's packing.

"I don't do everything my daddy thinks I ought to do," and she turns around and smirks at me. "As you should know better than anybody."

"Point taken," I say, and I pat her once on her perfectly rounded rump as she bends over her suitcase and I go in to check the weather again—as though it's going to be anything but hot and dry—before we leave. I have taken to watching the Weather Channel in the same fashion that I once watched sports, as though my fervent hopes could alter outcomes; although it's been a peaceful summer for Audrey, we desperately need rain, which seems to be falling regularly in West Texas and New Mexico but hits some invisible barrier and disappears before it can reach us. It has rained in Dallas, one hundred miles to the north, and in Abilene, to the northwest, and often, of course in Houston, down on the

Gulf Coast, but not a drop have we seen since early June, and according to my favorite weatherwoman on the Weather Channel, it looks as though that will be the case again today.

"Now you take good care of yourself while I'm gone," she says when I drop her off at the Waco Regional Airport so she can catch the flight to Dallas that will be the first leg of an extended trip.

"Why does everybody tell me that?" I grunt, hoisting her bags onto the scale at the American commuter counter inside the tiny airport.

We wait for her departure to be announced—there is only one gate and one plane on the runway, so it should be hard to miss—and when she walks out onto the tarmac I kiss her good-bye. Once home, I down a tall glass of a new carbohydrate-loading drink Becky has bought for me at the local health food store. I am supposed to drink it before, during, and after my rides to replenish my minerals and crucial enzymes or something like that.

Anyway, it does taste good, Becky's logic makes a certain amount of sense, and it makes her happy; if it does at last turn out to be a fraud, it is no worse than other frauds I have perpetrated in the interest of making someone feel good.

After my ride, I take a long lukewarm shower—it's the time of year again when even the cold water is hot—and then I drink a couple of beers and watch a Rangers game. Will Clark still looks odd to me in a Rangers uniform, but he has one of the most beautiful swings in baseball, so as long as he's decently clothed, I don't honestly give a damn what uniform he wears.

1994 has been an interesting baseball season for me so far. The Rangers are doing well. My Cubs are, in a word, awful.

I haven't been keeping up with the Rockies, though Rockiemania continues and the mall sports shops are full of Colorado Rockies hats, jerseys, and jackets. I don't want to think about the Rockies. In fact, I can't even hear the word "Colorado" without thinking of Richard. The guys and I talk about him less and less, and it seems like a betrayal of some sort. I'd like to hold onto that pain, that suppurating sense of loss, because when someone is dead, what's left after you've lost loss?

But all the same, there are days when I don't think about him at all, even during baseball season, and someday soon his face will begin to fuzz around the edges in my memory, and a hundred years from now we'll all be dead, furry blurs in the memories of people we don't even know yet, so what does it matter?

Only it does matter, it *has* to matter, or maybe nothing matters, although I just can't let myself believe that.

Jackson calls during the late game from the West Coast, Atlanta and L.A., and I am a little brusque with him because David Justice is batting, another lefty who has a swing Leonardo da Vinci could have designed.

"What?" I growl when I pick up the phone.

"Don't 'What' me, young man," he says. "I'm calling to ask a favor, so don't make me crawl any more than I already am."

"Okay," I say, watching Justice step out of the batter's box and look up the line at the third-base coach. Hit and run. "Crawl away." I almost remind Jackson that I owe him a favor for his help on the basketball goal some months back, but if he has forgotten, I am not about to call it to his attention. I play dumb.

"I need you to help make up a foursome tomorrow," he says. "Note the word. Not *want*. *Need*. I'm meeting with two investors from California, brothers, who are thinking about buying a stake in Cannon Construction."

"And you want to close the deal on the golf course?" Justice goes down to pull a slider into right field and Gant scampers from first to third despite Strawberry's strong arm.

"Nowhere better. This is your future we're talking here. You've got a vested interest in this meeting."

"And you can't play with just three people."

The silence is ominous. You'd think I'd asked that he sodomize the Queen of England on a public beach.

So I tell him I'll come. It'll be early in the morning, not my best time of day, but at least the weather will be cool; Jackson wants to play on his favorite course, out near the V.A. Hospital, and it's a course I know—and have played—well; I am not expected to participate in the business conversation but simply to be amiable, nod occasionally, and not louse things up for him. I think I can handle it.

We tee off at eight-thirty, Roger Kramer and me in one cart, Jackson and Tad Kramer in the other. Tad is the eldest, and as such, the business-talker; Roger is my age, with a tan almost as dark as mine and absolutely perfect teeth.

I do admire that in a man.

We don't have much to talk about, of course. Roger has a real head for business, but is lousy on the golf course. I play surprisingly well after such a long layoff, not so well that it looks as though I'm showing everybody up, but I am an almost effortless four under through the front nine and have made some beautiful shots: a twenty-foot putt on a cross slope on Number Three; a chip shot from a sand bunker to within two feet of the pin on Five; a drive off the Seventh tee over towering pecan trees that would draw some oohs and ahhs if we had a gallery, which, unfortunately, we don't.

"Brad is quite a golfer," Tad says to Jackson as we approach Eleven, a short hole with green water partway across the fairway that's meant to intimidate duffers into wasting their time going a long way around it. The distance to the green is shorter than it looks, the water doesn't take up that much space, and I have been negotiating more difficult water hazards all day long.

"He has his moments," Jackson says.

"You're up," Roger says, and I tee up, address the ball, swing naturally, and the ball hooks terribly and unerringly into the water.

Kerplunk.

Roger and Tad look at me, then at Jackson.

"Shame to ruin such a beautiful game," Roger says. "Why don't you hit another one?"

"I'll take the penalty," I say, but they persist, and I load up, get set, and hit again.

And again the ball soars high, straight, and true for the water.

Suddenly I become aware of the pounding of my heart. I'm starting to get a little scared; usually when you mishit a ball you can feel it from the outset, you know from the time it leaves your club that it's wrong. But I haven't felt that on either of these shots, and it worries me.

Without asking permission or even looking up to get their reaction, I load up another tee, and then another, and yet another, until I run out of balls.

Plunk. Plunk. Plunk.

My approach is flawless, my follow-through is perfect, I look up expecting to see the ball sailing straight for the pin, and each one instead steers infallibly for the water, the surface of which is now a series of concentric circles colliding and eventually disappearing.

I walk back to the cart and sit, heavily, while the others tee off. I am through for the day, and while I make light of it, claim I was saving all my shank shots for one hole, I honestly don't know what to make of it. It's as though someone has greased the bottoms of my feet, and something that has always been as simple to me as walking has now become well nigh impossible.

"What the hell happened to you out there?" Jackson asks me after lunch, after we have dropped the brothers back at the Hilton, after they have agreed to buy into Jackson's business despite my heartless drowning of so many defenseless little white orbs.

I shrug.

"I guess you're just a few bubbles off plumb today," he says. "Probably mooning over that girl."

"What girl?" I say, but again he doesn't listen, which is too bad.

I still have no idea what plumb is, much less how I could get back to it. I have not solved that puzzle before I get home, check the mail, and get another shock, an almost equal take-a-seat shock, in fact. It's a cream-colored envelope that I think can't be—but is—from Madelyn, an invitation to the party celebrating Colby's new book from Cambridge University Press. I can see the trembling hand of Dr. Martin Fuller behind this invitation: I haven't seen Colby or Madelyn since she laid the Hand of Doom on me at Hugh's wedding, and this invitation has obviously been sent with a minimal regard for whether I attend or not: the party is tonight, at seven o'clock, and further, there is no handwritten addendum from Madelyn, as though I expected one.

"Tough luck, Dr. Fuller," I mutter, and I crumple the envelope into a tidy sphere. Audrey at least is happy to see me, and if I read the signs, is actually relishing our time alone. Becky diverts too much of my attention away from Audrey and doesn't give much in return, so she and Audrey dance a wary step around each other. But Audrey and I—we understand each other. Together we have faced the invisible fears, the night frights, and if we haven't overcome them, exactly, we are still here, doing the best we can.

"We don't need anybody else, do we, Audrey?" I say, ruffling her auburn hair, and she wags happily in response. Although I could do without the shedding, which continues unabated, I could not ask for a better companion: loyal, affectionate, accepting. I like to think that in this way, at least, some good has come of Richard's death, although I would give up Audrey in a moment if it would bring him back.

As her reward for being so wonderful, I take her for a long walk out past the new barbecue restaurant which I have wanted to try but have been afraid to enter because it's so far out here in the country that I feared they would seize on me as the solitary customer and place the sole weight of their success or failure on my head. I didn't ask them to build a restaurant out in the middle of nowhere, and I refuse to take responsibility.

On the way back, Audrey lags behind a bit; although she goes out with enthusiasm, like I do on my bicycle, her return is much more subdued. I give her a dog biscuit once we're inside the house, open a beer, and sit down to pet her as she crunches the biscuit between her teeth, then quests for any missing pieces on the hair-laden carpet.

The Cubs are on tonight from Shea Stadium, home of the hated Mets. I've got a package of ground sirloin thawing and have been looking forward all day to the way those hamburgers are going to taste fried in chopped onions and sopping with grease, topped by a couple of slices of sharp cheddar, some sweet pickles, Creole mustard and barbecue sauce. Pure heart attack heaven.

I have every reason to stay home and absolutely none to go off to some stuffy academic party no one even wants me to attend.

All the same, at seven-twenty, I find myself showered, shaved, and standing in front of the Clarks's front door, focusing all my willpower into a simple act: raising my finger to press the doorbell.

And I can't do it.

It's ridiculous. I've come this far without thinking, so why shouldn't I go that last mile? I should just push that button and bring matters to a head.

All the same, I can't. Sweat is running down into the small of my back. Under my linen jacket, I can feel the shirt sticking to my back.

Nope. Nope, nope, nope. I can't do it. I give up, drop my arm, turn to go, and just as I do so, several of Colby's colleagues—including Dr. Fuller and his wife—sweep up the sidewalk and welcome me.

"It was so kind of you to wait on us, my boy," Dr. Fuller says. He seems to be the only one who isn't surprised to see me.

"My pleasure," I lie, shaking hands left and right with people who won't meet my eyes, and then stepping forward with them as Colby opens the door.

I feel his gaze wash over me like cold seawater, but that's all there is to it. He says nothing, he doesn't stare, he simply invites us in, and I pass in as part of the group.

Madelyn is not so timid about expressing her feelings, if that is what Colby is being. When she spies me across the living room she gets immediately to her feet and walks back to the kitchen. I try to act as though I haven't noticed this, when actually it is the only thing I have noticed. I chew numbly on anything passed into my hand, sip from my glass, nod dumbly at everything said in my vicinity.

Madelyn doesn't come back. I begin to wonder if she's ducked out the kitchen door, if she's run screaming down the street. Surely she's not afraid to see me.

Maybe it's not that she's afraid. Maybe she's ashamed. Maybe she's finally come to her senses, seen me for what I am, and can't believe her own gullibility.

I take another glass of champagne. I can wait as long as she can. Longer, maybe. She has to come out at some point, be the cordial hostess, while I am under no such constraints. All I have to do is stand—I am good at standing—and wait.

Dr. Fuller works his way around to me at last; this is the unfortunate but unavoidable part of my plan. I am not hard to get to, since almost no one has talked to me this evening. I'm sure most of the people here recall what happened the last time the Clarks and I got together, with the obvious exception of Dr. Fuller, who probably doesn't remember what he ate for breakfast. The long list of people who have not talked to me includes Colby, who is drinking champagne like water and has begun to laugh, too loudly, at something Dr. Parkinson from the Religion Department has said.

"Well, my boy," Dr. Fuller says, "I hope you're getting plenty to eat and drink."

"Yes, I am, thank you," I say, and trying not to be obvious, I glance back over his shoulder to see if anyone has emerged from the kitchen. Nope.

"We're very proud of young Colby," Dr. Fuller is saying, and I turn back to him and nod politely. "Very proud indeed. He just became the youngest full professor in the university, you know."

"No, I didn't know," I say, darting my eyes back to the kitchen door.

"Someone like Colby would be a prime candidate for an endowed chair, wouldn't you think? I believe he'll continue to do the university real honor if we can manage to keep him."

"Keep him?" For the first time I give him my full attention.

Martin Fuller looks to left and right—there is no one near, of course—and goes through a little hand-wringing routine. "Well, I'm not supposed to know this, of course, but one finds out things—"

He pauses, gauges my trustworthiness. "I understand he has accepted some interviews with other schools. That he's not completely happy here."

I look across the room to where Madelyn isn't, and I begin to see a whole future made up of such absence, and my stomach seems to fold in upon itself. "Not happy? Why not?"

"I believe it's partly Madelyn," he ventures, and you can see

Dr. Fuller's frustration with his lack of knowledge even through the age and wrinkles. "I don't possess the whole story, you understand, but she's apparently asked him to check into teaching situations elsewhere."

I shift my gaze to Colby, who is chuckling, still, a little too loud. "And you think he might stay in Waco if he had an endowed chair?"

"Why, think of the prestige, my boy," Fuller says. "There are so few of them in English these days. With a suitable endowment, we could pay him more than other schools, could offer him research money, a reduced course load—"

"I'll talk to my grandfather about it," I say suddenly, and Dr. Fuller blinks twice in surprise, as well he should; this is the first time I have ever displayed any interest at all in his pet project.

"You are a fine alumnus," Dr. Fuller says, pumping my hand up and down with surprising briskness. "I'm sure something good will come out of this. I'm just sure of it."

"Sure," I repeat, but he has already lurched excitedly away through the crowd, perhaps to tell his wife, perhaps to find a bathroom. At least it wasn't to tell Colby, who he passes with only a simple pat on the back. The more I think of it, the less likely it seems to me that Colby is going to accept our money; I don't think his considerable pride would permit it. But maybe I'm wrong. Maybe Colby Clark would delight in taking our money. It can't hurt to try.

And speak of the devil, Colby Clark now weaves toward me, and it seems the room takes up its collective breath because it's apparent now that Colby is totally sloshed. Blotto. Extinct.

"See here, old man—" he begins. He sways for a moment, his head almost dropping to his chest, and then he recaptures his train of thought and lurches back erect. "See here, old man. What is this between you and my wife?"

I don't know if Colby realizes, but this is a scene—slightly cock-eyed, I'll grant you, but a scene nonetheless—straight out of *Gatsby,* and since I've read the book, I know that it is bound to end badly, no matter how I respond. I take a step backward and prepare to run for the door.

He matches my step and raises me one, edging closer and speaking in a low, oiled tone: "What do you say, old man? Have you been boffing my wife? Have the two of you—"

He breaks off as I look across the room and away from him, and he follows my gaze to spy Madelyn standing in the doorway of the kitchen.

He waves her away, and the party-goers are hard-pressed to pretend that they aren't paying attention to us. It gets harder. "Under control, darling," he calls back to her. "Go on."

She doesn't go on, but Colby turns around, and now he moves even closer and I feel his hot breath. "What about it, old boy? What do you have to say for yourself?"

He stands there swaying in front of me, waiting for an answer.

Maybe he deserves one.

Really, there is only one answer that explains it all, and I am seven kinds of fool not to have understood it before now. The knowledge floods through me, and I have to smile, even with the crowd gathered and waiting, the jealous husband invoking Marquis of Queensbury rules, Madelyn horrified across the room.

"I love her," I tell him, so softly I'm not sure it can be heard, so I repeat it. And I raise my hands in front of me, palms up, and shrug. What else is there to say?

"You love her?" he says, and then he throws his head back and cackles. "Do you hear that, old girl?" he calls back through the wide-eyed throng. "He says he loves you."

Madelyn is properly appalled, of course; although she preserves the placid face she always presents to the world, her eyes are stricken. The guests—even Dr. Fuller—have given up any pretense of not watching the floor show, and now they look avidly from us to her and back again like spectators at a tennis match.

Colby has turned away from me and is bent over and clasping his sides with laughter. Occasionally "loves her" comes out between chortles.

Madelyn isn't looking at him, though.

She's looking at me, and when our eyes meet, I nod. Yes. It's true. We hold each other's gaze for a moment, and I try to let her read that truth in my eyes, try to let her see that whatever else I have done or haven't done, whatever else I have said or haven't said, that love is a fundamental and unalterable truth of my universe.

Colby seems to be getting over his little laughing jag—now he is coughing, but not so often or so loudly as he was laughing—and Madelyn turns her head away, bites her lip, and slips back into the kitchen.

I too turn my head away, and something burns in the corners of my eyes, but one thing I can do is go, and go I shall. Once I'm outside I can catch my breath, clear my thoughts, decide how I'm going to live the rest of my life.

My shoulders slump, the air leaks out of me like a wounded tire, and I head for the door.

It isn't hard to hear him coming—his charge is hardly subtle—but I am sunk so deep into myself that at first I don't make the connection between the approaching noise and its source. The source, of course, is Colby, stumbling toward me, and despite his laughter and his Anglo-cool, he is more than loopy enough to take a drunken poke at me, wife-boffer, violator of the home. His punch is awkward, a long roundhouse that only connects with my shoulder—a glancing blow at that, since I hear him coming—but that impact is sufficient.

Someone should have warned Colby Clark never to come at me from behind.

I flatten him. There's no other way to put it: it's not a conscious act, or at least, not completely conscious, but I wheel, swing, and connect solidly with the right side of his head, just below his ear, and he takes three sudden steps backward and sits down for at least an eight-count. I'm surprised it didn't take his head off. I wish it had.

I don't wait to see if he gets up, though, because I have lost this fight, even if I won it. I take a quick survey of the faces—shock, amusement, horror—this last especially prominent on Dr. Fuller's face—throw open the door and walk down the sidewalk, then come to almost as sudden and stupid a stop as Colby just did in his living room.

Madelyn is sitting in the driver's seat of my car, her hands resting on the steering wheel at ten and two.

"What are you doing?" I say, softly.

"I'm your designated driver," she says. "You'd better give me your keys."

I take a giddy step forward and then catch myself. "Are you sure?" I ask. We are on the verge of making a decision that could be life-altering, heartrending.

"Are you?"

I look at her, sad face and beautiful brown eyes, and then I turn and look at the house we both recently exited. There is, as yet, no sign of pursuit, although a posse may be forming as we speak.

"Do you know how to pop the clutch?"

She nods, and for the first time this evening, a smile shoots across her face like a shaft of sunlight through dark clouds. I push the car away from the curb and then vault into the passenger seat. We build up speed going down the hill, Madelyn expertly pops the clutch, the engine starts with a throaty roar, and with a brief shared look—affection? commitment? sheer terror?—we motor off into the coming night.

20

That sounds something like an ending, and maybe it would be, in a different story, for a different person. Thing is, I have known all along that a woman—even a woman like Madelyn—is not the answer, have known that a woman will not complete me or give my life meaning. So while I read our escape together as a good sign, even a liberation of sorts, I am still monitoring myself closely. I want to see if I've changed something more fundamental than my female companion. I don't know what would tell me that I am ready to live life in a fundamentally different way, but I'm pretty confident I will know it when I see it.

We drive that first night in unexpected and unplanned directions, from Madelyn's house onto Highway 6 and on until we reach I-20 and then on into West Texas. It's a beautiful night, warm, clear, and dry, and in between towns, the stars seem remarkably close. We get gas in Abilene, trade places, and keep driving on, not talking much, although the things we do say seem to be of some importance.

"I told myself that if you came tonight I would know," I hear her say shortly after we leave Waco, but when I ask her, "Know what?" she just shakes her head and doesn't answer.

And after Abilene, she turns and looks at me, and finally shouts, above the roar of the wind, "I still have no idea who you are!"

"I'm not sure I know myself," I tell her, and she bites her lower lip—maybe it's not too late to turn around—and then says brightly, "But that's good, don't you see? Because now you can be whoever you like." And she turns back toward the front of the car and crosses her hands primly in her lap. When I glance over at her, although she doesn't look at me, she has the slightest of smiles still shaping her lips.

There is a near-total void on the radio for some time, nothing but crackling static whenever I lean over to check. We do occasionally pick up a Cowboys exhibition game being broadcast from the West Coast, and once out in the total desolation—nothing but flatland and dark clumps of mesquite and sagebrush as far as we can see in the moonlit night—we began to pick up all sorts of AM signals: Tejano dance music, a Hispanic radio evangelist singing the joys of Jesu Cristo, a country station from Lubbock, stations from Tulsa and Des Moines and New Orleans.

It is well past midnight when we stop for the night in Odessa, and it is an event of some historical significance: it is the first time I have ever checked into a hotel with a woman not my wife and tried to pass her off as such. I am unaccountably nervous—in the face of everything else, this seems like small potatoes, but there it is—and I am ready to invent elaborate lies, spin a skein of marital untruths.

But the hotel is part of a huge chain and the desk clerk seems only to want to get me out of the office so he can go back to sleep.

I myself can't sleep, and Madelyn is likewise restless, although she falls into a fitful slumber around four. I sit across from her in the uncomfortable thing the hotel calls a chair and watch her until I too doze.

It's a bad dream, the black car dream, and I wake shuddering, wake to Madelyn kneeling beside me and holding me as if I'm an Audrey. Somehow I have slipped to the floor without waking, and I'm lying half under the dresser.

"You were crying," she says. "I've never seen you cry."

"No," I say, and I sit up. "I don't guess you have."

She lets me stand up, and I walk over to the window, pull back the curtain, peer out into the widening daylight.

And she stands behind me. I can feel her standing there, waiting. I think I can outwait her, but I have not reckoned with her stamina. And of course, she is a woman who has just jumped out of an airplane at night and would really like to know something about her parachute.

So she stands. I can feel her presence, her eyes on me.

And at last, I turn around.

"Would you like to hear a story?" I ask.

She remains stock-still, but her lips curl upward slightly. "Is it a happy story?"

"No." I take a deep breath. "Not until now, anyway."

"But it might have a happy ending?"

"Anything's possible," I say.

"Then yes," she says. "I do want to hear a story." She sits, straight-backed, on the edge of the bed, and waits for me to begin.

There's so much I want to say, I hardly know where to start. But I smile a rueful grin, and I find a place: "Once upon a time," I tell her, "there was a miserable little shit named Brad Cannon."

I tell her about losing my family, Mom and Dad and Carter. I tell her how I was supposed to go to the Baylor/UT game with them in Austin that Saturday. "It was my brother Carter's birthday, you know. But I had a big fight with my mom in the morning, and so I told them I wasn't going. I told them that I wanted to spend the night at my friend Arlo's. He had a huge comic collection and a beautiful older sister who never wore a bra."

"Now the truth comes out," she says gently.

"They were so mad at me." I shake my head. "My mom wanted to ground me. My dad drove me around for over an hour trying to talk me into going with them. We listened to his new Boston eight-track twice all the way through. He just kept saying, 'Brad, it's Carter's birthday.' I didn't budge."

"So they went without you," she says.

"They went without me. They dropped me off at Arlo's, and Carter gave me this pathetic little wave as they drove off. Like he didn't understand me, but he still loved me."

"I know the feeling," she says, and I try to smile to reward her. This is the first time she's told me she loves me, if that is, in fact, what she's just done.

But when I start to tell her how my grandparents pulled up in front of Arlo's house while we were playing tetherball, how they got out of the car so slow and so stiff that I thought, Something's happened, something really bad; then I find that I can't smile anymore. "It was like a dream. No, like when something happens and you know that just a second one way or the other and it wouldn't have happened. And you think, if it didn't have to happen, then maybe it hasn't. Maybe it could be, like, some kind of cosmic mistake."

"I know that feeling," she says. She takes my hand between hers. "Only it wasn't."

"No. It wasn't. It was real and permanent. They were gone forever."

"Do you think it was your fault?"

"The wreck wasn't my fault. It could have happened anyway. But I didn't have to be such a shit to them. I could have apologized to my mom. I could have been kinder to my brother." I look down at the floor. I have thought these things my whole life, but this is the first time they've ever traveled outside my head. "I could have listened to my dad."

She nods, slowly, and I go on. "He told me that people had a responsibility to make other people happy, even if sometimes they had to give something up to do it. I told him I didn't want to give things up. He laughed, but it was a sad kind of laugh, you know? And it serves me right, I guess. I've been giving things up ever since."

I turn and look out the window again. "You know, my dad and I never talked about the things he didn't want to do. About his responsibilities. But Jackson told me once that my dad's greatest dream was to play baseball. 'Damn fool,' Jackson called him. 'Idjit.' Didn't he know a man had to have a reliable job to support his family? My dad graduated from Baylor with an engineering degree. But he taught me to read a box score. He took us to baseball games in faraway cities. And he never said a word to me about what he'd lost. Men in my family didn't talk about such things."

"They do now," she says, and I turn to her gratefully.

"Yes," I said. "They do. I think maybe my dad and I were more alike than I realized. But somehow he lost things without living his life like I've lived mine. It seems like maybe I could have figured this out before now."

"They weren't all you lost, though."

"No." I sigh. "They weren't."

And so I tell her the last of my story, the part everyone already knows—how Susie Bramlett died—and the part no one knows—that with her death I lost all hope. That I gave up. That I believed the world was a dark and angry place, just waiting to strip things out of your hands.

"It feels like my life is haunted," I say, words I have never said out loud in my entire life. "Cursed, maybe. Like the black car is still out there, somewhere, and he's not finished with me. That there will always be something new it can drag away from me."

She stands up and looks in my eyes and then takes me in her arms and holds me as though I am a newborn, holds me with gentleness and strength that will not let me fall.

And then, at length, she steps back and she herself steps over to the windows, pulls the curtains all the way open, and peers out over the vast expanse of parking lot and West Texas.

"What are you doing?" I say, blinking at the brightness.

"Is he out there?" she asks, stepping back beside me.

"Who?" I say, although I know full well who she means.

"Do you see a big black car in the parking lot?"

"Of course I don't."

"Are you sure, Brad?" She extends her hand like Vanna White indicating some goofy game show prize.

"Maddy, of course I'm sure."

She leans in close, so close that our faces are separated by inches, and she looks into my eyes. "Do you want to spend the rest of your life holed up in here just in case he's out there somewhere?"

I shake my head slowly. No. I do not.

"Do you want to spend the rest of your life checking the rearview to see if something is back there?"

I shake my head again. But it's not that simple; logic has no power over magic, and I've been afraid a lot longer than I've been hopeful.

"Think about it," she says, and she busses my cheek, and then she walks into the bathroom and closes the door. I hear the shower running. At last, I go in there and sit on the toilet.

"If you love someone, you're just going to lose her," I say. "That's all I know about life."

"What?" she says. "I'm washing my hair."

"If you love someone, you will lose her."

"Someday," she says, and she pulls back the curtain to look out at me, her head covered with suds. "But not today."

"No?" I say.

"Nothing is going to drag me away from you today. I promise."

"Okay," I say. She pulls the curtain closed and hums as she rinses off.

Before we leave, Madelyn stops me at the door, raises a hand to her mouth, and says, "What about Audrey?"

And of course, she's right. Becky won't be back for days, and once she gets there, I daresay she won't hang around, not even long-suffering Becky. I feel a momentary twinge, the same twinge that has made it impossible all along for me to break her heart face-to-face. So, like the total heel her father has always believed me to be, I guess I will have to do it from a distance.

I call Jackson, collect. He can afford it.

After he accepts the call—and I can hear the merely grudging acceptance in his voice—he asks, "Where are you, son? We're just on our way to church."

"You haven't heard yet?"

"Heard what?"

"Nothing," I say. "I just need you to go by and get Audrey, put her up for a while."

"What? Where are you?"

"Odessa, I think." Madelyn nods confirmation. "Yeah. Odessa."

"What—" He decides it's not worth another heart attack and asks a different question. "Well, how long you figure to be gone?"

"How long?" Good question. I look at Madelyn, who shrugs.

"I don't know," I say. "I can give you a better idea later. Don't worry about us, though. Everything's fine."

"Us?"

I hear Evelyn griping in the background, something about

how late they're going to be, and Jackson puts his hand over the receiver and is saying something about how her damnfool grandson has run off with some woman and Evelyn is giving him hell either for saying "damn" or for referring to her grandson in such fashion. I hang up. I'll call them back when they've had a chance to digest things a little better. At least I know that Jackson will swing by and pick up Audrey after church. Anything else can wait.

At Pecos, we get off the interstate so Madelyn can get a midmorning Diet Coke and I can get a Dr Pepper, and on a whim, we head north on 285. The country we are driving through is flat and dry, with patches of grass and scrub here and there, dotting the rocky reddish soil. We drive across wide sandy draws that probably fill up with heavy rain.

We eat lunch and gas up in Artesia at an Allsup's convenience store. The landscape has changed slightly as we've continued north into New Mexico: better dirt, more trees, even pecan groves.

"Where to now?" I ask, as we eat the burritos—not bad—and plot our next move.

"Mountains," she says. "Definitely mountains."

"I've never been to the mountains."

"Well, then, you haven't lived," she says, and maybe she's right.

Since I don't know what to expect from mountains, Madelyn has volunteered to drive so I can enjoy the view. Heading west on U.S. 82, they appear first, from about fifty miles out, as only a bluish ribbon on the horizon. As we draw closer, though, they become unmistakable: the features of the mountains become distinct, with gradations of color, browns, tans, and greens. By midafternoon we have climbed to the village of Cloudcroft, almost nine thousand feet high. The temperature, in the nineties when we left Artesia, is a good twenty degrees cooler up here, and there's a line of dark storm clouds approaching from the southwest that promises—can it be?—rain.

We do some shopping that night in Albuquerque, and after we've settled into our hotel, I call Jackson back. "Now where are you?" he asks.

"New Mexico. Did you get Audrey?"

"Of course. She's out back now chasing squirrels. Son, what's going on? Have you completely lost your mind? Running away is not going to solve anything."

"We're not running away."

"What would you call it, then?"

I take a deep breath. "There's two kinds of running, Jackson: away and to. I think of myself as something of an expert on the first variety, and let me tell you, this ain't it." There is silence; he would like to believe me, but it is difficult, I know. I do not have a track record which inspires confidence. "You're just going to have to trust me."

"When are you coming home, Bradford?" It's Evelyn. She has probably elbowed Jackson out of the way to assume control over the situation herself.

"Don't expect me for a while," I say. Madelyn has dropped some cryptic comments about watching the leaves change; for my part, I have checked the paper, and although I haven't cleared it with Madelyn yet, I notice that the Colorado Rockies have a good long homestand coming up. Maybe we'll take in a ball game in Denver. That seems only right and proper.

She clears her throat delicately. It is the strongest sign of skepticism she will permit herself. "Do you know what you're doing, Brad? Do you really?"

"I don't know, Evelyn." I sigh, and then I turn and cannot help but smile. Madelyn has just come out of the shower wrapped in a towel in that wonderfully self-conscious way of hers and turned her back to me to slip into her panties—white, of course. "I'm doing the best I know how."

"Well, I suppose," she says. She is not, somehow, reassured by my words.

"I'll call again soon, Evelyn," I say, "I promise," and as I'm preparing to say good-bye, I picture her standing in her kitchen, perched shakily on her high heels just a lurch away from broken bones, imagine the rouge spreading unsteadily across her wrinkled cheeks, and suddenly I feel a tremendous warmth grow up into my chest that cannot be contained and I speak the name I have never used, the words I have never spoken: "I love you, Grandma," I say, across the miles between us. "Both of you. Always have. Always will."

And I hang up before she can say anything in return. Perhaps she would say nothing, or would remark that she couldn't spend all night on the telephone talking to her reprobate grandson, or would simply advise me again to be careful; my family has never been much for expressing feelings. But just like Madelyn needed to know, maybe they need to know too, and one thing I have finally learned is that time passes, that things change.

Madelyn and I get an early start from Albuquerque. It is going to be a beautiful day, and we are driving through majestic country, tall shadowy peaks off to our right, a line of purple mountains ahead of us and to our left. I look over at my beautiful passenger, her new hiking boots propped up on the dash, her eyes covered by new sunglasses, and can't help saying, "I don't deserve this. I don't deserve you."

"I don't deserve you either," she calls back. "Nobody deserves love. That's not how it works."

"I want to deserve it," I say, and I shrug. "Is that so wrong?"

"You know," she says, tapping her chin facetiously with her forefinger as though she's trying to remember something, "there was a term we learned in my religion classes. What was it? Something about unconditional love granted purely as a gift. A chance for redemption. Not something you could ever earn. New Testament concept, I seem to recall."

"Grace," I say quietly, but not so quietly that it goes unheard, and somewhere behind those Foster Grants I sense her eyes trained on my face.

"That's the one," she says, as if I've won a prize.

"A gift," I say, wonderingly.

"That's it," she says, and her finger trails onto and off my forearm.

We are climbing up an enormous hill—Madelyn calls it a mesa—and I am suddenly struck with an overwhelming desire, something like the powerful craving that pregnant women are said to have for spicy foods after midnight. As I pull over to the shoulder, cracked with heat and dry desert air, something is beginning to take shape in my head. I'm hearing words, recalling familiar images, and for once, they are welcome.

"Pass me that notebook," I say, and without question, wearing that hint of a smile she has carried throughout our journey, Madelyn pulls my latest blank notebook from the map pocket and passes it across to me.

I click my pen, balance the notebook on the wheel, and then, in large and uneven letters, I write: *It is mid-August in Waco, Texas, the Year of our Lord 1993. The mercury stands at one hundred for weeks on end, the grass goes first brown and then gray, and the parched ground cracks open.*

Madelyn glances over it and nods encouragement. "Is there more?"

"There will be," I say, and our eyes meet, and she nods again, slowly and seriously this time.

Then her lips curl upward slightly, and she can't help but ask, "And am I somehow involved with this story?"

"You are," I say, "or you will be," and when I hand her the notebook to put away for now, our fingers intertwine and our eyes meet again. "I think it's going to be about us. About second and third and fourth chances." I seize her slender hand almost as hard as if I'm giving birth, and a ridiculous grin breaks across my face like sunrise across the mountains.

I do not know what is going to happen next, or what I will do with these new beginnings. The road stretches before us. But this I do know, this I promise to myself and to anyone else who may be listening:

For once, I will do something.

Author's Note

Given the checkered ten-year history of the novel that you hold in your hands, I have, again, a long list of people I want to thank for support, care, and inspiration. Here are some of them: Tom Hanks, Chris Seay, Rajesh Solanki, Robert Olen Butler, Scott Walker, Lee Smith, Bret Lott, W.P. Kinsella, Jack Butler, Will Campbell, Joan Logghe, Fredrick Barton, Elizabeth Dewberry, Vicki Marsh Kabat, Jane Hirshfield, Bruce Hornsby, Carol Dawson, Andy and Rachel Moore, Blake Burleson, Trisha Mileham, Angela Baker, Bob and Mary Darden, Linda Germain, Scott Cairns, Greg Wolfe, Frank Leavell, John Ballenger, Mike Beaty, Vicki Covington, and Dennis Covington.

My family sustains me. My life would be bleak indeed without my sons, Jake and Chandler, and without Chandler's mom, Tinamarie. They have been my great loves over the years that this book was written and written and written. Thanks to my parents, brothers, sisters, grandparents, and on to the second cousins once-removed: for all my relations.

Thanks to Trisha and Laura, who were models for two of the wonderful women in this book. Years pass, but you're still in my heart. Dawn Adams and Ann Rushing are my biologist friends, and though neither works in primate sexuality, their seriousness of purpose and love for knowledge helped shape Sandra's character.

Blessings on my communities of faith, Seventh & James Baptist Church in Waco, Texas, and St. James Episcopal Church in Austin, Texas. May you preach peace and justice for years to come.

Richard Jackson, Marian Young, Philip Spitzer, and Greg Michalson made the book better with their care and suggestions for earlier drafts; I am grateful. Many thanks also to Joe DeSalvo, Rosemary James, and the Pirate's Alley Faulkner Society of New Orleans for their years of affection and support—I would not be writing these words without them—to the Writers League of Texas for their good work in supporting the work of Texas writers, and to the Texas Book Festival, one of the nation's great literary events.

Thanks also to the real Baylor University in the real Waco, Texas, where my work as writer and teacher has been supported by Baylor's real president, Robert Sloan, real provost, Donald Schmeltekopf, real deans, Bill Cooper and Wallace Daniel, and real English department chair, Maurice Hunt. The real Arts & Sciences Sabbatical Committee saw revisions of this book come up in nearly every report I've ever written them; many thanks to them for giving me the invaluable gift of time to write. Thanks also to my real students at Baylor, the real reason I remain a teacher. I am grateful for their insights, energy, and affection. Sic 'em, Bears.

As you've gathered with my use of "Baylor University," all actual people, places, institutions, and things mentioned in *Cycling* are used fictionally, and furthermore, are seen through the jaundiced eye of Brad Cannon. Please don't hold me responsible for anything he might have chosen to say in this book unless, of course, you happen to agree with it.

No author could expect greater support than I have received from the people at Kensington Publishing. I want to thank my publisher, Laurie Parkin; Creative Director Janice Rossi Schaus; Doug Mendini and all the wonderful folks in sales who get my books into stores across the country; my beloved publicist Joan Schulhafer, and her assistant, the lovely and talented Mary Pomponio, who manage to get me into stores across the country and then back again; and, of course, my dream editor, John Scognamiglio, who understands what I'm trying to do and believes in me while I try to do it. What more could a writer ask?

Well, okay, he would also want an agent like my agent, Jill Grosjean, who also believes in me, holds my hand when I need it, chews me out when I need it, helps me shape a career as a novelist, but considers me a friend, not just a client. Thanks, J.

Many thanks to the booksellers and stores who hand-sold *Free Bird*. I'm especially grateful to the Barnes & Noble stores in my part of the world—to Linda Germain, regional CRM, who loved my work and sent me out into the rapidly expanding world of the Southwest Region, and to the CRMs of Austin, Texas, with whom I'm sometimes privileged to work, laugh, and tell stories. People who work at many chain bookstores are not reputed to love books; these people do.

I still play Yamaha guitars, Fender amps, and Martin strings. My harmonicas are from Hohner.

Musicians on the soundtrack for this book would be Bruce Hornsby, Bruce Springsteen, Shawn Colvin, Goo Goo Dolls, Eliza Gilkyson, Sting, Steely Dan and Donald Fagen, Bob Schneider, Kasey Chambers, and Stevie Ray Vaughn. Thanks, all, for the inspiration. Reader: go out, buy their music, and put it on while you read back through the book again. It'll be even better this time.

Grace and peace,
Greg Garrett
Austin, Texas